Praise for *The Meq*

"An astonishing, inventive, and addictive book . . . Steve Cash's incisive storytelling runs the gamut of the emotional spectrum, touching upon love, hate, joy, loneliness, and despair."
—*January Magazine*

"This is a fantasy novel without swords and sorcery, a vampire novel without vampires. . . . His impressive debut crosses understated fantasy with an elegant, not-quite-coming-of-age story."
—*The Guardian* (London)

"*The Meq* is a deep and entertaining fantasy that promises to develop into a rewarding series, as the story of this enigmatic people continues through the twentieth century and on into the future."
—*BBC Book News*

"*The Meq* is a charming fantasy written by new U.S. writer and country singer Steve Cash. A tale of immortal children, this is superbly written and comes with my highest recommendation."
—*SFRevu*

THE MEQ

STEVE CASH

BALLANTINE BOOKS
NEW YORK

A Del Rey® Book
Published by The Random House Publishing Group

www.delreybooks.com

Library of Congress Cataloging-in-Publication Data
Cash, Steve, 1946–
   The Meq / Steve Cash.—1st ed.
      p.   cm.
   ISBN 0-345-47092-3 (alk. paper)
      1. Immortalism—Fiction. 2. Children—Fiction. I. Title.
   PS3603.A865M47 2005
   813'.6—dc22   2004055111

Manufactured in the United States of America

9 8 7 6 5 4 3 2

First American Edition: February 2005

Book design by Kate H. Kim-Centra

This book is for Star and Cody

It is dedicated to the memory of my good friends

Gary McCullah (1946–1970) and

K. G. Wells (1948–2001)

ACKNOWLEDGMENTS

I want to thank my longtime friends Frances Bissell and her husband, Tom, for making this possible. I owe an invaluable debt of gratitude to my true and able assistant, Anne Logan, for believing in the story and urging me on. I want to thank my friend and partner, John Dillon, for his keen eye and ear, his patience, and always helpful suggestions. I want to thank my daughter Star for insisting that I write it all down. I want to thank my son Cody for his support when I most needed it, and also for marrying the beautiful Allison and producing the equally beautiful Chloe. I need to thank Sydney Cash because I never have, and I want to thank my sister, Linda Baird, who has put up with me for a lifetime. I also want to thank Cheryl Coates and Elizabeth Byrd at First Impressions because I said I would if we ever made it to print.

THE
MEQ

BOOK
ONE

PART I

The Child is father of the Man.
—WILLIAM WORDSWORTH

1

EZEZAGUN

(STRANGER)

The kindness of strangers. Is it true? Most often, probably not, but invariably in everyone's life there is a moment, a window in time, where only a stranger will make sense of a senseless thing and pull you out or through or wherever you need to go and do not have the power to do so alone. It will feel as gentle and effortless as an angel's touch. It will come unasked and unannounced. It will come from someone whose name you may or may not recall, whose face may blur with memory, but whose deed, in one way or another, saved you. It will be a stranger.

For me, that window was May 4, 1881. It was my twelfth birthday for the first time. I was traveling with my mama and papa on the last leg of a long journey west from St. Louis to Central City, a boom town in the mountains above Denver. We were jammed into a noisy, crowded train filled with people of all sorts and sizes. My papa was going to be the "*lapur de urre,*" the "thief of gold" in all the great Rocky Mountains. He knew nothing of mining, but he always liked to say he knew everything about gold. "The Basque," he said, "will never steal your purse, they have the mountains." My mama always laughed a little when he said these things, but she never disbelieved him. She loved him in a special way, a way as old and wise and silent as the mountains themselves. A way, as you will see, that is unique to them and to me.

My mama said, "Zianno, put that baseball glove down and leave it be. You make me crazy with the rubbing, the rubbing." That's my name—Zianno. My mama sometimes called me "Z" because her name was Xamurra and my papa's name was Yaldi and he liked to think of us as "X," "Y," and "Z," the three unknowns. My mama made the baseball glove by hand in St. Louis. It was my most treasured possession. It was crude and rudimentary, but in 1881, so was baseball.

I kept that glove with me at all times on the trip west. I used it as a pillow at night and rubbed it constantly with my spit to "break it in." My papa had made me a baseball—actually two, one I kept with me and tossed around and the other he kept with him. We never played with that one.

"Mama," I said, "you know I've got to make it soft. The softer the better."

"Soft is one thing, my child. Crazy with rubbing is another. But never mind, there is something much more important I want to talk about today."

The train was inching its way through a mountain pass. Outside, there seemed to be hundreds of waterfalls, some small, some large; a result of heavy spring rains. Papa had made his way to the front of our car in order to listen to a fat man ramble on about recent gold strikes. I put my glove down and looked at Mama's face. I loved to look at Mama's face. She had creamy skin and her features were round and small. Round nose, mouth, and eyes that were coal black and always laughing. But not that day. She was serious and I knew it.

I said, "What, Mama? What's important?"

Mama looked hard into my eyes and reached up with her hands to touch my face. She ran her fingers over my eyebrows and down the line of my cheekbone and traced the outline of my lips. I sat dead still. She touched me often with much love, but not often in this way. It was as if she was trying to remember me with her fingers. The train lurched suddenly from side to side. We were beginning the descent from the pass and picking up speed. It startled Mama, but she wasn't scared and neither was I. We were sick of trains. She put her hands back in her lap.

"You must listen to me, Zianno. This is your birthday, your twelfth birthday."

"I know that, Mama, and when we get to—"

She cut me off with a hand gently placed on my mouth. "Now listen, my son. Your birthday is different, this birthday, this one today is different, just as we are different; you, me, and your papa."

"Different? How are we different, Mama? Because we are Basque?"

"We are Basque, yes, that is true, Z, but we are more than just Basque, we are . . . older."

"Older?" I was confused. "You mean you are older. I am twelve, Mama."

She let out a long sigh and her eyes glanced out of the window, then back to me.

"I mean our . . . our people are older, different, not like the Giza, the other people. Your papa will tell you everything you need to know, everything about us when we get to Central City."

"Mama," I said, "I don't know what you are talking about."

She leaned forward and kissed me on the forehead, then sat back in her seat. "I know, my child, I know. I said the same thing to my mama a long time ago, a very long time ago."

The train was gaining speed. The men gathered at the front of our car were laughing loudly at something the fat man had said, my papa included.

Through the window, the space between our train and the mountain wall opposite was widening. I could clearly see the river racing beside us, swollen from the runoffs and waterfalls I had seen at every turn higher up the mountain. I was trying to make sense of what Mama had said and I wanted her to tell me more, but she was staring out of the window at the rushing water. I started rubbing the pocket of my glove and leaned my head closer to the window. Up ahead, we were coming to a low bridge over a narrow section of the river. Then I saw something very strange.

"Mama, look!"

"What, Z? What?"

"Look up there, Mama, by the bridge. There's a scarecrow waving his arms."

She moved closer to me and followed my finger to where I was pointing. Up ahead, next to the bridge on the embankment, someone or something in an enormous black coat was waving like crazy at the train.

"It's a scarecrow, Mama."

"That's no scarecrow," Mama said. Her voice was low and even, as if she were talking to herself. She rose slightly out of her seat and stared harder at the scarecrow. He was getting larger as we were getting closer. In a blink, we were passing him and I could see that he was not a scarecrow at all. He was a man, a tall man with a beard and a small, round cap on his head. His long arms in the great black coat dropped to his sides as we passed. I saw his eyes, which were wide open, and his mouth in the shape of an O. So did Mama. She grabbed my hand, jumped up out of her seat, and screamed, "Yaldi, Yaldi!"

The train was already on the bridge. Through the noise of the train and the men laughing, my papa heard Mama's voice and turned toward the back of the car. I saw him catch her eye and I turned to look at Mama too. Her eyes were a bonfire of black, but without panic. I turned back to look at Papa. His eyes were the same. Their eyes were locked on each other, and for an instant, there was no sound in my world. No voices, no laughter, no metal screeching as the train tried to brake and avoid the washed-out track on the other side of the bridge.

I felt something pass through me, something that can only be described as Time. The weight of Time. Years upon years, people, places, joys, sorrows, and journeys, endless journeys. I was weightless, empty, and they were filling me, telling me. My mama held my hand, and she stared at my papa and he stared back, in that instant they gave me the weight of their lives.

All the cars of the train were uncoupling and falling from the tracks. There was nothing we could do. Bodies were being tossed around and Mama and I were flung through the window on our side of the car. I never saw Papa. He was somewhere in the middle of a tumbling mass of arms and legs and screams.

I saw the waterfalls. Hundreds, thousands of them; spinning, shining, falling upside down, trailing diamonds and gold, they were like comets. I watched how they spun and fell. I tried to reach out and touch them, but my arms wouldn't move. I felt cold somewhere. Then there was only one waterfall and it was warm. I opened my eyes.

I was wedged between two boulders and Mama was above me, face down on the rocks with one arm dangling over my face. The waterfall was blood, blood that was gushing out of her neck where a large piece of glass was embedded, and running down her arm into my eyes. She was moaning and trying to speak. I forced myself to move and, in moving, felt the pain in my right arm. It was bent at a crazy angle and pieces of glass were sticking out everywhere like darts in a dartboard. But I could only think of Mama. I crawled up to her and gently rolled her over. It was easy, too easy. She was no more than a rag doll broken on the rocks. The blood was pouring out of her neck. She tried to speak, but it was low and hoarse. I leaned down closer.

"Yaldi . . . Yaldi," she whispered.

"No, Mama, it is Z."

She opened her eyes for a moment, those beautiful coal black eyes. She stared straight at me the same way she had been staring at Papa in that last instant on the train.

"You must find Papa, Z. You must find him now." Her voice was weak, but clear and determined.

"No, Mama, no. You're bleeding. You're . . . you're . . ."

"I am dying, Z. But I will not die yet. You must be strong. You must go and find Papa and come back to me." Her voice was so calm and I was shaking, trembling from head to foot.

"Go, now. Go, my son."

Somehow, I did what she said and got up from beside her and made my way through the rocks and boulders, stumbling, crying, yelling, "Papa! Papa!" I was lost in a dead world, a world of broken glass, twisted metal, splintered wood, and bodies, dead bodies everywhere, torn and crushed and split apart.

I couldn't find Papa and probably never would have, except for a tiny sound, a sound that was barely there, but so different from everything else around me I couldn't help but hear it. It was singing. Someone was singing.

I followed the song, the voice. It was a sad and simple song, not in English, or Basque, or any language I had ever heard. It was . . . it sounded . . . older.

Then I saw him. Underneath several mangled seats from the train, my papa was impaled, flat on his back with a jagged piece of wood from the sideboard of the train jutting up and through his chest. And he was singing. With his eyes closed and blood running from his mouth, he was singing.

"Papa!" I yelled.

I tried to move the seats, but I couldn't. I was too small and only my left arm would work. My right arm was broken and useless. I got on my knees and tried to crawl between the seats. It was too tight. I reached down with my left arm and stretched my hand out as far as it would go, but I still couldn't get there, I couldn't touch him. Then the tears fell from my face to his. He opened his eyes and stopped singing.

"Z," he said, slow and soft, like someone whispering just before sleep.

"Papa," I said. "I . . . I heard you. I heard you singing."

"It was Mama's song."

"But it was . . . I mean . . . I didn't understand it."

"You will, my son, you will." He coughed violently and blood shot from his mouth. I started crying again because I could do nothing to help him. Then, through an opening in the tangle of debris, he somehow raised his arm and I saw that tightly gripped in his hand was the baseball that he had made for me in St. Louis.

"Zianno, quickly, listen to me."

"What, Papa? I'm here."

"Zianno, you must listen now and listen with all your mind. Take this ball, this baseball, and never lose it, always keep it with you. Do you understand?"

"Yes, Papa." I was still crying, but I was listening hard. His voice was very weak.

"Z, my son, my blood. Remember, we are . . . we are . . . the Dreams."

I took the baseball from his hand and held it next to me. He began to sing again, but only got through one line, then his head fell to the side and my papa was gone.

In the distance, a train car was coming apart, sliding down the rocks and crashing into the river. I could hear the wood cracking and splitting. I stood up dazed, numb, blank. Mama, I thought. Mama.

I ran back to her through the wreckage and mud and rocks and death. I couldn't feel my arm. I couldn't feel anything. I fell down on my knees beside her. She was covered in blood and her head was bent back on the slope of the boulder. Not six feet away was my baseball glove; I reached for it and put it gently under her head. The glass was still in her neck.

"Mama," I whispered. "Mama, Papa was singing. Papa was singing and I heard and I ran and I . . . I . . ."

"I know, Z. I could hear him." Somehow, she was alive, but her voice was hollow and distant. "Zianno, come close, my child."

I leaned down and put my face against hers so that her lips touched my ear.

"There is so much, Z, so much we never told you. So much you will need to know. You must be strong. You must not stop. You must find Umla-Meq. You . . ."

Her voice trailed off. I rose up slightly and saw that her eyes were closed.

"Mama? Mama? Please, Mama, don't go away. Don't go away . . ."

She moved her lips again. She tried to open her eyes but her lids were fluttering and when she did get them open, her gaze was dull and cloudy. "So tired," she said, "so tired . . . the Dreams . . . tell Papa . . . Zianno . . . Zianno."

"Yes, Mama, yes. I love you, Mama."

She drew one long, slow breath and then, using all the strength left in her, she pulled me even closer and with that last breath whispered, "Find Sailor."

The Window opened. All of Time and Space narrowed to a single, black dot. A dot that became a tunnel rushing toward me, growing larger, gaining speed. I screamed, but no sound escaped. I tried to run, but I had no legs. Then I turned and fell somewhere dark and deep; a nameless place beyond borders, a place of loss and terror, a place so empty and hopeless, I thought I might never return.

Four days later, I awoke near what is now Limon, Colorado. My first memory of that moment is sky; the endless western night sky filled with the Milky Way. The Silence. The Brilliance.

I smelled smoke. I turned my head from the fire in the sky to a fire on earth—a campfire. Someone was bending over it, rattling pans and mumbling. His back was to me, but somehow he seemed to know I was conscious and turned to look at me.

"So, kid, you live. Zis is good."

My head was propped against a log and I was lying on my back wrapped in a blanket from neck to toe, except for my right arm, which was in a sling across my chest. I couldn't feel it. My lips were dry and cracked. I tried to speak, but my lungs just pushed out an empty, raspy sound. I couldn't form words. He was leaning over me.

"Here, kid, here. Drink zis."

I drank the water. I looked up into his eyes, big and black as walnuts.

"You're the scarecrow," I said.

He scratched his beard and laughed a low, strange laugh, almost a gurgle.

"Scarecrow?" he said. "Scarecrow, no. Man of vision, weaver of wisdom, muleskinner, singer, miner, tailor, rabbi, yes. Solomon J. Birnbaum I am, was, and shall be. Yes . . . yes, indeed. Do you have a name, kid?"

"Yes."

"Zis is good. And what is it?"

"Z," I said. "My name is Zianno Zezen. My mama and papa call me Z."

"Ah, yes. Your mama and papa. Yes, of course."

Solomon was a big man, a tall man, maybe six feet five, and when he knelt down, as he did then, he did it slowly. He had large feet and hands and my own right hand disappeared as he took hold of it with his.

"Listen, kid." He paused and looked away from me into the darkness. He pulled and scratched his great black beard. He turned back and spoke slowly. "Do you know what has happened? Do you know what has happened to you and your mama and your papa?"

For a moment I just looked at him. What a stupid question, I thought. Of course I knew what had happened. I knew Papa was dead and I knew Mama was dead, but was I dead? I could still hear Mama's voice, a clear whisper, "Find Umla-Meq . . . find Sailor." But it was an echo with no source. I was scared. I looked up at him. He held my hand tighter.

"Yes, mister," I said, "I know my mama and papa are dead."

"Zis is good. But first you do not call me mister. You call me Solomon. For now, for all time, you call me Solomon."

I said, "Am I dead, Solomon?"

"No, kid, no." He stopped, cleared his throat, and went on. "Now, listen . . . Zianno, is it? Yes, well, now listen to me, Zianno, you hear what Solomon says. I try to stop the train by waving with my arms but train is going too fast. It wrecks anyway. I scream out loud, I pray to God, but it is too late, train cars everywhere, upside down, sideways. I unhook Otto, my mule, and go to see if anyone lives. No one does. I hear singing and go to see, but I only find dead man and little boy running away. I follow him. His mama is dying. He stands up to run again, but he spins and falls. I catch him. I put him on Otto to take out of zis place, zis horrible place. He is passed out but mumbling something. 'Baseball,' he says. Over and again he says, 'baseball.' At his mama's side, there is a baseball, so I pick it up. Under her head I see baseball glove, so I take it too. I bury his mama there where she has died. I know now the dead man was his papa, but he is under too much train. I leave him. I lead Otto out with the boy on top. He is bleeding and his arm is broken. I take out pieces of glass and sew him up good. I put his arm in splint and make sling for it. We take my secret way through the pass. All night we are walking. All the next day and the next and the next. Then I am cleaning my pans by the fire and poof! he wakes up. Zis is you, Zianno. Zis is what happened. Do you understand?"

Yes, I understood. I was still dulled and numb, but I understood. My mama and papa were gone. It was the most sure thing I had ever known or understood. Then something struck me, a question as much about fate as about fact.

"Why were you there?"

"Zis is my business," he said without hesitating. "I go there, not to that place, but beyond there, to Central City. I sell the things to the miners that the miners need, some they know they need, some they don't. So, I rejoice with them, I invoke the spirit of Yahweh, we sing, we dance, and poof! they find out they need these things. Simple, sweet. Zis is good. Then I return and do the same thing again. I was returning when the train came, Zianno. I don't know why I was there, except I am on business."

He started to rise, then knelt down again and with his huge fingers spread my eyes open and searched them thoroughly. Then he straightened up, adjusted the small, round cap on the back of his head, and said, "Let's have a look at zis arm."

When he untied the knot on the sling and unwrapped the bandages, he gasped and said, "Great Yahweh!"

I looked down at my arm. There were no cuts, gashes, stitches, nothing; only a few faint red lines marred my smooth, twelve-year-old skin. I moved my fingers. I stretched my arm out straight and opened and closed my fist. I had total movement and strength. Nothing was wrong. It was as if nothing had ever happened.

The big man looked at me closely, up and down, as if I had appeared from nowhere. Then he unwrapped the blanket and said firmly, "Stand up, kid."

I did and I was unsteady at first, but in a moment I felt fine.

"I have heard of zis," he said.

"Heard of what?"

"Zis thing, zis trick, zis gift of Yahweh."

I didn't know what he was saying. I didn't know anything. All I knew was that he had found me, taken care of me, and I was physically healed. I was a million things inside, mostly sad and lost, but unasked and unannounced, this man, this stranger, had saved me.

"The old, old rabbis from Germany told stories, stories of wondrous children who lived in mountains by the sea." He was talking to me, but his eyes were remembering long-forgotten men and places. "What are your people, Zianno? What were your mama and papa?"

"Basque," I said. "Sort of."

"What do you mean, 'sort of'?"

"My mama was telling me on the train we were more, or different, or older. She was telling me just before—"

He cut me off and said, "Never mind. We will not talk of zis now. We will talk later. Now we rest. Tomorrow, we start our journey and we will talk on our journey like many women at once."

"But—"

"No," he said. "There is only sleep now."

He kicked dirt on the fire to douse it and eventually settled down in his blankets. I did the same and lay there sleepless for a time. Then I said, hoping he was still awake, "Where are we going . . . Solomon?"

Without a moment's hesitation, he answered, "St. Louis, kid . . . St. Louis."

The next day we were on our way, sitting on the bench of his wagon, the Solomon J. Birnbaum Overland Commodities Co., being pulled by Otto and his stablemate Greta. We mainly followed the rail-road tracks, but occasionally Solomon had his own trails and shortcuts. It was a long journey that is a story in itself and on that journey we talked about many things. I never once thanked him for saving me and he never asked. Strangers never do.

2

EGURALDI

(WEATHER)

Weather. We talk about it all the time; the mess, the beauty, the dread, the joy, past, present, future, the common event, and always the uncommon. We talk about it, think about it, worry about it, and take it for granted. We journey toward it, through it, around it, away. It has power over us, but we are powerless, except for our flimsy attempts at shelter. It rains, we run. Weather is power because it is unknown . . . unpredictable. It is a force that influences me greatly. The power of Weather and . . . the Weatherman.

We arrived in St. Louis in the late summer of 1881. The last four days of our journey had been in a constant, steady rain. We were wet and miserable and the mules were stubborn and feisty. Still, we went out of our way to meet a friend of Solomon's in Washington, Missouri, who had a makeshift ferry. We somehow got the mules and wagon on board. In the rain, we made our way down the last stretch of the Missouri River and around the bend into the Mississippi, docking in the dark somewhere in south St. Louis. When I asked why we had gone to so much trouble, Solomon just said, "Zis is good business."

He had many strange routines concerning business, especially when it came to arrivals and departures. Solomon had anxious creditors at every stop. He was a fair man and always paid his debts eventually, but his ideas, appetites, and love for all games of chance came first.

We made our way to a boardinghouse Solomon was well acquainted with. The house seemed huge to me at the time, but really was only ten or twelve rooms. The landlady was Mrs. Bennings, an Irish woman with black hair pulled back in a bun, sky blue eyes, creamy white skin, and a figure Solomon described as "ripe as a great melon." I never saw a Mr. Bennings, nor was he ever discussed, and courtesy was her strong point.

"Good evening, Mr. Birnbaum. And what might you be doin' out on a night when all right-thinkin' persons are safe and warm inside somewheres?"

Solomon shook the rain from his great black coat. I just stood there, dripping silently. He put his hands together as if in prayer and made a full bow from the waist.

"Please, call me Solomon, Mrs. Bennings. It is good to see your bright face again and on such a dark night as zis."

"And yours too, sir. Will you be needin' one room or two, seein' how you sprouted a son since I seen you last?"

She glanced over at me and gave me a look that had more questions in it than anything else.

"No, Mrs. Bennings," Solomon said, "zis is not my son. Zis is my . . ." He paused and looked at her and she at him, ready for this latest explanation of himself. "Zis is my silent partner, Zianno Zezen."

"Well, then, you'll be needin' two, won't you, sir?"

"That is correct, Mrs. Bennings, that is correct. Partners need privacy. Zis is good business."

"It is, it surely is, Mr. Birnbaum." She was smiling to herself and turning to get room keys and towels. She stopped and looked at me.

"Do you ever speak, child?"

"Yes," I said.

"Well, then, what do you say?"

"Very nice to meet you, Mrs. Bennings."

She laughed out loud and sneaked a look back at Solomon. Her laugh stopped abruptly and she said, "Do you still have them stinkin' mules and that damned old wagon, Solomon?"

He was already at the door, halfway out. "That I do, Mrs. Bennings, that I do," he said.

"Well, then, put 'em where you usually do."

He made another short bow and, with a wink, said, "That I will. That I will."

We settled into our life at the boardinghouse. Every morning, we had breakfast with Mrs. Bennings and she made sure I always had enough to eat and was properly clothed. No one asked her to do these things. She just took it upon herself to do them. Some mornings I could smell whiskey still lingering on her breath, the same whiskey I smelled on Solomon's. They spoke little in the mornings and I was quiet myself, so nothing was ever said about these things.

The rest of the day was spent in the busy streets of St. Louis. Solomon and I in the wagon, the mules in front, crisscrossing south side to north side, over to midtown, back to the river; all in pursuit of "business." Some days, it was simple bartering; some days, gambling on fights, dice, cards, horses, baseball. The world turned and Solomon gambled. Some days we would just watch the river traffic, the coming and going of the big barges and pleasure boats. Solomon would say, "Zis is where the money will be, Z. On the water, you watch."

He left me alone a lot, not out of negligence, but just because that's the way it was for Solomon. Aloneness, not loneliness, was a natural and pleasant state for him. Many times while he was doing "business," I wandered through St. Louis. I found our old neighborhood once and ended up playing baseball with a few kids I had known. I told them all that we had moved and never mentioned what had happened. I played with Mama's glove and kept Papa's baseball in my trouser pocket. I always kept it with me just like he told me. I tried not to think about Mama and Papa too much. I didn't know how. Every time I thought of them, I thought of them as living and talking and laughing. I couldn't think of them as dead. It didn't make sense and what they told me didn't make sense—"Find Umla-Meq . . . find Sailor . . . we are the Dreams." It didn't make sense, but their voices were still living within me and, somehow, I would do what they asked of me. I always had.

Solomon and I became best friends. He never tried to be a papa to me and I never tried to be a son. We were equals, silent partners.

There were other children around, gangs of them, especially in the south side, but I preferred Solomon's company. He told me stories and taught me to love books. He told me jokes most twelve-year-olds would never hear. He taught me simple mechanics and went on at great lengths about exotic religious rituals. He pointed out the different dialects and accents that we heard everywhere in St. Louis. He taught me all the games of chance and what to listen for when making a deal—any deal. And he never mentioned the train wreck or the curious way my arm had healed afterward, except once.

Fall had turned to winter and it hit hard. Off and on for six weeks, the whole south side was frozen in. A fever had spread street to street, house to house. Nearly everyone came down with it, including Solomon and Mrs. Bennings. I wasn't sick yet, but I was worried that if I got sick we were in trouble, because there would be no one to do the chores and tend to the mules. Solomon called me to his bed and he said, "You will not get zis, Zianno. You will not get zis fever."

I said, "What do you mean? How could I not?"

"No, no. Listen to me," he said, "remember your arm?"

"Yes," I said, but it was really more like remembering a dream.

"Well, listen to Solomon. Your kind does not get sick. Ever. The old rabbis knew. They knew . . ."

Then he trailed off and went to sleep, but Solomon knew something. He knew something I didn't. Later, when he got well, I tried to talk about what he had said, but he waved me off and seemed uncomfortable with it. He just said, "Zis is not good business, not now."

I was different and I felt it, though I didn't know why. Mama had said I was—we were—different and I felt more that way every day. Not just because I was Basque and didn't look Italian or English or black or German or Chinese. And not because of my small size and quiet ways. My dreams had changed. They were deeper, richer, farther away. When I woke, I felt less in this world than another and sometimes this world became a dream. And I was alone. I felt alone with this difference.

Then I met the "Weatherman."

It was March. A fierce, cold wind still blew out of Canada and was freezing the Midwest. In St. Louis, solid ice spread out a quarter of a mile from the riverbank into the Mississippi. All major trade virtually stopped. Solomon and I still made our rounds, but not as often. He hated the cold and so did his mules. And he hated missing his other "business," his daily card games and gambling.

A friend of his told him of a poker game in which Solomon might be able to play mainly because he was German. It was held each day in the back room of one of the saloons favored by the new beer barons of St. Louis. In fact, the friend told him, Solomon looked quite a bit like one of the Lemp brothers, one of the players who would surely be there with lots of money in his pockets. But he would have to trim his beard, take off his little Jewish cap, and keep his opinions to a minimum. Solomon thought this to be a minor inconvenience in order to do "good business." And with Mrs. Bennings's help in the trimming and tailoring, he was physically transformed into a man he thought had the look and figure of a beer baron. He turned this way and that in front of the mirror, admiring the change.

"Not bad, eh, Mrs. Bennings?"

"Not bad at all, sir, but I've got to ask. What will you be playin' with? Them fat old fellas got more in their pocket than you got on your whole person."

He looked at her sharply, then back to the mirror. "I have enough to begin. After a few hands, zis will not be a problem." He turned and looked to me as he was lighting a cigar. He said, "Zianno?"

I just said, "You look the part, Solomon."

We took the wagon and mules to the address he had been given. The sky was dark, even though it was just after noon, and a hard wind was blowing. Ice still covered most of the streets and the mules were slower than usual.

Solomon wanted to be let off in the alley leading to the back room, probably so no one would see the mules and the wagon. As he stepped down and took his first few treacherous steps on the ice, I heard a voice, a boy's voice from somewhere in the alley, say, "There he is. There's Lemp."

I looked around and saw no one but Solomon. The boy thought Solomon was the beer baron, loaded with money, arriving for his daily poker game. Solomon didn't even look up. He was still concerned with the ice. Suddenly there were three of them, then five, then six.

Half of them were about my size and age, but the others were bigger
and older, maybe sixteen or seventeen. Before Solomon could do or
say anything, they had him pinned against the brick wall of the saloon.
They were yelling and shouting at him to stand still and when Solomon
did try to speak, one of the older ones pulled out a baseball bat and
swung it hard against Solomon's legs. The smaller ones were tearing at
his pockets, looking for money.

This all happened in half a minute. Then one of the older ones
glanced back over his shoulder into the darkness of the alley and said,
"Ray, he ain't got but a few bucks. Should we do him, anyway?"

I knew what that meant and, without thinking, jumped out of the
wagon. I was scared and mad. I didn't know what to do. I reached in
my trouser pocket and grabbed hold of Papa's baseball. I pulled it out
and held it up, ready to throw at the first boy that moved . . .

Then a strange and magical thing happened.

"Get away from him now," I said. "Turn around and get away from
him."

Everything went silent, except for the wind, which was still howling around us. They all looked at me bewildered, entranced, as if
some great clock had reached the hour and they were waiting for it to
chime. But what clock? And for what reason? I didn't have a clue.
Then, without a word, they let go of Solomon, the one boy dropped
his bat, and they turned and walked away, puzzled as to why they were
even there in the first place.

I watched them leave. I was still filled with rage, but somehow
calm. Solomon was slumped against the wall, moaning. I went over to
him and asked if he was all right. Before he could speak, I heard something move in the darkness, back in the alley where the boy with the
bat had glanced. At first, I couldn't see anything, then a shape appeared. It was another boy, one who looked just like me or at least
enough like me that we could have been somehow related. He walked
over to me and stared in my eyes, searching for something. Then he
looked at my hand holding Papa's baseball.

"You are Meq," he said.

I said, "What? Who are you? Why did they do that? Do you know
who this is? This is Solomon J. Birnbaum, that's who."

The boy looked at Solomon, then back to me. He was listening, but not so much to what I said as to how I said it. He came a step closer.

"How long?" he said.

"How long what?"

I looked at Solomon. He was hurt, I could tell, but he wasn't saying anything. He was just staring back and forth between the boy and me.

"You don't know, do you?" the boy said.

"Look, I know you know those punks—you tell them they got the wrong man and they'd better . . . they'd better watch out."

He laughed to himself, a strange laugh for a child, almost bitter. He took two or three steps backward, still looking at me until he was out of the alley and in front of the wagon and mules. Then he took off running. Fast. He literally ran like the wind; fluid, compact, graceful, like no boy I'd ever seen, and he was on ice.

Solomon finally spoke. He said, "Great Yahweh."

I helped Solomon into the wagon and I grabbed the reins and drove us back to the boardinghouse. Solomon's legs weren't broken, but he was badly bruised. Mrs. Bennings and I helped him into bed and I could tell she had seen and touched the results of violence before. She was gentle and efficient and hardly spoke a word until later, when she asked me what had happened. I was confused, mad, even a little guilty for some reason, and I told her everything, even about the other boy, the one who looked like me.

"Well, don't that beat the devil? I never heard such a thing. And them boys just walked away like that, peaceful and all?"

"Yes," I said, "they did."

"Well, then let's just let it lie, eh, child? Best we tend to Mr. Birnbaum and get him standin' on them long old legs of his."

I agreed with her and tried to "let it lie," but I couldn't. I thought about it all that night and the rest of the week. Even my dreams were no refuge. They were filled with strange faces, animals, and voices. They all merged and separated, changing, dancing like images seen through a fire on the wall of a cave.

When Solomon began to recover and get his strength back, he

came and woke me from one of my dreams. I was sweating and shaking and gripping Papa's baseball so hard my fingernails had broken through the hide. He held me gently by the shoulders. He said, "Zianno, we go find that boy. You hear me? You must do zis. Tomorrow, we find that boy."

But we didn't have to find anything. He found us.

At breakfast, Mrs. Bennings asked why I had been up so early wandering the neighborhood. I told her I hadn't been anywhere and Solomon and I exchanged glances.

"When did you last see him—or me, Mrs. Bennings?"

"Why, not ten minutes ago, child. And what do you mean 'him'?"

I got up from the table and went to the door. I looked at Solomon. He wore an expression as serious as I'd seen since the train wreck.

He said, "Go with caution, Zianno. Remember what those others did."

I walked out of the boardinghouse and down the hill to the nearest corner. It wasn't more than a hundred yards. For some reason I knew he'd be there, and he was, leaning against a stone post. When I was no more than ten feet away, I could see how much we looked alike, but up close, in better light than there was in the alley, I could also see our differences. He had green eyes, where mine were almost black, and his lips were fuller, rounder than mine. He had no scars or blemishes that I could see, but neither did I.

I said, "How did you find us?"

He just shrugged and looked out over the houses around us. Then I thought how easy it would be to find us. I'd told him Solomon's name. All he had to do was ask around.

He looked down at his feet. He kicked a loose rock and we both watched it arc and tumble down the hill. I waited for him to speak.

"You're the first one I seen in a long time," he said. "That's all. And you got the power of the Stones. I thought that was somethin' my old lady made up."

"Look," I said, "I don't know what you're talking about. All I know is that those boys hurt my friend bad and that one boy was asking you if he should do more."

"Yeah, well, they're Giza, that's what I'm tellin' you."

"Giza?" I said and then I remembered. When my mama was trying to tell me something on the train, she said we were not like the Giza, the other people.

"What's your name?" I said.

"Ray, Ray Ytuarte. Yours?"

"Zianno Zezen. My mama and papa called me Z."

"Called?" he said. Then he bent down and picked up another loose rock and threw it down the hill. He had a good arm. "Where are they now?"

"They're dead. So what?"

"No what. I was just askin'."

I wasn't sure if I liked him or not, but I was curious. So was he.

"How long have you been twelve?" he said.

"How long have I been twelve? How do you know I'm twelve?"

"Because we all are."

I got a sudden chill. I thought it was the wind, which was still coming out of the north and bitterly cold. I turned my back to it and said, "Listen, why don't you follow me. We can go in the boardinghouse. I've got my own room." I didn't know why I was saying this, maybe it was dangerous, but I had to know more. "It's too cold out here, anyway," I said.

He looked around and up at the sky nonchalantly. "Yeah, maybe, but it'll be nice tomorrow and almost hot in three days."

"How do you know?"

He just shrugged and laughed that same, strange laugh.

We came in the same way I had left, through the kitchen door. Solomon and Mrs. Bennings were still sitting at the big table. Solomon looked the boy over, knowing he was seeing something he'd only been told about as a child, something he thought was a tall tale told by a crazy old German rabbi. Mrs. Bennings's mouth had dropped open and she was speechless.

If someone, anyone, had looked in my room for the next half hour, they would have thought they were just seeing two boys, maybe two brothers, talking. But it was more than that, much more.

The first thing Ray Ytuarte did was ask to see Papa's baseball. I took it out of my pocket and tossed it to him. I sat on the edge of the bed and watched him. He walked around the simple room and over to the only window. He turned the baseball over and over in his hands inspecting every stitch and the gouges my own fingernails had made. The window was completely frosted over. He blew on it and rubbed a clear circle with his fist. He stared down through the cold glass, then looked at me.

"You really don't know anything, do you?" he said.

"No, I don't. Why don't you tell me. The first thing you said to me was 'You are Meq.' What does it mean?"

"I can only tell you what my old lady told me and she didn't know much. It's the word we use for ourselves, the old word. She said the Giza have called us other things, in other times; the Children, the Flock, the Enigma. I don't know that much about that part. It's all lost."

"But what does it mean?" I said. My mind was racing with questions.

"Well, it means you ain't gonna get sick. It's in your blood. And you're gonna heal fast if you get cut or broken. And you'll stay twelve. You won't get any older, at least not your body." He blew on the glass again and this time traced a circle with his fingertip, then another circle inside that one. "It's called Itxaron," he said, "the Wait."

"Can you die?"

"Yeah, you can die. If you get your head cut off or stomped beyond recognition by somethin'."

"How old are you?"

"Older than that old man downstairs."

"You mean Solomon?"

"Yeah, Solomon. Solomon J. Birnbaum. I seen him around years ago, but he didn't see me."

"You are actually older than Solomon?"

He laughed that hard laugh and blew more of his breath on the glass. He wiped the sleeve of his jacket across the circles he had made. He answered in a low monotone.

"I was born in 1783, in Vera Cruz. That's Mexico. I turned twelve in New Orleans. Spent a lot of years there. It was easy for a kid, but not so good for my old lady. My old man was killed in a zipota match for money. Had his brains kicked in. My sister didn't know how to stay twelve too good. She took to the brothels and slipped out somewhere.

I ain't heard a word of her since. I learned how to run gangs and that's what I did. They called me the 'Weatherman.' But you gotta keep movin' when everybody's gettin' older and you ain't. You'll learn that quick. My old lady tried to live like the Giza and got her throat cut in a fancy hotel. They never found the guy. I just made my way upriver, town to town, city to city, until I got to St. Louis. I been here to this day. In all that time I only seen a few of us and none could do what you did in that alley. My old lady told me only an Egizahar could do that. She said they're the only ones with the Stones. I thought it was just another one of her crazy stories about us."

He stopped talking and tossed me the baseball. I caught it and sat there in a daze.

"Where'd you get that?" he said.

"My papa made it."

"Well, if my hunch is right and it usually is, that ain't just a base-ball. Did he tell you what to do with it?"

I looked down at the baseball, remembering Papa. "He said 'never lose it.' "

"That's because you're Egizahar. You gotta protect the Stones."

"What does it mean," I said, " 'Egizahar'?"

"It kinda means 'old truth.' According to my old lady, there's two bloodlines: the Egizahar and the Egipurdiko. 'Diko' for short, which kinda means 'half-assed truth.' The ones who Waited and the ones who didn't. I don't really know what it means. She was crazy, but I don't know; I ain't so sure now that I seen you and what you did."

"What did I do?" I said.

"You stopped the Giza. You made them all forget, turn around, and leave. They wouldn't—couldn't have done that on their own. That's old magic, old power, and for us, there ain't nobody that can do that without the Stones. We got other things we can do, but not that."

I still sat on the edge of the bed. I hadn't moved. I was lost . . . over-whelmed. It was like one of my dreams. I felt as if I had stepped into a shallow pool only to be dragged out to sea.

He stepped away from the window and took something out of his pocket.

"Look, kid," he said, "I know what that baseball probably means to you, but . . ."

"Don't call me kid," I said. "It's ridiculous. You look just like me. Why don't you be Ray and I'll be Z."

He put his hand out to shake. "Deal," he said.

I looked down at Papa's baseball. "So, Ray, you think this baseball is magic?"

"I don't think the baseball is magic, but I think what's inside is."

"Inside?"

"That's right. I think your papa put the Stones in the middle of that ball. Why don't you give it to me and let me cut the stitches. I got a penknife right here."

"No," I said, but I didn't say it with much heart. I wanted to find out myself. I had to. I tossed him the ball.

He didn't waste a second. Without a word, he sat down on the bed and put the baseball between us. He cut the stitches one at a time and carefully peeled back the flap of hide. He took out the coarse hair and fiber underneath and suddenly there it was. Like a single egg in a bird's nest, there it was. In fact, it was shaped like an egg. A dark, pock-marked stone in the shape of an egg that would easily fit in the palm of your hand. And like the four points on a compass, there were four tiny gems embedded in the Stone. In the light, they all reflected a different, brilliant color. I lifted the Stone gently and it was heavier than I expected. The gems were a mystery, I had no idea what they were. But Ray did.

Ray said, "That one there at the top, that's blue diamond. The one on the bottom is star sapphire. The other two are lapis lazuli and pearl."

I turned it over and over in my hands. I touched the gems with my fingertips, then I put it in my palm and closed my hand over it. I shut my eyes and thought about Mama and Papa. I couldn't touch them anymore. I couldn't run up to them and ask them a thousand different questions. I opened my eyes and looked at the cold glass of the window-pane. The light coming through was low and faint. I turned and looked at Ray. He was putting his knife back in his pocket.

"What do I do now, Ray?"

"I don't know," he said, "but I got a hunch you're gonna figure it out."

★   ★   ★

Three days later it was almost hot, just like the "Weatherman" had predicted. Solomon was on his rounds again, doing more bartering than gambling, now that he was getting prepared for his annual trip west. I went with him and tried not to let him see what I was thinking and feeling. I should have realized he knew me better than that. He said, "You don't go with me out west, kid. You stay and find zis thing, zis thing inside you."

We had never discussed me going west with him, but I think we had both assumed I would.

"You know about me, don't you?" I said.

He barked at his mules, then turned to me.

"I know what I know, Zianno. No more than that."

I made him stop the wagon and I told him I had discovered something special, something I didn't understand, something from my papa. I told him I had to find something else now. I had no choice. I had to find someone named Sailor; it was the last thing my mama had said and maybe Ray Ytuarte could help me do it. He said he understood and that he'd already made arrangements with Mrs. Bennings for me to stay with her. Of course, I'd have to earn my keep and maybe watch over her a little for him. He said he might go all the way west this time, maybe to California. I told him that sounded like good business.

In the next few weeks, Solomon and Mrs. Bennings made no more pretense about their relationship. She knew he would be away for at least six months and they spent most of their time together.

I spent a lot of that time with Ray. Every day we met somewhere and I asked him about the Meq. Ray still ran his gang, but I could tell he was drifting away from that. He was starting to need me as much as I needed him, for what I didn't know. Some days he actually seemed like a twelve-year-old and some days he was just strange and distant. One day, for no reason, he told me his sister's name. He said it was Zuriaa, a beautiful old Basque name, but she had changed it to something else.

I asked him about us, all of us. How could we even be born if our parents stayed twelve. I knew babies didn't come from storks.

He said there was a ritual, something only the Meq did, called Zeharkatu. He didn't know much about it because he'd never done it, but after the ritual the Meq became like the Giza, the other people. They could have babies, get sick, grow old and die, just like the Giza. But their babies would be Meq. He wasn't sure when or how the ritual was done. He said it had something to do with the Itxaron, the Wait. He said there were all kinds of old stories and legends, but his old lady only knew a few and since he'd been on his own, he'd learned very little. He heard that some of us were old, older than you would believe, and some were not to be messed with. I asked him if he'd ever heard of one named Sailor and he said he had, but it was more like a ghost in one of his old lady's stories. I asked if he'd ever heard the name Umla-Meq, but that name was unfamiliar. We both wondered about the Stones I carried—Ray a little more than I.

Finally, the day came for Solomon to leave. St. Louis was turning green with spring and it was a fine bright day. He and Mrs. Bennings said their good-byes inside, she acting as if it was just another day, but I knew better. Outside, after he'd hitched the mules and climbed in the wagon, he tossed me the little round cap off his head. "Here, kid," he said, "zis will make you safe, smart, and rich." He waved once and was gone.

Four days passed and I hadn't seen or heard from Ray. Then, he burst into my room one morning and wanted to know which way Solomon had headed west. Had he taken a northern or southern route? I said I didn't know, but probably northern, because he had mentioned a man in St. Joseph named James he wanted to see and if he went that way, following the railroad as was his custom, he would stop at the Missouri–Pacific Railroad in St. Joseph to check on new lines and track. Ray said this was bad because there was a big storm about to form and there would be tremendous rain and flooding in that part of the country. I almost laughed, but he was serious, so we told Mrs. Bennings that she ought to wire St. Joseph and warn him. She thought that was silly, but when it came to Solomon her feelings were clear—"better safe than sorry."

She sent the telegram and we waited for a reply, but none came. One day later, news broke of a devastating storm that raged through the Great Plains and created hundreds of flash floods and destruction everywhere. Mrs. Bennings feared the worst. Two days after that, Ray disappeared without a word. I looked for him in the pool halls, outside the saloons, around the levees, and all his usual street corners. He was gone. We never heard from Solomon.

I felt lost again and I didn't have the faintest idea what to do next. Solomon had asked me to "watch over" Mrs. Bennings and that's what I would do, but somehow, I still had to find Sailor.

That night, my dreams were filled with driving rain and mules and baseballs and pistols and wind. Everything kept splitting apart and everyone was screaming and crying and running for dry ground and a safe place to hide. In the middle of it, calm as could be in a bowler hat, there was a boy waving to me and saying something I couldn't quite understand. I woke up soaking wet from my own sweat and took a deep breath, then a thought crossed my mind . . . even if you can predict the weather, you can't predict the "Weatherman."

The next day was May 4, 1882. I would be twelve again.

3
ARMI-ARMA
(SPIDER)

Imagine a warm summer afternoon. You're sitting on a porch swing or in the grass leaning against a tree. Caught in a ray of sunlight, out of the corner of your eye, you detect movement. Not sudden, yet quick and graceful. You turn toward it and see nothing at first, but you wait and watch. Then you catch a silver flash, then another, descending in the light. You follow it with your eye and there, dangling in space, she sits, stands, hangs, you can't tell. She is the spider suspended in space. Alone, defying gravity, she spins her magic home and trap. You are mesmerized. You watch her in a silence filled with power. Her power of will and perseverance and the slow knowledge that what she weaves will work. The beauty is incidental. Or is it? You watch her until the light fades and she blends in with shadow and darkness. You rise and leave by ways familiar to you, but you know that behind you, back there, she has spun her web and, in darkness, waits.

It was Independence Day before Mrs. Bennings and I really talked about it. Solomon's absence in body and spirit, by wire and by letter, was absolute. We hadn't heard a word from him or about him. Mrs. Bennings kept busy and never mentioned it. She might have had an extra nip or two in the evenings from her bottle of Old Bushmills, but that was the only outward sign I could see that she was worried. After chores, I spent most of my time combing the piers and levees looking for traces of Ray. He had vanished as completely as Solomon.

At breakfast that morning, Mrs. Bennings suggested I accompany her to Sportsman's Park for the day. She had tickets to the baseball game between the St. Louis Browns and the Chicago White Sox and after the game there would be a fireworks display. I told her I'd be glad to go. I loved baseball and she loved fireworks.

There were several thousand people there and after she bought us both lemonades and we made our way through the shouting, sweating crowd, we sat next to each other in the grandstands. That was my first professional baseball game. I took in everything at once. I loved it. I still think the few minutes just before a game starts are the most exciting. Mrs. Bennings turned to face me, oblivious to the hoopla around us.

"I think it's gettin' to be downright rude of Mr. Birnbaum to not be tellin' us whether he's alive or dead."

"I think we'll know soon," I said. "I think we'll find out he's just fine."

She looked out at the field, started to say something else, then didn't. She watched the whole game and never spoke. The Browns won and the sun went down and the fireworks began. She took off her wide-brimmed hat and some of her black hair fell loose from the bun on top. Her blue eyes flashed in the fireworks. For a few minutes, she looked more like a child than I did. Then she said, "I'll not be waitin' to learn."

"Learn what?" I asked.

"The truth," she said.

After that, Mrs. Bennings's spirit changed. For better or worse, only time would tell. She still worked hard, but her heart wasn't in it. She spent more and more evenings in the saloons and taverns on the south side. I followed her for a while, "watching over her" as Solomon had asked, but after a time, I quit. It was her life and she seemed to want it that way.

I spent all of my free time at the ballpark, hanging around with other boys, sneaking into a game when we could and trying to get the ballplayers to talk to us. Most of them would and I became good friends and errand boy for one of the most notorious players, the "Whirling Dervish," Billy Covington. He was a great second baseman and a wild man on the base paths. He'd tell me stories about baseball and growing up in the South and how he'd love to have his twin girls see him play, but he couldn't afford to keep them. I'd listen to everything he said and then run to get him a sandwich and a bromo. He always needed bromo, because he had a reputation as a "whirling dervish" on and off the field. Billy got me my first job as a bat boy in a weekend series against the Phillies. I'll always be grateful to him for that and for something he had nothing to do with at all, except for dying.

It was a Saturday in late summer. The game started at one o'clock, so I was up early and at the ballpark by ten to watch batting practice. I noticed right away that Billy wasn't on the field. I asked around and Charlie Sweeney, the pitcher, said he was out by the ticket office talking to his girls. I wasn't sure exactly what that meant, but I thought I'd go and see anyway. When I got there, Billy was still in his street clothes, holding the hands of two girls who looked completely lost. They were both blond and skinny, about twelve years old, and wearing dirty print dresses. Billy saw me coming.

"Hey, kid," he yelled, "come here, I want you to meet my girls, my daughters."

They both looked over at me. One of them smiled and one didn't. I could tell they were twins, but they weren't identical.

"This here's Georgia," Billy said, pulling the smiling one forward and patting her head. I nodded and so did she. "And this here's Carolina," he said. He pulled her forward and she looked me up and down.

"Hey," she said.

"Hello," I said. I was smiling, but she kept a straight face. Both girls looked tired and worn-out. Billy knelt down so he was on our level.

"Listen, kid. I been waitin' for you. I got a game to play and these two, well, they been through a rough time. You know your way around, so you stay with 'em, will you, 'til after?"

"Sure, Billy," I said, "do you want us to just stay here?"

"No, no. I got y'all tickets."

He slipped me a silver dollar and kissed both girls on the forehead, then he did one of his "whirling dervish" moves and went in to dress. They watched him leave with blank expressions. Carolina picked up her sister's hand and turned to me.

"Who are you?" she asked. Her face was still blank.

"Zianno," I said. "Z for short."

"What are you doing here?"

"I don't know. I love baseball, that's all."

"That's silly."

I didn't say anything and turned and motioned for them to follow me. We went inside and watched the game. I bought roast beef and lemonade for all of us with the silver dollar Billy had given me. Billy had one of the best games he'd ever played. He went five for five and scored the winning run in the bottom of the ninth. After the game, a bunch of players carried him off the field on their shoulders. They took him out of the ballpark and down to Chris Vonder Ahe's Beer Garden, where he drank fifteen beers and chased them with fifteen whiskeys, then did one "whirling dervish," passed out, and never woke up.

The manager, Charlie Comiskey, was told about the girls and the fact they were waiting for Billy back at the ballpark. He found them sleeping by the ticket office next to me. He'd seen me around.

He leaned over and said, "You with them, kid?" There was whiskey on his breath and he was louder than he thought he was.

"We're waiting for Billy," I said.

"Well, he ain't coming back." He pulled out his handkerchief and wiped his nose. I couldn't tell whether he was just drunk or he'd been crying. "The good Lord threw him a curve and struck him out for good," he said.

I looked over at the girls. Georgia was still asleep, but Carolina had opened her eyes. In her eyes was a look I knew myself. That afternoon she'd told me why they came to St. Louis. They had only seen their daddy twice in four years, but their mama got sick with consumption and when she died she left just enough money and instructions for the girls to take a train to St. Louis and their daddy, the only place she knew to send them. Now he was dead. I looked up at Charlie Comiskey and lied.

"Well, sir, they're really with me, not me with them. Billy set it up for them to stay at Mrs. Bennings's boardinghouse."

"Then you best take 'em on over there, kid. We'll sort all of this out later."

He glanced down at the girls, blew his nose, and left.

I stood up and Carolina did the same. We looked at each other, but neither one of us said anything. She woke Georgia and whispered something in her ear, then she turned to me, but all she said was, "Which way, Z?" Georgia never did speak, but she cried most of the way to Mrs. Bennings's.

Some girls don't have to explain themselves or have things explained to them. They walk into rooms and know where to sit, what object to pick up or leave alone, what to say without speaking. Carolina was like that and Mrs. Bennings loved her for it immediately. She welcomed her and Georgia into her home as if she'd been expecting them. She asked her if Georgia ever said a word at all and Carolina said, "No, she hasn't said a word since birth, but she doesn't need to. I can read her eyes."

Mrs. Bennings gave the girls their own room and within two weeks had taught them everything she knew about how to run a boarding-house. I think just having them around filled a void for Mrs. Bennings, a void I was sure that Solomon had left. She especially took to Georgia and her simple, quiet ways. Every night after all her chores were done, Georgia would go to Mrs. Bennings's room and brush her long, black hair. The two of them shared a common need; Mrs. Bennings had found a daughter and Georgia had found a second mother.

I became friends with both girls and at every opportunity tried to take them on some new adventure in St. Louis. Carolina loved seeing new things, going to new places, watching people, and she really could "read" her sister. Georgia never once had to tug on her sleeve to get attention or point her finger to say where she wanted to go; Carolina "knew."

The girls filled a void for me as well. All summer I had tried not to think of Solomon or Ray and what had happened to them. I tried not to think of Mama and Papa and finding Sailor. I tried not to because, when I did, I got confused and angry at everything. I didn't know what to do. I was alone with mysteries beyond my comprehension.

I told Carolina about some of it. I told her how Mama and Papa had died and I told her about how I got to St. Louis. She listened and understood because she'd been through it, but I never told her about the Stones and about being different, being very different . . . being Meq.

Every night I held the Stones in my hand and wondered what they meant, but they were mute, like Georgia, and they never spoke. My dreams were, as always, full of people and places I had never known, never seen. I dressed in the mornings and put the Stones inside Mama's glove. I never took them with me anymore. It was a habit that would change.

On the last day of the baseball season, Chris Vonder Ahe, also known as the "Old Roman," decided to combine two events into one. Since he owned both the St. Louis Browns and the Beer Garden, he felt somewhat guilty about the circumstances surrounding Billy Covington's departure. To ease his guilt, he came upon the idea of having the last game of the year followed by a special circus performance all the way from Europe. Two great events for one slightly elevated ticket price, the difference being donated to the unfortunate orphaned twins, Carolina and Georgia Covington. The whole day would be in Billy's honor and he could rest in peace and pride knowing he was still contributing to the welfare of his loving daughters.

Mrs. Bennings thought it was a grand idea and a very good deed. She was already in love with the girls and could always use the money. She wasn't greedy, but there were three extra boarders now, even if they were just children.

She took charge of everything, finding two pretty dresses for the girls and making sure we were all washed and clean. She and the girls took turns fixing each other's hair and then we all climbed into a carriage that the Browns had arranged to take us to Sportsman's Park.

We took our seats, which were right behind the Browns bench, and enjoyed the game. Mrs. Bennings knew nothing about baseball, but was constantly asking about the players, especially the veterans. I kept looking over my shoulder the whole game with the strange feeling someone was watching me. Carolina saw me and turned to me in the sixth inning, saying, "What's the matter with you?"

"I don't know," I said, "something, nothing, I don't know."

"You're crazy," she said.

Georgia even leaned over and pointed to the side of her head with her finger and made a twirling motion.

After the game, Charlie Comiskey and Arlie Latham came over and escorted the girls out to home plate where Charlie made a speech about the legendary "Whirling Dervish," which nobody could hear past the first few rows. Mrs. Bennings was clapping loudly and even whistling, something no lady ever did, and I'd certainly never seen her do. Then, Charlie Comiskey made a big deal out of waving a wad of bills in the air, the money for Carolina and Georgia, and putting it all in a cigar box and handing it over to Carolina. Both girls seemed shy and out of place, but she thanked him and they came back over to our seats. Charlie Comiskey gave Mrs. Bennings a big wink as he left.

Most people in the stands were restless and unsure whether to get up or stay seated, because they hadn't been told anything about the big special performance that was supposed to follow the game. There was only a huge hand-painted poster, hanging by the ticket office, of a spider, to give any clue of what was to come.

Just then, a man walked out to home plate. He was a skinny man in a black suit and a black string tie. His hair was slicked back and he had a megaphone in his hand which he held up and used to announce to the crowd that his name was Corsair Bogy, the St. Louis promoter who was bringing to the city and the ballpark today the only Midwest performance of the great Geaxi, Spider Boy of the Pyrenees! The performance would take place just after dark, he said, and then we would all witness the defiance of gravity itself.

Everyone was excited and Mrs. Bennings remarked that this might be the perfect time to introduce herself to a few of the ballplayers and thank them personally, along with the opportunity to wet her thirst just a bit. She left in high spirits, reminding us not to wander too far and meet her back in our seats for the big show.

Carolina, Georgia, and I decided to take a walk down Grand Avenue. Carolina tucked the cigar box under her arm and off we went, with Georgia leading the way doing a sort of "whirling dervish" dance all her own.

After a few minutes, Carolina turned and said, "Didn't you say your mama and daddy were Basque?"

"Something like that," I said.

"Well, don't Basque people live in the Pyrenees . . . you know, in Spain?"

I had been thinking the same thing, wondering if the Spider Boy might be Basque.

"Yes, they do," I said.

"Well, don't you think you ought to talk to him, find out if you got something in common?"

"I was thinking about it, but I don't know. It's probably a hoax anyway," I said.

Carolina stopped walking and looked at me. She said, "Why do you think it's a hoax?"

"It's simple," I said. "Geaxi in Basque is a girl's name, not a boy's."

Carolina started to speak, but didn't get the chance. Out of nowhere two boys grabbed her from behind and one of them put his hand over her mouth. A moment later two more grabbed me and did the same. I struggled, but they were bigger and stronger. They were dragging us into an alley filled with broken bricks and loose stone. Out of the corner of my eye I could see they had Georgia too. There must have been eight or nine of them and I didn't recognize any of them. In thirty seconds, they had us back in the alley and underneath a scaffolding that was set up between the buildings. They threw us on the ground and surrounded us. Carolina cut her knee as she fell, but she didn't say a word and she held on to the cigar box. Georgia crawled over to her and they huddled together. One of the boys was talking to me.

"I been watching you, bat boy," he said.

I looked up at him and had no idea what he was talking about, then I remembered his face. He was the boy from Ray's old gang, the one who had hit Solomon with the bat.

"I don't know what happened last time, but it ain't goin' to this time," he said. He looked over at Carolina and grinned. "And I know what's in that box too."

He motioned at two of the boys and they started for Carolina. She and Georgia crawled farther back against the wall. I thought of my Stones and reached in my pocket, then remembered that I'd left them at the boardinghouse. The two boys going for Carolina bent down and picked up bricks and the one talking to me said, "Let's get 'em."

Just then, in one of the few shafts of sunlight penetrating the alley, I saw a glint of color, a bright blue, and then another, a red, descending through the light, down the scaffolding. I followed the movement and saw a shape around the colors, a body, arms, legs, I couldn't tell, climbing down the scaffolding in the blink of an eye. When it reached the ground there was a voice from its direction. It was a girl's voice, but low and droning, like a sad and ancient ballad sung many times.

"Hear ye, hear ye now, Giza. *Lo geltitu, lo geltitu.* Go like lambs, now. You will forget. *Ahaztu!*"

The boys put down their bricks. Their faces all had the same blank, puzzled expressions. Without another word or even looking at each other, they all turned and walked out of the alley at an even pace.

I watched them walk away. Carolina and Georgia watched them too, then we all stared at the figure left standing in the alley. Dressed in black leather leggings and a black vest held together with strips of leather attached to bone, wearing ballet slippers for shoes and a black beret for headwear, there stood a child—a child who could have been my twin.

"I am Geaxi."

"You're the Spider Boy, aren't you?" Carolina said. She didn't even mention what had just happened or the fact that we looked just like each other, except Geaxi's hair was cropped even closer than mine. She went on, "But you're not a boy, you're a girl."

"Yes, I am a girl."

I looked at her more closely. Around her neck was the source of the colors I'd seen reflected in the light. Hanging from a simple, braided leather necklace was the black egg-shaped rock that held the gems, what Ray had called the Stones. It was the same as mine. I was staring at it. She saw where I was staring.

"If you had yours with you, young Zezen, this would not have been necessary," she said.

I looked up at her face. She was smiling. She turned and looked back toward the entrance to the alley.

"Tell the girls to wait for you there," she said. "We must talk."

I looked over at Carolina and she seemed to understand. Without being asked, she and Georgia helped each other up and walked toward the street. Carolina's knee was bleeding badly. I watched them until they got to the entrance and leaned against the wall. I turned and looked at Geaxi. She was still smiling.

"You are surprised, no?"

I still hadn't said a word and she went on before I could think of anything to say.

"You should always wear the Stones," she said. "Later, as you get older, you will learn a sense of danger that will help protect you, but not like the Stones. You protect the Stones and, in turn, the Stones protect you. You are Zezen, through the tribe of Vardules, protectors of the Stone of Dreams. I knew your mother well and—"

"You knew my mama?" I blurted.

"Yes, I did. And your father and your father's father when I was a child."

"But you are a child," I said.

"No, young Zezen, I am not. I am old in a child's body. But we are great friends, myself and this body of a child. We know each other well."

I started thinking back to something Ray had said—"Some of us were old, older than you would believe"—and now I knew he was telling the truth. I was standing next to one. I looked in her eyes. They were a child's eyes and yet they weren't. There was a calm and compassion not possible in the eyes of a child; an innocence drowned in experience.

"Tell me who you are," I said.

"My *deitura*, my family name, is Bikis. I am Geaxi Bikis, Egizahar Meq, through the tribe of Vascos, protectors of the Stone of Will."

"I don't know what any of that means," I said.

"You will learn it," she said, smiling again.

There were so many things I wanted to ask her, so many things I needed to know. She walked over to the scaffolding and every step was purposeful and graceful with no wasted movement.

"How did you find me?" I asked. "And why?"

"I have my ways," she said and climbed ten feet up the scaffolding in one effortless move. "You will too, in time. I had to see if the Stones were safe."

"What about the Stones? Are there many of them?"

"There are five, at least there were five when Umla-Meq saved them in the time of Those-Who-Fled." She climbed up ten more feet diagonally. "They were given to five separate families for protection."

"Did you say Umla-Meq?"

"Yes, Umla-Meq."

"One of the last things Mama said was 'find Umla-Meq.' "

She was already up the scaffolding another ten feet. I could barely see her in the shadows. She shouted down at me, "Then you better get busy."

"But where? How?" I shouted back. "And who's Sailor?"

I could hear her laughing somewhere up in the darkness, a spider safe inside her web. Suddenly she leaned her head into a lone shaft of sunlight and looked down at Carolina and Georgia. They were leaning against each other at the entrance to the alley. She shouted to me, "Beware for that one."

I turned and looked at the girls, then up to her and yelled, "Which one?"

Geaxi was gone, probably up and over one of the buildings, but gone. She never answered.

Georgia and I helped Carolina walk back to Sportsman's Park. The bleeding had stopped and she balked at our helping her, but we did it anyway. We found Mrs. Bennings in our seats sitting with two of the St. Louis Browns. She was glad to see us, but several rounds of beer and the attentions of two baseball players sort of made us invisible. I told her I was taking the girls home, because Carolina had cut her knee and Mrs. Bennings thought that was a grand idea and said she'd be right behind us. Several hours later she made it home and, before she passed out, told us that the Spider Boy of the Pyrenees never showed and Corsair Bogy had been booed and showered with debris. Several fights broke out and that's when she said she took her leave. "After all," she said, "public brawlin' is nothin' but bad manners."

That night, Carolina asked me the first of a thousand questions about what she had seen. I don't remember my answer, but I clearly recall the dream I had later.

I was in a cave or cell made of stone. I was staring at a single opening in the wall above me. I felt desolate and defeated. I saw a spider crawl into the open space and begin to spin a web across it. Four times she spun her web only to see it break and fall. On the fifth try the web held. I reached up to touch it and the strands were razor sharp. I cut my fingers and the blood poured out and kept pouring out until it covered the floor.

I kept bleeding and the blood around me kept rising. I was sure I was going to drown in blood. Just before it reached my mouth and nose, I looked up and saw the spider, alone in the center of her web, waiting.

I awoke then and one word filled my mind—Meq.

4

MUGALARI

(SMUGGLER)

By the dim light of a new moon, his ship slips through the dark and deadly rocks of the headlands and sails into the secret cove. He navigates by instinct and memory and every sense is alive and alert. He is familiar with the delicate balance of fear and calm. He expects the unexpected. His ship is fast and sleek and manned by a loyal crew who know their mission well. He is a smuggler, as was his father before him, and his father's father before that. His contraband is not gold or guns or rum. He carries something else; stowed safe and warm, waiting for the swift moment of exchange, is the Dreamer. The Dreamer, who must be delivered in darkness, entrusted to another with only a silent nod and never spoken of again. He has done this before. In his dreams, he has never stopped.

For the next few months, Mrs. Bennings ran the best and most respectable boardinghouse in south St. Louis. The girls had willingly handed over to her their "welfare" money from the Browns and Billy's fans. She used most of it on improvements to the house and a brand-new, hand-painted sign out front that read: "Mrs. Bennings's House— A Proper Place—Visitors Welcome." A good sign and a simple sign that reflected perfectly the character of the owner. She was a good woman, a loving woman, and I think maybe her only flaw was the hole in her heart created by the total absence of Solomon. She was haunted by it, I could tell, but still we never spoke of him.

Along with improving the state of the boardinghouse, she grew obsessed with improving the minds and manners of the girls. She bought new clothes and books and enrolled both of them in school, making sure everyone from the principal on down understood that even though Georgia was mute, "her mind was as sharp as the sting of a bee."

For some reason, maybe something instinctual, Mrs. Bennings never mentioned the possibility of me going to school. It was not discussed, nor was the fact that the girls were changing physically and I was not. But all around me I was sensing and learning what Ray had told me—"You gotta keep movin' when everybody's gettin' older and you ain't." I could feel the lingering stare of a neighbor or hear the unasked questions if my name was brought up among the boarders. I began to stay away from the boardinghouse more and more, especially during the day, and spent most of my time wandering through Forest Park or Henry Shaw's gardens, alone, thinking about who I was and what I was. Carolina went with me sometimes and it was there in Forest Park on the first day of winter that I finally told her everything I knew about myself and the Meq. I told her everything, but naturally she thought I was crazy.

"I don't believe you," she said, "something like that just can't be."

"Well, it is," I said.

We were walking in the heart of the park, not along the laid-out paths, but through and around the trees, kicking dead leaves as we went. She stopped and looked at me, waiting for me to explain. I couldn't.

"You mean you're just going to stay twelve and that's it?" she asked.

"I guess so. I don't know." I wanted to tell her more and make it clear for her. She was my best friend and we shared everything, but I knew I couldn't. She was Giza, I was Meq, and I was learning the difference.

"How do you know any of that stuff is true," she said, "and how do you know what we saw that girl do in the alley wasn't just some trick?"

"Because I know."

"But how?"

I took off my jacket and rolled up one of my shirtsleeves. I reached into my trousers and pulled out my penknife. I opened the blade and held it up in front of her. Sunlight glinted off the steel blade. She started to speak, but I made a motion for her to keep quiet. I slowly dragged the sharp edge of the blade across my forearm. Carolina jumped back.

"No, Z, what are you doing?" she screamed.

She put her hands to her mouth and looked at me wild-eyed. I stared back at her with as steady a gaze as I could hold. The knife blade hurt.

"Wait," I said.

"Now I know you're crazy," Carolina hissed with real anger.

We both watched as the blood poured out of the cut and down my arm. A minute passed, then Carolina said, "Please, Z, stop this now. Let me put something around that."

"Wait," I said again.

In less than three minutes the bleeding had stopped and the wound began to close. Carolina stared in fascination. In another minute there was only a dark red line where there had been an open wound. I knew that even that would be gone by the next day.

"You see," I said, "I'm not like you, Carolina. I'm something different . . . something else."

Carolina stood still and straight, barely breathing. I watched her face. She had a band of freckles that crossed her cheeks and nose and were barely visible unless she was flushed. Right then, I could count every one of them. She was still angry, but confused and amazed at the same time.

"I don't believe it," she said, "I saw it, but I don't believe it. It doesn't make sense."

"I know it doesn't make sense. That's why I've got to find some things out," I said.

"But, Z, that's a miracle. It's something out of the Bible."

"It's not out of the Bible," I said. "It's in my blood."

She reached down and grabbed a handful of leaves, then walked over to me. "Give me your arm," she said. I let her take my arm and she wiped the last traces of blood off my skin with the leaves. "Is that girl, Geaxi, like you?" she asked.

"Yes," I said, "and a lot older. I've got to find out some of what she knows. My mama said to find Sailor and I've got to do it. I don't know how yet, but I've got to do it."

I looked into Carolina's eyes. They were a gray-blue with little flecks of gold reflecting sunlight. She took my hand in hers.

"I'd go with you," she said, "if Georgia wasn't so happy here."

"Well, I don't know if I'm going anywhere yet."

We started walking toward home, kicking leaves again.

"You'll go," she said.

She was right. Not six weeks later Mrs. Bennings and a lady friend of hers, who introduced herself only as Natalie, came home late one night accompanied by two men. I should say that although Mrs. Bennings was running a successful and respectable boardinghouse at the time, she was becoming more and more drawn to a life after dark, a life of saloons and whiskey and men. Georgia was troubled by this and always stayed up late, waiting for her, ready to brush her hair and help her to bed. Carolina and I were up with her that night, sitting by candlelight at the long kitchen table when the foursome arrived, loud and drunk.

Mrs. Bennings led the way, almost crashing through the door, arm in arm with a skinny man I'd seen before, but couldn't place. Behind them and laughing like hyenas were Natalie and a shortish, red-faced man with a full beard and wearing a tam-o'-shanter tilted at an angle.

"Hush now, darlin's, we'll wake the boarders," Mrs. Bennings said to the others. She was trying to put her finger in front of her mouth, but she was swaying too much to find it.

"Let the buggers wake up and piss themselves!" the skinny man yelled.

I recognized that voice. I looked closer at the man's face. I remembered the slicked-back hair and the gaunt, sunken cheeks. I was sure of it—he was Corsair Bogy, the promoter who had brought Geaxi to St. Louis only to be booed and humiliated when Geaxi disappeared.

Mrs. Bennings said, "Shhh! I'll not be hearin' that kind of talk. I'll have you know, we don't—" But she never finished her sentence. Instead, she stumbled into the kitchen table and suddenly saw the three of us. "Children!" she said.

Corsair Bogy was drinking whiskey straight from the bottle. He wiped his mouth with his sleeve and looked at us. He smiled at the girls . . . then he noticed me. Suddenly all his features narrowed into a look of fierce rage.

"Why, you little son of a bitch," he snarled, "I don't believe you got the nerve to come back around here."

The other man and Natalie stopped laughing. Mrs. Bennings looked at Corsair Bogy, completely baffled. I stared straight into his bloodshot eyes. He went on. "Well, Spider Boy, I think you owe me about five hundred dollars." He turned to the other man and said, "Ain't that right, Mr. Woodget?"

I glanced at the other man. He was looking hard at me, but said nothing. I unconsciously moved my hand up and grabbed hold of the Stones, which I now wore all the time, around my neck and under my shirt, just like Geaxi.

"Or maybe I'll just take it out in pleasure," he said, taking a step toward me and smashing the whiskey bottle on the edge of the table.

Mrs. Bennings tried to cut him off, but she tripped and fell on the floor between us. Georgia and Natalie both rushed over to her. She looked up and said, "No, no, he ain't no Spider Boy. He's Zianno."

Corsair Bogy held the neck of the broken whiskey bottle in one hand and with the other he took hold of Mrs. Bennings's arm and tried to jerk her out of the way.

"I'll decide who's who," he said. "Now, out of my way!"

I glanced quickly at Carolina. Her eyes were wide open and scared. I held the Stones tighter. "Stop right there," I said. "You will leave this place now and you will harm no one."

My voice was steady and firm. Corsair Bogy looked at me as if he were looking at a blank wall; no more, no less. He gently placed the broken bottle on the table and stared at it, as though he had no idea why he'd picked it up in the first place, then turned and walked out of the door, paying no attention whatsoever to anyone else in the room.

After the door shut behind him, there was nothing but silence, then

Natalie said, "Why, Mrs. Bennings has passed out." She looked at
Georgia and said, "Help me take her to her room, will you, missy?"
They got her to her feet and she murmured something, then they half
dragged, half walked her out of the kitchen and up the stairs. The
room was empty except for Carolina, me, and the other man, Mr.
Woodget.

I looked over at him. He was still red-faced and his eyes were
bloodshot, but they were staring directly at me, steady and focused. I
wondered what he thought about what he'd seen. It was the first time
I had knowingly used the Stones.

Then, still without saying a word, he bent down and started picking up pieces of broken glass, stacking them neatly in a pile on the
table. He pushed the pile to one side and sat down slowly, deliberately.

"That was a close call, eh, boy?" he said, pulling out a long-stemmed
pipe and lighting it. He glanced up at me.

"Yes, it was," I said.

I watched him. Carolina watched him. He took two long pulls on
his pipe and exhaled. He was in no hurry.

"The name's Woodget, Caleb Woodget," he said, "and in twenty-
five years at sea, I have only seen what I just saw twice, both in the last
year. And both times, the parties involved that did what they did were
children, children that looked so much alike they could be twins.
Now why do you suppose that is? Eh?"

"I couldn't tell you, Mr. Woodget." I tried not to show concern or
give away anything. "But could you tell me the name of that other
child? Was it Sailor?"

"No, no, it wasn't. I never got the name," he said, "but Bogy called
him the Spider Boy. Only thing was, he was no boy. He was as female
as that one there," he said, pointing toward Carolina with his pipe.

I looked at Carolina. She was twirling a strand of hair between her
fingers.

"Why was she with you?" I asked.

He tapped his pipe on the table, refilled it with tobacco, and lit a
match.

"I smuggled her into the country for Bogy. Picked her up in Port-
au-Prince and slipped her in through Biloxi," he said. "Easy job, good

money, but it was in the harbor at Havana that I saw her do something I have never seen before or since. Until tonight. You want to tell me what it is, boy?"

"I can't do that, Mr. Woodget. Why don't you tell me what she did."

He sat back in his chair and looked at me. I could tell he wasn't sure whether to go on or not. He took several long pulls on his pipe.

Finally, he said, "I am captain of a fine and fast clipper ship, the *Clover.* Twelve years I have been her skipper now. A smuggler I am and proud of it, but that day we were taking on a legal load; cane sugar, it was. Next to us in the harbor was a ragged old ship I had never seen nor heard of before called the *Pisces.* I was busy with the load-in and not paying much attention, but on board the *Pisces* there was a mean and sinful thing taking place: a flogging. If you have ever seen one, you will never want to see one again. The unfortunate man receiving the lash was stripped to the waist and bound to the rigging, hands tied above his head, legs spread apart, and ankles secured. The boatswain's mate wielded the cat-o'-nine-tails. I could hear the dull whacks followed by the poor fellow's low moans.

"I should have done something, maybe called out the captain or stopped it myself, but I did nothing. Flogging has been outlawed since the sixties and I knew it, but still, in my business, you often lend a mute conscience as well as a deaf ear and a blind eye.

"But to the point. That Spider Boy, who I soon found out was a girl by the sound of her voice, had somehow sneaked up my own mizzenmast and was dangling there in the rigging, looking down on the *Pisces* and the flogging. No one saw her but me and I don't think anyone else heard her issue instructions to the boatswain to put down that cat-o'-nine-tails and walk away, even though he was a good sixty feet away and had no way of hearing her. She said it nice and steady, just like you, and in a low voice that was more a chant than anything else. But put it down he did, and walk away he did also, knowing, I suppose, that his own captain would probably have him flogged for doing it. After that, the Spider Boy—what did you say her name was?"

"I didn't say, but her name is Geaxi," I said.

"Yes, well," he went on, "she looked down at me and, I swear by

Neptune, she knew I had been listening and watching, but we never spoke of it and I delivered her safely to Bogy in Biloxi."

He looked down at his pipe, saw that it had burned out, and tapped it again on the table. Whether it was the circumstances or he could just handle his liquor, I didn't know, but he now seemed completely sober. He was a patient man, I could tell, and he was going to wait until doomsday for a response.

"What do you want from me?" I asked.

He looked me squarely in the face and leaned forward.

"Can I speak openly in front of her?" he said, nodding toward Carolina.

"Yes."

"I want to hire you, boy. I want you to come and work for me. I will take you on as an apprentice, so you don't have to bunk with the crew and you can do what you do, however you do it, when I need it. I need your power, or whatever it is, to protect me. There are a great many scoundrels in my profession, let me tell you. I will show you the high seas and a fine life of adventure. You will not regret it."

I looked at Carolina. A million things were going through my mind. Was this it? Was this my chance to do what Mama said and find Sailor? Carolina was tight-lipped, but she was nodding, as if to say, "Yes, yes, do it. This is your chance."

I looked back at this odd man in his tam-o'-shanter, holding his long-stemmed pipe. He wasn't going to say another word or persuade me in any way and, in that respect, reminded me of Solomon. I liked him for that.

"Yes," I said, "I'll go with you and I'll do what you said when it's needed, but I've got to tell you now, I'm going for another reason."

"And what would that be?" he asked.

"There's someone I've got to find; another one like me named Sailor."

"Aye, that would be the one you asked about. Well, not to discourage you, boy, but almost every man at sea has, at one time or another, been called Sailor."

"I know," I said, "I've thought about that."

"Well, never mind, we will find what we can find, that I promise you. I expect to leave for the Gulf bright and early in the morning. Can you be ready?"

"Yes," I said.

He got up to leave and stopped at the door.

"By the way, what is your name, lad?"

"Zianno," I said. "Call me Z."

He tipped his cap to Carolina and said, "In the morning then, Z." And he left, leaving Carolina and me sitting by the light of a single candle, staring at each other.

We sat like that until dawn, talking and trying to imagine what my life was going to be like. Carolina saw it as the adventure of a lifetime and I did too, but I couldn't escape another feeling; I felt guilty about leaving and not "watching over Mrs. Bennings" as Solomon had asked; and I felt guilty about leaving the girls alone after Geaxi's warning. Carolina said Mrs. Bennings would be fine, she'd see to it and she would always be there for Georgia. I said, "Yes, but who's there for you?"

She said not to worry, everything would be fine, and we both acted as if I'd be back in a few weeks. It was a lie. We both knew that too.

I stopped by Mrs. Bennings's room before I left. Natalie and Georgia were asleep in chairs, but Georgia had pulled hers next to the bed. Mrs. Bennings was curled up on her side in the center of her bed with the sheets tucked all around her. Her right hand was at an odd angle beside her cheek. She was snoring. She had something clutched in her hand and I bent over to see what it was. I recognized it immediately, but I hadn't seen it in a long time; I thought I'd lost it. It was Solomon's cap, the one he'd tossed to me when he left.

I walked out of the boardinghouse into a pale gold dawn light. It was the winter of 1883. It was cold. Carolina and I stood shivering in it.

"You know that when I come back it will be completely different between us, don't you?" I said.

"Why is that?" she asked.

"Because you'll be older . . . different . . . a woman . . ."

She just laughed and turned to run back inside. She got to the door and as she went in, leaned her head back out.

"Well?" I said.

She laughed again. "What difference does that make?" she asked, and closed the door.

Two weeks later I was at sea, after traveling with Captain Woodget, as he now liked to be called, down the Mississippi by steamer to New Orleans and then to Biloxi by train. We slipped out in the dark of night by longboat and met the *Clover,* anchored in the Gulf about a mile out. We set sail for points south by southeast, headed for Key West, Nassau, and ports unknown.

The *Clover* was one of the last of its kind, nearly ninety yards long with miles of rigging and a well-drilled crew. Steamships were beginning to vie for trade with the clippers and the days of the great merchant sailing ships were numbered. Captain Woodget didn't agree with this fact and never backed down from a challenge to race with one of the "tin crates," as he called them.

He made sure that everyone on board understood I was his apprentice and not a cabin boy. No one ever doubted him and I was given free rein on the ship. He was a good captain, hard but fair, and he was an expert in sail-making, rigging, and navigation. He had the respect of every seaman on board and each one knew that things would be done one way—Captain Woodget's—no matter how trivial it might seem.

I got my sea legs early and never got seasick, even crossing the Gulf Stream, which was rough. I made friends with many of the crew and most called me Z, but I also got a nickname from our Portuguese cook, who called me "Pequeño Basque," or "Little Basque."

Captain Woodget became a friend and helped me search for Sailor in every port, as long as I remembered my primary task, "watching his back."

I loved the life at sea; the wind and the smell of the constant spray and the stars at night, ten million more than I'd seen when I woke up to the Milky Way in Colorado. I was kept busy most of the time, but I also had endless hours to think about Mama and Papa, Solomon, Ray, Georgia, and Carolina; people I had loved and somehow lost, much too quickly.

Time has a different pace at sea. Days turn into weeks and weeks into months so easily. It rolls under you and you sail through it as you would the sea itself. It is vast and broken only by the light, the weather, the next harbor, a memory of lost things. Sailor, if he existed, must have felt this way a thousand times, I thought.

I hadn't found a trace of him. After Captain Woodget had taught me how and where to look, I talked to seamen of all colors and nations. I stopped and hounded dockworkers, barmaids, whores, kitchen cooks, anyone and everyone. Months went by, then a year, then two. My Meq blood and sensibilities concerning Time didn't seem to notice; only my obsession with finding Sailor mattered. We took on cargoes of tea, wool, coal, jute, redwood, brown sugar, dyes; hundreds of different goods from hundreds of different ports. We anchored off West Africa, Brazil, Madagascar, Nova Scotia, Bermuda, the whole rim of the Atlantic and Indian oceans. Most of our cargoes were legal, but the *Clover* always had one hold, or at least part of one, filled with contraband, and a cabin was always available to the occasional revolutionary or murderer at a price. Holidays and birthdays were never celebrated; smuggling is mainly business and the demands on the men who do it are relentless and never romantic. Two years became four and four became eight. I saw Captain Woodget and most of his crew through two separate cholera outbreaks, where dozens died. I learned to speak bits of French, Spanish, and Portuguese, enough to ask, "Do you know a boy named Sailor?" But no one did. Twelve years passed and I was as lost as I'd been when I first went to sea; twelve years of searching I felt were wasted. I still wore the Stones, though I hadn't had to use them, not once. Captain Woodget and the crew never mentioned how I looked the same. I was just "Little Basque," another unexplained mystery of the sea.

Then we anchored in a cove on the coast of Bermuda, not in the main harbor, but near it. It was New Year's Day 1896, and twelve years were about to feel like twelve seconds.

Captain Woodget and I came ashore after dark with his first and second mates. "This is a human cargo," he said, "a job beneath me, but still worth the money."

As we made our way up a rocky path, he told me we were transporting the mistress of Antoine Boutrain, a well-known captain of the French shipping firm Bourdes, to New Orleans.

"Seems the good captain has a beautiful and loving wife at home," he said, "but he likes to have this one meet him in different ports around the world. She cannot sail with him, so this time she sails with us. He is a warped man, I tell you, probably from trading that damned Chilean nitrate, but he pays well and guess what more is in it, Z?"

"I think I know," I said.

Captain Woodget stopped on the path and turned to look at me. It was dark all around us, but I could feel his eyes bearing down.

"What do you mean?"

"I don't know," I said, "I mean, I'm not sure, but then again, I am."

"Damnit, Z, say what you mean!" he fumed.

"This woman," I said, "this mistress you're picking up, she has an entourage; two of them, two Basque like me, right?"

"Holy Trident and dammit to hell! How did you know that? Only Captain Boutrain told me and I told no one."

I looked in Captain Woodget's face. He knew me as well as anyone by now.

"I don't know," I said.

We left the rocky way and started on a path of sand between the seagrass and weeds. The ground leveled out. We could see the house ahead of us, alone and lit by candles, white against the black sky.

I heard the song first. The lonely notes. The ancient melody and words woven into the night. Two voices exchanging lines, sad lines in a forgotten language; singing, swelling, falling. I knew that language. It was Papa dying, singing Mama's song.

Captain Woodget asked if I was all right. I nodded and we walked toward the house.

The captain introduced himself and his first and second mates to the mistress, whose name was Isabelle, and was ushered in. I hung back in the shadows. The singing had stopped, if it had even begun. I turned and made my way in the dark around the house to the rear, which sloped down through the marsh and rocks toward the Atlantic, a thousand yards away. I stood in the silence.

Then I felt them. I couldn't hear them, but I felt them. I felt them closing in, coming nearer. I knew they would and they knew I would feel them. It was what we knew. It was knowledge I had never been taught, but now could never forget.

"I am Unai," he said.

I turned to my left.

"I am Usoa," she said.

I turned to my right.

I looked back and forth between them, our eyes exchanging greeting and welcome. They had come to within ten feet of me and never made a sound. They were both dressed in loose black trousers tucked into leather boots laced to the knees. They wore broad-collared cotton shirts and no jewelry, except that he had a necklace around his neck and she a priceless blue diamond in her pierced right ear. They looked like twins, and if they were twins, I could have been their triplet.

"I am Zianno," I said.

"We know," they said in unison.

"I heard you singing, I think. What is it?"

"It is an old Meq song," Unai said, walking over to Usoa and taking her hand in his.

"It is about Home," Usoa said, "and return, the longing for return."

"It was beautiful, but I don't know the language."

"You will," Unai said.

"It will come to you," Usoa said.

"But how?"

"Be patient," Unai said, "you have come a long way, Zianno. You are learning, believe me, but I should introduce myself formally. I am Unai Txori, Egizahar Meq, through the tribe of Caristies, protectors of the Stone of Silence."

He lifted Usoa's hand. "And I am Usoa Ijitu, Egizahar Meq, through the tribe of Autrigons," she said.

I didn't know what to say. It had been over twelve years since I'd seen one of my own kind and the last time had been almost too short to remember. But there was a presence, a kinship . . . something.

"You're wearing the Stones around your neck, aren't you?" I asked Unai.

"*Très bien,* Zianno. You are learning recognition. Later, you will learn more than any of us—more than your father."

"You knew my papa?"

"Of course," he said, "and your mother."

"And you know Geaxi?"

"*Oui,*" he said.

"Then you know that I look for Sailor and Umla-Meq."

He glanced at Usoa and they exchanged a bewildered look. "Both?" he asked.

"Yes," I said, "it was the last thing my mama told me to do."

Usoa looked at me and said, "Sailor is the wind, Zianno. He finds you, you will not find him."

I looked at Usoa and then over to Unai and understood that I would get no more directions to Sailor from them; that somehow I was to find Sailor myself.

They turned together, holding hands, and started back toward the house. I went with them.

"I see you have learned the Giza," Unai said, "and you work well among them."

"Yes, I have," I said.

"It is a good way to travel; to be with one who needs the Stones. We do the same for the woman, Isabelle, and we have our freedom."

"Do you travel together always, you and Usoa?" I asked.

"Yes, always," he said. "We do the Itxaron, the Wait, together. We will cross in the Zeharkatu when it is time . . . when we have finished something. Until then, she is *ma chérie.*"

We had reached the stone steps at the back of the house. I looked at them. Their black eyes were shining in the light. They were absolutely quiet and still.

"How old are you?" I said.

They both laughed, sounding just like two children giggling.

"On the way to New Orleans, Zianno. There is time for everything."

"Why do you go to New Orleans?" I asked.

"Because the woman Isabelle goes there," he said, "and Usoa and I seek an evil one. Let that be that."

Captain Woodget, his two mates, and Isabelle appeared that moment at the door and we set off—first to the *Clover,* then to the Gulf, and eventually to New Orleans.

On the voyage, I learned many things about the Meq and heard tales of adventure that trailed back to the courts of Charlemagne and beyond, but I wanted more. I wanted to know everything; I was hungry and thirsty for any and every detail. I asked about Mama and Papa and they told me of caravans and crusades, journeys to the East Indies with the Portuguese, all manner of people and places and times they had witnessed together. I listened to it all and still wanted more. They sang Meq songs and once, while my eyes were closed, I caught myself singing along without any idea how I even knew the words. Usoa laughed and told me it was common, a trait we carried inside ourselves from the time we were painting horses on the walls of caves in the Pyrenees, caves that were still unknown to the rest of the world. "*Oui,*" Unai added, "it is true, Zianno. Not even the Visigoths were aware of the caves, and believe me, some of them preferred caves." We all laughed together at the inside joke and I could only marvel at the fact that it was based on real experience.

The captain sailed the *Clover* at her usual pace, but it seemed too swift for me. I wanted the sea itself to stop and let me catch up. And yet, for the first time since I had been on my own, I felt the connection that was in the blood, our blood, and I knew it was alive and ancient. As Unai told me one night when I became impatient, "You are Meq, you are Egizahar Meq. Learn your Stone. The Stones speak; we are silent."

We arrived outside New Orleans on a late afternoon in March, not long after Mardi Gras. It was snowing—strange weather that was just beginning. We decided to drop anchor and not disembark until morning. Captain Woodget wanted to make sure all his papers were in order, both legal and illegal.

I was supposed to stay on board and only Captain Woodget would accompany Isabelle and her entourage ashore and through customs, acting as her escort. This was as close as I'd been to St. Louis in more than twelve years and I thought about it most of the day. I felt anxious and after dinner I asked Unai and Usoa who was the "evil one" they sought. Their answers were vague, only telling me that he was "diko" and "aberrant."

I fell asleep in an agitated and frustrated state of mind. Outside, it kept snowing, and inside, I came apart.

I dreamed I was in the stone cell again, only this time there was an opening in the wall and a hole in the floor. I walked over toward it and saw that it was really a well, a dry well, with no borders around the edge. I had to watch my step. I heard a voice or thought I heard a voice, coming from inside the well. I got down on my knees. I crawled to the edge and looked over. Down in the darkness, floating in space, was Carolina's head. Her eyes were wide open and she was trying to scream, but there was only a faint cry coming from her lips. I reached down and couldn't touch her; her head kept floating away. I yelled "No! No!" but it was drowned out by another sound, a sound like a train roaring through the night, and Carolina's head spiraled out of sight, disappearing into nothingness.

I awoke in terror. I knew what I must do. I had to get to St. Louis and get there quick. Carolina was in danger and a dream as sudden and clear as lightning had told me so. I thought of Papa's very last words, "We are the Dreams."

I ran to Captain Woodget's cabin. I knocked and woke him from a sound sleep. I told him of my dream and the absolute necessity for me to leave at once. He was calm, just as he was at sea. I never remember seeing him anything but calm in dirty weather. He told me to wait and slip ashore when he and Isabelle disembarked. He would create a diversion, and as a child, I could easily get lost in the chaos.

I waited. Morning came and the rare snowstorm had disappeared. Captain Woodget and Isabelle, along with Unai and Usoa, went ashore. The captain immediately created a ruckus concerning the luggage and the customs agents came running. I slipped easily through the confusion and shouting, acting as if I were lost and looking for my sister.

I was in the United States, in New Orleans, and on my way to St. Louis.

For over twelve years I had smuggled goods and valuables in and out of countries. Every time, the cargo was something someone wanted or treasured. This time, I only smuggled fear.

5

ETSAI

(ENEMY)

Sometimes, an enemy is just an adversary, no more than an opponent in a game, such as chess. Rules are followed and expectations are familiar, as is the enemy. Other times, an enemy is discovered by surprise; a flame flares up and hatred ensues, intense, obsessive, then a violent end and the enemy disappears—the only trace—a scar you carry somewhere, inside or out. But what if the enemy doesn't disappear? What if the enemy appears again and again? What if the enemy becomes your son's enemy? And your son's son, following a bloodline that follows your own, he advances, carrying a single purpose behind ever-changing identities, he knows you and your kind better than he knows himself. What if the enemy is one of you?

It was more difficult than I expected picking up a ride to St. Louis. I finally hired on as a cabin boy on a barge hauling coal to Dubuque. In a little more than a decade, river trade had begun to decline due to federal regulations and competition with the railroads, I was told. Maybe Solomon was wrong when he said the money would be on the water.

Whatever the reasons, I was being delayed and in my mind the fear kept growing that I might be too late, but too late for what, I didn't know. I only knew that up ahead, upriver, there was danger, and the closer we got, the more I felt its presence.

After stops in Natchez and Memphis, we docked in St. Louis late at night. I collected some of the wages due me and said I'd be back in an hour. I never returned. I made my way through an unfamiliar St. Louis to the south side, walking hills and streets I knew from memory, but feeling like a stranger.

I rounded the corner where I had met Ray and saw the boarding-house. I walked toward it. The sun was just rising. I saw the sign out front and it still read "Mrs. Bennings's House." I walked around the back to the kitchen door. It was unlocked and I opened it.

She was in the kitchen, in the dark, but I saw her in the half-light that shone through the windows. She was standing by the stove put-ting water on to boil. Her blond hair was piled on top of her head. She tried to tuck a strand of it behind her ear. I watched her in silence. She was in her mid-twenties and beautiful, even in a worn old cotton robe and unlaced boots. She was at least six inches taller than I was. She watched the stove. I watched her.

"You know it won't work like that, don't you?" I said.

She jumped back, kicking over a chair and landing against the table. She regained her balance and looked over toward the door. "Who's there?" she yelled.

I said, "You can't boil water and watch it too. You know that."

She didn't make a sound for several moments, then she got on her knees and sort of half crawled toward me and the light from the open door. She stopped and looked at me, started to rise, then sat back down on the floor and crossed her legs, never taking her eyes from mine.

"Hello, Carolina," I said.

"God, Z, I knew it. I knew you would come back just like this, just this way. I didn't know when, but I knew how."

I stared at her. I had seen the gold flecks in her eyes before, but now those eyes were in the face of a grown woman, a beautiful woman. Suddenly we both laughed, not a nervous laugh, but a real out loud laugh. It felt so good to see her.

"How's Georgia?"

"She's fine, she's fine."

She reached up and put her hand on my cheek. It was a woman's touch. It was my mama's touch. This was crazy. Inside, I was a man who had traveled fifty thousand miles at sea for twelve years; outside, I was a child being touched by the fingers of a beautiful woman.

"Should we talk about this?" I asked.

"This? What do you mean—this?" She put her hands in her lap and rubbed them together. She nodded at the door. "Why don't you shut the door . . . it's cold."

I shut the door. "But what about—"

"Come on," she said, cutting me off and taking my hand. "I've got something for you."

I wouldn't quit. "But what about—"

"This?" she said, cutting me off again. "I told you a long time ago, Z, 'this' doesn't make any difference."

She took me out of the kitchen and through what had once been the front room. Walls had been knocked out and the whole space was one big parlor with velvet couches and chairs, a full bar at one end, a card table, and an upright piano between two windows hung with thick, blue velvet. There was one gas lamp lit, next to one of the couches where a woman in a full-length red gown was sleeping, snoring heavily.

"What the—"

"Shhh," she said, covering my mouth.

She took me up the stairs and down the hall, which now had a runner of rich blue carpeting down the center and tiny gas lamps over every door. She pulled me into her room.

"Carolina," I said, "you want to tell me what I just walked through?"

"A lot has changed, Z." She knelt down by a chest in front of her bed. She opened it carefully and brought something out. She stood up and hid it from me behind her back. "I've got something for you," she said, "something I think you forgot."

She smiled and held out Mama's baseball glove. I took it from her and put it on my hand, smiling myself. I pounded the pocket with my other hand and rubbed it as I'd done a thousand times before. "I didn't forget it. I left it so you wouldn't forget."

She sat down on the bed and looked directly in my eyes. "That would be impossible," she whispered.

I sat down on the bed next to her. Everything felt strange, yet familiar. I looked around her room. A few pictures were new, and perfume bottles, and clothes, lots of clothes, but many things were the same. The bed we were on was the same one we had sat on as children . . . when we were both children. A lot of things were the same, but now I was the only child in the room. I stood up and walked over to one of her pictures and turned around.

"Look," I said, "I've been around a little bit and this place— downstairs I mean—it looks like, well . . . uh . . . a whorehouse."

"Yes. It is," she said.

Just then, Georgia burst into the room. At first, she didn't see me. She ran over to Carolina, picked up both of Carolina's hands, and spread them apart. Then, she waved them back and forth, one at a time, in front of her own face, acting as if Carolina were slapping her. Carolina nodded and took her hands back, then she smiled and pointed to me. Georgia turned and saw me. She cupped her hand over her mouth to stop a scream that never came, never had. She sat down on the bed next to Carolina and stared at me, her eyes welling up with tears.

"How are you, Georgia?"

She didn't answer, but she looked over at Carolina.

"She can't hear you," Carolina said. "She started going deaf about three years ago. Now, she can't hear a sound. It's funny, though. It seems the more she gets cut off from the world, the more she gives back. She plays the piano now, real well, and she never did before she went deaf. And she's the only good thing Mrs. Bennings has got left."

I looked at Carolina and Georgia. So alike, so different. They were Giza, "the other people," Mama had said, and I was Meq. But it was like that among us too. So alike, so different. I cleared a place on the floor and sat down. I motioned for them to do the same, like we used to, and they did. I looked at Carolina's face and thought of my dream.

"Tell me what has happened," I said.

Carolina glanced at Georgia and Georgia slowly closed and opened her eyes, then nodded her head once. Carolina could still "read" her.

"It happened by degrees," she said. "After you left, Mrs. Bennings seemed to unravel. I don't know whether it was you leaving or you taking with you the last reminder of that man you told me about, Solomon. But, either way, she started drinking heavily; drinking to get drunk, and going around more and more with Corsair Bogy."

I looked at her with alarm and straightened up, unconsciously reaching for the Stones beneath my shirt.

"No, no," she said, "he hasn't done anything to us. Yet. But I am scared of him, Z. He's not a good man and I think he's hired someone—"

"Wait, Carolina," I interrupted, "you're way ahead of me. Tell me the rest . . . from the beginning."

She went on. "Mrs. Bennings got worse and worse. Corsair was with her all the time, and for a while, I guess he was good for her. At least he paid attention to her, but in time he sort of took control of her; told her what to do, what to wear, who to see, and who not to see. Georgia and I were in school most of the time and it was during the day, during that time, that I think Mrs. Bennings was finally worn down and let him have complete control of her and this place. Within a year, he had turned it into a house of prostitution and Mrs. Bennings into a madam. A madam with good manners. That was the only thing she insisted on, that all the girls have good manners.

"Corsair is from an old Creole family that lost its money decades ago, but he still has connections and a whole slew of 'cousins' in New Orleans. For years, all the girls came from New Orleans. Now, almost all the girls are from here in St. Louis, trained by me."

I stopped her right there. "You mean, you and Georgia . . . work here?"

"Of course not," she said. "We run it."

I looked in her eyes. She stared back at me. I didn't know what to say, but I knew there, in her eyes, she hadn't changed.

"I am not ashamed of what I do, Z. It is a good business and I learned . . . we learned," she said, nodding at Georgia, "how to do it well. We are not deprived or made to do anything we don't want to do. We take good care of our girls and we take good care of our 'visitors,' as Mrs. Bennings likes to call them. I like everything about it except for Corsair. He's got out of hand, Z. Two months ago, he finally talked Mrs. Bennings into marrying him and now he wants control of everything. He's dangerous. I know he hates me and my influence and lately he's been slapping Mrs. Bennings for no reason at all."

"Is that what Georgia was trying to say?"

"Yes." Carolina stopped talking and gave me a strange look. She pointed her finger at me and made a circling motion. "Z," she said, "why did you come back now?"

I looked down at the floor, then up at her and Georgia. "I had a dream," I said. "The rest is a little complicated."

We sat in silence. I stared in wonder at these two young women, these Giza, sitting on the floor talking like this with a Meq, a child.

"Have you found Sailor?" Carolina asked.

"No," I said. She turned to Georgia and shook her head, saying no, as if they had talked of this before. "Why did you say Corsair had hired someone?" I asked.

"I said I *think* he has hired someone. I can't prove it."

"To do what?"

"I don't know," she said, "but I'm afraid for Mrs. Bennings."

I thought about my dream again. I was much more afraid for Carolina. I knew that Corsair Bogy was the source of my fear. Everywhere around me I felt an invisible, prickly net descending. It was a heightened sense of danger; an awareness of it that I was learning, as Geaxi said I would. But it felt like waking up. "Don't tell Mrs. Bennings I'm back," I said. "I have a plan."

It was a simple plan. Corsair Bogy had to be watched; all the time, everywhere he went, inside the house or on the town. But Mrs. Bennings couldn't be told. Carolina agreed—if I wasn't here, he wouldn't see me. We could not alert him. Corsair Bogy was a snake, but he wasn't stupid; whatever he had in mind for Mrs. Bennings or Carolina, he would not do it himself.

I stood up to leave. I wanted to be gone before anyone in the house saw me. Carolina handed me Mama's glove. "Don't forget this," she said.

"I never have." They both walked me back through the house to the kitchen door. "Be careful and watch him like a hawk," I said. "I won't be far away."

It was a cold morning, but spring was in the air and I walked into it, glancing back once at the two women I had known so long ago as girls. They were holding hands.

★   ★   ★

I got a room in the Italian neighborhood known as "the hill," just off Hampton Avenue. It was a place where I could easily blend in and live cheaply. No one noticed another dark-haired boy on "the hill."

Every day, I followed Corsair Bogy wherever he went. Most of his time was spent in the saloons or at Sportsman's Park. The baseball season had started and Bogy had box seats, three rows up on the first base side. I hadn't seen a baseball game in years, except for a few crude games in the Caribbean, and it was exciting to smell the smells, hear the sounds, and watch the players. Sneaking in was no problem; under Captain Woodget, I had learned to sneak into any place. The Browns were terrible. They had a great slugger at first base, though. His name was Roger Conner and he held the record for most home runs until Babe Ruth broke it. I thought about being a bat boy again, at least for a game or two, but that would make me too visible. Instead, I hung back in the shadows and watched Bogy.

At night, I stayed outside the boardinghouse and spied on those who came and went. I had seen whorehouses before, almost everywhere around two oceans, but never one like Mrs. Bennings's House. There was no red light over the door or girls leaning out of the windows. From the outside, it looked the same as it always had.

Carriages pulled up and left, dropping off gentlemen in fine dress and top hats. I suppose that not all were gentlemen, but they looked the part. Every once in a while I thought I heard Georgia playing the piano. She was good. I could tell that Carolina and Georgia ran a genteel business, and except for the traffic, it could still have been a boardinghouse.

Each night I met Carolina somewhere outside and asked her if she had seen anything or anyone unusual around Bogy. For three weeks, she didn't. Then, on May 1, she told me something that sent a chill through me. I was on the corner and she ran to meet me.

"I just heard him talking to someone," she said, out of breath. "It was out back, just beyond the kitchen door. I don't know who it was, it was too dark to see, but whoever it was said that Bogy had to come up with more money. Bogy said, 'A deal is a deal,' and the other voice said, 'Not if there is more than one body to do.' Those were his exact words—'more than one body to do.' And, Z, here's what scared me.

When he turned to leave, I got a glimpse of him. He was a boy, Z, a boy like you, only with green eyes."

One name flashed in my mind and one name only—Ray Ytuarte. It didn't make sense, but he was the only one of us I knew who might think like that. He had made his living from violence, I knew that too, but an assassin? It just didn't make sense. I felt that prickly net descending again; the danger. If it was Ray, what could I do about it? Ray had shown me to the Stones and told me about them, but would they have any effect on him? On us? On the Meq? I looked at Carolina and knew it made no difference. Whatever I had to do, I would.

"Who is he?" she asked.

"I don't know," I said. "But Corsair will have to see him again, about the money. Then I'll know. You stay with Georgia. Go to Mrs. Bennings's room. Lock the door if you have to. Just stay together."

"Where will you be?"

"I'll be here, close, unless Bogy leaves."

"All night?"

"Yes."

She was still upset and anxious. I could see the band of freckles across her face standing out in the faint light. She turned and started back, then stopped.

"Do you still get scared, Z? Or is it different for you?"

"I turn twelve again this week," I said. "What's so scary about that?"

The night passed and Corsair Bogy never left the boardinghouse. I saw nothing unusual and the sun rose in a cloudless blue sky. All over south St. Louis the dogwoods and redbuds were in full bloom. I was tired, but edgy and alert, and for some reason the image of Captain Woodget came to mind. I could see him holding on to the weather rigging in his yellow oilskins and long leather sea boots, watching aloft and hanging on until the last minute. I had to keep that same resolve. I had to find the will of Geaxi and the silent strength of Unai and Usoa. I had to bury fear and wait . . . something I knew the Meq could do very well.

Corsair Bogy appeared around noon and headed straight for the saloons adjacent to Sportsman's Park. Before I left to follow him, I saw Carolina standing in the window of Mrs. Bennings's room. She put two fingers to her lips and pressed them against the glass. I nodded once and went off after Bogy.

He visited three saloons, the first two for only minutes and the third for over an hour. He played cards with his cronies and I only lost sight of him once, for a few minutes, while he was in the men's room. After that, he and two men walked the short distance to Sportsman's Park to watch the Browns play Cincinnati. The sky was still blue, but the temperature was dropping.

I stayed close to him in the park, closer than I had before, so I could hear him talk. Mostly, he drank beer and yelled at the manager of the Browns, Harry Diddlebock. He was loud and the drunker he got the more he yelled and bragged to his cronies about women and money; but that was Corsair Bogy all over and such behavior was nothing unusual.

About the seventh inning, a low bank of clouds appeared to the southwest. Gusts of wind blew loose paper and debris around the stands. I felt something else—a presence. I glanced around quickly through the crowd and thought I caught a glimpse of something or someone familiar. I wasn't sure.

I made my way to one of the exits, where I could scan the whole crowd, and turned in a slow, full circle. Nothing.

Suddenly I heard Carolina's voice. "Z!" I heard her scream. She came running toward me, through the crowd. "He's here," she said. "He came to the house, the one with green eyes, and he wanted to know where you were."

"Did he hurt you?" I asked and looked her up and down.

"No, no. It was strange. He just wanted to know where you were. I didn't say a word and he took off running—fast."

It was Ray all right. That proved it. "Why did you come here?" I said. "You should stay with Georgia and Mrs. Bennings."

"I had to do something. I had to warn you."

Then a thought struck me. If Ray was hired by Corsair and Corsair didn't know I was around, why would Ray ask about me and show himself at the same time? It didn't make sense.

The wind was blowing harder and fat drops of rain began to fall. I could hear Corsair's voice yelling over the crowd at an umpire. Then I heard something else—a haunting, bitter laugh I hadn't heard in years. I turned and saw him, standing with his legs spread in baggy black trousers, a white shirt with the sleeves rolled up, and a black bowler hat, staring at me.

"You're lookin' the same, Z," he said and laughed again. "Ain't that odd?"

I stared back at him. If he was running one of his games on me, I couldn't tell. "How are you, Ray?"

"About the same. How 'bout you?"

He took a step toward me, holding on to his bowler hat. The wind was blowing much harder and hail was starting to fall. Carolina came closer, never taking her eyes off Ray.

"Why are you here, Ray?"

"I was in Cincinnati and I had one of my 'forecasts' come to me. I thought about you, Z, so I thought I'd come and save your ass, if you were still around. I hitched a ride with the ball club and I been lookin' for you ever since."

"When did you get here?" I asked and glanced at Carolina.

"This morning," he said. "Look, Z, I don't know how much time we got." He put both his hands over his eyes and looked at the sky. "You mean, you weren't here last night?"

"No. Hey, Z, let's get out of here. Now."

I was confused. If it wasn't Ray, then who . . .

"Now, Z, now!" Ray yelled.

"What? Why?" I looked at him dumbfounded. He pointed to the sky.

"A tornado's comin'. A big one. I saw it three days ago."

I looked at Carolina. I couldn't tell what she was thinking. She didn't know Ray, she didn't know the "Weatherman," but I did. She probably thought he was crazy, but I knew he was never wrong about the weather, and he was no assassin. I kept looking at her and her face seemed to change. I was in my dream again and her head was floating, only it wasn't her head and her face . . . it was Georgia's.

"Let's get to the house!" I shouted.

We turned and headed out of the exit, but everyone else was doing the same. The storm came in so fast that the umpires had no time to call off the game. All the players and four thousand fans were trying to leave at once. It was chaos. We squeezed, pushed, and ran through the crowd, finally making it to Grand Avenue, where we ran straight into Corsair Bogy. He looked at me. He looked at Ray. Something about us stunned and shocked him, then he saw Carolina.

"You bitch, you're supposed to be at the house!" he screamed.

"Come on!" I yelled and we took off, leaving Bogy in the driving rain and hail.

The streets were filled with people running for shelter. Streetcars with bells clanging were racing to make it back to their stations. Some fences were already falling down and the blooms of the dogwoods and redbuds were being blown through the air like snowflakes in a blizzard.

A block from Mrs. Bennings's House, Carolina stopped in her tracks from a dead run. She was gasping for air and so was I. Ray wasn't even out of breath. She put her hands over her ears and her eyes seemed to be staring into some unknown hell. "Georgia!" she screamed and tears poured down her cheeks.

I took her hand away and dragged her toward the house. She was no longer herself. She had fallen somewhere dark and deep inside. I knew the place. Solomon had caught me falling there.

Suddenly the rain and hail and wind stopped. There was a strange, eerie calm. I glanced at the sky and it was green and black.

"It's comin'!" Ray said.

We made our way around back and I saw the "girls" running from the kitchen to the cellar door. I told Ray to take Carolina down into the cellar with the others. I stopped one of them and asked her where Mrs. Bennings and Georgia were. She said they were still in Mrs. Bennings's room, the door was locked, and they wouldn't come out or answer. She ran on toward the cellar and I looked at Ray.

"Someone is in there or he's been there, Ray. He was hired to kill and he's one of us. He's got green eyes, like you."

"There's only one like that," Ray said. "He's somehow related to me on my old lady's side."

"Who is it?" I asked.

"The Fleur-du-Mal."

I stared back at Ray. I reached inside my shirt and pulled out the Stones; holding them, showing them to him. "What about these?"

"They won't make any difference," he said, "not on the Meq, not on him."

I turned to go inside and glanced back at Carolina. "Watch out for her," I said.

He nodded once. "You'd better hurry. You ain't got much time."

I walked through the kitchen and into the large room that was the parlor. A few gas lamps were lit, but the room was empty and silent. The piano stool was on its side, as if someone had stood up suddenly and kicked it over. I reached the stairs and started climbing the steps one at a time, trying to stay close to the wall. Outside, I could hear a faint but distinct sound, like a distant train.

I got to the top of the stairs and saw Mrs. Bennings's door wide open. The girl had said it was locked. I started to call out, then stopped myself. I took a step toward the door, then another. It was then that I heard the laugh. Inside the room, someone was laughing; a low, mean laugh, like Ray's, only . . . different . . . older.

I ran to the open door. I looked inside and saw Mrs. Bennings slumped on a couch, her dress split open from the back, blood covering her chest and her throat slit from ear to ear. Next to her, Georgia sat with her head held back by the hair, screaming in silence, a knife blade at her throat. She saw me and her eyes grew even wider. Behind her, holding her, laughing, was the Fleur-du-Mal.

He looked up at me and smiled. His teeth were a brilliant white. He had deep green eyes, a short ponytail tied with a green ribbon, and two red ruby earrings. He was slightly taller than I was but that was the only other difference.

"I know who you are," he said.

I stood there in silence. I felt a sense of evil and danger I had never known.

"The weather is bad, no?" he said, laughing that laugh.

"Let that one go," I said.

"No, no, no, *mon petit, mon Pequeño Basque,*" he said bitterly. "You cannot protect her with your precious Stones."

"She's not the one you want."

"No? Then who is she?"

Just then, the front door downstairs crashed open and a ferocious wind blew in along with Corsair Bogy. He saw me and started for the stairs, yelling, "You little son of a bitch!"

A tremendous roar followed and the house began to come apart. I looked at Georgia. Her eyes were frozen with terror. The Fleur-du-Mal laughed again, but I couldn't hear him and he cut Georgia's throat in one motion from ear to ear.

After that, I remember nothing. Nothing but the dream; the dream of endless falling through a black hole, of floating heads, trains, and spiders dangling from the masts of ships being torn to shreds in the black winds. And there were stars in the winds; stars made of red rubies, diamonds, and lapis lazuli. I fell through a thousand lifetimes, spinning, weightless, like ash from the fire in a cave.

They found me with my arm and shoulder under the corner of the piano. My arm and collarbone were broken and I had dozens of cuts and bruises. I knew all that would heal. They found Corsair Bogy under the rest of the piano.

There was no more Mrs. Bennings's House. The tornado had raged through south St. Louis and cut a swath a half mile wide, wiping out whole neighborhoods and leaving nothing.

The Fleur-du-Mal had vanished with the tornado.

Ray found Mama's baseball glove not far from where he discovered the bodies of Georgia and Mrs. Bennings. When I was able to look, he showed me something on their backs. It was a signature of the Fleur-du-Mal. He had carved a rose on their backs with the point of his knife before he slit their throats. Ray said his own mother had been killed that way in New Orleans.

Carolina was in shock and we took her and the other girls to a brewery warehouse where a temporary shelter had been set up.

Ray and I returned to the wreckage and rubble of Mrs. Bennings's House. We sat there through the night, the following morning, and the rest of the day. It was May 3, 1896, the day before my birthday. During that time, we talked about where we'd been and what we'd done in the last dozen or so years. He told me he had left the way he had because he'd received information through his network of contacts that his sister was in the Far East, working with a famous courtesan. He combed most of the western Pacific looking for her, but never found a trace. He asked me about Carolina and I told him as much as I could, but I found I was barely able to talk about her. I was becoming consumed with a thought and feeling I had never experienced. It had many images and shapes, but only one name—revenge.

I asked about the Fleur-du-Mal and he told me what he knew. The Fleur-du-Mal was an old one, how old he didn't know. He had come to America with the Portuguese and had been the only survivor when the ship went down in a storm off the coast of Florida. He had many nicknames, one of which was "Sugar," because he had a habit of eating whole pieces of sugar and the Giza thought it odd that his teeth stayed a brilliant white. His real name was Xanti Otso, but the Meq only referred to him as the Fleur-du-Mal, the flower of evil. He was an assassin, a good one, and had been for centuries.

We watched the sun come up and it lit a broken, battered world. We checked on Carolina and she said she was fine and wanted to leave. She wanted to see the house even though we told her nothing was there. Arguing was pointless and so we walked through littered streets back to the house.

Standing in the sunlight, staring at what had been her life and her sister's life, she scanned the debris until she saw it. To no one in particular, she said, "We'll save the piano."

At that moment, a formal carriage pulled by two stately draft horses turned the corner and stopped in front of us. The driver, who was Chinese and wearing a long, braided pigtail, jumped down from his bench and opened the door facing us. A man stepped out; an old man, tall, with white hair and a white beard. He was dressed in a finely tailored black suit and held a top hat in his hand.

"Zis is not good business," he said, taking in the whole neighborhood with a slow turn. He looked at me. I looked at him.

"Come here, Z," he said, "there is someone in the carriage I would like you to meet. I think you call him Sailor."

PART II

If only I could be like the tree at the river's edge
Every year turning green again!

—HAN SHAN

6

MAMU

(GHOST)

Some moments in life are remembered uniquely. They are most vivid in the mind not because of the event or person or place itself, but because of something that surrounds it, something in the background that only you perceived and yet, when you recall that moment, it is the first thing you think of and the last thing you will forget. It is the moment outside the moment. It is the ghost of memory.

I remember the sound of a dog barking; more than anything else I remember that. As I walked toward Solomon and the carriage, I heard in the distance a dog barking in a steady cadence, like a chant, and urgent. I was sure there was someone trapped in the wreckage, but alive, and the dog was barking for anyone to come and look; find them; save them. No one else seemed to hear it. I stopped walking and looked past the carriage in the direction of the sound. Then he spoke and the barking stopped.

"It is long time since we see each other—eh, Zianno?"

Was it really Solomon standing there speaking to me? I didn't know until that moment how much I had truly missed my good friend.

"I must say, Z, my partner, you look much the same." He winked and made a formal bow, waving his top hat in a low arc across his body before placing it carefully on his head as he rose.

I laughed out loud. "I wish I could say the same for you, old friend."

"What? You must mean these rags?" he said, pulling at the trousers of his very expensive suit. "Or zis?" He yanked on his full white beard. "I am same man, Z. Solomon J. Birnbaum I am, was, and shall be."

"We thought you might be dead. You know that, don't you?"

"Dead I am not." He paused and took another slow turn, surveying the refuse and debris that had once been a neighborhood and Mrs. Bennings's House. Speaking more to himself, he said, "We should have been here two days ago. We were delayed . . . by the weather." He looked once at Carolina, who was staring at him hollow-eyed, and he glanced at Ray standing easy in his bowler hat. He turned back to me. "We will talk of all zis later. Now, come. Come and meet Sailor."

The sun was glinting off the polished black surface of the carriage. Shading my eyes, I stepped between Solomon and the Chinese man holding the door open. As I passed Solomon, I whispered, "How did this happen?"

He pursed his lips and shrugged. "Business," was all he said.

A single shaft of light cut through the darkness of the carriage, catching as it did a hand reaching from the shadows; a hand just like mine but for a small ring on the first finger. It was a ring made of star sapphire set in silver and six different rays of color shot out from it in the light. I grabbed the hand and was helped into the carriage and onto the bench.

"Happy birthday, I believe, is a proper opening."

The voice came from the shadows. It was a measured voice; a voice that accented each syllable evenly; a voice that had studied this language and learned it as it had a hundred others.

"I had forgotten," I said. "As you probably know, they start to seem the same."

"Ah, but that is not true, Zianno." He leaned forward out of the shadows, putting his elbows across his knees. I could see him clearly now. "Birthdays are not the same, not a one of them. Whether out of longing or loathing, you must remember each of them fully, if for nothing else—a testament to your survival."

I heard him talking, but I wasn't listening. I was finally seeing, in the flesh, this man-boy I had been looking for half my life. I ran my eyes over him. He wore leather boots like Unai and Usoa, laced to the knees. Tucked into them, black silk trousers held at the waist by an old leather belt with a brass buckle. He wore a burgundy silk tunic open at the neck, and hanging from a single leather strap worn as a necklace were the Stones. His hair was dark and cut short, except for one braid that hung from behind his left ear down to his shoulder, tied with a tassel and an oval of lapis lazuli. His eyes were dark as coffee beans and one of them, his right, had the only physical imperfection I'd seen in any of us. Around the iris, his eye was gray and cloudy instead of white. He was smiling. It was a shy smile, unexpected but genuine.

"I call it my 'ghost eye,' " he said, aware that I was staring.

"Your name is Sailor?"

"Yes, most call me that."

"I have been searching for you for much of my life. Now I don't know what to say. The last thing Mama said was 'Find Umla-Meq; find Sailor.' Now, at least, I have found you. Umla-Meq remains a mystery to me."

He was still smiling. "Then your journey is over, Zianno."

"What? How do you mean?"

He reached into his pocket, pulling out something small and holding it in his fist. "Let me introduce myself," he said, dropping his smile. "I am Umla-Meq, Egizahar Meq, through the tribe of Berones, protectors of the Stone of Memory."

"You mean, you're the same person?"

"Yes. Your mother, Xamurra, must have been trying to tell you, but there was too much to tell and too little time."

I looked out of the window of the carriage. I thought, "I am here, Mama, I have made it. I have done what you asked." I felt something touch my hand and I glanced down at it. Nothing had.

"It was her touch," he said, "it is common."

I looked at him and then out of the window again. Solomon was talking to Carolina, holding her hand. Ray was kneeling down listening to him, but stealing glances at the carriage. The dog was barking again somewhere in the distance. I turned to look in the face of this boy, this ancient boy who I realized had found me, just like Usoa had said. I had not found him.

"Open your hand, Zianno. Open your hand and hold it out, palm up. I wish to give you the oldest Meq greeting and exchange."

I held out my hand and he placed a cube of salt in it and closed my fingers. In a very low voice he said, "*Egibizirik bilatu.*"

I asked him what it meant and he said it roughly translated as "the long-living truth, well searched for." I told him I had so many questions I didn't know where to start. He said he would be glad to answer anything he could because that was part of the exchange in the giving of salt. It was the first exchange and the most important; when others are lost and questions asked, answers will be given. Then he did something strange. He told me to turn my head and look in the light. He knelt down and came in close, searching my eyes.

"You have seen the Fleur-du-Mal, have you not? He has burned himself inside you, has he not?"

I lowered my eyes and eased back against the seat, out of the light. "Yes," I said. The same rage and sense of vengeance I had felt talking to Ray came rushing back to the surface.

"I have an offer to make to you, Zianno. It will involve the feelings you have toward the Fleur-du-Mal."

Suddenly there was a commotion outside and I heard Solomon's voice rising and coming toward us talking to the Chinese man. The door swung wide and Solomon thrust his head in.

"Zis young woman needs food and rest, Z!" He was red in the face and his eyes were watery. "She told me everything, everything that happened. Great Yahweh, Z! If only . . ." He trailed off and turned to the Chinese man, talking belligerently about having enough room and not to worry. I looked at Sailor and he was smiling again, but not at me, at Solomon. Then Solomon was waving his arms for Carolina and Ray to get in the carriage and for the Chinese man to jump on top and get going.

"Now, Li! No more protests! Up you go!" he yelled.

In a matter of thirty seconds, we were all in the carriage and on our way. Solomon removed his top hat and, huffing a little bit, said, "You will all come and stay with me. No questions, no worries. Zis is good business."

Ray and Carolina were sitting next to me. I looked at Ray and he shrugged, as if to say "why not." I looked at Carolina and she seemed worn-out; inside and out, she was beaten down. Almost in unison, we all turned to look at the boy sitting next to Solomon.

"Carolina, Ray, this is . . ."

"Call me Sailor," he said, saying it as easily as if he'd said it a hundred thousand times.

"We go downtown. We stay at the Statler Hotel," Solomon said. "We have many, many things to talk about."

Just then, Carolina jumped in her seat and turned sideways, craning her neck out of the window. "The piano!" she screamed.

Solomon and I leaned over and pulled her back in and he caressed her face with the palm of his hand. He spoke softly to her. "Don't worry, my child. I will have Li take care of it." He looked over at me suddenly with a puzzled expression. "By the way, Z, where is your mama's baseball glove? Do you still have it?"

Ray reached behind his back and pulled it out, saying, "I figured you might not want to leave it."

Sailor leaned forward; he looked at the glove and then at me. "Would you mind if I held that?"

"No. No, I wouldn't mind at all."

He took the glove and studied it all the way downtown. He turned it over in his hands, feeling the stitching and smiling, almost as if he were touching Mama's own hands.

Passing Freund Bros. Bread Company, Solomon lamented the loss and the unavailability of his favorite German rye bread. No one else spoke. We stared out at the aftermath of the tornado and drove on. North of Soulard, there was little storm damage and we pulled up to the hotel in the middle of the everyday traffic and frenzy of downtown St. Louis.

Footmen and bellboys rushed the carriage. The Chinese man, Li, jumped down and barked orders to all of them in badly broken English.

"What is Li's full name?" I asked Solomon.

Grimacing, he said, "He calls himself Li Wen-ch'eng because he thinks he is great White Lotus rebel reincarnated. His real name is Po, but he won't answer to it. I tell you, Z, he is more stubborn than Otto, only he save my life, so now I think I try to save his."

"Solomon, you have much to explain."

"I know, I know. Zis is true for all of us. Now, follow me!"

We were led through the large and well-appointed lobby of the Statler Hotel. Solomon and Li conferred with the concierge about the transfer of all his luggage from Union Station, where he had left not only his luggage but his private railroad car as well. He was boisterous and generous with everyone and even though most of the patrons and passersby stared openly at our strange little troupe, the staff and management's curiosity was kept to a minimum by Solomon's deep pockets.

He had us booked into a suite on the top floor. Each of us had our own room and they all opened onto a central parlor filled with fine furniture, paintings, mirrors, electric lamps, and a huge walnut table in the center. The floor was polished hardwood and covered with Persian rugs. I told Solomon I had a few things left in a room on "the hill" and he said, "Unless they are important, leave them. I will make sure everyone has what they need. Now we all rest and clean up. Tonight, we have big meal in zis room and tell our tales."

Carolina welcomed the chance to rest and bathe, but before she left the room, Solomon asked her for all her sizes from hats to shoes and sent them on to the concierge with instructions to go to Barr's and "buy properly."

Ray went straight to his room, tipping his bowler hat to the rest of us. I waited until Solomon retired to his room, then walked over to where Sailor was examining one of the electric lamps.

"I am still amazed at this magic," he said, holding his fingers close to the light, expecting to be burned.

"Mr. Edison wouldn't call it magic; he'd say it was electricity."

"Ah, but I would wager that if you asked Mr. Edison where he discovered this electricity and he was honest, he would say it was like magic—someone showed it to him and he found it for himself."

"Like you found me?"

"Exactly."

I watched him in the light. His ghost eye shone like the Milky Way with a black hole in the middle. He was calm. He waited for me to speak. Finally, I said, "I want to find the Fleur-du-Mal."

"Yes, I know. Is it because he killed the Giza, the sister of Carolina?"

"Yes."

"Do you wish to kill him when you find him?"

"Yes, I mean, I think I do, I don't know, I've never felt these feelings."

He took a step toward me, searching my eyes, then turned and walked to the door of his room. I spoke to his back.

"You said you had an offer to make—an offer concerning my feelings toward the Fleur-du-Mal. What was it?"

He ignored my question, opening his door and speaking over his shoulder. "Your father had more reason than that to kill the Fleur-du-Mal and he let it go, he gave it up."

"My father?"

"Yes."

"Why?"

He walked the rest of the way into his room and turned to face me with his hand on the doorknob. I could see his ring reflecting colors in the lamplight.

"Which why?" he said. "Why did he want to kill him or why did he let it go?"

"Both," I said. My tongue felt thick in my mouth and I couldn't swallow.

"The Fleur-du-Mal murdered your grandfather," Sailor said, "and your father wanted revenge for three hundred and sixty years."

Without thinking, I touched the Stones around my neck. Sailor saw me and nodded slightly. "You are Egizahar Meq," he said, "you are the Stone of Dreams."

I drew in a long breath. "Why did he let it go?"

He shut the door, but behind the door I heard him say, "To have you."

I stood in silence staring at the door. Minutes passed, then I turned and walked to one of the large windows looking downtown. The sun was setting in the west and I watched the black smoke from the hundreds of factory smokestacks and chimneys swirl up in the fading light. It was blowing east, over the river, and it took me with it.

Somewhere—east, back, behind, before, I don't know, but some-where, and while everyone was resting, I had the first of my Walking Dreams.

I walked across the Persian carpets and down to the lobby. I walked out of the lobby and onto the street toward something or someone, I wasn't sure, but I seemed to know where I was going, and as I walked, I was a canal, a stream, a passage, and the people, wagons, horses, trolley cars, and bicycles on either side were oblivious to me.

I walked to Union Station and stood under the Whispering Arch. I heard something flapping and looked up to see a bird, a finch, trapped up near the ceiling with no exit and no perch. I thought I heard a voice whispering. I watched the people passing. They didn't see me. I looked up again and the bird was gone. The voice was louder, but still whispering; moaning. It said, "Beloved, hear me!" Over and over, for several minutes I heard the voice, then it faded like an echo in a canyon and disappeared into the steady hum of a busy train station.

I was awake. I walked back in the twilight to the hotel and up to my room. I lay on my bed and waited for dinner. The waiting felt natural.

I heard Li's voice first, then Solomon's, telling waiters and busboys where and how to set the places. I quickly washed and walked into the central parlor where a royal feast was being carried in and presented on the big walnut table. There were two silver candelabras holding a dozen candles each, surrounded by oysters on the half shell, shrimp, roast pheasant, prime rib, fresh peas, corn, squash, and a mountain of mashed potatoes. Solomon had arranged our place settings evenly around the table.

Everyone was in the room, but I only saw Carolina. She was radiant in a dark blue, almost black, velvet dress and a single strand of pearls around her neck. She wore long velvet gloves, which I'd never seen on her before, and she was smiling, which I hadn't seen her do in a long time. She saw me and walked over, not smiling now and pinching at my clothes as if they were filthy rags. Then, in her most aristocratic voice, she said, "You simply must learn to dress for dinner, Z.

What will the waiters think?" She maintained her stern look for a few moments more, then broke into a full, robust Carolina laugh, a laughter whose return I welcomed.

"You look beautiful," I said.

"Why, thank you, sir."

"Solomon has good taste. I never knew—"

"Then you should have paid attention," Solomon burst in. "You would have known, Z, I have best taste in all things beautiful, especially women." He took her arm in his and led her to the table. "Now we eat," he announced to all of us and one of the waiters held a chair out for Carolina. Another waiter uncorked a bottle of champagne and filled her glass, then moved over to fill Solomon's. "Champagne for everyone, young man!" Solomon barked at the waiter.

"The children too, sir?" he asked, glancing at Sailor, Ray, and me.

"Yes, I believe so," Solomon said with a smile. "I think everyone is old enough." After the waiters had filled our glasses, they were shooed out of the room by Solomon. We were alone in the room, except for Li, who sat in the corner as still as granite. I caught Solomon's attention and nodded toward Li. Solomon waved his arm, dismissing any concern. "He won't eat with me," he said. "The damn man thinks I am beneath him." Then, rising from his chair, he motioned for everyone to stand and toast.

Ray stood up first, glass in hand, and I noticed that he had actually removed his bowler hat. I don't think Ray had ever sat down to such a meal.

Sailor seemed calm and comfortable at the gathering and rose up slowly. I could tell he had done this many times, whether at a campfire or the courts of kings.

Carolina and I stood up together and it was to her that Solomon turned and began his toast.

"Zis is first and last time I say zis. Here is to Mrs. Bennings; a woman I loved, but from too great a distance; a woman of good manners and taste and a woman I wished to see once more, but was denied by fate and the whims of Yahweh. May she rest in peace."

Everyone drank from their glass and Solomon continued. "And here is to Georgia, the sister of Carolina I never met, but in knowing

Carolina, I know her presence too. May she rest in peace. I give them both grand funeral, I promise." He gave a solemn nod to Carolina and everyone lifted their glass to drink.

"Wait," I said, "I want to add a toast—a toast to you, old friend, for coming back and for helping all of us."

"Hear! Hear!" everyone said and we all leaned across the table to touch glasses.

Solomon looked at Sailor, Ray, and me one by one, then he said, "You are the children the old rabbis spoke of, the 'Children of the Mountains,' the children of Yahweh, and one of Yahweh's greatest mysteries. It is my honor to help."

I looked at Sailor who silently toasted Solomon himself. I looked at Carolina who had tears in her eyes and she made me think of Georgia, which made me think of the Fleur-du-Mal and I had a sudden flush of anger, but I pushed it out. I looked at Ray, who was grinning and clearly enjoying himself. I was sure he had never been treated like this by anyone, Giza or Meq. And I looked at Solomon, white-haired and bearded, full of gladness, sadness, and pride. I knew this was the time to ask him.

"Well, Solomon, are you going to tell us?"

"Tell you what, Z?"

"Oh, not much, just where you went, how you got rich, and why you ended up back here with Sailor, who I couldn't find a trace of in twelve years at sea. That's all."

He laughed out loud. "Let's eat zis wonderful meal and I will tell you while we eat. It is simple, really." He picked up an oyster and let it slide out of the shell and down his throat, gulped an entire glass of champagne, and began to tell his story.

"I left St. Louis to become rich man. How? Where? I didn't know, but I told myself, 'Solomon, you will not come back same as you are leaving!' Zis much, I knew, but first I was to meet a man in St. Joseph named James. You knew about that, Z."

"Yes," I interrupted. "Did you get our telegram?"

"What telegram?"

"The one we sent, actually Mrs. Bennings sent, warning you about the big storm."

He looked puzzled. He pulled on one of his earlobes. "No, no," he said slowly, "I never receive telegram, but I was delayed in Booneville two weeks because of that damn storm. I lost Otto and Greta because of that damn storm. I hated that damn storm, but I finally get to St. Joseph and things have changed. The man I was to meet is no longer. He had been killed, shot in the back by someone he knew."

"Who was the man?" I asked.

"Jesse James."

Carolina lurched forward in her chair, staring at Solomon. "*The* Jesse James?"

"Yes, yes, he was good man; outlaw and robber, but he was always good man to me."

"How did you meet him?" Carolina was fascinated, leaning forward with her elbows on the table.

"That is another story, but I will tell you I met him after Civil War in a card game in Kansas, where I, uh, how should I say . . . advised him. He went his way, I went mine; that is life, but we stayed in touch, occasionally. Then, in that spring of 1882, I get letter from him saying he wishes me to transfer something for him to California, where he will start a new life. He has made 'a deal,' he says. I get to St. Joseph on April 19 and check into the World Hotel, where we were to meet. There is big hoopla and craziness going on, so I ask the desk clerk what zis is about. He thinks I am crazy and tells me Jesse James was killed April third and zis is the day they are auctioning off all his things just down the street. Then, he gives me letter, unmarked, that was left for me some time ago.

"I go to my room and the door is unlocked. I walk in and there is already another man staying there. He is a funny-looking man with long, wavy hair and wearing clothes even I could not have tailored. We introduce ourselves; his name is Oscar Wilde and he says he is there to watch the auction from the window. He says, 'Americans love their heroes and they usually love them criminal.' I tell him yes, but zis auction, zis is bad business. I take my leave, saying there must be a mix-up about the rooms and wish him well."

"*The* Oscar Wilde?" Carolina burst in.

"Yes," Solomon said and continued. "I get a new room and sit down to read the letter that was left for me. It was from Jesse and dated April first. He said he couldn't chance a meeting with me in public, but he had made a deal, through a lawyer named Hardwicke, with Governor Crittenden and the Pinkerton Detective Agency that they would let him and his brother Frank alone if they would change their names, give up crime, and simply disappear for good. However, they couldn't take anything with them, except their immediate family and personal belongings. They especially couldn't take any ill-gotten gains with them and that is where I came in. I was to take the keys that were taped inside the letter, go to the bank in Liberty, Missouri, and open several safety-deposit boxes using the name Solomon Barnes. Then, I was to go to San Francisco with the contents and wait for him to contact me through the Union Pacific Railroad.

"Well, I cannot believe what I am reading. I walk to the window and look down on zis ugly auction taking place, insulting my dead friend. I say to myself, 'Do zis, Solomon! Why not? Yahweh smiles!' The whole situation was backward, upside down. It made me think of the old proverb, 'War makes thieves and peace hangs them.'

"The rest was simple. I check out of hotel, go to Liberty and collect $163,575 in gold and cash, catch train in Kansas City for San Francisco, and when I get there, I book passage to Hong Kong on the first steamer leaving.

"Once in Hong Kong, I ask around, find out what's what and who's who. I meet a French sea captain, Antoine Boutrain, who loses a great deal of money to me in a game of chance. In lieu of payment, he wishes to give me business tip, the 'deal of a lifetime' he says."

The name was familiar to me somehow, then I remembered—Isabelle—Unai and Usoa. I glanced briefly at Sailor and he returned my glance with an enigmatic expression. Solomon continued.

"He says to go south to Shanghai and he will give me proper introduction to Sheng Hsuan-huai who will welcome my investment in the China Steamship Navigation Company. In two years' time, he says, I will be rich man; he was right, except it took five. In one year, I make my money back; in two, I double it; in five, I am a millionaire. I always said the big money would be on the water, eh, Z?"

"Yes, you did, Solomon, you did indeed. But how did you meet Li? And when did you meet Sailor?"

"Ah, first things first," he said and stopped to refill everyone's champagne glass. He turned and looked at Li, sitting like a human stone in the corner. Solomon lifted his glass in a silent toast to him. "A few years ago," he went on, "things began to change in Shanghai for me and for all foreign investors. China wanted in on all the action. Most investors sold out and moved on; I stayed, maybe a little too long. A comprador there, Cheng Kuan-ying, who was a liaison between the mandarins and the foreign investors, wanted me out— poof!—for good. I knew zis, but ignored it.

"Li was working as a laborer on the docks and quays of the Whangpoo River. I did not know him personally, but I knew others like him; workers who were also members of some damn crazy sect who thought they were White Lotus rebels reincarnated. They were violently opposed to the 'Old Buddha,' the Empress Dowager Tz'u-hsi, and all her mandarins and their compradors.

"One night, I am walking from ship to office and Cheng sends four men to take me out. Li, who was there by chance, he told me later, sees them pull out knives and clubs and steps in. Like lightning, he cracks all four of their skulls in seconds. I thank the man, try to pay him reward, but he won't accept; he has some crazy fool belief that once you save a man's life you are responsible for his safety until he dies; and if you don't do zis, you will succumb to a nine-headed, soul-swallowing dragon. He is a crazy man, but as you can see, still to zis day, is concerned for my safety, even though, I am sure, he would love to see me croak and die so he can get on with his life."

Solomon raised his glass to Li once more in silence. I looked around the table and most of the food was eaten. Ray had one leg slung over the arm of his chair and a toothpick in his mouth; he looked fat and happy. Sailor sat back in his chair holding his champagne glass on his knee. The ring on his forefinger danced in the candlelight. Carolina sat enraptured with Solomon and his life and had barely touched her meal.

"So, you and Li left Shanghai then?" I asked.

"Yes, it was a good time for leaving. For both of us. We went to Macao and I liquidated everything from there.

"I stayed in Macao another seven years, living quietly, and still making investments, only they were investments of a more high risk and, how should I say . . . independent nature." He bent over and lit a cigar on one of the candles. Leaning back, turning toward Sailor and exhaling, he said, "Six months ago . . . we meet."

"But how?" I asked. "How did you find him?"

Solomon leaned forward again and cupped his hands around his mouth. In a false whisper, he said, "I do not think I found *him*. I still think he found me."

Sailor laughed and, pointing his glass toward Solomon, said, "No, no, my friend. If you remember, it was you who walked up to me."

"You were too easily found," Solomon said.

They both laughed and Carolina, who was sitting up cross-legged in her chair, said, "How did you meet?"

Sailor spoke. "As I remember, it was outside the Pomegranate, a Taoist refuge and restaurant, in the center of Macao. I was there waiting for someone. There was a fierce sun overhead. I was sweating and, despite the heat, felt something warm bearing down on me through the crowd. I looked among the faces and saw Solomon staring at me. I stared back. He walked straight toward me without hesitation and asked, 'Is your name Sailor?' 'Yes,' I said. 'Do you know the family Zezen?' 'Yes,' I said again, and he said, 'There is one looking for you.' We went inside the restaurant and shared tea. He told me of Zianno and this place, St. Louis. He said he felt like a ghost, but wished to return. I told him he was no ghost and that he should return. He agreed it was time and offered to take me with him and, alas, here I am."

Just then, not a second apart, Ray laughed and there was a loud knock at the door. Solomon and Li rose to answer the door; the rest of us looked at Ray. He hadn't said a word all night.

"What's so funny?" I asked.

"I don't know, I guess it ain't really funny," he said, rolling his bowler hat around in his hands. "It's just that this used to be a big world. That's all."

Solomon opened the door wide to allow four men to roll into the room a slightly damaged, but still sound, upright piano—Georgia's piano. We moved couches and chairs out of the way and Solomon had it positioned in an appropriate and honored place in the room.

Carolina walked over to him as the men were leaving and placed two fingers on his lips. Then she pulled a chair up to the piano and sat down. She bent over, spreading her arms and laying her cheek on the keys.

I watched her, but let her alone. She was fine. She didn't need help, just healing.

Solomon suggested we call it an evening and we all agreed. Li began snuffing the candles and we exchanged good nights. Solomon walked Carolina to her room. As I was passing Sailor on the way to mine, I said to him, "I had a new kind of dream this afternoon."

He smiled his shy smile and said, "You shall have many."

An hour later, I was awakened by music. From a sound sleep, I gradually became conscious of a melody, a simple five-note melody, being played over and over on a piano. I stood up and walked toward the sound. It was coming from the big parlor, from Georgia's piano. In the faint light, I saw Sailor and Carolina also leaving their rooms and walking toward the piano. We got there at about the same time and the melody went away.

"You heard it too," I said, looking first at Sailor, then Carolina.

Carolina started trembling. "That was Georgia, Z. It didn't just sound like her, that was her."

Sailor and I held her arms and helped her into the chair she'd pulled up earlier. She tensed slightly, then relaxed. "It's warm," she said.

I looked at Sailor and he smiled. "There are ghosts all around us, Carolina," he said. "Some we chase, some we embrace." Then he looked up at me and said, "It was her touch . . ."

"It is common," I said.

7

ARTZAIN

(SHEPHERD)

A good shepherd is a vigilant man. He is on constant lookout for danger and opportunity. To him, a shift in the wind is information; a common sound a warning; a drink of water a story of what has passed and what lies ahead.

He guides and guards his flock with patience. He endures drought, blizzard, predation, snakebite, accident, and illness—but most of all— Time.

He stops at the source of solitude and moves on, often leaving a mark of his passing. In the mountains it may be a carving on an aspen tree, a sapling that will grow and expand, bringing out his image. In the desert it may be a pile of rocks on a barren windswept ridge, "stone boys" he calls them.

A good shepherd knows Time like no other and a good shepherd sleeps well, even while dreaming of wolves.

During the late spring and early summer, before the real heat and humidity arrive, there is no better or more beautiful place to be than St. Louis. To the east, with the rising sun, the wide Mississippi seems even wider and more majestic in its slow roll around the city. By midday, in the heart of the city, there is the sweet scent of Forest Park. Baseball, music, laughter, and commerce of all kinds surrounds you. To the west, at sunset, the Meramec River curls below the limestone

hills and cliffs like a lazy, blue ribbon. It is a place of converging waters, highways, and railroads; a place easy and exciting to live in, but
during that time between seasons, difficult to leave. And yet, by the
end of the second week in June 1896, that's just what I was doing.

After the big feast, and for the next few weeks, we made a sort of
home out of the Statler Hotel. We came and went like some extrava-
gant and eccentric family on vacation. Solomon and Carolina went
shopping everywhere, with Solomon tipping heavily from a wad of
bills that Li carried. We all went bicycling in Forest Park many times
and ate lunches on the veranda of the Cottage Restaurant. I insisted
that we see a baseball game and we watched the up and coming Cardinals beat the Philadelphia Phillies. As the game went on, I explained
it to Sailor and he was fascinated, especially with the fact that the game
had no time limit. Ray took us to a "private" club that sponsored their
own prizefighting matches. Solomon loved that, but Carolina was
bored stiff, agreeing with Mrs. Bennings's axiom, "Public brawlin's
nothin' but bad manners." We even went to the Grand Opera House
to see Verdi's *La Traviata* and drew inquisitive glances from all around
as we took our seats. Dressed in formal attire, we must have looked
like some lost cast from another opera. Sailor seemed unaware of the
attention and even sang along with the aria, "Di Miei Bollenti Spir-
iti," under his breath. We were all busy enjoying life in St. Louis. We
were shedding skins and it felt good.

Carolina already had her plan for the future in place along with the
full approval and promise of financial backing from Solomon. I found
out about it late one afternoon on a bicycle ride through Forest Park,
something we tried to do together almost every day. Carolina had the
lead and took me through and out of the northeastern entrance, past
Laclede's Pavilion and into the "old money" neighborhoods around
the northern edge of the park.

"Where are we going?" I yelled ahead. She just looked back over
her shoulder and smiled.

We were in the four thousand block of Westminster, an elegant
tree-lined street with one Victorian stone mansion after another. We
pedaled through bars of sunlight and shade cast by the huge oaks. It
was a rich and silent street; a sanctuary. Suddenly a boy appeared out
of the shadows and began running alongside us. He was a handsome,

skinny boy, younger-looking than I was, but somehow older than his years, and he had obviously seen Carolina before. He wore knicker-bockers with a white shirt and tie and he was smiling as he ran.

"Hello, Thomas!" Carolina shouted.

"Hello, Miss Covington!" the boy shouted back as he tried to keep up. "Will you be stopping this time?"

"No, no. Now, watch where you're going or you'll run smack into a tree, Thomas."

"Don't worry about me, Miss Covington," he yelled, but his voice was already behind us. I looked back; he had stopped and was stand-ing in the street and staring at the receding image of Carolina on a bi-cycle. We rode on a bit and I asked who that was and how he knew her.

"His name is Thomas Eliot," she said. "He's a nice boy—wants to be a writer." She stopped her bicycle and I pulled up alongside her.

"Well, I think you've already inspired him to write something," I said.

She laughed and pointed toward the brick and stone mansion in front of her. "Look at this place, Z. Just look at it."

I looked at it and it was magnificent, with three stories, climbing vines, big leaded windows, stone verandas, and a driveway that led under a brick arch back to a carriage house half the size of the main house.

"Thomas told me the family that owns it has it quietly up for sale," she said.

I was still confused. "How do you and Thomas know each other?"

She leaned her bicycle against a tree and started pacing back and forth, looking over the property. "I've been riding through here and thinking, Z, about a lot of things. One day, he just came up to me, right here where I'm standing, and we started talking. He's home from boarding school and I think he was just lonely. He and his family live back there where we saw him and he told me about most of the fami-lies in the neighborhood. Most of the things I need to know."

"You need to know for what?"

"To start a new life. Right here."

I turned in a circle and looked around at where we were. I saw nothing but wealth couched in castles of abstinence, discipline, and propriety—very conservative, very Victorian.

"Doing what?" I asked and Carolina looked right at me. Her eyes were bright and her freckles stood out.

"I thought about it, Z. It came to me the other day when I read in the newspaper that there's going to be two national political conventions in St. Louis this summer, and Union Station's got more railroads coming in and out than any other point in the United States, and 'old money' like their vices close by, they don't like the risk in risqué, and then, at the opera, I was sure of it; I studied the faces around me and I knew, *I knew,* this was the right place."

"The right place for what?"

"A whorehouse."

I looked around again. "Here? In this house? On this street?"

"Yes. That's the beauty of it. What they can't get at home, they can get right next door, or at least down the street, or down the street from someone they know. Private. Expensive. Very discreet and filled with beautiful, intelligent women who *want* to be there, not *have* to be there."

"You've thought about this."

"Yes."

"And Solomon agrees?"

"Yes."

"Does Thomas Eliot know he's going to be living in a red-light district?"

She laughed and said, "No, and don't tell him either. He'll think we're the Muses. And we will be."

We got back on our bicycles and rode until we turned on McPherson and stopped for chocolate at Bissinger's. I was still thinking about her plan, seeing only disadvantages. "Seriously, Carolina, is this what you want to do? It is against the law, you know?"

"It's what I know how to do, Z. It's what Georgia and I learned. I can't just quit because Georgia's gone and it's illegal. I never make anyone do anything they don't want to do and I won't allow anyone around who does. I'll have Li close by to make sure of that. I'll also bet 'the law' is our best customer."

"I guess it is better than having babies."

"Don't make fun of me, Z. Just because I'm for one thing doesn't mean I'm against another."

"I'm sorry, that was stupid."

"I love babies," she said.

There was an awkward moment that passed between us. It happened rarely, but it did happen; the unspoken knowledge and fact that our difference wasn't just in our remarks, it was deeper in the blood, further back in time. It was a difference that we ignored, but would forever keep us apart, a difference we could not change. Carolina used the tension to tell me more.

"Another thing, Z. I know you've been thinking about that evil one, that one that did those things to Mrs. Bennings and Georgia. I want you to stop. I want you to let it go and remember Georgia, not avenge her. I know Sailor wants you to do something, not about that, but about something else. I don't know what it is, but I think you ought to do it. For your own good."

Her words hit me hard. Inside, underneath everything else, I knew she was right. I was changing, but all I was really changing was one obsession for another. In my heart of hearts, chasing Sailor had turned into chasing the Fleur-du-Mal, and for all the wrong reasons. I knew she was right about Sailor too. I knew he wanted me to do something, but he hadn't mentioned his "offer" since that first day.

"I hope you have lots of babies," I said, "and I hereby bestow Mama's baseball glove upon your firstborn."

"You're crazy," she said.

We rode our bicycles back the way we came and turned them in at Forest Park. We walked back to the Statler Hotel in the twilight, a long walk, but a good one at that time of year. The next day Sailor made his "offer."

We took the train west out of Union Station to the Meramec Highlands, an amusement park that the Frisco Railroad had a direct line to, hauling five hundred passengers a day. Once there, you could ride horses, pedal bicycles, row boats, or swim in the Meramec River. "Privacy in Public" was their motto.

Solomon, Carolina, and Ray chose horseback riding. Sailor said he wanted to row a boat and he asked for my company. As we launched our boat, I asked him if he didn't think the name "Mera-mec" was ironic, considering the circumstances. He said no, he hadn't thought about it, but that was in the area of what he wanted to discuss. We set out on the water, Sailor rowing easily, gracefully, better than any twelve-year-old in the world.

Several minutes passed. I watched his concentration and the way every stroke was complete, none more important than the other, each with a meaning all its own. While still rowing, he said, "I am reminded of the first time I rowed with passion. It was 2,737 years ago, 841 BC by the Roman calendar. It was the time of 'Those-Who-Fled.' " He stopped rowing and looked at me, trying to catch my reaction. I sat still. I hadn't asked him about these things, but I wanted to know. He started rowing again and went on. "I was escaping a Phoenician ship in what is now the Bay of La Concha, near the Basque village of Gipuzkoa. We left in the dark when the tide was right so we could float in silence before we had to row. There were forty-three of us, all that would fit in the tiny boat. Others had to stay behind. Choices had to be made. It was decided that the five Egizahar families carrying the Stones would leave and the rest would escape later, somewhere, somehow. There was someone very important to me that we left behind on that ship. Someone whose absence from me made me row with hatred for the Phoenicians and fury against any power that would let this happen. They had violated my family, betrayed our Basque protectors, and stolen my Ameq."

"What is Ameq?" I interrupted.

"My beloved . . . the one for whom I waited. Deza was her name. I tell you this now because you feel hatred for the Fleur-du-Mal and the way he has violated your family, your Giza family. I want you to go with me and meet some of your real family, your own blood, your own protectors, and then make a decision about the Fleur-du-Mal. You may still seek revenge. It will be your decision, but I ask you now, Zianno, to go with me first. There is another way to defeat the Fleur-du-Mal. He knows something we need to know and he thinks we are unable to find it without him. You may have the power within you to find it yourself."

"What power?"

He stopped rowing altogether and drew in the oars, crossing them over his knees. He leaned forward, closing his left eye and searching my eyes with his right, his ghost eye. "Your dreams," he said. "You are the Stone of Dreams. Your father and six fathers behind him have carried the Stones since we left that Phoenician ship so long ago. They have all gone deep within their own dreams, but none has found what we need, none has broken through."

"What do you need?"

"The fifth set of Stones and the Bihazanu of the one that wears them."

"Bihazanu?"

"It is an old word, a Meq word; it means heartfear. I will tell you of this and much, much more if you go with me to your western United States, to the high desert. There are people there you should meet, people there you must meet."

"What people?"

"Your protectors; Basque shepherds from the tribe of Vardules and others, old friends of mine."

He smoothly slipped the oars back into the water and turned us around in an easy, practiced motion. We headed back to the dock and I noticed that all the rowing boats were painted exactly the same. Coming and going, each one, just like the other.

"Yes," I said suddenly, "I will go with you."

After that, events moved swiftly. Solomon arranged for us to use his private railroad car and have access to any line on any railroad in the United States; money was no object. We were to meet a man, Owen Bramley, in Denver, and he would make sure everything went according to Solomon's wishes. Solomon said Bramley was "his man" and would handle everything with efficiency and discretion. "He is one of those damn Scottish men," he said, "he will pay you no mind and get the job done and done right."

Even with Ray going, which Sailor had insisted upon, we had very little luggage. I left my baseball glove with Carolina, this time with her full knowledge, but for the same reasons. We spoke very little on the way to Union Station. It was a beautiful, clear green and blue day. This parting seemed natural, expected, and we were both comfortable with it; but leaving is still leaving.

"We have done this before," I said.

"Yes, we have." She wore a yellow dress and carried a yellow parasol, unopened. She was sitting on a stranger's trunk that had been left alone on the platform and she was attracting stares from a few passersby; ladies simply did not sit on trunks.

"I'm not sure why I'm leaving this time."

"It's not the why that concerns me, Z. It's the where. I don't want to lose touch with you for another twelve years. I'm not a vain woman, but even I might be too old for you by then."

We both smiled and watched Li and Solomon conferring with the conductor.

"Write to me," I said. "Solomon told me Owen Bramley will be able to find us anywhere." I turned to get on the train. Sailor and Ray were already on board. *"Egibizirik bilatu,"* I said.

"What? What does that mean?"

"It has something to do with a long-living truth."

"I agree," she said, standing up and opening her parasol at the same time.

As we pulled out of the station, I waved to Solomon and he gave me the new sign he had been using for "good business"; he gave me a thumbs-up.

Sailor smiled his sly smile and gave a silent nod through the window and a kind of salute to Solomon. Ray was pacing back and forth in the railroad car anxiously looking out both sides and taking his bowler hat off and on. He was nervous about something.

"What's the matter, Ray?" I asked.

"Nothing. Nothing's the matter. Why?"

"You seem edgy, that's all."

"Well, maybe I am, a little, I don't know. It's just that I . . . I never been to the mountains. Ain't that odd? All this time and I never been to the mountains."

"It's not the mountains, Ray, and you know it." It was Sailor who spoke and he spoke in a voice we hadn't heard him use before—a voice of authority. He was staring out of the window, but he was speaking to both of us.

I looked at Sailor and asked, "What is it then?"

He turned his head and motioned for Ray to sit down, close, so he could see Ray's eyes. He watched him as the train settled into a steady rhythm. We were nearing the western fringe of the city, where Victorian homes and trolley cars became small farms and cornfields and cattle.

"Ray is nervous because he knows where we are going. He knows we are going to meet some people, some Giza, who not only know who we are, but protect us. Not like Carolina and Solomon. He has known others like them. These people are Basque and he has only heard of them in legend or a story his mother may have told him. This makes him afraid because he is Egipurdiko, not Egizahar. Am I right, Ray?"

Ray looked sheepish. "Am I that easy to read?"

"No, no," Sailor said, "your anxiety is natural. It is always natural. I knew your mother, or at least I knew her family in the Azores hundreds of years ago. They and others like them have always thought these Basque tribes, if they exist, favor the Egizahar over the 'diko.' That somehow, if you are 'diko,' you will be found out and harmed. That is wrong. First of all, they do exist, and second, they make no distinction between us. Unfortunately, only *we* make a distinction between us. It is an old, tired practice and needs to be done away with.

"No, Ray, you have nothing to fear from these Basque we shall meet. They are good, honorable people descended from the tribe of Vardules, simple shepherds really. And they would all give their lives to save Zianno and what he wears around his neck. They always have, they always will."

I thought this was as good a time as any to ask him what had been on my mind for some time. "Why do they protect us? And if they do, why haven't they come to me?"

Sailor turned the ring on his forefinger, pausing, then looked me in the face. His "ghost eye" was cloudy and swirling. "The answer to that," he said, "is older than I. I only know that they know of us, they always have. The Basque and the Meq are like sky and water—each taking credit for the other's origin.

"There are few left; few of them and few of us. And the few who are left honor the old traditions. The first one of which is, Zianno, you come to them—they do not come to you."

"What do they know about the Stones? Do they know what we can do?"

"Of course. The Stones are a sacred mystery to the few Basque who know of them, as they are to us."

"What do they think of someone like you? Someone who outlives them all for countless generations and remains a kid? A boy?"

"We have worked that out," he said. "You will find out what I mean for yourself."

Ray got up from his seat and walked the length of the car and back. He rubbed his hands over the soft velvet of the furniture and the burl walnut finish of the cabinets. "You say they're shepherds, is that right?"

"Yes," Sailor answered.

"Damn."

The trip through Missouri went too fast. Every stream was blue and every tree was in full leaf and still colored a spring green, not the deep green they would soon be. We were treated like princes by the porters and given everything we needed. By the time we hit the endless, flat prairie of Kansas, we all agreed that if you had to cross this land, this was the way to do it.

In Denver, we were surprised to find that Owen Bramley wasn't there. After what Solomon had said about him I expected him to be opening our door before the train had stopped. He did leave a telegram for Sailor though. It was sent from San Francisco and said, "Sorry didn't make connection STOP Am waiting for extra cargo STOP Will meet in Boise STOP Owen Bramley STOP."

"What does that mean?" I asked.

Sailor folded the telegram in quarters and placed it inside his boot just below the knee. "I'm not sure," he said and then smiled. "We may have an unexpected guest."

Just then, I felt a presence, a presence laced with fear—the net descending. I looked at Sailor and Ray and they felt it too. We instinctively looked around and through the crowd. Someone was watching us and it wasn't the usual glance of curiosity. I searched the faces, at random, quickly, chasing the eyes that were following mine. And just for a split second, I thought I caught the razor-thin eyes of a man in a bowler hat, like Ray's, staring back, knowing me. Then he disappeared in the crowd.

"Was that the unexpected guest?" I asked Sailor.

"I think not," he said.

"Then what was that?"

"I do not know. Let's hope our train leaves soon."

"Does Solomon have any enemies?"

"I presume many, but that presence was directed at us. There is always danger when two or more of us who carry the Stones travel together. That is the first time I have felt danger since we met."

"Have they been stolen before? The Stones, I mean."

"No."

"Never?"

"Never, though it has been attempted a thousand times. The gems have always attracted the Giza's attention."

"But how would they know? How would they ever know where any of us were going to be?"

"Mistakes, inattention, carelessness, fatigue, taking time itself for granted, false security, the Fleur-du-Mal—"

"The Fleur-du-Mal!" I shouted.

"Yes, his greatest avocation is selling the Giza on a plan to steal the Stones, getting his money, and laughing as he leaves, knowing they will not succeed."

"What stops them?"

"Our . . . abilities . . . and the kind of people we are on our way to meet. They and their ancestors are tireless sentinels."

Solomon's railroad car was recoupled to the appropriate line and we departed for the spectacular route through the Rocky Mountains and into the Great Basin and Salt Lake City. I watched Ray watch the mountains and I could tell he really had never seen them before. As we snaked through passes, only to find more mountains, more passes, more of everything, he watched in silence and awe and truly became twelve years old again.

I thought briefly of Mama and Papa, but not in a sad or nostalgic way; I felt that their bones inhabited a good place; a place of clean rock and water, pine, aspen, and hawks. Their material passage back to dust would be a good place for their spirits to rise.

Sailor rode through the mountains in silence. He was alone in himself, but his memories were crowded. He turned the ring on his forefinger sideways and stroked the priceless sapphire with the smooth part of his thumb.

We made a connection in Salt Lake and turned north toward the high desert and Boise, Idaho.

We arrived in the late afternoon. It was hot, dry, and windy. Sailor opened a window and a fine mist of grit and dirt blew in. You could feel it like sand in your eyes and teeth. Our railroad car was uncoupled on a side track and left by itself as the rest of the train pulled back on the main line. We stepped down from the car and looked around for our hosts. I saw people scurrying in and out of the station, holding on to their fedoras, Stetsons, bonnets, and scarves, most keeping a handkerchief over their nose and mouth.

Ray was holding on to his bowler too. "I wonder if it's always like this?" he said.

Out of nowhere, a voice answered, "Not always, señor. In the winter it snows."

We all turned at once to see a wiry young man of about twenty years old holding a red beret in his right hand and motioning us toward a wagon with his left. He and three other men on horseback, all wearing red berets, had appeared silent as shadows around the corner of the station.

"This way, please," he said. "I will take you to the Aita."

Sailor took a step toward him, squinting with his ghost eye. "Are you Pello?"

"Yes, señor, I am."

"In the blink of an eye," Sailor said, "I swear, Pello, in the blink of an eye you have become a man."

It was odd. I had never seen it before, but the young man, who looked to be at least Sailor's older brother, maybe even a young father, was self-conscious and slightly embarrassed, as he would have been if an uncle or grandfather had made the same remark.

Sailor turned to me and told me he wanted to check and see if Owen Bramley had sent a message. He left for the station and the Basque men dismounted and loaded our things onto the wagon. Sailor was back in minutes and I couldn't tell from his expression whether there was a message or not. He jumped in the wagon and we headed south across the Snake River, trying to shield our eyes and mouths from the grit. The Basque didn't seem to notice.

I asked Sailor what "Aita" meant and he said it meant Father. We were on our way to see the Father of the western clan of the tribe of Vardules. Most of them were sheepmen and many had emigrated from Vizcaya and Navarra in Spain. Cousins, nephews, sons, and daughters, all came and went under the tutelage and blessing of their "Aita." Only this "Aita" hadn't always been a sheepman. He had been a sailor in his youth and toured the world many times before he became "Aita." Sailor knew him as Kepa, Kepa Txopitea.

We changed direction at a town called Riddle and headed east and south, crossing two small rivers. The sun was low and the mesas to our west cast shadows across the basin ahead of us. Just at sunset, we veered toward what appeared to be a single mesa at least twenty miles long, but as we came closer, turned out to be two mesas, running parallel and staggered.

We rounded the end of the first mesa on a narrow, well-worn trail and a world within a world came into view. Between the mesas, two miles wide and five miles long, was a valley, an oasis, a green world of pine, aspen, and spruce with a bursting spring-fed stream winding down the center. So unexpected and dreamlike was the sight that Ray whispered, "Damn."

We followed the trail that followed the stream back toward its source. Along the way, I saw thousands of sheep grazing in four different natural meadows angling up and away from the stream. I heard music at one point and Sailor heard it too. He straightened up sharply and we both looked in the same direction. It was behind the pines, among the rocks somewhere. Sailor smiled. It was the same melody I'd heard from a distance in Bermuda. It was Meq.

We slowed for the gate to a corral to be opened and closed behind us. We came to a sprawling set of buildings, all of them stucco with red tile roofs and supported with pine beams. Each was directly or indirectly connected to the other and together they loosely formed the shape of a horseshoe.

There was life everywhere. A campfire burned in the center even though there was still some daylight. There were men tending to sheep and horses; women carrying water and baskets of vegetables while yelling at children who were laughing and ignoring them; dogs, chickens, cats, and, on the veranda of what looked like the central building, an old man in a rocking chair, watching our arrival.

We pulled to a stop in front of him. Sailor got out first, then Ray, then me. The children gathered and surrounded us. Some were shorter than us and some taller. The men on horseback tied their horses and stood behind the old man's chair. A small woman with gray hair pulled back in a braid came from inside the building wiping her hands on a cloth and smiling. She walked over to the old man and stood beside him.

He rose slowly, but no one moved to help. I could tell that even if he needed help he wouldn't have asked for it or expected it. He was thin and wiry, but not weak. His hair was white and close-cropped and he had at least a seven-day growth of grizzled, white beard. He wore an old and unique vest of sheepskin and leather with colored symbols carved and dyed into it. Underneath the vest, he wore no shirt and there was a small tattoo of a bull on his left breast. Even in wide cotton trousers, I could tell he was bow-legged and he started walking toward us, then stopped abruptly.

"Miren!" he said, turning to the woman at his side. "My beret!"

She quickly ran inside and back, handing him an old red beret. He placed it on his head at a precise angle. Then, he walked directly to Sailor and said, "It is good to see you, old one."

"You too, Kepa," Sailor said in a monotone, then he smiled and added, "You smell like sheep."

Everyone broke into laughter and the real greeting began. Sailor already knew half the crowd that had gathered and was introduced to the rest. Then Sailor introduced Ray to Kepa, his wife Miren, his four sons, one of whom was Pello who drove our wagon, three of his seven daughters and their children, and several other cousins, lieutenants, nieces, and nephews. He turned to me then and spoke to Kepa.

"I brought someone else, someone I think you should meet. It is a good time of year for such a thing."

"It is a good time of year, indeed, old one," Kepa said. "We have fat lamb and fresh water from the stream and even a full moon tonight. Let us meet."

He walked over to me and looked down in my eyes. He was an old man, but still taller than I was and I met his gaze with my own.

"Your father was like a father to me," he said. "I miss him as a blind man misses touch—I want you to know that. I am Kepa Txopitea, Aita in the tribe of Vardules, protectors of the Stone of Dreams. I welcome you to our camp. We would have met sooner or later, but I am pleased it is now. Now is a good time of year."

"Yes," I said, "now is the best time of year."

We embraced and it was a formal embrace, but genuine. He backed up a step or two and opened his vest, nodding his head for me to look at his tattoo. I looked and it was magnificent; a bull as big as his fist in profile and drawn with skill and detail in now faded blues, blacks, reds, and golds.

"You see," he said, "Zezen, the bull. Your name, your family," and then he placed his open hand over his chest. "My heart," he said.

Miren elbowed him in the ribs and made him introduce her to me, then she insisted we be shown to our rooms and be given fresh towels, soap, and water. We were treated like family, not guests. I appreciated the feeling and told Kepa so. He shrugged it off, waving his arm, and said, "I know you have been to sea, Sailor has told me; so have I, but wait 'til you see the stars here, Zianno. There are more than in the Fijis."

"I've never been to the Fijis."

"Then remember these—they will be enough."

Our rooms were simple and clean. There was a single bed in mine with a window next to it looking out and across the space between the mesas. It faced west, and by turning your head from right to left, you could follow the stream all the way up the valley to where the mesas seemed to join and the stream found its source.

I sat on the bed to take in the view and almost sat on a cylindrical leather case lying on the blankets. It was very old, about eighteen inches long, and divided into two sections held together with brass clasps. Slipped underneath the case was a note folded in two. I read the note and it said, "For the Shepherd of the Izarharri—Good for wonder, good for wolves!"

I opened the leather case carefully. Inside and fitting perfectly in a molded purple velvet lining was a single-lens telescope in two parts, one sliding into the other. It was made of brass and highly polished. The craftsmanship was exquisite and there were no markings on it except for two tiny initials engraved near the eyepiece: A. L.

I held it in my hands and it felt somehow familiar. I extended the two sections and looked through it to the west where the sun had set and the first few stars were appearing. Old as it was, it worked perfectly.

I put the telescope back in its case and walked to Sailor's room where he had changed clothes and was lacing up his boots.

"This was lying on my bed," I said and handed him the case. "This was with it." I gave him the note. He read it and smiled.

"What does 'Shepherd of the Izarharri' mean?" I asked.

"Izarharri is the old word for Starstone. You are the Shepherd, the caretaker, of the Starstone. Kepa wants to give you something in recognition of this, something priceless to him. Therefore, he gives you his telescope; the same telescope that your father gave to him years ago."

"My father!"

"Yes, and it was given to your father in the seventeenth century by Baruch Spinoza, the Dutch philosopher, who in turn had it given to him by Anton van Leeuwenhoek. It is very rare and of very good quality for its time. Look, there by the eyepiece, you can read the etched A and L."

"I know, I saw it. I can't keep this, you know. Even if it was my father's, it must mean too much to Kepa for me to accept it."

"You must accept it. It would be an insult not to. It is because it does mean so much to him that he gives it to you."

I walked to Sailor's window and gazed out at the same view I had from my own. It was getting dark and light at the same time. The full moon was rising. Something basic and fundamental occurred to me. I suddenly felt light, almost weightless, as if I were a piece of paper no bigger than Kepa's note and I might, at any second, fly out of the window, over the stream, up the face of the mesa, and disappear in the western sky. I turned to Sailor.

"I don't know what I'm supposed to *do* here," I said.

"Do? You are not supposed to *do* anything. In time, you will have a dream, we hope. A dream your father and his father and his father never had."

"Why do you think I will have the dream?"

"I do not think it—I hope. There is no way to know, but there is also no reason for you to worry and doubt. Besides, tomorrow you meet Eder-Meq, my sister, and her Ameq, Baju Gaztelu, and their daughter, Nova. Nova is newly born and I have only seen her once myself. Kepa is planning a feast that will last all day and night. Do not worry, Zianno. You have time. You are Meq, remember? You have all the time in the world, so enjoy it."

"You have a sister?"

"Yes, it is strange to see her aging, but always good to see her, nevertheless."

"Was that her singing we heard? From the wagon?"

"Yes."

I remembered the melody, the ancient melody, and the way the notes rose and fell, hanging on to each other like hands across an abyss, lifting and swaying, never letting go.

"The song's about return, isn't it?"

Sailor had long since finished lacing his boots and he stood up, motioning toward the door for us to leave.

"Yes," he said.

"Return to where?"

"We do not know."

That night, we had what I'm sure was, for Kepa's clan, a quiet meal. There were but fourteen people at the table and it only lasted two hours. During the meal, I noticed Pello watching me; not in a menacing way or even staring—just watching.

Kepa talked about the problems the Basque sheepmen were having. More and more grazing land and forest were being federalized and made into reserves where the itinerant Basque and his sheep were not welcome. Some were called "tramp farmers" and discriminated against like the Chinese had been. No one wanted to do the work of the Basque, but no one wanted the Basque to do it either.

Afterward, I walked with Kepa to a low stone wall overlooking the long valley and the stream. The water was shining in the moonlight.

"The stream looks magic tonight," I said.

"Yes, it does," he said, then stepped up on the wall, looking back at me. "It is a small stream, but a good stream. A small stream that flows into another that flows into the Bruneau that flows into the Snake . . . not unlike ourselves, no?"

I told him I wanted to know more about my papa, about their times together, and he promised many stories and tales to come. He told me I was welcome here as long as I liked and would be for the rest of his life and his son's and his son's sons'. We said good night and I walked back to my room, thinking the long day was over.

There was a lamp already lit on the nightstand next to the bed. I spread the blanket out and sat down, dead tired and ready for sleep. I took the telescope out of its case, just to see it once more before I slept. I thought about my papa holding it, using it. I thought about where he might have used it and wondered if he kept notes and if he did where they would be and who might have them, and then I thought about Kepa and I opened his note and read it again—"Good for wonder, good for wolves!"—and I thought about the Fleur-du-Mal and I thought about Carolina and I wondered, wondered . . . then I fell asleep, for how long I don't know, but the telescope had rolled off the bed and hit the floor, waking me, opening the door to a Walking Dream.

I pick up the telescope and walk out of the room. I walk outside and back to the stone wall. I step up and over the wall and I land on four legs. I am heavy, but graceful. I am grazing, making my way down the slope toward the stream. I know my way, I have been here before, but this time there is something different, something new, something that has never been here before. I take a different path to the stream. I see the wolf ahead of time. He is surprised. The ritual is well known and understood. He is alarmed and I see it in his eyes. He starts upstream, loping through the rocks in the shallow water by the shore. I follow easily. He takes the familiar path, but this time I close the gap. I pick up speed and so does he. We run for miles and I see the jewels and dead bodies strewn among the rocks. I pay no attention. I close the gap even more. We ascend, climbing the mountain, toward the source of the stream and the place I cannot follow, the place I have never been allowed. I change shape and walk upright on two legs, but I continue to climb and gain ground. The wolf stops and turns and stares. He has never seen me, not this me. I start to cry out. The wolf turns and runs to where the stream pours out of the mountain; the dark pool and spring where I cannot go. He does not look back and leaps into the swirling abyss. I stop at the edge and look down. There is a trail of stars where he has disappeared. I remember the telescope. I take it out and extend it, looking through the veil of water and stars until I find the wolf retreating, changing; form became feeling and feeling became beauty and she was revealed . . . naked . . . innocent . . . and wearing the Stones. Then something else happened—something so outrageous, unknown, and unexpected that I woke up.

I was alone on a slab of rock jutting out over a four-hundred-foot drop. The sun was just rising over the mesa. I had no idea where I was or how I got there. The telescope was in my hand. From behind me I heard a voice.

"Do not move, señor. Before you stand, let me help you." It was Pello. He said he had followed me all night and watched me, keeping his distance, but at some point he lost me and didn't find me until that moment when I cried out. I asked him where we were and he said we were far to the south, miles from camp.

He helped me up and we started back along a narrow ledge, then down through brush and scrub cedar until we found a trail he knew by heart.

It took five hours to walk back to Kepa's camp and when we finally stepped over the low stone wall and were in the compound itself, no one seemed to notice. Most were gathered by the veranda of the central building, children especially.

They were surrounding a tall man with red hair and a bristly red mustache, wearing wire-rimmed glasses and showing everyone how to assemble a Chinese kite. Some other men were preparing several lambs for an open-pit cookout. I asked one of them who the red-haired man was and he said his name was Owen Bramley and he and someone I might know had arrived by train in Boise the night before and made their way here this morning. I looked at Pello and he shrugged.

I walked toward my room, and just before I went in, I saw Sailor talking to someone, someone our size. Neither one of them saw me approach. They were deep in discussion about something. Then I saw two things I hadn't seen in a long time, but they were still familiar—a black beret and black ballet slippers. It was Geaxi, and as I got nearer, I could just hear the end of her sentence ". . . but she is no longer there, she has vanished."

From behind them, I said, "I know who you seek."

They both turned at once and stared at me.

"You seek Opari," I said.

They both showed no surprise, but they continued to stare.

"And I know her Bihazanu, her heartfear."

"What is it?" Geaxi asked.

"Me."

8

IZAR
(STAR)

"Follow your Star."

The words are simple, but the real thing is a little tricky. Does it mean direction? Is it Destiny?

If you could chart the movement of the largest, farthest, fastest supernova and still find the smallest grain of interstellar matter—stardust—would it answer the why, the where, the who? Would it finally connect you in a line of time and circumstance to a singular continuum like the drawn lines of a five-pointed star?

If only it were that simple.

The trick in chasing Destiny is to feel it as a rider, a rider on a spinning ball waiting for a rare chance in time. Those few moments of balance between darkness and light where the Infinite is in motion and the motion is felt as a dance, as a solution that dissolves the question.

You are suspended, and yet, you have met Destiny. You have been eclipsed.

Sailor and Geaxi kept staring at me. They could have been two strange children, perhaps brother and sister, dropped off suddenly by someone and left without a ride. Their looks were a mixture of disbelief, bewilderment, and wonder.

Sailor walked over to me. He looked at my torn clothes, the caked mud on my face and hands, and the blood-crusted scratches on my arms that were healing and disappearing as he looked.

"You have had the Dream?" he asked, almost in a whisper.

"I have had *a* dream," I said. "Something—someone—was revealed to me. I know that her name is Opari. She has great strength, power, and cunning. She knows that you seek her and in her heart of hearts, somehow, for some reason, fears me. She doesn't know me, but she fears I will find her."

Sailor turned for a moment and glanced at Geaxi. Silently, gracefully, she closed the few paces between us.

He turned back to me and said, "Your father and your father's fathers never had anything revealed to them. They had to be told her name, and even then, she never revealed herself to them."

"I think I surprised her and I think I know why, but I can't be sure until I see her."

Once again, Sailor and Geaxi looked at me and smiled. I hadn't seen that smile since being surprised by her so long ago on that hot afternoon down that dark alley in St. Louis.

"Hello, young Zezen," she said and she reached in her vest and took out a cube of salt, placing it in my hand and closing my fingers.

"*Egibizirik bilatu,*" I said.

"Five fingers—one hand," she answered.

"I haven't heard that one."

"There are a million of them," she said. "Sailor probably knows two million. I cannot keep track. Now, tell me, can you find Opari?"

As tired and weary as I was, I still almost laughed. Nice, blunt, and right to the point—that was Geaxi. I did manage a smile and turned to look around me before I answered. It was midafternoon and the whole camp was alive. I caught sight of Ray standing among the Basque children watching Owen Bramley and his Chinese kites. Kepa was watching too, sitting in his chair with one of his grandchildren on his knee. Miren was standing next to him, her hand on his shoulder. Dogs barked everywhere from the excitement and activity. This was a day of celebration and feast for the Basque, all on account of us. But who were we? What were we?

I looked hard at Sailor and Geaxi and said, "I need to know now who Opari is and why you need to find her."

Geaxi started to speak, but Sailor cut her off and said, "There is a better one to answer your questions. Go and clean yourself and change your clothes. We will go to see Eder, my sister."

Geaxi nodded her approval, and even though I wanted an answer, a hot bath and clean clothes sounded good.

An hour later, the three of us and Ray were walking the same trail on which I had heard the singing back behind the pines. Sailor had insisted on Ray coming along. He liked bringing Ray into a circle of friends and family he had never known. He wanted Ray to feel good about being Meq.

Sailor knew the trail well and, at some point only he could see, took us up through the pines and scrambling around boulders three times our size until we entered a natural clearing hidden from the world and open to the sky.

At the far end of the clearing and slightly up the slope from us, there was a small, well-constructed log cabin. In the middle of the clearing, standing by itself on a leveled stone platform, was something I had never seen before—a sundial. It was amazing. Sailor said it was an early Roman sundial that Baju had taken with him from Spain when he and Eder moved to America. It was so incongruous and yet it seemed always to have been there. Sailor said Baju had been known for centuries among the Meq as "Stargazer." Now that he and Eder had crossed in the Zeharkatu, he preferred just Baju. He was from the mountains of Bizkaia where they respected time and silence and the night sky. He had the ability to foretell certain "events," as Ray could the weather, and Sailor hoped Nova would inherit the trait. "One never knows," Sailor said. "That part is tricky."

We walked past the sundial and approached the cabin. There was a covered veranda on all four sides and standing on the one facing west and waving to us was a young man and woman with a small child perched on the man's shoulders. As we drew nearer and I could make out their faces, I caught my breath and stopped abruptly. Except for clothes and hairstyles, they could have been my mama and papa. Geaxi seemed to know what I was thinking and turned to me. She said, "Familiar, no?"

I couldn't reply, but I walked on with the others and when we got to the cabin, the young couple met us on the steps.

Sailor made the formal introductions and I found out Baju was also through the tribe of Vardules. Our families shared a long history. When Sailor introduced Ray, a very unusual thing happened. The little girl, Nova, who was about eighteen months old and clinging to her papa's neck with her arms and legs, suddenly opened her arms wide and begged Ray to take her. Ray got that sheepish look again, as if he'd been caught doing something he had no idea he'd done, but he let her swing over to him and sit on his shoulders and play with his bowler hat. She was attached to him and stayed that way the entire time we were there.

Sailor's sister watched and waited her turn. As Sailor began the words, she waved him off and came over to me, embracing me with no words at all. I held her tight. It was as natural as embracing Mama and, unexpectedly, I felt tears sliding down my cheeks. She whispered in my ear while we held each other.

"Your mama was my closest friend. I never got to say farewell."

Slowly, we eased our hold on each other. She backed up taking my hands in hers and examining me like a rare but familiar coin. As she studied me, I studied her. It was strange. If I had been Giza and looked my real age, she would have looked younger than I did. I could even have been attracted to her, as any man would to a pretty young Basque woman, but that was not the way it was. It was a kind of Meq paradox. I was in a child's body, and until recently she was as well but she was much, much older.

"Come," she said. "Come with me."

She kissed Baju and Nova, gave Sailor a lingering glance, and led me off the veranda and into the pines. We followed a winding, well-worn path up and away from the cabin until we came to an outcrop of rocks with a few boulders in the middle lying flat on their sides. They formed a gigantic, natural table with a view of the horizon at all four points of the compass. The sun was low in the west. We climbed up on the huge stone table and she sat down cross-legged, reminding me for an instant of Carolina and Georgia. The air was cool and dry, but the wind was swirling. She reached up and adjusted her hair, taking out two ivory barrettes with strange markings on them.

"Eder? Should I call you that?"

"Yes, of course," she said. "I forgot. We never exchanged names. I have always known yours, but you must never have heard of me before today."

"Yesterday, actually."

She laughed a little and turned her head to the side, sliding one of the barrettes into place. "Those barrettes are beautiful," I said. "Where did you get them?"

She held one out in front of her, turning it over in her hand and rubbing her fingers over the markings. Then she handed it to me, saying, "My mama gave them to me on my twelfth birthday—my first one. They are the oldest things in my possession. Mama said they were made in the Time of Ice, when the ice was retreating and we lived in its shadow."

She took my other hand and rubbed my fingers over the markings. The tiny lines and half circles were etched deep in the ivory.

"That is Meq writing," she said.

"What does it mean?"

"We do not know. We have lost the ability to read it. Perhaps you will dream the code, no?"

She stood up and looked toward the sun in the west. It was almost over the horizon, but still glowed like a round, bloodred ruby. She walked in a circle around the stone table. "Your mama would have liked it here. Your papa too. He and Baju could have watched the night sky and had all their old arguments about the stars. I miss them. I wanted them to see Nova. I wanted . . ."

Her voice trailed off and she stopped to watch the sun finally set. After a few moments, she turned toward me and I knew it was time to ask her. I wanted to hear more about Mama and Papa, but that could wait. "Tell me about Opari," I said.

Suddenly she smiled and then put her hand over her mouth. She stared at me in disbelief. "You have had the Dream?" she whispered through her fingers.

I looked away from her for some reason and saw Venus rising in the east. "I have had *a* dream," I said and turned back to face her. "Sailor said I should ask you about Opari."

She sat down slowly, cross-legged again. She leaned forward a little with her hands folded in her lap.

"Then I shall tell you," she began. "I shall tell you what I know as best I can because I have never seen her. Sailor is the only one of us to have seen her and that was long ago in the time of Those-Who-Fled. It is rumored that the one we call the Fleur-du-Mal has also seen her, but this has always been speculation."

She stopped for a moment with a peculiar expression on her face. "Did Sailor tell you anything? Anything at all?"

"No."

"Ah, I see. Well, that should not surprise me. It is still difficult for him, even after all this time. He carries too many memories."

"Go on, please," I said. "I need to know everything you can tell me."

She went on, speaking quietly, but urgently. "Opari is the oldest among us, if she still exists. She is over three thousand years old. At the time she was born, all Meq lived in the Pyrenees. Her family lived in the hills of Oiartzun, through the tribe of Autrigons. They wore the Stone of Blood, as you wear the Stone of Dreams. Our histories and traditions, our customs, rituals, and ceremonies were known to all the Meq and were intact and used. Our written language was still practiced and passed down. It was an ancient culture even then, and known only to a few Basque of the five tribes. Our 'differences' and 'abilities' were totally unknown to the rest of the world. Then the Phoenicians came.

"At first, the Basque in the coastal villages treated them the same as they had the Celts and Picts, who had come by sea from the north, as equal and respected traders. The Phoenicians came seldom and generally left the Basque alone. Then, their visits became more frequent and they left men in the villages with the Basque to mine tin and other metals they could trade in the East. The Basque became less and less enchanted with their presence. This was new to the Basque, who had been isolated in their land for thousands of years. The Phoenicians had sophisticated weaponry and fortified ships, however, and they were

practical and more interested in good business than conquering lands.
A few leaders of the five tribes of the Basque approached the Phoenicians with an offer. If the Phoenicians would remove their men from
the mines and their standing armies from the villages and only trade,
in the future, from their ships in the coves and harbors, the Basque
would trade exclusively with the Phoenicians. But they were naive.
The Phoenicians never planned on staying in the first place. The cost
of mining and the distance of their routes were becoming less profitable. Nevertheless, they told the Basque they would agree to these
terms if the Basque could offer them something as a 'gift,' something
that would be treasured and desired by the rest of the world and only
the Phoenicians would have it. And whatever it might be, it would
be the bond that would seal the promise between the Basque and
themselves. The Basque believed them. After many meetings among
the leaders of the tribes, an Aita of the Autrigons suggested a 'loan'
rather than a 'gift.' He said there was no gold, tin, silver, or anything
else as rare as the 'Children of the Mountains.' He suggested that a few
of us could travel with the Phoenicians, serving as ambassadors and
symbols of the magic in the Basque homeland and also represent the
power of the Phoenicians. No one else could think of a better alternative and they sent the Aita to talk with the uncle of Opari. What
was said is not known, but for some reason he agreed and he spoke for
all the 'children.'

"The families gathered in a central village and were told of the
situation and opportunity. We were also naive and many thought it
would be an honor and a chance to travel beyond the Pyrenees, Opari
and her sister Deza included." Eder stopped and asked, "Do you know
of Deza?"

"Yes," I said, "a little, mainly just the name."

She nodded and went on. "Opari and Deza had been in the Itxaron,
the Wait, for hundreds of years. Neither had met their Ameq. They
both hoped to be chosen for the voyage, but Opari wore the Stones
and early at the gathering it was decided that the five who wore the
Stones would be the ones to go. The disappointment Deza felt did not
last long, however. At the gathering, Deza met her Ameq—my
brother, Umla-Meq.

"He and I had been in the Itxaron for only a few years, like yourself, and he never expected it. I was not at the gathering, but he told me later about the shock of the experience. A thousand years later, I found out myself."

"What exactly is the Itxaron?" I interrupted. "No one has ever really told me."

She looked in my eyes, searching, as Sailor had. I saw Mama turning her face toward me on the train. Slowly, evenly, she said, "It is the one thing that makes us—the Meq—different from all other species. The Egizahar *must* do it; the Egipurdiko do it sometimes, not often. We do not know why. It is in our nature to wait, physically and spiritually wait through Time for our Beloved, the one and only other with whom we are complete. This may happen soon, as in Sailor's case, or it may take centuries, as in my case, or Deza's, or Opari's. And once you find your Ameq, it is still a conscious choice when and if you will cross in the Zeharkatu and become like the Giza and mature and have children of your own and be vulnerable to accident, disease, age, and death.

"Trumoi-Meq, an old one, once said, 'The Wait is a wheel with spokes of discipline, frustration, silence, and love. It takes great patience and perseverance to keep it turning.' Not all can do it, especially now, since we are so few and those few are in all corners of the world."

"So, you never know when it will happen? Ever?"

"You never know. And it may never happen. The wheel may be more like the stone of Sisyphus and only turn to return to the beginning. Or you may live on, like Sailor, after your Ameq dies."

"Deza."

"Yes, Deza."

"What happened?"

"On the day they were to set sail, the Phoenicians pulled their ruse and tricked the Basque and us. They only knew of us through a few of the Basque leaders, but they had heard of the Stones and the power of the five who wore them. In a ceremony of pomp and circumstance and surrounded by their own fully armed soldiers, the Phoenicians gave the Basque grain, wine, beautiful urns of all sizes, and robes and fabrics, each dyed their distinctive shade of purple. In return, they only asked to see the Stones and hold them for a moment.

"The five wearing the Stones foolishly, trustingly, took the Stones from around their necks and handed them over to the Phoenicians. Then, on command, the soldiers charged in, holding the Basque at bay while they forced as many of us as they could onto their ship. In the hours that followed, a hasty plan of escape was devised, but only a few could go. At the same time, Opari's uncle was stealing back the Stones. He was quick and cunning, like Geaxi, and an excellent choice for a thief. Sailor was put in charge of the escape even though he was considered 'very young.' He wore the Stone of Memory and that would be essential. Deza was not among those chosen to leave. This was a tragic and bitter moment for Sailor, but he made a vow to Deza that somehow he would save her and the others. Opari was beside herself with terror and loss and had to be dragged from the Phoenician ship.

"The escape was dangerous, but successful, and the Phoenicians sailed away thinking they had the Stones and a captive cargo of magic children they could parade through the cities and temples of the Mediterranean.

"As their ship sailed west and south on the long trip around what is now Spain and Portugal, Sailor, Opari, and a few others made the trek across the Pyrenees to the easternmost point of our land, the Cape of Higuer. There, they were given a Basque fishing boat and crew and sailed for Carthage, the largest Phoenician port in the western Mediterranean. But they were too late. The Phoenicians had arrived with their prize two days earlier and promptly discovered that the Stones were missing along with forty-three of us. They were furious, but took no particular revenge. They were only interested in money and prestige and now the 'Children of the Mountains' could provide neither. Instead of parading them, they decided to sacrifice them. They had a temple that served as a sanctuary and was called a 'Topheth.' Inside, in a ceremony and sacrifice called 'Molk,' they killed children in the belief that the children would be possessed by their deity, Kronos. It was barbaric and idiotic, but Carthage was rich and decadent and such practices were common.

"The temples were filled with scribes, servers, musicians, barbers, sacred prostitutes, and priests and priestesses. When Sailor and Opari found the 'Topheth,' there was not a chance of getting close enough to save anyone without risking capture themselves. They watched in horror as, one by one, the Meq were decapitated and disemboweled. Sailor will not speak of it. He never has. Others who were there told me later that Sailor put his arms around Opari and his hands over her eyes and mouth. He held her so tight she nearly suffocated and did fall unconscious before Sailor realized it and let her go.

"Since then, Sailor has had an underlying hate for all Giza, no matter the language, race, or place. He will trust one occasionally, but never completely.

"Opari didn't speak on the entire journey back to the Cape of Higuer. She stayed at the bow of the boat, holding on to the lines and staring at the sea. Once they were ashore, she turned to Sailor and told him she blamed the Meq and him for her sister's death. She said they all could have escaped from the Phoenician ship—there was no reason to leave anyone behind. She said it had all been about the Stones instead of lives, including her sister's, and if Sailor had truly been Deza's Ameq, he wouldn't have left her. She said these things and much more in a calm, dispassionate voice. Sailor said she had gone inside herself to somewhere cold, somewhere barren, where no one was welcome, especially the Meq.

"It was the time of Those-Who-Fled and Opari was one of them. She turned east and told Sailor never to follow, never to look for her. If he or any of the rest of us tried, she said we would only find the footprints of a ghost. We would not find her. She was no longer Meq, she said, only the ghost of one.

"And since that day, no one has seen her. Her presence has been rumored in many places at many times and, ironically, we think it was Opari who used the Stones the one and only time they have affected history. Giza history. It was when Attila the Hun had amassed his armies on the boundaries of the Roman Empire. He was ready to strike and at any moment could easily have taken the city in a bloodbath. But he didn't. He suddenly changed his mind and his armies retreated. Christians said it was a miracle due to the divine presence of Pope Leo I. However, we now know it was Opari. Attila, though it is not widely known, was a dwarf. Opari traveled with him as an omen, a charm, a magic child with a bold sexual presence. He always kept her near. On that day, evidently after she had seen enough of his pillage and murder and knew what was to come, she withdrew the Stones from around her neck and used them on Attila, telling him to turn around and go home. We know this because, through the ages, Opari has kept with her and trained as courtesans orphaned Meq girls, usually Egipurdiko, and one of them, Aurkene, told us this occurred. Aurkene didn't call her by the name Opari, but she described the Stones and what happened perfectly.

"After that, Opari continued traveling east, always protected by royalty; sheiks, sultans, maharajahs, and even emperors in China have hidden her, lied for her, even stolen from their own families to appease her and her unique 'charms.' She has never been found by us. She has power, perhaps because of her age and isolation, but if ever we get near, she is gone. She can sense our presence long before we sense hers. That is why your papa and his papa and all before have tried to use dreams to find her. It is the only way. We must catch her unaware or she will always be a step ahead.

"It is also said the Fleur-du-Mal might know where she is. We don't know for certain, but we think he may have 'found' orphaned Meq girls for her in the past.

"It has been a long search, a long wait, and still we seek Opari. We do not even know if she still exists."

She stopped talking and we both looked up at the sky. Night had fallen and there were ten million stars wheeling around us.

"She exists," I said. "But I still don't know why you need to find her."

Eder looked over my shoulder toward something behind me and nodded. "Ask one of them," she said.

I turned and sitting behind me as silent as stones themselves were Sailor, Geaxi, and Baju. I had not heard or felt them approach and had no idea how long they had been there.

Baju rose to speak. I could not get over how much he reminded me of Papa, especially under starlight.

"You look at me and think of Yaldi, no?"

"Yes, I do," I said. "How did you know?"

"I did not know for sure, but it is good, because your papa would have told you this himself, someday.

"In a little over a hundred years from now, there will be a time, an occurrence, that is sacred and unique to the Meq. It is the reason your mama and papa crossed in the Zeharkatu when they did, so that you could be born in preparation for it. It is the same reason Eder and myself crossed and were blessed with Nova. We know of it through legend and story, but also through Sailor's family and the Stone of Memory. It is even mentioned in fragments on a stone in the Pyrenees called the Idol of Mikeldi. The language is a transitional language between Meq and old Basque, but the name is the same. It is called the Gogorati, the Remembering."

He paused and looked at the others, not sure how to continue.

"What is the Remembering?" I asked.

Geaxi rose from her squatting position and said, "We do not know. We only know that all five sets of Stones are to be together at a certain place and time. The place is called Egongela, or the Living Room. We also know it is a cave somewhere in the Pyrenees. The time is the time during the Bitxileiho, or the Strange Window. We know when that is and Baju will tell you what it is later. The important thing, nay, the imperative thing, is that we find Opari. Without her, we cannot know, we will never know . . ."

"The truth," Sailor finished.

He had circled behind me and stood opposite Geaxi. Baju and Eder stood together in front of me and slightly to the side. We almost formed the shape of a five-pointed star with one point missing. The configuration did not go unnoticed by Sailor. He said, "We must find her, Zianno. Geaxi is right. It is imperative. The Gogorati will come and go and we must be there with the five Stones or we may never know who and what we are.

"I will tell you that before I met Solomon and came to you, Geaxi and I were in the Far East on the trail of Opari. Through various and disparate contacts, we learned that someone of her 'description' was living outside Shanghai with another one like herself called the 'Pearl.' They were protected by a secret cadre sent from the Empress Dowager, or the 'Old Buddha,' as she is called by her enemies. But, as you heard Geaxi tell me earlier, she has vanished.

"And now that you know her story and ours, have you indeed . . . 'seen' her?"

"I don't know where she is," I said, "but if I could get close enough, and I don't know why, she will not sense my presence, at least not in her usual way. I could find her then."

"Then we shall go back to the Far East," Sailor said. "And pick up her trail."

I wasn't sure I believed what I'd just said, not completely. I felt lost in what I'd heard, lost and small, like a grain of dust in a great wind, one star blurred by the Milky Way and Time itself. But I also felt a sense of family, blood, and connection to my own history that I had never felt before. They were Meq and now, finally, so was I.

I looked at Eder and suddenly thought of Nova. "Where is your daughter?" I asked.

She laughed and took my hand again. "We only have to find Ray to find Nova," she said. "I am afraid my daughter is literally physically attached to Ray."

We came down from the clearing and back to the cabin to discover just that. Ray and Nova were on the floor playing a game that mainly involved Nova sitting on Ray's bowler hat and pulling on various parts of his face while giggling to herself.

Ray looked up at me in obvious pain and joy. "Damn, Z, where you been?"

We rested that night in Eder and Baju's cabin and returned in the morning to Kepa's camp. He welcomed us as if we'd never been gone and all that day and night the festivities continued. There was accordion music and dancing and roasted lamb and games of competition among the Basque like stone-lifting and wood-chopping. Old men played a card game called Mus and Ray played pelota, or handball, with the children.

Kepa introduced me to everyone I hadn't yet met and gave me a long diatribe about each of their faults and virtues. I even taught a few, including Pello, the basic rules of baseball and we had a makeshift game in the center of camp. It was a good day, a full day, and though everyone was happy enjoying a day of play, I saw Sailor only once, and that was at sunset walking toward the stream with his head down and

Geaxi's arm gently folded in his. I found Eder and asked if he was all
right.

"Sailor is fine," she said. "As fine as he will ever be." She watched
the two of them walk down the slope, disappearing into the pines.
"Geaxi is good for him. She knows his darkness."

"Is it because of Deza still?"

"Yes. Did you know that he was not born with his 'ghost eye'? It
became cloudy when he saw Deza murdered and dismembered in
front of him. He says that Deza is in his eye now. She is the 'ghost' of
his vision. But Geaxi is the quickest and brightest among us. She
knows when to comfort him and when to leave him be."

"Does Geaxi still do the Itxaron?"

"Yes. A long time now."

"Has she never met her Ameq?"

"No, and she will never speak of it. She and Sailor have different
demons, but the same will and perseverance to survive. She is the
Stone of Will and he is the Stone of Memory. Those two things together keep hope alive."

As Eder was speaking, I caught sight of the one person I hadn't
met, the one person present who was neither Meq nor Basque—
Owen Bramley. He was just leaving a group of men gathered around
a corral admiring horses and saddles. I excused myself from Eder and
walked over to him. He saw me approaching and stopped to face me.
He was a good foot and a half taller, but I could see in his eyes that he
considered me no less than equal. He nodded to me without speaking.

I spoke first. "My name is Zianno Zezen."

"And mine, Owen Bramley," he said, holding his hand out.

We shook hands. He had a strong grip and his shirtsleeves were
rolled up above his elbows. He was freckled, a thousand times more
than Carolina, from fingertip to forehead.

"Solomon told me you were 'his man,' " I said.

"That sounds like Solomon. You are either 'his' man or you are
someone else's."

"He also said you were Scottish."

He laughed out loud. "I am Scottish, at least my parents are, but
I'm from Chicago. I think Solomon likes to call me Scottish, as if

it were a curse, because I know how much he spends and I tell him when it's too much."

"Now *that* sounds like Solomon," I said.

He laughed again and I wondered what he knew about me, about us. He seemed at ease, so I asked.

"What did Solomon tell you about myself and the others?"

"He said to treat you as I would him—with respect—and to keep an open mind and enjoy myself."

"Did he give you any special instructions?"

"No, only to make sure you and Sailor have anything you need, anytime, anyplace. And if I can, prevent any . . . accidents." He took his glasses off and cleaned them with the front of his shirt. "You're probably wondering why Solomon would trust me with this," he said.

"Well, yes, I was."

He chuckled to himself and said, "I don't know, really. Based on our first meeting years ago, I would think he might trust me least of all."

"What happened?"

He waved his arm, dismissing the thought, and said, "It is a long story, but just let me say, it was Solomon who saved my life and I am forever grateful to him. If it is only trust he asks of me, then he shall have it without question or doubt."

"I know that feeling," I said, meaning every word and missing the old man as I said it. In the distance, I could hear a Basque woman singing a beautiful ballad accompanied by a guitar and accordion.

"Sailor says we must leave this place soon," he said, "and we may have a long journey ahead of us."

"Yes, that is true."

"I will miss these people and this place, even though I have only just arrived."

I looked around at the joy of life and sense of place that was everywhere in Kepa's camp. "And so will I," I said.

We spent the next two weeks at Kepa's camp making plans to leave. Owen Bramley left early to secure our train and steamship schedules in Boise, where we would rendezvous later. It was decided that Sailor would go by himself with one of Kepa's sons to San Francisco and then on to Shanghai. Geaxi, Ray, Baju, and myself would go north through British Columbia to Vancouver with Owen Bramley, Pello, and one of his brothers, Joseba, as "chaperones." It would be easier for Ray and me to have identity papers made in Canada and Sailor said Baju had advised him there was something in Vancouver I must experience as an Egizahar Meq. He said it would be good for Ray to know of it as well, since many Egipurdiko do not even know it exists. He wouldn't elaborate except to say the time and place were right and we must take advantage. It was absolutely essential that I go "to it and through it." Whatever it was, Geaxi was not that excited about it, saying, "Once is enough," but she agreed it was essential and "since it no longer affected Baju, we were safe." Baju himself was mostly silent, saying only "we must be on the ship in Vancouver by the morning of August 9."

When we left Kepa's camp, everyone gave their long thanks and embraces to Kepa and his wife, Miren. Kepa told me Pello was the youngest and the best and that was why he was sending him with Joseba. He leaned into my ear whispering and asking, "Did you take your telescope?" I whispered, "Of course, it will always be with me as your tattoo is with you."

Ray had a harder time leaving than the rest of us. Nova wouldn't let him go. She was laughing and pulling on his nose and shirt. Finally, he gave her his bowler hat and she let go and he jumped in the wagon. Still laughing, she threw sunflower seeds at him as we were pulling out. He caught nearly every one of them. The last image I saw of Kepa's camp was Eder and Nova waving, and Eder and Baju exchanging a look I had seen before only on the faces of Mama and Papa.

In Boise, we met Owen Bramley and went over our plans, times, and routes to meet finally in Shanghai. Sailor's train left first and even though he was alone, except for Kepa's son, I knew he would be safe. He had traveled this way for longer than any train or road that carried him had even existed. Only the sea was older. He gave Baju an extended embrace and stepped onto the train without a backward glance. Now that I knew about Deza, everything Sailor did seemed to have something else attached to it. I glanced at Geaxi and instead of watching Sailor depart, she was watching me. I walked over to her and said what I was thinking.

"He pays a price for his memories, doesn't he?"

She paused a moment and said, "No more than every breath."

A short time later, we boarded our own train and headed north. We crossed the border into Canada, stopping briefly at a small station with a single agent and no customs. Owen Bramley took care of the paperwork and we were on our way. We passed through a wild and beautiful town in southern British Columbia called Kelowna. Huddled between mountain ranges in a valley made from receding glaciers, it was a paradise of the north with peach trees full and ripe all around. Geaxi was napping, but I woke her up as we passed through and it was the only time she smiled during the whole trip.

On the afternoon of August 8, 1896, we arrived in Vancouver under a steady rain. An hour later, the sky was clear and the sun was shining. We were told this was a daily occurrence. Ray, the "Weatherman," said he would be too busy to live here. Baju looked worried and said he hoped it would be clear in the morning.

We went directly to the docks and the ship on which Owen Bramley had booked passage, the *Lotus,* a steamer registered in Singapore and owned by Bourdes, the same firm that had employed Antoine Boutrain all those years before. Baju made sure our cabins were on the starboard side, facing east. Pello and Joseba stayed close the whole time, watching every face, but staying slightly out of sight themselves. I knew they were nervous and I knew why. Vancouver was a rough place.

Still in the midst of the Klondike gold rush and already known as an international port, Vancouver was a new town, a frontier town with all the cardsharps, punks and thieves, whorehouses, saloons, and backstabbing that goes with it. You felt free in such a town, but not necessarily safe. And with Geaxi and me both in the same place, and after what we had sensed in the Denver train station, there was cause for concern. I admired Pello. He showed patience and calm, but kept a steady and keen alertness amid the chaos. I was sure he'd never been in a place like Vancouver.

We ate in a little saloon on Water Street near Carrall on the edge of the Burrard Inlet. It was called Gassy Jack's. Someone was playing a loud, out-of-tune piano the whole time we were there. The place was filled with men and women of all kinds from all ends of the earth. It was one place where a group like ours was nothing unusual.

Owen Bramley ordered for everyone, but it didn't make any differ-ence, since a huge piece of salmon and a bucket of beans were the only things on the menu. During the meal, I changed places at the table and sat next to Baju. I had to know more about the next day.

"Tell me what will happen tomorrow," I said.

He stopped eating and looked around the table. No one else could hear us over the general racket and discordant notes of the piano. "I will tell you more and we will talk again afterward, but I will tell you this"—he paused and wiped his mouth with a hand towel—"the sun will rise and appear tomorrow and then disappear."

I looked at him as if it could not be that simple. "You mean an eclipse?"

"Yes, an eclipse. A total eclipse of the sun will occur here tomor-row. But to us it is more than that. To the Meq, it is the time of the Bitxileiho, the Strange Window.

"For reasons we have never known, or have known and forgotten, during an eclipse of the sun, there is a strange"—he paused again and took a drink from a large mug, then went on—"thing that we, the Meq, experience. It is similar to what happens to the Giza when the Stones are used on them, only for us it is more difficult; a deeper place; a wider gap. But it is necessary to know this place, because it is there that you cross with your Ameq in the Zeharkatu. To the Meq, the Bitxileiho is as strange and common and magic and sacred as a drink of water."

"Will I feel—"

He cut me off and said, "We will talk of your feelings afterward, Zianno. It will be the same for you as all others, yet uniquely your own. Since Eder and I have crossed, I will not be affected. This is also not understood, but I am like the Giza now, and Pello, Joseba, and I will be there while you, Geaxi, and Ray are . . . somewhere else. This is all I have to say now—afterward, afterward we will talk."

Geaxi got up suddenly to go to the ladies' room and was escorted by Pello and Joseba through the rowdy crowd. I thought I caught a glimpse of Ray ahead of her, but I turned and saw him still in his seat scooping up the last of his beans with a piece of bread.

On her return, I noticed Geaxi looked extremely pale and I asked if she was all right. She could only point to her stomach and say "the food." Ray looked at her with an expression of bewilderment.

Owen Bramley paid the bill and we walked the short distance back to the ship. There was a low fog hovering over the whole town and out on the Burrard Inlet. I walked alongside Geaxi. I was nervous, uncomfortable, and I didn't know what to say or what not to say. She looked over at me.

"Do not worry, young Zezen. I know that you are anxious, but Sailor is right—it is time for you to gaze in the Window."

Back on the *Lotus,* it was a quiet night with only a few passengers outside their cabins. Baju said to get a good night's sleep and rise early. It would happen in the morning just after the sun crested the mountains to the east.

I mostly lay on my bunk wide awake with thoughts tumbling one into the other. I did drift off once and dreamed I was playing catch with Papa in a bright green field with the sun high in the sky above us. I was wearing Mama's glove. Papa was tossing the baseball to me, higher and farther each time until once he tossed it so high I lost it in the sun and turned my head, afraid it would hit me. It did hit, but it hit the ground, splitting open and spilling out the Stones. The gems sparkled in the sunlight. I tried to yell to Papa. I tried to yell "I broke it, Papa, I broke it!" But I couldn't yell. I couldn't even speak. Then Mama was talking to me. She was saying something over and over, but I couldn't take my eyes off the Stones and the gems sparkling in the light.

"Wake up! Wake up, Zianno!" It was Geaxi. "It is almost time."

I dressed quickly and met her at the railing on the deck, not twenty feet from my door. Baju was there with Ray. He said he wanted us close to our cabins. It was light, but there was no sun yet and a fog still clung around the ship.

I looked up and down the deck on the starboard side. I saw Pello standing out of sight under some stairs to my right. To my left, Joseba was walking casually beside the railing. Past Joseba were the only other passengers on deck, a group of men setting up tripods, cameras, charts, and graphs, all speaking at once in a rapid and excited French. Baju said they were members of some obscure French astronomy society. Owen Bramley was nowhere in sight.

Then it began. First, the sun rose above the horizon of the mountains and the fog gradually burned off. The air was cool, the sky became clear. Baju lined up three deck chairs behind us. "You may have to sit down," he said. "You will notice nothing at first, but during totality you will not be able to move."

We were in an eerie half-light. The moon was sliding into place. I looked out across the water and there were low-contrast bands of light and dark racing over the seascape. The amateur French astronomers began to cheer and whistle at the other end of the deck. I glanced quickly at Baju. He was smiling. I looked up and there was only a thin bright crescent of the sun remaining. I was hypnotized by that crescent. The horizon around us was yellowish or orange, the zenith a pale blue. The seconds ticked down—five—four—three—two—one— Incredible! It was the eye of God. A perfect black disk, ringed with bright spiked streamers stretching in all directions. I could see a few red peaks in the ring and a star or two behind this wonder, this window blazing in the surrounding blackness at midmorning.

And half of me fell away. There is no other way to say it. Part of me was open, weightless, nothing there. I could see, but what I saw went on without me. I could feel nothing, move nothing. Why move? There was nothing to move. I was at the other end of a strange telescope, a tiny point, a speck of . . . what? It was cold and dark, so dark. I wanted to sleep, but I heard a voice, a whisper. It said, "Beloved, wake." I felt a fluttering of wings. I looked back through the telescope, this window, and saw movement. I saw Geaxi and Ray sitting in chairs and a figure approaching them. Everything was in slow motion, but it still happened quickly.

The figure slipped behind Geaxi and in one practiced motion removed the necklace with the Stones from around her neck. Then he moved behind me and I could feel a tickling sensation as he took my necklace and Stones. I couldn't move. I felt trapped in a thick, invisible sand. All I could do was watch.

He bent down in front of us and was holding the Stones on the deck with one hand and prying out the gems with the other, using a uniquely designed pointed tool. At the same time, Baju, Pello, and Joseba were rushing forward from three different directions. When they got to within a few feet of the man, three shots rang out from a pistol. In the grand silence of a solar eclipse, they sounded like cannons from another world.

Baju and Joseba went down, both hit hard in the chest. Pello fell against the railing, hit in the thigh and unable to move. The man who had fired the shots walked through the darkness and over to Pello. It was the man I'd seen in Denver in the bowler hat with the razor-thin eyes. He lowered his pistol and pointed it at Pello, but didn't shoot. Instead, he looked up the deck toward the French astronomers. Owen Bramley was out of his cabin and running toward us. The man with the pistol yelled something in a strange language to the man picking at the Stones. Owen Bramley was gaining ground. Finally, the kneeling man had all the gems picked from the Stones and leaped up, running past the man with the pistol. Backing up, the man kept his pistol aimed at Owen Bramley who had closed the gap and was going to charge the man, gun or no gun.

Light returned—bright only an instant after totality. I could move again and just as the man with the pistol cocked the hammer to fire, I reached for the Stones, which were no more now than a black rock shaped like an egg and I held this rock with both hands and I turned to the man and said, "Stop now, Giza! Stop and forget! Turn and go!"

Then, as if a switch had been turned, the man dropped his pistol where he stood and walked away in the direction in which the other man had fled. I looked at the pitted, black rock in my hands. There were deep gouges where the gems had been picked out and stolen. It was now only a rock—an old, old black rock. Geaxi was staring at me. Owen Bramley was out of breath and crimson-faced. He didn't have his glasses on and he was squinting in the bright light. "What happened?" he gasped.

I looked for Ray and he was kneeling by Baju, who was still alive. Joseba had been killed instantly. Pello was hanging on the railing and losing consciousness. Owen Bramley went to look after him. Geaxi and I ran over to Baju and knelt down next to him. Geaxi took off her beret and held it with her hand under his head. She shook her head slowly, sighing, and said, "Baju, Baju."

He opened his eyes and coughed. There was a dark bloody hole in his chest. He looked at Geaxi and said, "This was supposed to be my last time, old friend. Did you know that? I was going to teach Nova and the next—" He broke off in a coughing spasm and blood ran out of the corner of his mouth. His eyes were closed, but he opened them again and looked at me. "Zianno," he whispered, "come closer." I bent down so that his mouth touched my ear, as I had for Mama, and he said, "This was not about theft. This was—" but he never finished. Baju Gaztelu died on the morning of August 9, 1896.

I looked at Geaxi. She had tears streaming down her face, but said nothing. This was the second time I'd seen someone murdered and both were senseless.

I said, "Someone will have to tell Eder and Kepa about this."

Ray said two words and I knew he knew everything that went along with them. He said, "I will."

Owen Bramley had Pello leaning against his shoulder. He was conscious, but bleeding badly. Owen said, "I will make the arrangements to get all of us back to Kepa's safely."

Geaxi and I exchanged glances. "We won't be going with you," I said. "Geaxi and I will go ahead to Shanghai and meet Sailor."

Owen Bramley gave me a long look. "After this? Are you sure?"

Geaxi answered for both of us. "Yes."

We talked to the police and the officials of the shipping firm, giving our explanation that the eclipse must have driven a madman over the edge and he had shot at random the first phantoms that appeared in his delusion, who happened to be our friends and uncle. All agreed it was a misfortune and a tragedy.

One of the members of the French astronomy society, the photographer, told Owen Bramley a strange thing might have happened. As the shots rang out, he had been startled and bumped his tripod, swinging the camera to a different position, one that caught the madman directly in his lens. He had squeezed on his bulb without realizing it and may have taken the madman's picture. He couldn't be sure until it was developed, but it was very possible, indeed. I overheard and asked Owen Bramley to get his name and address. We wanted to see that photograph.

Later, when Ray, Geaxi, and I were alone, Ray said, "The Fleur-du-Mal?"

I shrugged and looked at Geaxi. She didn't respond to that, but she reached into her vest and held out the two egg-shaped black rocks. "I do not think it matters any longer which is which," she said. "Do you, Zianno?"

We looked at each other with a hard truth and new understanding of what we had seen.

"No, it does not," I said.

"You know the Basque have always had the true name for these," she said and tossed me one of the rocks. I caught it easily. She held hers in her fist with her arm pointed straight up.

"What is it?" Ray asked.

She brought her arm down and opened her hand, staring at the object she had been born to wear and had worn for so many centuries. Was it a blessing or a curse? She had always thought the "secret" to be in the gems. She looked at Ray with a sad smile.

"Starstones," she said quietly.

9

HERENEGUN

(DAY BEFORE YESTERDAY)

You are a child. All your life, inside, behind the clutter and refuse you must acquire to live in this world, there is a child. Everyone knows this, but rarely admits it. The child is too busy hiding and playing amid the clutter. Occasionally, usually after the clutter has been hoarded and stacked, moved from place to place, displayed and then forgotten, the child will tire of play and tell us to throw things away, clear the room, make things the way they were the day before yesterday. And therein lies the conundrum. We have spent our lives constructing gates and fences, protecting this clutter, preparing for the day after tomorrow. We cannot find the day before yesterday. Even the child cannot remember what we need to know . . . where it was . . . how it was. The gift of Time is time and it cannot be given back. The day before yesterday is a place of dreams where even children are strangers.

The departure of the *Lotus* was delayed a full twenty-four hours due to the "incident," as the captain referred to it. During that time, Ray and I picked up our passports and other false documents that Owen Bramley had prearranged for us. He also bought coffins for Baju and Joseba and wired Solomon, telling him briefly of the events and the change in plans. He asked if we should try to wire Sailor and Geaxi said that would be impossible, because when Sailor traveled alone, he was virtually invisible. No one would find him on any passenger list.

Of course, Ray wouldn't need his passport anymore, except to reenter the United States. He and I talked a little about him joining us again soon somewhere in the Far East, but neither of us knew when or where that might be. Something in Ray had changed or maybe it had always been there and I was just now seeing it, but Ray took the death of Baju personally. I could see it in his eyes. For the first time, he had a sense of purpose that was, without a doubt, his own. We had been through a lot. We were true friends and I would miss him, but there is something odd and wonderful about true friends—farewells are easy. The feeling that true friends share is always in the present. Time in any direction is not the point.

As we pulled out of the Burrard Inlet in patchy fog with broken clouds overhead, Ray was on the docks, standing between Owen Bramley and Pello, who was in a wheelchair. Pello waved meekly and Owen Bramley stood ramrod straight. Ray reached up to tip his bowler hat to us, but then remembered he'd thrown it to Nova. He tipped an invisible one anyway. I felt a hand tap me on the shoulder and turned around to see who it was. There was no one there and I had to remember . . . "it is common." I was looking west toward the horizon and beyond, toward China. I had the same feeling I'd had so many years before on a pale cold winter morning when Carolina and I had been kids, real kids. An overwhelming sense of leaving and barely a trace of return.

The voyage across the Pacific was long and made even longer by a series of storms off the coast of Japan. The *Lotus* eventually steamed into Yokohama, our first port of call, badly in need of supplies and repairs.

Geaxi and I had stayed in our cabins for most of the trip—the less seen, the fewer questions—a lesson both of us had learned a long time ago. I did tell her what Baju had whispered: "This was not about theft." We both had plenty of time to think about what had happened and what it meant. In Yokohama, we talked about it.

The *Lotus* docked for three days, not only for repairs but also because she had to be thoroughly searched. The Japanese had been at war with China and any ship going there was suspected of carrying contraband. I thought we might be asked several questions that would be difficult to answer, but Geaxi spoke fluent Japanese and made it easy for us. She said she spoke an old dialect, but the official understood her perfectly and whatever lies she told him, he believed her and bowed to her with great respect. For some reason, I wasn't even surprised.

We went ashore and Geaxi found directions to a teahouse. Along the way, I kept thinking that two Western children on their own, one of them a girl in black leather leggings and a beret, would draw attention, but no one gave us a second look. We were merely two more strangers weaving their way through traffic. Geaxi said, "It will not be this way in China."

We arrived at the teahouse and were taken to a low table in the back that faced an open area with a small stone garden. The fence around it was old and rickety, but the garden itself was beautiful and well tended. Geaxi ordered for us and then caught me staring at the garden and the odd placement of stones with sand around them raked in perfect but natural lines, resembling waves.

"Like islands in Time, no?" she said.

I looked at her, and even though she was in shadows, I could tell that something in Geaxi had changed since Vancouver, something subtle that softened her expression and came through her eyes.

"What do you think Baju meant?" I asked.

She looked out over the garden herself. "I do not know," she said. "I only know that finally the Fleur-du-Mal has gone too far. This time, his obsessions have killed one of us."

"Sailor told me he murdered my grandfather."

"That is true, but that was personal."

"So you think the Fleur-du-Mal is behind it?"

"It has all the hallmarks of his sick sense of humor. No one but he would know our movements or anything about the Window. However, one thing bothers me."

She stared at me strangely, then looked away as the hostess brought our tea and silently poured out two cups. The girl was not much older than we appeared to be and Geaxi was extremely polite and respectful to her. As she left, bowing, I said, "What thing?"

Geaxi sipped her tea, holding the cup with both hands. "We will have to ask Sailor when we see him if he has been harassed or followed. If he has not, and what you said about seeing the man with the pistol in Denver is accurate, then there is only one conclusion."

"What?"

"They were only following you."

She looked at me for the first time since I had known her with an expression that said, "*You* tell *me*, Zianno, what do *you* know that *I* don't?" But I didn't know. I only had my Dreams and they came and went as they pleased. I looked at her and had no idea what she wanted of me.

Two Russian sailors sat down near us and loudly ordered sake. They were already drunk, but were obviously not ready to stop drinking. They looked our way and laughed at some inside joke between the two of them.

Geaxi said, "How did you know the Stone would work for you without the gems?"

"I didn't."

"But somehow you knew it would, you believed it would."

"Yes, that much is true, but I don't know how. There wasn't time. I simply acted."

One of the Russians spat out his sake and yelled something at the hostess. She bent down to wipe up the sake and he threw his cup at her, kicking it when it bounced off the floor. She crawled on the floor to retrieve the cup and he yelled something else at her in Russian.

"There is still so much we do not know about ourselves," Geaxi said and she reached in her vest and pulled out the Stone, clenching it in her fist. She started to turn toward the Russians and I stopped her, putting my hand over hers and holding it to the table.

"Not here, not now," I said. "We *must* find Opari. We can't take chances. Even you said it was imperative."

Her hand loosened under mine and her eyes looked away toward the stones in the garden. Then she smiled. "You are too young to sound so wise, Zianno. Shall we leave?"

"Yes," I said, and as we rose to leave, Geaxi helped the girl up and out of the drunken presence of the Russians. Walking past them she whispered, *"Alu hori!"* and then out loud in Russian with a smile, *"Das vadanya."* She'd told them in her tongue and in theirs that they were assholes and to go with God. Only Geaxi could do that.

The *Lotus* finally made it to the Whangpoo River and then docked in Shanghai after three more weeks' delay due to two more unscheduled stops for reasons that were never fully explained. I was beginning to learn the ways of the Far East and I hadn't even entered China. One step forward and two steps back seemed to be the rule.

The delays did give me more time to spend with Geaxi. I found out when and where she was born (51 BC on the island of Malta) and when she met Sailor (AD 480 after the Fall of Rome). I learned her parents had died naturally after living long lives among their friends in Malta, tending a large olive grove where she had practiced her climbing skills as a real child. I found out little else about her personal history, but still enjoyed her company.

I asked her many questions about the Fleur-du-Mal. She answered some, but admitted that, until recently, she had considered him irrelevant. She told me that Unai and Usoa were the experts on the Fleur-du-Mal and one other whom we might or might not meet, Zeru-Meq, his uncle. When I heard the names Unai and Usoa, I immediately asked how and where they were. I had often wondered, but never inquired. Geaxi said they were in New Orleans, or had been, following the movements of the Fleur-du-Mal. Then she corrected herself and said they had been following the "rumors" of his movements. She said the Fleur-du-Mal was often harder to track and find than Sailor. He was unpredictable, completely unpredictable. But he could be a connection to Opari and so they persisted, as they had for centuries. Geaxi said she doubted he was a connection, but now, after Baju, he might be capable of anything. I had my own memories to verify that.

We disembarked, secured what little luggage we had, and made it through customs easily. After that, it was a madhouse. All China and half the rest of the world seemed to have docked in Shanghai. There were ships of every size and shape coming and going. The docks and wharves were filled with anything and everything that could be bought or traded. I heard languages I'd never heard, saw faces I'd never seen. This was Shanghai, the true gateway to China, and it was chaos.

We looked for Sailor and would never have seen him, even though he stood just fifty yards away, except he was the only thing not moving. He was standing next to a rickshaw and staring at us. He wore a bright red and gold robe with wheels or circles embroidered around the edge and a round straw hat with a flat top and a drawstring pulled tight under his chin. He looked like a circus puppet. I glanced at Geaxi and she didn't seem to think it odd in any way.

We made our way over to Sailor, dodging through the maze of people and goods, and without a greeting except to look in our eyes, he said, "This way." A man with the thinnest shoulders I'd ever seen loaded our luggage on the back of the rickshaw and then pulled the three of us to a section of Shanghai known as the Chinese City, the oldest part. We were almost twenty-five days overdue and I wondered if Sailor knew about Baju and what had happened.

We stopped in front of a shop crowded next to a hundred others on a street crowded next to another street just like it. There were a thousand sounds and smells, a few of which made you want to know the source, but most of which didn't. It was a shop that sold nothing but funeral trappings. And far from being grim and somber, it was bright with color everywhere. Crimson satin coverings for coffins hung aloft and around on the shelves or under glass cases there was apparel for the dead; richly embroidered robes, slippers, and headgear. There were priests' robes and white cotton raiment for the mourners. Somewhere in the shop there was everything for a proper and glorious Chinese funeral.

Sailor led us quickly to the back of the shop and through a door to the private living quarters. It was cramped but fairly clean, with a single window that opened onto a narrow alley and very little light. He took off his straw hat, laying it carefully on a nightstand, and without being asked, gave me answers to the questions I had been pondering.

"There was a cable waiting for me when I arrived," he said, "from Owen Bramley. It was good that I had not let Kepa's son, Gotzon, sail with me."

"Were you assaulted?" Geaxi asked.

"No," he said and looked at her strangely. "I was thinking of Gotzon and how he would have felt if he had heard the news of his brothers here, so far from home. It has been a long time since I have lost someone as close as Baju. I know Gotzon would have felt helpless, as I have." He fell silent and stared at the sapphire on his finger, rubbing it with his thumb and turning it around and around. Then he looked up at Geaxi. "Did they get the Stones?"

Geaxi glanced at me before she answered. "Yes and no," she said.

Sailor looked puzzled. "I do not understand," he said and looked over at me.

Geaxi told him the whole story, leaving nothing out except the few moments we were in the Bitxileiho, for which Sailor needed no explanation. She slowed down when she told him about me and the Stone with no gems and the man with thin eyes dropping the pistol. Sailor did not react and she went on until she got to the part about Baju. She took her beret off and clenched it in her hands. She started to speak again and then stopped, looking away from both of us toward the single, airless window.

I let a moment pass and then told Sailor what Baju had whispered to me as he was dying. Sailor's puzzled expression returned, but he said nothing. He walked the few steps over to Geaxi and took her hand in his. Then he spoke to me.

"I have often suspected this about the Stones," he said. "Your father and Baju and I used to discuss it, but we would never have defiled a sacred trust merely to satisfy our curiosity. It is ironic, no? That we have solved this mystery in such a horrid manner and for such an empty purpose."

I watched him. I watched him look inside himself and I could almost see him sitting with Baju and my papa and others on a cliff somewhere in a remote part of the world, talking of the mysteries of Life, and the Stones, and of being Meq. I could see them all sitting there, knowing so much, sharing so much, and being careful with each other and the Truth. Now, another one from that circle, another friend, was gone.

"Tomorrow we begin our search," he said. "This news, more than any other, tells us who we seek first. We must find Zeru-Meq. It will be difficult, yes. He is unpredictable, completely unpredictable, but I know he is in China."

"That's what Geaxi said about the Fleur-du-Mal," I said.

"It is true. That is where he learned his unpredictability, from his rather unusual uncle. Fortunately, his uncle is not 'aberrant.' There is a difference. If the Fleur-du-Mal is responsible for Baju's death, he will tell Zeru-Meq about it. He will be compelled to do so."

"How do you know?"

"You will have to ask Zeru-Meq the source of that. It has always been so. When the Fleur-du-Mal has acted 'badly' and is proud of himself, he always finds his uncle to boast and brag of it. It is a mystery."

"What about Opari?"

"We have exhausted every lead, rumor, and trace of her in Asia. If she is still in China, Zeru-Meq is the only one who will know it. There is a problem, however."

"What is that?"

"Zeru-Meq is nearly as difficult to find as Opari herself."

I looked at Geaxi. She was not despondent, but as close to it as she had ever been. Sailor let go of her hand and sat down on a bed that was really no more than a bench. As he did, the sash holding the red and gold robe came undone and the robe opened. Underneath, he was wearing a cotton shirt, trousers, and his leather boots laced to the knees. I said, "What are you supposed to be in that robe and that straw hat?"

"The same thing you will be starting tomorrow. A Tibetan Buddhist monk. It is not unusual for their monks to be children. We will say, if we are asked, that we are from some obscure sect, which could also explain our Western features, and we are traveling together on a sacred pilgrimage.

"We are on our own now, as it should be. We must use our wits, skills, and powers in a controlled and muted fashion. I will cable Unai and Usoa tomorrow before we leave and tell them who we seek and why. They will need this news of the Stones. I will tell them to watch for any appearance of the gems in the purlieu and underground world of the Fleur-du-Mal. We will find Opari and then turn our attention to the Fleur-du-Mal." He paused a moment, looking back and forth between Geaxi and me. "Do you both agree?"

We agreed and told him so, but inside I wished the order of our search could be reversed.

The next day, our journey began. It was the fall of 1896. Sailor had secured passage with an old Chinese man from the south, Ling Kai, and his even older Chinese junk to take us up the Yangtze River as far as we needed to go. Ling Kai considered it an honor, saying he had long been a devout Buddhist and mystic himself. He also smoked three bowls of opium a day.

Our long Buddhist robes were uncomfortable at first and we now looked like three puppets instead of one, but in time we all adapted to wearing them. And they served us well. Before we had gone a hundred miles upriver, we were stopped or boarded four times by Chinese and British officials. I wondered if this was the way it was going to be, but within another hundred miles, we were just another vessel sailing upstream and back in time on a river that was once known as the "River at the Center of the World." And I believed it when Geaxi translated a poem for me. It was carved into a five-foot stone pillar that served as a bollard for securing boats on one of the little docks in one of the endless villages along the Yangtze. It seemed to be centuries old and I asked Geaxi if the author had signed it. She said no. The inscription read, "Upriver, downriver—it is nothing to disappear in China."

Our destination was the sacred Taoist mountain of Hua Shan in the province of Shensi. Sailor said it was a good place to start because of its inaccessibility. Zeru-Meq loved impossible places, he said, especially places as contradictory as Hua Shan. The mountain had been held sacred in China since very early times and often appeared as a backdrop in scrolls because of its spirituality and isolation. It was a trip which by junk, train, and donkey should have taken no more than a month. It took us three. One step forward, two steps back. China.

Hua Shan lies to the east of the ancient city of Sian and looms over the Yellow River and the narrow valley below it. It is surrounded by the Tsing Ling mountain range and the mountains of Shansi to the north. Hua Shan itself is a jagged circle of sharp peaks around a patchwork of flat land and small plots. It is beautiful and dangerous, foreboding and inviting all at the same time. The peaks rise two to three thousand feet and are very steep. It seemed ironic but fitting that the last leg of our difficult journey was a short and easy train ride to the nearby hamlet of Hua Yin, which means "under the shadow of Hua Shan." Along the way, I thought of Zeru-Meq and what Geaxi and Sailor had told me about him.

Born premature in 356 BC, the same year as Alexander the Great, he was so tiny his papa could literally hold him in the palm of his hand. He was Egipurdiko and his family were fishermen and gamblers in equal parts. They were known but rarely seen in every thriving port of the western Mediterranean. Most of them died or were killed in a violent manner, some even taking their own lives, a phenomenon Sailor said was unique to the "diko." Zeru-Meq and his sister, Hilargi, were eventually left with no one but themselves and traveled together, surviving that way for more than a century. Then, when Hannibal, the Carthaginian, was making his ill-fated march toward Rome, they joined his armies and entourage, becoming elephant handlers. During Hannibal's retreat to North Africa, according to Geaxi, they both met their Ameq and Hilargi crossed in the Zeharkatu, but Zeru-Meq did not. The reason has never been known. Eventually, Xanti, the Fleur-du-Mal, was born to Hilargi in a ruined village somewhere in North Africa. They were staying as far away as they could from the murdering Romans, who were killing anything or anyone associated with Hannibal. After that, something happened. It has never been explained, but Zeru-Meq appeared in what is now Barcelona with the infant Xanti, saying Hilargi and the father were dead. He handed Xanti over to an old Basque family that had once done business with him and returned to North Africa, disappearing for the next few centuries in the deserts and mountains. Sailor said that since then Zeru-Meq had had so little contact with other Meq you could count the occasions on one hand. It was known he first went to China with Marco Polo in the thirteenth century after coming out of the African desert with a strange passion for all things mystical in Giza religions. He stayed in China, seeking out the old Taoist poets and mystics, which he does to this day. Geaxi said he knew of Opari and our search for her. However, it might not matter. He thought the Remembering and the Meq themselves were insignificant and irrelevant. She said that was why they had not sought Zeru-Meq before; even if they did find him, he might decide not to help. But, she added, now we had no choice. The Fleur-du-Mal himself had made it so.

We walked the fairly short distance from the station to the Jade Spring Temple, which was the start of the ascent of the mountain. Our long robes and hats were dirty and worn and we truly looked like three tired and road-weary pilgrims. Geaxi asked the monks who greeted us if there was a head priest we could have counsel with and ask a very private question. They were cordial and did not treat us as children at all, but as equal seekers of an immutable truth, even though we were Western and dressed as Buddhists. They told us there was no head priest, but five priests had permanent residence on the North Peak. They would be the ones to ask.

The way up the mountain took most of the rest of the day. At one point, it was so steep that the path led up nearly perpendicular rock faces in which steps had been hand-cut and iron chains were set in rock to provide handholds.

Finally, we emerged on the North Peak, which was really a knife-edged ridge with a few temple buildings and a monastery perched on top. The ridge was so narrow that the path had to pass through the buildings, with no room on either side. From the ridge I took my first full view of the plain below, the mountains of Shansi in the back-ground and the great Yellow River flowing in between. All around were daggerlike pinnacles and rock walls, the whole scene continually changing through the dance of sunlight and drifting mist.

Walking slowly, we started toward the monastery. We passed a monk sitting on his haunches and painting an elaborate rendering of a Chi-nese character on a scroll. I asked Geaxi what the character meant and she said "shou," or longevity. I was nervous with energy. I wondered inside what Zeru-Meq might be like.

The monastery itself was a simple stone structure with a steeply an-gled tile roof. Two twisted and gnarled pine trees somehow clung to the ridge beside it and hung suspended over a three-thousand-foot chasm. There was no one inside except a boy about our size sitting by an altar. He had his back turned to us, but we all knew he was not Zeru-Meq. We walked through an open door at the other end and there, sitting cross-legged on a rounded boulder against a background of clouds and mist, were five Taoist priests. They wore full-length blue-

black robes and small four-cornered caps set back high on their fore-
heads. They each held a fly whisk in their hands. Their expressions were
indifferent, but the one in the middle motioned for us to approach, as
if he had been expecting us.

Sailor stepped forward and spoke to him in Chinese. He introduced
himself and told him it was an honor to visit the mountain and
thanked him for receiving us. The priest said it was indeed their honor
to receive pilgrims who had come so far and then they spoke of the
monastery and Sailor asked about the boy we had seen inside. The
priest said the boy had been sent there from Shanghai by his parents
for the benefit of his health. Just then, I saw the boy appear out of the
corner of my eye and take a seat behind and to the side of the priests.
Sailor went on to ask the middle priest if he knew of another boy, one
that looked like us, with the name Zeru-Meq. The priest shook his
head, but at the mention of the name, for just an instant, I saw the boy
smile. Sailor thanked them all again and we turned to leave, bowing
first to show respect. As we walked back through the monastery, I
glanced at Geaxi to see if she had seen what I had. She nodded.

Once we were out of sight and sound of the monastery and were
about to make our descent, the boy appeared again. Geaxi spoke to
him. He said he knew the one we asked about and that Zeru-Meq had
taught him to play cards and even written a poem while he was there,
carving it in a pine tree. He took us to the tree and there it was, recently carved and in Chinese. Geaxi translated. It said, "Time is only
fire and spark knocked off flint. Let's play."

Sailor asked the boy when Zeru-Meq had been there and the boy
said we had just missed him. He had been there the day before yesterday. I was confused. The five priests had told us they had no knowledge of him. Sailor looked at Geaxi and then at me. "I was afraid of
this," he said.

And so it was. We set out on a trail that followed whispers, rumors, in-
timations, and outright lies. We eventually made pilgrimages to all of
the eight remaining sacred mountains in China. We were delayed for
weeks and months at a time by floods, mudslides, tornadoes, and snow-
storms. We were forced to make detours again and again by washed-

out bridges, transportation strikes, misinformation, and the overall chaos of a changing and disintegrating empire. I often thought of the old inscription on the stone anchor post I'd found on the Yangtze and how true it was—it is nothing to disappear in China.

Sailor asked me regularly if my dreams had revealed anything: a name, a place, or direction. But my dreams were as chaotic as the country we were in. Once, I dreamed Mama and Papa and I were staying in the Statler Hotel in St. Louis and we went to a baseball game in a rickshaw. The grandstands were full of screaming fans, but there were no players on the field. I turned and asked Mama what all the cheering was for and she said, "Watch. Just wait and watch, Z. It's a good game!" When I looked back to the field, the bases were being swept away by torrential rain. It was raining everywhere, but we stayed completely dry. I watched and watched until I woke up.

Our search for Zeru-Meq became an endless cycle of discovery and disappointment, almost always ending with the revelation that he had been there the day before yesterday.

For three and a half years we ate simply, traveled lightly, and criss-crossed China in our hunt for the enigmatic Zeru-Meq. We went as far west as the isolated fishing village of Shigu, where the Yangtze makes an impossible hairpin turn from south to north within a few hundred yards. And we went as far east and south as the island-city of Macao, where we could finally take off our Buddhist robes and blend in with Macao's large Portuguese population. And everywhere, at every temple, village, monastery, shipping dock, and gambling house we found only a trace, a poem, a riddle, or an odd anecdote concerning the missing Zeru-Meq. I was tired of tracking him. It seemed pointless, hopeless, and fatigue overtook perseverance more than once. Then something wonderful happened.

It was May 5, 1900. My birthday had come and gone the day before and would have passed unnoticed except that Sailor had mentioned it and reminded me that each one counted. "The Meq must count birthdays," he said, "the way bankers count money or else we will own nothing of ourselves."

We had recently left the town of Ch'u Fu, where Confucius had lived and was buried, and traveled north to T'ai An, which lies below T'ai Shan, another sacred Taoist mountain in the province of Shantung. The roads were heavy with traffic and there was generally more chaos than usual. We had heard rumors of revolution and violence throughout the province and that the Germans had taken control of Kiachow peninsula. We were taking tea at a monastery outside T'ai An and the monks were telling us what a dangerous future there was in store for China and the monasteries if the foreign devils came inland. I had learned enough Chinese to understand what was being said, but I was drifting and paying no attention. Half a mile from where I was sitting, a train had stopped on the tracks at a small crossroads. It was not a regular stop, and as I watched, I could see several men working on the wheel of the car just behind the engine. There was nothing unusual about that. But then I noticed, on the other side of the train and rising above it, one by one, Chinese kites. I had seen hundreds, maybe thousands, of kites in China, but these I had only seen in one other place. Kepa's camp.

I got up without a word and started walking toward the train as if I was being reeled in by an invisible line. As I got closer, I could hear the voices of children laughing and shouting, some in Chinese and some in English. I knelt down and easily crawled under the train. On the other side, in the middle of an open field and twenty or so children, stood Owen Bramley patiently assembling his kites and helping the children to fly them.

I watched for a moment and then started toward him. He saw my bright red and gold robe immediately, but the hat must have fooled him. He turned back to his kites, then paused and slowly turned around again, staring at me and adjusting his glasses. He gave the kite he was holding to a boy about my size and walked to meet me.

"My God," he said. "She was right. She said I would find you when I least expected it."

He looked the same, maybe a little thinner, but then so was I. He wore the same white shirtsleeves, rolled up, and his trousers were held up by suspenders. He was grinning and shaking his head back and forth.

"How are you, Owen?"

"I'm fine, I'm fine," he said, at the same time turning and looking around anxiously. "Come, let's walk somewhere. I've got something for you."

He took my arm and we walked about a hundred yards away from the tracks where a long, shaded walkway to the monastery's Hall of Incense began. There were ancient cypress trees on both sides and it was paved with square-cut stones. We walked a short distance and stopped. We were standing between two massive stone lions, facing each other across the walkway. The late afternoon light was broken and made the lions look as freckled as Owen Bramley.

He unbuttoned his shirt and reached inside for something. "Carolina Covington gave this to me for me to give to you. I told her I would, but until now, I never knew how." He grinned again and handed me a letter. It was coffee-stained and wrinkled, but still sealed and intact. There was only one thing scratched across the back. "Z."

I know of nothing more treasured than a letter from someone you love. Its very presence has power. I held the letter from Carolina as if it were older and rarer than the bones of the one who had carved the stone lions I was standing between. I was astonished. I couldn't move. I looked up at Owen Bramley.

"How did you . . . when were you . . . what are you doing here?" I stammered.

He laughed and took his glasses off, wiping them clean.

"I met her in St. Louis while visiting Solomon," he said. "A re-markable woman, that one. When I told her I was coming to China, she took me in her confidence and entrusted me with the letter. She was ecstatic that I might see you, though privately, as I told you, I had my doubts. Anyway, there you are and here I am. How are you . . . progressing?"

"There are good days and bad," I said, trying to be honest, but having no real way to answer him. "Why are you in China? I know it's not just to find me."

"Actually, I came as a favor for my parents to begin with, but now it has turned into something else. We have relatives, my aunt and uncle, the Reverend William and Daphne Croft from Cornwall, who moved to China thirty years ago as missionaries. When my parents heard the rumors of this uprising in China and that Christian missionaries were being slaughtered by the Boxers or whatever these hooligans are called, they asked me if I would help get the Crofts out of China. Of course I said I would, but I had no idea I'd be taking out twenty-nine children as well." He paused for a moment and looked toward the train, which was close to being repaired. "Z, as a foreigner, you should be very careful in China these days. It is dangerous and it's going to get worse. There may be a war."

"The Chinese think we're Tibetan Buddhists," I said.

"Just don't slip up. These Boxers are fanatics. I don't trust a one of them. Tz'u-hsi, the Empress Dowager, thinks they might bring the old China back with their lunatic magic. She might be as crazy as they are. Anyway, it's time to leave China, not stay. Have you thought about it?"

"No, it's not possible. We still have unfinished business. But tell me, how is Pello and . . . how did Eder take the news?"

Just then, Sailor seemed to appear out of nowhere and walked up beside us. He acknowledged Owen Bramley with a nod and said, "Please, go on."

Owen Bramley hesitated for a moment. Then he answered. "Pello is fine. He walks with a limp, but he is well and back at Kepa's." He turned to face Sailor directly. "Eder is . . . brokenhearted. Kepa said she is well, but very sad. However, Ray is with her and Nova keeps them both very much alive."

Sailor looked down at the cracks between the ancient paving stones, then up to Owen Bramley. "Good," he said.

The train blew its whistle long and loud, signaling that the repairs were finished and it was time to board. We all looked in the direction of the children and they were frantically trying to pull in their kites. Geaxi was standing next to the boy Owen Bramley had handed his kite to earlier. They were both looking our way, the boy almost frozen, like one of the stone lions.

We started back toward the train. Owen Bramley said, "Listen, Z, I have a contact, don't ask me who or how, but it's the best, inside the Forbidden City, inside the imperial palace itself. If I ever have to reach you outside normal channels, I will use this contact and I guarantee you will get my message. How soon is another matter."

We reached the train and it was five minutes of Chinese chaos gathering kites, counting the children, and making sure all were back on the train. The boy Geaxi was standing by barely moved the whole time and seemed to be transfixed by me. In five more minutes, they were all accounted for and the train steamed forward toward the hills and eventually Tsingtao. Owen Bramley waved once. The same boy leaned out of his window and stared at me until the train was completely out of sight. I turned to Geaxi and said, "Who was that kid? And why was he staring at *me*?"

A mischievous grin was spreading across Geaxi's face. "His name is Willie Croft," she said, "and I told him you were Buddha."

Sailor chuckled and we all stood there, staring up the empty tracks and listening to the last echoes of the disappearing train. Six hours later, I was on a cot in the monastery and I tore open Carolina's letter. By candlelight, I read it slowly, five times.

My only Z,

I am writing to you, hoping and praying this will reach you. Solomon said not to worry, that Owen Bramley would somehow accomplish the task. He is a nice man and told me as he took the letter that it would not leave his person until he handed it to you. If you are reading this, then our luck still holds and he has found you.

I ache for you, for your presence, but not in a sad or painful way. I am so happy, Z, I feel so wonderful I am about to burst with joy.

I have met a man, a good man, a man I can love. I know you would approve. He is a sportswriter for the Post *and loves baseball. And me, of course!*

I met him out of the blue while attending a game at Sportsman's Park (the Cardinals need pitching, by the way). Solomon and I have got box seats and season tickets, but that day I was alone. In the third inning, he simply sat down, unasked and unannounced, and passed me a box of Cracker Jacks, never taking his eyes off the field. I never said a word, nor did he, and I was in love by the fifth inning. That was last year. I would have written to you sooner, but I wanted to wait, wait and see if what I felt was real. It is real, Z, and now I have even more wonderful news. I found out the day before yesterday I am going to have a baby. A baby, Z! Can you believe it? And I always thought you were the crazy one.

God, I wish you were here. I have so much more to tell you, so much I wish I could share with you. I pray every day that you are well and will remain so.

*I do miss you terribly. I even think Georgia misses you, wherever she is. I don't
hear her playing as often as I used to.*

From my heart of hearts,
Carolina

    *PS. His name is Nicholas and the "business" is doing well, thank you very
much.*

That letter cleansed my soul and cleared a dark window I'd been
afraid to look through. I'd thought of her so often, worried and wondered, and now I knew. I was overjoyed for her. I carried that letter
and read it every day for six months. It became a talisman, a lucky
charm, and it served me well.

Owen Bramley was right about war. Through June, July, and August, there was a war, of sorts. They called it the Boxer Rebellion, but
it was really an ineffectual attempt by China to stave off the inevitable.
China was an old woman falling down and the Western powers were
going to help her, not to get up, but to stay down. The Boxers and
their belief in old magic and the notion that bullets would turn away
from their holy bodies as they killed Christians were only crazy exam-
ples of China's refusal to accept change, both good and bad, especially
the imperial family and the "Old Buddha." The Boxers could be dangerous, however, and we tried to avoid them. And cities. And trains.
Sailor said the Meq had no place in Giza politics and their penchant
for barbarism and war. I said what about the Fleur-du-Mal and Sailor
said that was what made him "aberrant."

We did learn something, however, as a result of an encounter with
the Boxers. We were in the remote province of Kansu following another "clue" about Zeru-Meq's whereabouts. It was long after the
"Rebellion," late 1901, and these Boxers were on their own, no longer
connected to anything political or even righteous. They were roaming
and raiding, murdering and torturing at random in the poorest towns
and villages of Kansu. In all our years in China, it was the first time we
were forced to reveal ourselves as Meq.

We had stopped to rest at a small inn and get some relief from a bitter wind that seemed never to stop blowing. The Boxers arrived suddenly, maybe thirty in all, and a few came inside and ordered the

innkeeper to give them whatever they wanted or be dealt with as a nonbeliever. They wore the symbolic red sashes and turbans they were known for, but theirs were old, tattered, and stained. Outside, the rest of them were noisily torturing some poor innocent. They were calling their victim a "liberal old crow" and we could hear the high-pitched screams as the Boxers delivered their blows.

In a very few minutes, whether it was the immediate situation or an accumulation of our years in China and the futility of our search, I don't know, but Geaxi had had enough. She was out of the back door and up on the roof in a matter of seconds. Sailor and I followed, but neither of us was as quick as Geaxi. When we got to her, she was on the edge of the roof looking down on the Boxers and the beating that was taking place. She had the small, pitted black rock, the Stone, in her hand. I took mine out as Sailor and I came up beside her. With just a glance toward me and a nod, she looked back down on the Boxers. We both raised our hands and spoke low in unison, "Hear ye, hear ye now, Giza! *Lo geltitu, lo geltitu, Ahaztu!*"

The Boxers were carrying everything from ax handles and home-made swords to government-issue carbines. They laid them all down immediately and walked away. In less than a minute, they were gone in five different directions. Sailor stared at us in mute fascination. This was the first time in twenty-six centuries he had seen the Stones used without the gems.

We climbed down the front of the building into the little courtyard surrounding the inn. The person the Boxers had been beating sat huddled against the wall and trembling. It was a man, but as Sailor approached him he let out a piercing, high-pitched screech like a crow. And as I approached, I could smell something foul about him, not from lack of hygiene, but something else. He was a eunuch and, judging from the robes he was wearing, an imperial eunuch. He, and thousands like him, had run the daily palace affairs and served at court for centuries. They were known, at least some of them, to be masters of deceit and intrigue. Eunuchs like him, who sounded like crows, were usually castrated after puberty. Others had a softer tone and had probably been castrated as children. The Boxers hated them and blamed them for a long list of imperial wrongdoings, especially the liberal ones who believed in Western influence.

Sailor stopped and told him not to be afraid. He looked at Sailor, still trembling, and in Mandarin replied that he was not afraid, he was thankful, and he had screamed only because an ancient legend and rumor in the imperial palace had now come true. Sailor asked him what that was and he told of a tale that had been passed among the eunuchs down the years. That Li Lien-ying, the chief eunuch, and the Empress Dowager herself, Tz'u-hsi, harbored a girl, a girl with Western features who was known for her powerful presence, sexual and otherwise, even though she was physically immature herself. And she supposedly had a hypnotic effect on others whenever she wanted them to stop what they were doing. The legend held that she was called the "Hare" and sometimes the "Jade Hare." He said that when he heard us and saw the Boxers leave it was the same thing.

Sailor looked to Geaxi and then to me, barely suppressing a grin. We knew the "Hare" had to be Opari.

We helped the man up and he gathered his sensibilities, then departed in a flurry to who knows where. On the spot, we discussed if our search for Zeru-Meq should continue or whether we should go to Peking and explore other avenues. Sailor said we should keep looking for Zeru-Meq. "Without him," he said, "we will get nowhere in Peking. If Opari is behind an imperial gate, Zeru-Meq will know the gatekeeper." Geaxi and I reluctantly agreed.

After that, we stepped up our search, traveling faster and resting less. We covered Honan province and Hupei to the south. We doubled back through Shensi and north as far as Ningsia. At every stop, whether riverfront opium den or mountaintop shrine, Sailor thought we had learned something, inched a bit closer, or didn't have long to go. He had started asking certain questions in a certain way, so that he could read between the lines of the answer and anticipate Zeru-Meq's movements. The longer we kept at it, the more obsessed he became.

For two more years we searched in vain. Then, in a remote Taoist monastery near Yushu, at the far west end of Szechwan, not far from Tibet, which was supposed to be our country of origin, we gave up.

It happened suddenly. After our arrival and a few inquiries, we were taken back to the kitchen and shown an ancient slab-oak table, twelve feet long and four feet wide. We were told it was used for everything from the preparation and serving of food to communal meetings and prayer. On the far end and carved into the edge was a poem. We were informed, after asking, that it had been written "the day before yesterday." It read:

> The oyster folds over the Pearl
> The Hare stays put in the nest
>   Your steps are loud
>   Your thoughts are thunder
> Why do you still hunt?

Sailor turned bright red and pounded his fist on the table. The monk who had shown us the carving jumped back and then excused himself, not knowing how to respond to such a violent reaction. Then, just as suddenly, Sailor broke into laughter, loud and long, more than I'd ever heard him laugh before. When he stopped, he said, "This game is over. I will not play any longer. Do either of you have anything else in mind? Anything will do. We must try something else."

I suggested we go to Peking and cable Unai and Usoa. They might know something of Zeru-Meq through the movements of the Fleur-du-Mal. While we were waiting for their reply, we could try and find a hint of Opari. What could we lose except time?

Geaxi agreed and Sailor was open to anything. The next day we started on the long trip to Peking. It was spring of 1904 and we had been after Zeru-Meq for almost eight years.

We traveled by train as often as we could. Now that our priorities had changed, we were anxious to get to Peking. We were silent for hours on end. I think all three of us were disillusioned, but when we did speak, I noticed Sailor was much more pleasant. We watched the vastness of China pass around us, and in our Buddhist robes we probably looked more like the young monks we were supposed to be than we ever had.

When we were still a good distance from Peking, maybe two hundred miles, the train made an unscheduled stop close to Ta T'ung and near the ancient Yün Kang caves that contained thousands of Buddha statues, images, and carvings. We were there for at least twenty minutes and outside I heard men shouting and yelling while they loaded something heavy into a car farther down the train. People inside were grumbling about the delay, but once we got going, everyone settled back into the stupor of a long train ride.

I was dozing myself when I was suddenly jolted awake by a boy falling into me. He was carrying an armful of umbrellas and he fell across my lap and rolled into the seat next to me, forcing Geaxi to squeeze up against the window. He never once dropped the umbrellas, holding them with both arms in front of him like a bundle of trees. I couldn't see his face, but he was apologizing profusely in Chinese. Sailor was sitting across from us, facing the boy. Then the boy began placing the umbrellas between his knees, lowering them one at a time. After two or three, Sailor could see his face.

"It is not so," Sailor said. "Please, say it is not so."

The boy lowered the rest of his umbrellas and I could see his face. He had curly black hair, green eyes, and he was definitely Meq.

Geaxi laughed out loud.

"*Egibizirik bilatu,*" the boy said with a smile. "Do the Meq not say that still?"

Geaxi, still laughing, said, "And five lights shine at the birth of every Buddha."

The boy laughed along with Geaxi and said, "I am afraid I am out of salt," then he looked directly at Sailor and said, "Hello, old one."

Sailor stared back at him and without taking his eyes off the boy said, "Zianno Zezen, meet Zeru-Meq."

The boy turned and focused his concentration on me. He looked me over thoroughly. "I did not know your father," he said, "but I knew your grandfather. A tragedy." Then he nodded toward Sailor. "Did this old wanderer tell you I was 'unpredictable'?"

I looked at Sailor, who was shaking his head. "Actually, he said you were 'completely unpredictable.' "

Zeru-Meq started laughing again and trying to find a place to put his umbrellas, as if we had all been planning to meet and he was just a little late.

Sailor said, "Why now? Why here? What's the point?"

"The point is, old one," Zeru-Meq said, finally putting up the last of his umbrellas, "that to find something while one is still looking is to lose it, but to find something after one has stopped looking, that is discovery. Anyway, it is I who need your help at the present. We can discuss your needs later. Do you still carry those wonderful Stones?"

Sailor, Geaxi, and I all glanced at one another, unsure of how much information we wanted to share. Sailor solved it, saying simply, "Yes."

Zeru-Meq said "very well," and went on to tell us that during the decay of the Ch'ing dynasty, open vandalism and looting were taking place at many sacred temples and shrines such as Yün Kang, which we had just passed. That was why the train had stopped, he said, to pick up stolen heads from several statues of Buddha to sell to foreign museums and art collectors. Zeru-Meq said this was an abomination to him. He told Sailor that just outside Peking, where the shrine robbers had planned their drop-off, he had planned his own pickup. Once they had unloaded their sacred contraband, if we could make the scoundrels "forget," then his men would be there to return the heads to their rightful owners in Yün Kang. He also said that doing this would make Sailor "feel better."

Geaxi stifled a giggle and we all agreed to help. Sailor was silent for most of the remaining journey, but I spoke to Zeru-Meq about many things and in the course of our conversation brought up the Fleur-du-Mal. I asked him what he was capable of and, straight out, if he had heard from or seen him recently.

He looked at me openly and smiled. He had the same brilliant white teeth as the Fleur-du-Mal, and his eyes were the same deep green, but there the similarities ended. I sensed no evil in Zeru-Meq.

"The Fleur-du-Mal," he said, "is a righteous man. He does only one thing based on one way of thinking—that which is forbidden. He is not a grand thief or even a good murderer. He is a common man, as clear as a mountain stream, only he does not think he appears this way because of his obsession with the forbidden. If starving were forbidden, he would never eat another egg. The Fleur-du-Mal, Xanti Otso, is a pilgrim. A sad, dangerous pilgrim."

"But have you seen him in the last eight years?" Geaxi asked.

"No," he said, "I have not spoken with him since the 1860s."

I thought about this and what Sailor had said about the Fleur-du-Mal and his habits. I glanced at Sailor to see his reaction, but he was staring out of the window.

We arrived at the station Zeru-Meq had said was the rendezvous point around dusk. A strong wind, laden with grit and sand, was blowing out of the west. Our plan was simple: surround the scene of the exchange at three equidistant positions and use each of our Stones together, simultaneously mouthing the words the way Geaxi and I had done at Kansu. In a matter of minutes it was done and Zeru-Meq had all the Buddha heads carefully loaded into two-wheeled peasant carts and "his men" discreetly hauled them away and back to the caves of Yün Kang. The other men, the thieves, wandered off aimlessly.

Later, Zeru-Meq mentioned that he hadn't seen any gems imbedded in either my or Geaxi's Stones, only in Sailor's, yet they all seemed to work as they always had. He asked Sailor about it and Sailor was silent. He smiled and said, "This puts things slightly askew, doesn't it, old one?"

Sailor finally said, "You know what we seek, Zeru-Meq. And you know we would never ask for your help if there were any other means. Will you help us find Opari?"

"If I had not seen what I just saw with the Stones, I would say no. And I have always thought you and the others were wasting your time with your fixation on the Remembering. We are who we are. The Remembering will not change that."

"You have your opinion," Sailor said.

"Yes, I have," Zeru-Meq said and paused a moment. "Anyway, I can only arrange an audience with Li Lien-ying, the chief eunuch, and even then, an audience of only one. Three would never be allowed. Once inside the Forbidden City, whoever it is will be on their own. I would be very careful. Li Lien-ying and Tz'u-hsi herself are the only ones that know of Opari and another one with her called the 'Pearl.' They are very jealous of their magic children and protect them accordingly."

We entered Peking and I saw everything from dogs and children sharing the same scraps of food in the street to wide avenues lined with peach trees in full bloom.

Zeru-Meq helped us locate rooms near the Forbidden City and we finally took off our Tibetan Buddhist robes for good. There seemed to be hundreds of thousands of children on their own in Peking and four more like us would alert no one.

That night, it was decided that I would be the one to visit Li Lien-ying. I was still convinced that it was Opari's heartfear that made her vulnerable and her heartfear was me. "Why" was a question I couldn't answer. All those years in China and I hadn't heard one voice or dreamed one dream that made anything any clearer. But I was excited. I knew I was close. There were only a few miles separating us that night and I knew that soon even that gap would be closed.

The next day, Sailor went to cable Unai and Usoa. No matter what happened in Peking, he wanted news of the Fleur-du-Mal. Zeru-Meq went to arrange the audience with Li Lien-ying. He said it could take five minutes or five hours. There was no way to know until it was done. Geaxi and I began to walk around the Forbidden City, but the wind was still full of grit and sand and we returned to our rooms. It was odd. Whole years had swept by me, barely noticed or counted, and now a few hours seemed a lifetime. I was nervous. Geaxi laughed at me and said, "The one thing you should be able to do, and do well, is wait."

Sailor returned at about four in the afternoon, saying only, "Peking has lost its charm." Zeru-Meq arrived at six and said I was to be outside the east gate at eight o'clock sharp. An audience had been accepted. He said he had had to give my name, it was required, and the truth seemed most appropriate. He said "the truth" from now on would be my ally; it was so rarely heard inside the walls of the Forbidden City.

We had tea together at a small café as the sun was going down and the wind with it. Outside, however, the Peking traffic remained constant. Sailor went over everything I should say to Opari if the chance arose and reminded me that I would be the first to do this. "Do not be the last," he said.

I was met at the gate by four eunuchs, two in front to escort me and two behind for no reason other than ceremony and ritual, the way it had always been done.

We walked through the massive gate and along the wall to another smaller gate, through that and across a courtyard into a large hall with two huge doors, painted a brilliant vermilion. All around the building were hundreds of intricately carved lattice windows. Inside, there was electric light, which somehow seemed incongruous.

I was handed over to four other eunuchs in slightly more elaborate dress and led down a corridor alongside the hall. It must have been the living quarters for hundreds, maybe thousands, of eunuchs. The same sour odor of decay I had detected in Kansu was overwhelming.

At the end of the hall, we crossed another courtyard and I was left alone on the steps of a smaller, but just as magnificent, structure. It was a two-story pavilion with stone dragon heads peering over the up-turned corners of the roof.

The building was dark inside and around me the sounds of Peking were only a distant murmur. The door opened gently and a small man asked me politely in English to come in.

It was deathly quiet. I followed him to the center of the large room where a man was standing with his back to me: a tall man, taller than any of the other eunuchs I had seen. He was standing beside an ancient cherry and teak wood desk with a single candle on top. It was the only furniture in the room. The small man moved slightly to the side, into the shadows. I was not introduced, so I stood where I was, waiting.

The tall man said something in Chinese I couldn't quite catch. His voice was high-pitched, but not the screech of a crow The small man spoke immediately after, interpreting. "Your name is Zezen, is that correct?"

"Yes," I said, speaking to the tall man.

He spoke again, still with his back to me, and the small man interpreted. "Is it Zianno Zezen?"

"Yes, it is."

"Do you know a man, a Chinese man, named Po?"

I thought for a moment, trying to place all the names with all the faces I'd seen in China. Then, I thought again. "I know a man named Li who used to be called Po. He lives in America with a friend of mine."

"Then our meeting is most fortuitous," he said, turning around as the small man was translating.

"I am—" he started, then caught his breath in his throat and his eyes widened slightly. He was startled at seeing me and I thought if he had known of the Meq, then he hadn't known many. He composed himself and continued. "I am Li Lien-ying, chief eunuch for the imperial court of Ch'ing, and please tell me, how is my cousin?"

I almost laughed out loud, but managed to keep a straight face. "Li, I mean Po, is your cousin?"

"Yes, my first cousin on my mother's side. We would have starved as children if it had not been for his family. He has always been opposed to my chosen profession, but I have always owed him a debt of gratitude. I have promised to deliver what was given to me."

I was confused. I wasn't sure what he meant. "You mean, you will take me to Opari?" I asked.

At the mention of Opari, he was genuinely surprised and looked down on me with a cruel, paranoid stare. "No, no," he said rapidly. "That would be impossible."

"Then what did you promise to deliver?"

"This!" he said and pulled open a drawer in the desk, drawing out a letter and handing it to me.

I looked at it. It was very familiar. There was nothing written on the side facing up and I turned it over. In the middle, scratched in black ink, was a single letter. "Z."

I ripped it open and read it by the light of the single candle.

Z, my only Z, please get this! I am afraid. I don't know what to do. I don't know who else to tell. I have seen the evil one, the one that killed Georgia and Mrs. Bennings. I saw him in the French Pavilion at the World's Fair. And he saw me!! I had my baby with me, Z, and he gave me a look that was like a knife in the chest. I am so frightened. I know he will do something, I can feel it, but what? And when? I can't bear this with my baby around, Z. I am more afraid for her than me. Please, Z, I don't know what you can do, but you are the only one who understands. The only one. I pray this gets to you.

C.

I looked up and glared at the chief eunuch. "When did you get this?"

He looked over at the small man, as if to confirm it, and said, "The day before yesterday."

At that moment, the door to the large room opened and in the darkness we could hear the rustle of robes followed by a sharp command in Chinese. Li Lien-ying and the small man stood frozen in their slippers.

Shuffling toward us with tiny steps and gradually becoming visible was an old woman dressed in a priceless robe of yellow, orange, and purple. Embroidered with seed pearls and coral, it was covered with ideograms and images of bats and dragons. A girl about my size, with a translucent scarf over her head for a veil, accompanied the old woman and held her arm gently. It was Tz'u-hsi herself, the Empress Dowager of China.

She stopped not three feet in front of me. Behind me, Li Lien-ying said, "Good evening, madam."

She stared at me, up and down, as if I were an exotic animal. "It was," she said, "until We were informed of certain proceedings. We would think that We would be informed when such a special guest is in Our midst."

She tried to smile at me, but the right side of her face sagged and her eye and cheek began to twitch violently. She turned away from me and barked, "Why does this 'magic child' come to Us?"

Li Lien-ying answered, "He seeks one of his own kind, madam."

Still hiding her face from me, Tz'u-hsi said, "And who would that be?"

"Opari," I said.

"Silence!" Li Lien-ying yelled.

Tz'u-hsi raised her hand and said, "There is no need for that." Then she reached over and lifted the scarf from the girl's head and revealed her face. She was Meq. She had green eyes. She was somehow familiar. "This is Opari," Tz'u-hsi said. "Tell her what you seek."

I looked down at the letter I was still holding in my hand. Suddenly all I could think was "I may be too late. I've got to get there." Then, I thought I heard a bird crashing against the lattice windows, somewhere in the darkness. It was loud and I looked all around me, but no one else seemed to hear. I looked at the girl who was staring back at me, expressionless. There was something about her, something in the eyes. Then it made sense.

"You're the 'Pearl,' aren't you?" I asked her. She took a slight step back. "But your real name is Zuriaa, isn't it? You're Ray's sister!"

The girl's eyes opened wide and her pupils rolled up and disappeared in the back of her head. She fainted and fell at Tz'u-hsi's feet.

Li Lien-ying let out a piercing cat scream and Tz'u-hsi shouted into the darkness, "Seize him!" Hidden doors that looked like windows opened on all sides and government soldiers with rifles and long-robed eunuchs with swords started toward me. I reached into my pocket as slowly and casually as I could. I felt the Stone in my palm, cold and solid. I turned first to Li Lien-ying, whom I knew would have a weapon. He was pulling a long stiletto out of his brocaded sleeve and I raised my fist with the Stone in it. In a droning cadence that was loud enough to fill the room, I said, "Hear ye! Hear ye now, Giza! All stop now!"

I looked in Li Lien-ying's eyes, and where they had been burning into me a moment ago, there was now a softness, a dullness, staring back. He dropped the stiletto and I started backing away, looking around me and trying to find the door and still chanting, "*Lo geltitu, lo geltitu*. You will forget. You will go like lambs now. *Ahaztu, Giza!*"

The soldiers dropped their rifles and stopped in their tracks. The eunuchs let their swords fall. Tz'u-hsi was kneeling over the girl and seemed somehow unaffected. She watched me turn and walk through the dreaming soldiers, more in wonder than fear.

I hurried out of the door and into the courtyard, stopping for a moment to locate the large hall of the eunuchs. Every building looked the same. I was lost. I started to pick any path, any direction, then I dropped Carolina's letter and bent to pick it up. Before I could, I heard the Whisper.

It was soft but strong, like incense or perfume. It had texture. It had fingers and stroked my hair and touched my eyes. I breathed it. It filled my heart and mind with mist and musk. It spoke no word. It said no name, but it was speaking to me, as it always had, as it always would.

I looked up and from behind a life-size statue of some forgotten emperor she stepped out in a plain blue silk robe. She was my height and looked about twelve years old. Her hair was black and cut straight at the shoulders. Her eyes were dark and set wide over high, round cheekbones. Her nose was short and round at the tip. Her eyebrows were as black as her hair and thick. She wore no earrings, but her robe had an open neck and I could see a necklace with the Stones attached, sparkling in the lamplight. I could see the vein in her neck throbbing and I could feel her heart beating from where I stood. I could see her lips, her beautiful lips, tremble.

I knew two things instantly. I knew she was Opari and I knew she was my Ameq.

I heard men shouting somewhere and saw more lights coming on. I heard a deep ringing bell from another courtyard, an alarm of some kind. I knew there was no time. Not here. Not now. I picked up the letter and glanced at her just once more. She moved her lips and mouthed one word. "Beloved."

I turned and ran, climbing over rock gardens and under bridges like Geaxi, racing through halls as fast as Ray. I was lost, but kept running until I found a gate that was still open with several foreign diplomats and their wives straggling through. I lost myself among them and, once outside, lost myself on the streets of Peking.

One day later, I was in Tientsin, and two days later, I was on board a ship bound for San Francisco. I had spoken to no one. I could only keep thinking, "I may be too late. I've got to get there." And then another thought occurred to me. I was already hundreds of miles from Opari, from my Ameq, and I had only met her the day before yesterday.

10

GURPIL

(WHEEL)

Wheel and deal. Do you want a hit? Wheel and deal. It is a game. It is a ride we sometimes take with fate as our companion, strolling through a carnival of circumstance and fortune. It is return. It is a circle spiked with fear and spoked with dream and spun with love and will. It is a cycle. It is completion. It is the motion of our birth and death, our sweet crop of secret corn, sown in light and harvested in darkness. It is a song, it is a refrain. You know how it goes and comes again. It is a wheel. Take a spin. Spin the real. It is your turn.

The tramp steamer *Cartagena* took five weeks to cross the world's largest ocean. I had no luggage except what I had on me, which was my passport, the Stone, and a few British banknotes and Chinese coins. I had lied to get on and I would lie to get off. An innocent-looking child with half a lifetime of experience and a good story can slip through many locked gates and still be left alone. I talked only to the captain and spent all my time obsessed with the moment a beautiful girl had walked out from behind an ancient statue and looked into my eyes.

In a split second, I had felt her inside me, felt it in my chest physically, and everything I had ever thought about this world changed forever, because now I knew she was in it. It was the most urgent and powerful feeling I had ever felt.

On the long crossing, I watched the spray of ocean as our ship cut through the Pacific, I stared at a rose in the old-fashioned wallpaper of my cabin, I looked up at the bright star Vega, shining at the top of the night sky, and only thought of Opari, only saw her eyes and her trembling lips. I could still hear the whisper, as you would a gentle, familiar voice waking you from a long and unsettling dream. Thoughts of Opari ran parallel or intersected with every thought I had. I understood why the Itxaron and the power behind it was so difficult to describe. It would be like trying to tell someone who only lived in the desert about the effects of a flood. And still I went east, away from her, toward St. Louis, toward Carolina. There are two things you are never prepared for: suddenly finding love and suddenly losing love.

I knew Sailor and Geaxi would have no way of knowing what had happened, and Zeru-Meq would have to call in many favors and ask endless questions, perhaps ultimately to find no answers. Whatever had happened inside the Forbidden City would have to be explained later.

Coming into San Francisco, I had the same anxiety and fear I'd had years earlier approaching New Orleans with Captain Woodget, only this time my fear had a specific name and face. The Fleur-du-Mal was a killer. I knew that now and I was determined that he had to be stopped. I knew who he was and I knew what he was and my fear increased with every passing second, because now I knew where he was.

I made it through customs with only a slight delay due to the fact that I was unattended and had no luggage. I told a long and pathetic story about my missionary parents and their wish to get me out of China as fast as possible to the United States and a Chinese Christian family in San Francisco that was to take care of me. I even spoke a little Chinese at one point and gave him Owen Bramley's name as an American reference. I was in the country and at the train station within an hour. I thought about trying to reach Owen Bramley and decided against it. I thought about wiring Solomon and Carolina to tell them I was coming and decided against that too. It was best, this time especially, that I come unannounced. If something had already happened, then I would find out soon enough. If something was about to happen, if Carolina was being stalked, then the best way to stop it would be to stalk the stalker. I didn't know how the Fleur-du-Mal "worked" or what he had in mind, but I could find out from a distance. Then, I could stop him forever, if I had to.

I boarded the first train with connections all the way to St. Louis using a similar story on the conductor that I'd used in customs. It worked again and I was able to gain free passage all the way through. He put me in a cabin "for looking after" with an unusual family of three also traveling to St. Louis. There were two men, one very old and one middle-aged, and a woman of about thirty. They were Ainu, an ancient people from northern Japan who are unique in their own right. They have Caucasian features, some are said even to have blue eyes, and the men have heavy, thick beards. No one knows why they are the way they are or where they originally came from. I felt an immediate kinship based solely on isolation and survival. The conductor told me they were part of an entire contingent of Ainu living in the grounds of the World's Fair. "Some promoter's idea," he said, "they got people from all over kingdom come living there." He told me the woman spoke very limited English and the two men hadn't said a word in any language. They all wore brightly colored tunics and wide trousers covered in simple but beautiful patterns. The woman watched me take my seat and made a slight bow with her head. I nodded back. The two men stared impassively out of the window. I followed their gaze and we stayed that way for hours. Together, we watched the twentieth century in the Western world pass by us for the first time. I thought about what Sailor had said, deep in China on the eve of the twentieth century. "We must look out for this century," he said. "Our kind must adapt quickly. The Giza are shrinking the world with their inventions in communications and travel and they have only just begun. Our old ways must change or we will be swept away, obliterated and forgotten. It will be very difficult for many of us, but we must do it or none of us will live long enough to see the Remembering. The twentieth century, if we are not alert, could be the extinction of children such as us." Going east, I watched the cities, farms, faces, fashions, noises, and spaces and I knew he was right. Especially, thinking of Baju and the Fleur-du-Mal, if we were going to kill our own kind.

The two men never spoke the entire journey, neither to me nor to the woman. She offered me a rice cake once in silence and I accepted in silence. Twice I exchanged glances with the older man, once while passing through Colorado and once while crossing the Meramec River, just before we arrived in St. Louis. As we were preparing to leave, the old man whispered something to the woman. It sounded like a series of low belches. She looked over at me and in very broken English said, "Grandfather say you have very old eyes for so young one."

I looked at the old man. He was looking out of the window at the traffic in Union Station. I said, "Tell Grandfather he has very young eyes for so old one."

We bowed to each other a final time and I thought I saw a trace of a smile on her face.

I stepped from the train and was hit by a wall of heat and humidity. I had almost forgotten the infamous St. Louis summer. There were people everywhere speaking in a dozen different English accents and in another dozen foreign. St. Louis had always been a hub for railroad and river traffic, but now it was the center of a wheel of international culture and commerce. The World's Fair was in St. Louis and St. Louis had attracted the world.

I tried to focus and concentrate. It had only been eight years, but for some reason I was disoriented and walked aimlessly through the crowd. The men all seemed to wear the same flat-topped straw hats and the women all had parasols, which reminded me of the last time I'd seen Carolina in her yellow dress with her yellow parasol in hand. I kept thinking the same thought I'd had for weeks—"I may be too late." I felt dizzy and couldn't catch my breath. I made my way the best I could through the noise and bustle and finally came to a halt, slumped against a cool marble wall. I let my head fall back and closed my eyes. What was wrong with me? Was it the heat? I tried to relax and breathe deeply. Somewhere in the back of all the noise in Union Station, I heard music and the unique sounds of a calliope. I opened my eyes and walked toward it. I passed under the Whispering Arch and looked up at the cavernous ceiling. There were no birds flying. Beyond the arch and in the open was a small carousel crowded with children and their families all around. As the calliope played, the children rode in a circle on painted lions, tigers, giraffes, and elephants. Vendors on either side sold pins, ribbons, and flags announcing St. Louis and the World's Fair. The strange, hypnotic sound of the calliope drew me

closer. I looked at the faces of the children on the carousel. One had
Opari's nose and lips. Another had her eyes and eyebrows. Still another had her hair and lips again. She was everywhere. I saw Opari
in a part of every child in front of me. My temples throbbed and
my breath caught again. I turned and looked back through the arch
and saw something else, something I never expected, something that
brought my mind into focus instantly. I walked back toward what I
saw. I wondered how close I could get without being seen or felt. I
didn't get far. Still thirty feet from them, they stopped what they were
doing, turned in unison, and stared at me. They stood next to a
woman speaking in rapid French to several porters at once. They wore
loose black trousers tucked into leather boots laced to the knees. Both
had white cotton shirts with broad collars. I smiled at them. Unai and
Usoa smiled back.

They nodded toward a shoeshine stand next to the wall and I
walked over to meet them. I could see the outline of the Stones with
the gems still intact under Unai's shirt. Usoa still wore the blue diamond in her ear. We stood three feet apart and looked at each other in
silence. The shoeshine boy, who was about our size and busy with a
customer, glanced over at us. He looked at our faces for a moment, astounded by our similarities, but then looked down in obvious admira-
tion of Unai's boots, which were of the highest grade leather and
craftsmanship and polished to a high sheen. He looked up again and
shouted over to Unai, "Man, where did you get those?" Without a
moment's hesitation, Unai turned and said, "In Barcelona, after the
Romans left." The boy turned back to his customer laughing and repeating the words, "Right, right."

Unai turned to me. "*Bonjour,* Zianno. You almost surprised us."

"Hello, Unai. Were you expecting me?"

Before he could answer, Usoa grabbed my hand and said, "You do
not look well, Zianno. Are you all right?"

I looked at her. How many years now since I'd seen them? Ten?
Eleven? She was exactly the same, only now she wore barrettes in her
hair similar to the ones Eder had worn. I was still amazed by us, by the
Meq. "I am fine, Usoa. Exhausted perhaps, but fine."

"I suppose coincidence occurs, even for the Meq," Unai said, "but
this is extraordinary. What brings you here, Zianno?"

I looked in his eyes, and Usoa's, and saw a blend of honesty and uncertainty. "How much do you know?" I asked.

Unai grabbed the front of his shirt, holding the Stones tightly. "We know about this," he said, "and we know about Baju. We thought you were somewhere in China with Sailor and Geaxi."

"Then you haven't heard from them recently?"

"No," Usoa said. "We have been in St. Louis for two months with the woman, Isabelle, and watching another."

"Another?" I asked. "Do you mean the Fleur-du-Mal?"

She paused a moment or two. "Yes," she said.

Instinctively, I looked around as if I might catch him darting between parasols and luggage. "Have you seen him?" I blurted out. "Has he done anything? Has he harmed . . . anyone?"

They exchanged a look between them, one that held a world of information. It was a look that I'd seen pass between Mama and Papa, between Baju and Eder. A look that held the deepest possible trust in each other and one that I thought I'd glimpsed in the eyes of Opari.

"He has gone," they said in unison. "He harmed no one, not even your Carolina Covington."

"You know Carolina?"

"We know of her," Unai said, "and of her sister's tragedy."

I looked hard at them both. I was slightly dizzy and my breathing was shallow. "He must be stopped," I said.

"He will be," Unai said, "at the proper time . . ."

"And in the proper manner," Usoa finished.

I looked over to the scene of the woman still struggling with the porters in rapid French. She was craning her neck, searching for Unai and Usoa.

"Is that Isabelle?" I asked. If it was, she had not fared well through the years. She was made up like a clown and had dyed her hair red.

"Yes," Usoa said. "Sad, is it not?"

"Yes, it is," was all I could manage.

"You know, old Captain Woodget is still her escort, after a fashion. He retired from the sea and lives across Lake Pontchartrain. He visits her twice a month and spends the rest of his time in his garden. A quite beautiful one, I am told."

I was glad to hear Captain Woodget's name and that he was alive

and well. He had helped and taught me a great deal. I let the moments
pass in silence, a state in which Unai and Usoa were most comfortable.
They were old ones. They had survived a very long time on will,
sharp wit, and the love they shared. It was strong and carried its own
presence. I couldn't believe they had not yet crossed in the Zeharkatu.
I looked them both in the eye before I said it.

"I have found Opari."

They drew in a quick breath. Together, they whispered, "Where?"

"It is complicated, very complicated. More than you know, more
than I can explain."

"But then, that brings me back to my initial question," Unai said.
"Why are you here?"

"That also is complicated, but the answer is the Fleur-du-Mal. I
will not let him kill again. It's as simple as that."

Unai looked at Usoa, then put his hand on my shoulder. "It will
not happen here, my friend. Be certain of that. Whatever 'business'
the Fleur-du-Mal had in St. Louis, it is concluded. We have reports he
is already back in New Orleans."

He paused a moment and Usoa continued. "Enjoy your visit to St.
Louis, Zianno. Then come to New Orleans and tell us of Opari and
we will discuss what to do with the Fleur-du-Mal, once and for all."

Just then, the shoeshine boy yelled over at Unai, "One of y'all better get back over to that lady before she gets arrested!"

Isabelle was frantic and both Unai and Usoa turned to leave and
rescue her. Unai said once more, "The Fleur-du-Mal is in New Orleans, Zianno. We will watch him closely. Adieu."

They walked back to Isabelle and the porters, arrangements were
made and tempers cooled, and they were gone, nodding to me ever so
slightly as they walked toward the trains. I looked over at the shoeshine
boy who watched it all with little expression. "What's your name?" I
yelled.

"Mitch," he yelled back. "Mitchell Ithaca Coates. What's yours?"

"Z," I hollered over my shoulder. I was already on my way to Carolina's. No detours, no waiting. I sneaked on a streetcar at Lindell Boulevard and took it west toward Forest Park. The streetcar was packed.
Most of the World's Fair was being staged in Forest Park and I over-
heard a passenger say a hundred thousand people a day were going to

the Fair. I picked up a discarded newspaper and read the sports page, trying to stay calm. If everything Unai had told me was true, and I had no reason to doubt him, then Carolina was safe and well. I was not too late! But I had to see her in the flesh to know for myself. I wanted to hear her voice tell me it was so. In the sports section there was an article about the Cardinals, why they were doing so poorly and what they should do about it. It was well written and whoever wrote it obviously knew a lot about baseball. I looked at the byline and saw that it was written by Nick Flowers. I knew that had to be Carolina's Nicholas.

I stared out of the window at the summer and St. Louis and the flurry of people. I tried to think about everything I felt. Nothing was left out, but it was all upside down. How can your heart be longing for one person and still be beating in anticipation of seeing another? It was a mystery, but I felt both emotions in me like a wheel turning over and over, like a source of light, as different and necessary as sunrise and sunset.

I hopped off the streetcar at De Baliviere and Lindell, near the entrance to the Fair. I walked through a throng of people, spilling out in the streets for blocks, on their way in. Every man, woman, and child was excited and thrilled to be there. This was the biggest event in St. Louis's history and it was in full flight, an amazing spectacle even from outside the fairgrounds.

I found the neighborhood and walked down the long streets of ancient oaks and stately mansions. A half block in, the noise from the Fair was only a faint hum in the background. I passed the Eliots's and thought about that first bicycle ride through this neighborhood. The "old money" had been sleeping soundly then. Since Carolina's arrival, I wondered if it still was.

Finally, I came to the house I remembered. Sweat was dripping in my eyes even though there was shade from every angle. I walked up the paved driveway and paused to look around. There was nothing in particular to distinguish this house from any of the others. No lanterns, no red carpets, no invitations of any kind. There was a formal front door with a brick walkway to it, but I kept walking, under the stone archway and back to where there were two massive oak doors that were obviously the "commercial" entrance. The paved driveway that once circled back to Westminster now went straight back past the carriage house and through the adjoining property to the rear and eventually on to the street beyond. A private alley. It was simple, discreet, and made perfect sense. She had purchased the other property so that people could arrive on one street and leave by another. I thought of what Owen Bramley had said in China: "A remarkable woman, that one."

Suddenly I heard a chorus of female laughter cut through the heavy silence. And even that was cut through by a high-pitched squeal that could only have come from a small child, either being tortured or having so much fun she could barely stand it. It was not coming from the Fair. It was coming from the far side of the carriage house. I followed the sound and came to a wall of forsythia, wisteria, and honeysuckle. The bushes were old and had grown together, standing ten to twelve feet high and forming a circle thirty feet across, with a small opening facing the carriage house.

I walked through the opening. Inside, in the private clearing made by the surrounding tangle of bushes, was a scene as absurd as it was beautiful. There was Li in a tuxedo, but barefoot with his trousers rolled up to the knees, and holding a huge barrel over his head while staring stone-faced into some unknown point in space. Around him in a circle were five women and a little girl; two wore jersey-knit bathing suits and bathing caps, and the other four were naked, including Carolina and the little girl. There was a hose attached to the bottom of the barrel and as Li held the barrel high and steady, gravity allowed Carolina to wave the hose and spray the women as they danced, leaped, shrieked, and laughed. It was unique. It looked like Buddha in formal dress, standing in the middle of the Garden of Delights.

I stood and watched for a few moments unnoticed, then Carolina saw me and dropped the hose. She started walking toward me. She was so beautiful, magical, and completely oblivious of her nakedness. One of the other women quickly grabbed a towel and wrapped her in it as she was walking. The rest stopped and stared. The little girl was the last to notice and she squealed, "Mommy?"

Carolina knelt down in front of me and spoke over her shoulder. "Come here, honey. I want you to meet someone." She looked into my eyes and I looked into hers. "My God, Z," she said, "you came back, you really came back." She put her arms around me and we held each other as tight as two people can without hurting each other. Her towel slipped loose and fell to the ground, but she didn't bother to pick it up. The little girl ran over and leaped on Carolina's back, giggling. "You're naked, Mommy," she said.

Carolina eased her hold on me and casually picked up the towel, swung the little girl around to her lap and covered them both in one wrap, giggling herself. She made sure the girl was looking at me and then said, "Star, I want you to meet . . . Uncle Z."

"Uncle Z," I said. "Please!"

"All right then. Z. Just Z."

I looked at the girl and she was staring at my face and features, but still giggling. "Hello, Star," I said. "Nice to meet you." The girl turned her face and buried it in her mama's chest, being shy, then grabbed Carolina's chin with her little hands and pulled it down, saying, "Mommy, he's a boy." Carolina kissed her on the head and smiled at me. "Yes, he is, honey. He is most certainly a boy . . . the rarest of boys."

I took Carolina's hand in mine and Star watched me carefully. "Are you safe?" I asked. "Have you . . . seen him?"

Carolina turned and gave Li a sign and he rounded up the other women and shooed them through the opening in the bushes. They left quietly, almost reverently, and for a moment it was like being in China again. Carolina kissed Star on both cheeks and handed her over to Li, who gave me an almost imperceptible glance as he was leaving. I said nothing to him, but nodded in recognition. Star left giggling and saying over and over to herself, "Z, Z, Z." She had discovered a new sound, letter, and name all in one. Carolina waited until they were all gone, then touched my cheek with her hand and traced my eyebrows, nose, and lips with her fingers.

Quietly she said, "Yes, I am safe, Z. I have not seen him." She paused and looked away, started to cry and then stopped herself. She turned back to me. "I can't believe you came. I feel like such a fool now. I sent that letter to Owen Bramley like a crazy woman, but I was so frightened, Z, seeing him out of the blue like that, and knowing that he recognized me, seeing it in his eyes. I had no idea what he might do. I could only think of you. I could only call out to you." She paused again and looked hard in my eyes, wanting me to know she was sincere. "But I haven't seen him since, Z. It's been three months and I haven't seen or felt a hint, a trace, or a glimpse. Now I'm not even sure he was the one I saw . . ."

"It was him," I said. "You would never be wrong about that. However, I do know from another source that he's not here. He's been seen in New Orleans, and logically, he should have no interest in you anyway. Unfortunately, I also know he's completely unpredictable. And he's dangerous. We both know that." I paused and looked at her face and shoulders, her hair and freckles, the shape of her body under the towel. She was so beautiful, so ripe and full of life. I breathed in the sight of her and the sight of her was as rich as the honeysuckle surrounding us. I had made it. I was not too late and she was safe and well. I looked in her eyes and said, "Your daughter looks just like you, I'm afraid."

She backed away slightly. " 'I'm afraid'? What does that mean?"

"It means I'm afraid she's got no chance. She's doomed."

"Z! What do you mean? Don't scare me. Doomed how?"

"She is doomed and bound to be beautiful, just like her mama. She's got no chance."

Carolina gave me that same look she'd given me as a kid, as if I was hopeless. "You're crazy," she said. Then she jumped up, holding her towel with one hand and taking my hand with the other. "Come on," she said, "let me change and I'll give you the grand tour."

As we turned to leave, I looked around the space we were in. It was odd. A perfect circle of sweet-smelling bushes at the back of a garden that was closed in on itself. There were day lilies and yellow roses planted at intervals around the inside. They were blooming, but a few other plants were not. They were all well tended. "What is this place?" I asked.

Carolina looked around with wonder and satisfaction. "I don't know," she said. "It was here when I moved in. I'm putting different plants all around the inside, so that something will bloom in every season. It's my private place. I call it the 'Honeycircle.' "

I groaned at the pun and let her lead me not in the direction of the main house but to the carriage house. She told me that was where she and Nicholas and Star had made their living quarters. It made it much easier to keep her "public" and "private" lives separate.

The carriage house was two-storied. The bottom level looked to have basically the same functions it had always had—a storage space for equipment and tools, and stables for draft horses. The upper level had been completely refurbished. Windows that opened outward had been installed all around and a long balcony was attached on two sides of the structure, with one overlooking the "Honeycircle." There were wide stairs leading up to the balcony, but before we could climb them we had to negotiate a path between all Star's toys and then remove the largest of them, a tricycle, from in front of the bottom step. Carolina said, "Her daddy spoils her rotten."

She started up the stairs and I said, "I suppose you've bought her nothing."

"Not a thing," she said.

We walked inside and it was beautiful, simple, and very comfortable, with the smell of honeysuckle wafting through the windows. It was a real home. Carolina went to change and told me to look around, especially Star's room.

At first, I simply stood and stared out of the windows, at the life she'd made all on her own, with only the support of Solomon to make it a reality. Remarkable. Then I turned to look around. There were fresh-cut flowers in vases, framed photographs on the mantel, Persian rugs, a few Tiffany lamps, and the constant, sweet smell of honeysuckle everywhere.

I found Star's room easily. The trail of toys was a quick giveaway. It was a normal child's room in every way but one. The walls were all painted a deep blue, and on the blue there were hundreds of painted stars. But not the cartoonish stars and moons that usually grace a child's walls. These were detailed, accurate renderings of all the major stars and constellations in the Milky Way, with their names underneath in bold reds and golds. It was almost a work of art. It was certainly a work of science and wonder.

Carolina had silently slipped in behind me. "Nicholas did this while I was pregnant. He said he wanted his son or daughter to have a real sense of place and not just know the address of their house."

"It's wonderful," I said. "Can she place the stars on the wall with the ones in the sky?"

"Not yet, but she knows there's a connection."

I turned and looked at her. Her hair was tied in a loose bun and she wore a simple skirt and blouse. No jewelry or makeup. She resembled a schoolteacher and mother much more than a wealthy madam. "How do you make this work with that?" I asked and nodded toward the big house through the windows.

"It's simple really, Z. I don't know any other way. Nicholas approves and when Star's old enough, I'll answer any question she's got. She's loved, well taken care of, and later, she'll be able to go to good schools. I can't hide it from her. I'll tell her it's a part of life, in my case a business, but certainly not all there is to life. What she does with that information will be up to her."

"You've done well, Carolina. I'm happy for you."

"Come here," she said. "I want you to see something."

We walked to the mantel and she lifted up a small, framed photograph and held it for me to see. It was a picture of herself and a young man with a mustache sitting at a café table and smiling for the camera. They were holding hands under the table.

"This is Nicholas," she said.

"That would be Nick Flowers to the rest of us, correct?"

Her mouth dropped open and she could only say, "How on earth . . ."

"I read the paper on the way over. You know me, sports page first."

She paused and looked out of the window for a moment, shook her head, then turned back to me. "This was almost five years ago," she said. "Look at my eyes and tell me what they say."

I looked again. "You are in love. That much is plain."

"Yes, and when I first saw you in the 'Honeycircle,' I could see it in your eyes. You have met someone, haven't you? Someone . . . like yourself."

I thought about everything I could say, everything I wanted to say, but that would just have made everything else less clear. I still didn't understand it myself. "Yes," I answered. "Yes, I have."

She looked at me strangely, curious for more detail, but knew instinctively to leave it where it was. She drew in a deep breath, placed the photograph back on the mantel, and said, "Where to?"

Without hesitation, I said, "Take me to Solomon."

"Right now?"

"Sure. Why not?"

She looked out of the window, confused at first, then laughed to herself and said, "You're right, Z. I've never been there, but sure, why not?"

I didn't get the inside joke. "You've never been where?"

" 'Chestnut Valley.' It's downtown along Chestnut and Market Streets near Twentieth. It's our 'red-light district.' "

"And that's where Solomon is?" I asked incredulously.

"Yes, but not necessarily for what you may be thinking. He goes for the gambling and the music. He knew the original owner of the Rosebud Café, 'Honest John' Turpin, and next door, over a drugstore I'm told, is a gaming room. He's got a permanent seat at 'the wheel,' as he calls it. He hardly ever wins, but he never fails to play. I've heard that the music coming from next door is terrific. Honest John's son, Tom, runs it now. Evidently, he's a gigantic Negro man, who is supposed to be very nice and play a very wicked piano."

"Why have you never been there?"

"I've heard that there's a certain amount of jealousy toward me from a few madams in the area. However, it's never been a real problem, because Solomon spends all his money there and I stay away."

Now it was my turn to laugh to myself. Some things, beside the Meq, never change. "How is the old man?" I asked.

"He's fine, but he drives me crazy. Of course, Star loves him and Nicholas thinks he's some legend out of the Wild West. I just wish he would slow down a little. Anyway, let's go, and go now, before I think better of it."

I followed her out of the door and down the stairs. She swung open the wide door at the far end of the lower level, and instead of horses inside, there was a bright yellow automobile. I didn't quite know what to say and laughed out loud.

Carolina looked it over with pride and turned to me. "Stanley Steamer," she said. "It's the latest thing, Z. But first, I have to check

on Star and I want you to come with me. I want you to see something."

She led me to the back of the big house and a separate, private entrance. She said it was Li's living quarters and the only place Star
would take a nap. I told her I had met Li's cousin, also named Li, in
China.

"Really?"

"Yes, really."

"Well, I hope he is a bit more sociable than our Li."

"He does what he can."

Carolina gave me a peculiar look and gently tapped on the door.
She paused for only a moment, then opened the door. "He never says
come in or go away. He never says anything to anybody, except I've
heard him talking to Star when he wasn't aware I was listening."

Inside, it was clean, simple, and spartan in decoration. Li sat in the
corner as still as a stone. He was gazing straight ahead at the opposite
corner. He looked like a prizefighter between rounds with perfect
posture. Star lay on the single iron-frame bed against the wall. She was
curled up on her side, sound asleep and sucking her thumb. Under her
head, as her only pillow, was Mama's glove.

I watched her sleeping. I knelt down and listened to her breathing.
Inside her breath, I could hear the steady clackety-clack of the heavy
railroad wheels and feel the rocking motion of the car, and all the
hours, and all the miles across Kansas resting in my mama's lap with
that same glove under my head.

"She won't sleep without it and takes it with her everywhere," Carolina said.

I got up and glanced at Li. He hadn't moved an eyelash. Carolina
kissed Star lightly on the cheek and we turned to leave. On the way
out, I spoke without facing him. I said, "Your cousin wishes you well."
I paused at the door, but heard no response.

Carolina cranked up the Stanley Steamer herself, put on a wide
bonnet that she tied securely under her chin, and we took off, loud
and elegant, through the heavy traffic of the World's Fair and downtown to Market Street and a different world. We didn't talk much on
the way. We couldn't, it was too loud, but I did find out that Nicholas

was in Pittsburgh with the Cardinals and the next day was Star's birth-day. A big celebration was planned along with a trip to the Fair. Caro-lina said I had to see the Fair without question. "There are no words to describe it," she said. "It is a visual encyclopedia."

Somehow, she found a parking place on Market Street. With the heat, the Fair, and all the action that follows such things, the streets and sidewalks were filled with people, mostly black and of every age from nine to ninety. Carolina shut off the engine and stepped down into the chaos as if she'd been there every day. People up and down the street took notice. Between Carolina and the setting sun glinting off the big yellow Stanley Steamer, I was invisible, or at least I thought I was.

"Z! Hey, Z, man!"

I heard my name being yelled from somewhere behind us in the crowd. I turned, and coming out of the shade of a storefront awning, I saw the shoeshine boy I'd seen at Union Station. He walked up to Carolina and me.

"Hey, Z, you remember me, man?"

"Yes, I do," I said and turned to Carolina, who was staring at me in wonder. "Carolina Covington, I would like you to meet Mitchell Ithaca Coates."

He wiped his right hand on his shirt and then held it out to her. "Nice to meet you, ma'am," he said.

Carolina shook his hand and said, "Nice to meet you, Mitchell. How on earth do you know Z?"

"We met this morning at Union Station," I answered. I didn't think this was a good time for him to tell her everything he might have seen.

"Yeah, that's right," he said. "But I got one question. What are you people doing here?"

"Do you live nearby, Mitchell?" Carolina asked.

"Yes, ma'am, at the moment, I do."

"Well, Mitchell, we are looking for a place, actually a man in a place. He's an older man . . ." She paused and Mitch was looking at her blankly. "He's a gambler," she added.

"Oh, you mean Solomon. Everybody knows Solomon. Come on, follow me. I know just the place he's at."

He took us down the street two blocks, past the Rosebud Café and around the corner, into an alley that had a flight of stairs rising up the side of a building.

"He's up there," Mitch said. "But you better tell 'em y'all are family. They're kinda funny like that."

"Thank you, Mitchell," Carolina said. "I doubt we could ever have found it on our own."

"I don't know about that, ma'am. I think you might be able to find whatever you want." He turned to walk back to the street and stopped halfway. "Tell you what," he said, "I'll watch your automobile for you for two bits. Make sure nobody harms it. What do you say?"

Carolina was already three steps up the stairs. "It's a deal," she said, laughing.

We walked up the stairs, and without really thinking about it, I put my hand in my pocket and found the Stone. I wasn't expecting trouble, but neither of us had ever been here before. Carolina knocked and a black man in a bowler hat, smoking a cigar, opened the door. My worries were unfounded, because as soon as she mentioned Solomon, we were let in and told he was sitting by the back wall, at the roulette table. The man did ask about me and my youth and Carolina told him I was a foreign boy who had been left in her charge for the run of the Fair and I couldn't be trusted to be left alone. That seemed to make sense to him and we walked into the noisy, smoky, crowded room.

Now I really was invisible. Every man and woman in the place turned to get an eyeful of Carolina. Some of them obviously knew who she was and the rest of them wanted to. She ignored all of them and leaned over toward me, shouting, "Do you see him?"

I started to yell "no" and then heard a very distinctive and angry "Great Yahweh!" coming from somewhere in front of us. I pushed through the crowd, ahead of Carolina, and there he was, sitting in a straight-backed chair, leaning his elbows on the railing of the roulette table. He was laughing, cursing, counting his chips, flirting with a woman named Yancey, and trying to light a cigar. He still had a full head of hair and a full beard, all white. Even his eyebrows were white. He was sweating profusely and wearing a formal tuxedo. I smiled to myself and got an idea.

Looking around quickly, I spotted a boy about my size, carrying a tray of cigars, snuff, matches, toothpicks, and other assorted items. He was making his way around the room, but hadn't yet reached Solomon's table. I glanced back at Carolina, then slipped between the tables and stopped the boy, telling him if he'd let me borrow the tray, the man at the roulette table would buy the whole thing. The boy agreed, but warned that he'd be watching me, just the same. I put the strap of the tray around my neck and made my way over to the roulette table, stopping beside Solomon and lighting a match. He leaned over when he saw the lit match, still talking and laughing, not noticing who was holding the match.

I whispered in his ear, "You can't beat the wheel, old friend. A muleskinner told me that a long time ago."

He turned, dripping sweat and dropping his cigar on the floor. Our eyes were level and we looked into each other's eyes. "Zianno," he whispered back.

Carolina almost crashed into us from behind and knelt down, laughing and smiling. She looked back and forth between us. Solomon turned to her.

"Is zis true? Is zis Zianno or an impostor?"

"I am afraid it's the real thing, Solomon," she said.

"Good to see you, old friend," I said. Then I glanced at the table and his dwindling stack of chips. "I see you are losing."

He gathered his chips, put them in his pocket, rose out of his seat, and told the woman, Yancey, to hold his chair, that he would return another time. Then, he turned and took both of us by the arm, leading us out through the crowd. "I am no longer losing, Zianno. Partners know when to call it quits."

Carolina and I both laughed and then I remembered the boy and the tray with matches. I told Solomon the situation. He found the boy and gave him a double eagle, a twenty-dollar gold piece. The boy said that was more than it was worth and Solomon told him, "So was the surprise."

We walked out of the door and down the stairs, slowing a little for Solomon. He was still tall and vigorous, but time and his body were betraying him. I could tell it annoyed him more than anything else. On the way to the Stanley Steamer, he asked Carolina if her being down here was such a good idea. She said she could ask him the same thing herself. It was obvious this subject had come up before.

We reached our parking place and Mitch was on patrol, not allowing a soul within three feet of Carolina's property, which looked golden in the light of the setting sun. She gave him four bits, tip included, and Solomon tossed him a double eagle when he turned around. Mitch looked at me and I gave him a wink. He winked back and Carolina drove the big car away, toward Forest Park and into the last light of a long day.

All the way home, Solomon went on about the wonders of the World's Fair, all the aboriginal peoples that had been gathered from the far ends of the earth, the architectural and engineering feats of the canals, bridges, lagoons, and fountains, the palaces, pavilions, the ice-cream cones, and the Observation Wheel, also called the Ferris Wheel, and named after the man who had invented it, George Washington Gale Ferris. He said it was remarkable and called it "structure in motion." He talked about Geronimo, the Igorots, the John Philip Sousa Marching Band, and the Pike with all its amusements. He said he'd leased a car all to ourselves on the Ferris Wheel, for Star's birthday, and a private tour of Jerusalem, which he said I'd love because they made it "more real than it ever was," whatever that meant.

He talked and talked and the more he talked, it seemed as if I'd never been away. Not once did he ask about my sudden appearance or the reason for it. I wondered how much Carolina, or even Owen Bramley, had told him. His sense of arrivals and departures, and the trivialities attending them, reminded me of Zeru-Meq.

After coming to a screeching halt in front of the carriage house, Carolina announced that "business" was closed for the evening. The big feast was on and everyone in the house was invited. I asked her if my presence needed explaining and she said it was not my presence she was worried about, it was my absence that needed explaining.

She immediately began taking charge of the preparations and suggested Solomon take me on the grand tour. I asked him if he would prefer a short nap and he said, "Nonsense."

He took me through the big house and introduced me to all the "ladies" who lived and worked in Carolina's home. There were five who lived there normally, but the youngest one, Lily, was visiting her ailing brother in New Orleans. They were gracious, bright, and obviously all in love with Solomon. I wasn't sure of their ages, but none looked younger than eighteen or older than thirty. Solomon's simple introduction to each one was the same, "Zis is Zianno."

He led me through all the rooms and salons, which were elegant and immaculate, comfortable with every nuance of taste and decoration, and definitely giving the impression of someone's home rather than someone's whorehouse.

We ended up in his room and Solomon eased himself into a beautiful burl walnut rocker set close to the window and facing west. I turned and looked around the room. It was a good room, a warm room. I'd never known him to keep photographs, but he had two of them, framed and displayed on his dresser. One was a formal portrait of Mrs. Bennings, which I'd never seen before, and the other was a blurry shot of Star trying to keep still in the grass of the "Honeycircle."

I asked him how he liked living in one place for such a long time. He looked through the window first, then rose out of the rocker and walked to the dresser. He picked up the photograph of Star.

"It is zis one, Zianno. Zis child has stolen my heart."

I looked at the picture with him. He was right. Her eyes were as bright and full of promise as a sunrise.

"She is lovely," I said.

"Yes . . . yes, she is," he said, almost under his breath. Then he smiled and said, "Do you remember your Plato, Z?"

I laughed. "I'm not sure, what do you mean?"

"Basically, Plato said all we really needed to do in zis life was to cultivate reason, honor, and passion. But zis one"—and he pointed at Star's photograph—"zis one has taught me that the first two can go poof! All we need is the last—passion—and we must rediscover zis passion every day. Star does zis without effort, as every child can, I know, but I tell you, Z, every day I watch in wonder. It is such a simple thing. I think Yahweh must have meant for us to go full circle. I see zis world more and more as Star does than as Solomon."

He carefully placed the photograph back on the dresser, then made his way to the other side of the room and disappeared into a walk-in closet. I heard some rustling and grumbling and he tossed the tuxedo to the floor. A few minutes later, he walked out in slippers, long, loose trousers, and a black velvet smoking jacket, tied at the waist. I didn't say a word, but smiled to myself, remembering that scarecrow I'd seen years ago in Colorado.

"Come, Zianno," he said. "You must eat if you want to grow up big and strong."

He put his arm around my shoulders and we both laughed all the way down the stairs.

Dinner was a feast in every sense of the word. The food was delicious, the women were beautiful, the spirits were high, and the tales were tall. Much of the conversation concerned the Fair and the life around it. The women talked at length about the international fashion they'd seen and, at the same time, the lack of it. Carolina brought me up-to-date on professional baseball a little, telling of the exploits of a few players and recounting the World Series, the first one ever, the year before. Star bounced back and forth between Solomon and Li and I could see that each was jealous of Star's affection for the other. Solomon told stories about China and held the women mesmerized. As he was in the middle of one particular tale in which he was pulling the wool over the eyes of a Chinese man, I glanced at Li, who was sitting as silent as stone in the corner and shaking his head from side to side, as if poor Solomon would never get it right.

The whole evening was loud and lusty, and as it began to wind down, the table thinned out. The women left one by one and Star fell asleep in Solomon's lap, with Solomon himself nodding off soon after. Li picked up Star to take her to bed and Carolina assisted a grumbling Solomon upstairs to his room.

I walked outside through the kitchen and, without thinking about it, wandered in the darkness back to the "Honeycircle." I took a few steps in, but stopped short of entering. I could see nothing except a faint light from above, inside the carriage house. The heavy, sweet scent of honeysuckle was overpowering. I took in a deep breath and let it out slowly, and as my lungs were nearly empty, I heard in the darkness someone else breathing in. I closed my eyes and opened them again, trying to see a form. I stood silent, waiting. Then, ahead of me, inside the darkness, I thought I saw a shape, a silhouette, something. I took a few steps forward, toward it. Something was familiar, something particular was forming and coming toward me. This couldn't be, I thought, but I could almost see them. I could see the lips, her lips, coming toward me. They were parted and trembling. Suddenly, from behind me, I heard footsteps, real ones. I turned and it was Carolina, carefully making her way through the opening.

"Are you all right?" she asked.

"Yes, yes, I'm fine."

"Are you sure?"

"Yes."

She took my arm and led me up the stairs to the carriage house. She showed me the room I was to stay in, and as she was fluffing up pillows and turning the bed down, I walked out to the balcony and looked down on the "Honeycircle." I don't know how many minutes passed, but I was lost, somewhere inside and far away. Without my knowing, at some point Carolina had slipped in behind me and was looking over my shoulder.

"What is her name, Z?" she asked.

"Opari," I said, after pausing only a moment.

"That is a beautiful name."

I turned and looked at Carolina. She was standing with the light behind her and her eyes were in shadow.

"Did you leave her to come to me?"

"Yes and no."

"If I have caused you pain in any way, I couldn't—"

"You have not," I interrupted. I took her hand in mine and moved to where I could see her eyes. There was a single tear sliding down her cheek over her freckles.

"Will you tell me more about her?" she asked.

"Yes, I promise."

"Good," she said. "Let's get some rest."

After a long overdue and dreamless sleep, I was awakened to Star's birthday by Star herself. She was leaning on my bed, shaking my knee, and saying, "ZeeZee, wake up! ZeeZee, come on! ZeeZee, we ride the Fierce Whale, we ride the Fierce Whale."

It took me a minute to figure out she meant "Ferris Wheel, Ferris Wheel," and then I remembered our plans for the World's Fair.

Everything moved quickly. We had a hearty breakfast in the kitchen of the big house, then all gathered under the stone arch at the top of the driveway. At first, we debated whether to walk to the Fair or not, thinking of Solomon, but he would have none of that, and away we went. There were six in our party: Solomon and I took up the rear; Li and Carolina walked in front of us, and leading the whole pack were Star and Ciela, the second youngest of Carolina's "ladies" and the most trusted. She was of Cuban descent and still had a trace of an accent. Star seemed to treat her like a sister and she was along to celebrate, as well as babysit, if Star got tired or sleepy.

Carolina and Ciela both carried parasols, and by the time we approached the main entrance near De Baliviere and Lindell, both were unfurled. The sun was already high in the sky and the day was hot and getting hotter.

We entered with a swarm of people, tens of thousands, and started up the main avenue, the Plaza of St. Louis. Solomon was right. The sheer size and magnificence of the fairgrounds and buildings took your breath away. As we walked, we passed a statue of Hernando de Soto, who discovered the "Father of Waters" while in search of the Fountain of Youth. I couldn't help but think of Geaxi and what she had told me once about De Soto. She said he was a fool who would probably have mistaken a horse trough for the Fountain of Youth.

On we went to Festival Hall, which Carolina insisted we see. Along the way, we passed lagoons with people in motorboats and gondolas, some shaped like Cleopatra's barge and some like swans' and serpents' necks. Other people rode in roller chairs and zebu carriages, in Irish jaunting cars and all kinds of oriental contraptions. There was also a scaled-down train on the fairgrounds itself, carrying people from point to point.

We stopped to watch the Cascades, a series of fountains and waterfalls, which tumbled down the hill into the lagoon. Star almost jumped in, but was restrained by Li.

Solomon took us through the Palace of Mines and Metallurgy, where there were workers actually mining coal in a full-size coal mine.

There was also an oil well, again full-size and working. The women were more impressed by the huge obelisks guarding the entrance.

Next, he guided us through a tour of the Palace of Electricity and everyone was astounded that, from here, St. Louis could communicate by wireless with Chicago, Springfield, and Kansas City. Solomon leaned over to me and said, "Zis is where the big money will be in zis century, Zianno. Communications." Then he winked and whispered, "Perhaps the 'Children of the Mountains' should become experts, eh?"

Carolina took us to our next stop, the French Pavilion. It was a re-production of the Grand Trianon at Versailles and set in a fifteen-acre garden. It was rich and luxurious and surrounded by espalier trees, which I'm sure no one in St. Louis had seen before. Inside, there were expensive tapestries and elegant furniture. At the end of one long hall and next to the twenty-foot draperies around a huge window, Caro-lina nodded toward a spot against the wall. No one understood, but I got her meaning—that was where she had seen the Fleur-du-Mal.

After touring the Palace of Machinery and the Palace of Liberal Arts, Star wanted a boat ride. We boarded one of the gondolas and cruised through the lagoons and canals, cooling off and listening to the gondolier serenade us with Italian songs.

We disembarked and Solomon declared it was time for lunch. We stopped at the Falstaff Inn, a two-story structure with flags waving on top and tables and chairs outside under an awning. We sat outside and didn't order off the menu. Instead, Solomon sent Li to purchase two of his favorite foods that had been introduced at the Fair for the first time, hot dogs and ice-cream cones. A few minutes later, we were all toasting Star's birthday with a hot dog in one hand and an ice-cream cone in the other. Star giggled and dribbled and gave Solomon a hug and a kiss that left traces of mustard and chocolate in his white beard. Even Li liked the ice cream and grunted as it melted and ran down his stone face.

Within moments of finishing her ice cream, Star was tugging on Carolina and saying, "Fierce Whale, Mommy, let's ride the Fierce Whale."

Solomon interjected and announced that our appointment for our private ride was at four o'clock sharp. Our appointment for our pri-vate tour of Jerusalem was at three-thirty and, therefore, we could not dawdle. "The Fierce Whale at four," he said, "and Jerusalem at three-thirty, but first—the Pike."

The Pike was easily the most crowded area of the Fair and the most fun. It was one long, wide boulevard with everything you could imagine from "Blarney Castle" and the "Tyrolean Alps" to the "Battle of Santiago" and the "Galveston Flood." The Pike was a living color picture of the world. Architecture, scenery, concessions. Anything, everything. We even saw a statue of Teddy Roosevelt made of butter and a bear made of prunes. We wandered in and out of everywhere, but Star loved Hagenbeck's Animal Circus best. There she got to see animals she'd only seen in books, roaming at large inside a huge compound. Except perhaps in her dreams, it was the closest she'd ever been to elephants and tigers. Solomon was as fascinated as Star, or perhaps because of her, and had to be reminded by Carolina that three-thirty was approaching.

We hurried down the Pike and reached the gates of Jerusalem just in time. A dark, heavyset man who seemed to know Solomon greeted us and escorted our entire party inside and to a tent where six camels stood saddled and in a line, one behind the other. We were introduced to our guide, who wore a long robe and turban, despite the heat. We were each given a robe and turban to wear and told, "Believe it or not, you will be cooler." The women were asked to wear veils, even Star, and we all looked very mysterious as our caravan set out through Jerusalem. Our guide was in front, followed by Ciela, Carolina with Star in her lap, Solomon, myself, and Li as a sort of caboose. The camels were each attended by two boys, one in front with the reins and one by the saddle for assistance. The camels snorted and baulked at first, but then fell into their lazy, awkward gait. Carolina and Star were laughing hysterically and Solomon looked like a long-lost Arab prince returning home.

Jerusalem was one of the largest exhibits of the Fair and the most labyrinthine. Streets led into streets that led back into themselves. Every passage was narrow and claustrophobic with people and dust. Dogs barked and merchants shouted in foreign languages. It was dream-like, exotic, and felt, as Solomon said, "more real than it ever was."

After several minutes, maybe ten, maybe twenty, we came to a particularly tight and congested corner. The camel boys slowed the

camels, but it was too late. A man had tumbled out of an open doorway into the street and surprised our guide and the lead camel. The
camel stopped abruptly and kicked the camel boy behind, who
screamed and fell, spooking Ciela's camel into a spin and tangling legs
with Carolina's camel, which lost its balance and fell sideways, throw-
ing Carolina and Star into the crowd.

Just in front of me, Solomon tried to get down from his camel, but
the crowd pushed against him, locking him in his saddle. I had to get
closer. I turned around and waved to Li and the both of us leaped into
the chaos and, with Li as a battering ram, made our way to Solomon.
I yelled up at him, "Can you see anything?"

"Yes, I can see Carolina," he said. "She is standing. She is all right,
but confused, a little dazed, I think. But . . . but . . ." He was straining
forward in his saddle, looking left and right, frantically. "I can't see
Star, Z. I can't see Star!"

Li and I pushed forward, finally making it to Carolina, who had lost
her robe, turban, and veil. She was shaken, but coming to her senses.
People speaking in Arabic were dusting her off and feeling her limbs,
making sure nothing was broken.

"I'm fine. Thank you. Enough of that, thank you," she was telling
them. Just then, she saw Li. "Find Star," she yelled, "find Star, Li!"

I got to her a moment later. "Are you all right?" I had almost to yell
myself.

She reached out for my hand. "Yes, yes, I'm fine, just scared.
Where's Solomon?"

"He's all right. He's stuck back on his camel."

"Good," she said. "Let's find Star, Z."

The camels had been secured and the panic of the crowd had dis-
sipated. Shouts passed back and forth between our guide and two
other men about who was to blame. Up ahead, there was a circle of
people gathered around a doorway. Li was on the outside of the ring,
waving to us. We ran toward him. He nodded at the circle and Carolina pulled at people's arms and shoulders, yelling, "Out of the way!"

In the middle of the circle, sitting on the stoop of the doorway,
Ciela was holding a trembling child, wearing a robe, turban, and veil
with her head buried in Ciela's chest.

"Is she all right?" Carolina asked in a kind of strained whisper.

Ciela nodded, but didn't speak. She held the child close, rocking back and forth, and softly saying, "Shh, shh."

We stood in silence, catching our breath, which was difficult. Dust was everywhere, kicked up during the melee, and the camel boys were still trying to calm the animals. I looked back for Solomon, and just as I saw his familiar white head above the crowd, I caught sight of something else familiar, a movement between the camels, but I couldn't pinpoint it. Then Solomon broke through and took charge.

"Is everyone in one piece?" he asked Carolina.

"Yes, thank God," she said. "We could have been thrown anywhere."

"Is Star unhurt?" He bent down and patted the child, who still clung to Ciela for dear life. "Star, honey," he said in his softest voice, "are you all right?"

She nodded, but kept her face pressed against Ciela's chest. Solomon stood up and looked around angrily for our guide, who had disappeared. "I shall sue them for zis," he said, then he helped Ciela to her feet. He and Carolina put their arms around her. "Come," he said, "if everyone is up to it, we go ride the Ferris Wheel. I guarantee in five minutes, Star will forget zis ever happened."

After several wrong turns, we eventually found our way out of Jerusalem and through the Japanese Gardens, just in time to make our prearranged ride on the Ferris Wheel. We were still flustered as we approached it. I could barely comprehend the sheer size of it. It was over two hundred and sixty feet high, had thirty-six cars that were almost thirty feet long and over twelve feet wide, an axle one hundred and forty feet above ground, and steel rods extending in pairs to the rim all around. To me, it looked like a giant, spinning spiderweb.

We walked up the platform and the doors to our car were opened. There were glass walls on all sides so the entire fairgrounds could be observed as the wheel turned in its great orbit.

After all the cars were loaded, the ride consisted of four revolutions. On our first revolution, we all stood in silence and gazed down on the Fair and Forest Park from a new perspective. At the top of the arc of our second revolution, Carolina, who had been standing next to Ciela, leaned over to kiss Star, pulling the veil away.

She jumped back, spinning and hitting her back against the glass wall. "That's not Star!" she shrieked.

Ciela tore off the turban of the girl she was holding and Solomon looked at Carolina, turning as white as his beard. "What did you say?" he asked.

My own throat went dry and I felt the old feeling of the net descending. We all looked at the child, who was staring back at us blankly. She was blond and female, but clearly not Star.

I went to the glass wall that looked out over where we'd been, over Jerusalem. Two hundred and sixty feet below me and boarding the small train that ran through the Fair, with Star frozen against him, paralyzed in fear, was the Fleur-du-Mal. He wore the same robe as one of the camel boys, but had taken off the turban. I could barely see the green ribbon at the back of his head. He turned and looked up at the Ferris Wheel and grinned. Even from that distance, his teeth were a brilliant white.

Solomon saw where I was staring and looked down. He found her immediately. He ran to the glass, pounding his fists on it, trying to break it, and screaming, "No! No! Zis cannot be!"

The big wheel wouldn't turn fast enough for him. He kept pounding and screaming as we made our descent. What was probably two minutes seemed like two hours. Before we got to the platform, he turned bright red and began to cough violently. Li and I tried to reach for him, but he slid down the glass wall and sprawled on the floor. He went into a seizure and his chest heaved in spasms. Carolina knelt down and loosened his shirt, but he started to lose color and his breathing stopped completely.

Finally, we got to the bottom of the arc and Li rushed out onto the platform to find water. I looked around at the crowd and asked if there was a doctor among them. There wasn't. Carolina shouted out that he'd started breathing again, but just barely. Then, two of the Jefferson Guard appeared and called to a third to find a stretcher. They were policing the Fair and I wondered for a moment if I should mention Star. Carolina must have thought the same thing, because she looked out at me, then quickly shook her head.

Li came back at the same time as the stretcher arrived. He sprinkled water on Solomon's face as we lifted him onto the stretcher and into the shade of the Falstaff Inn, a hundred yards away. His breathing was shallow and uneven and he drifted in and out of consciousness. Carolina decided we should get him home as soon as possible and have her doctor meet us there. A carriage was located and we were transported through the main entrance, with an escort of ringing bells to clear the way, and on to Carolina's, where she had him moved upstairs to the carriage house. She opened the windows wide on all sides and made sure there was a breeze getting to her sofa, where Solomon lay on his back. She propped his head up and, when he was conscious, tried to help him sip water. She didn't mention Star once, nor did anyone else. I looked at her eyes. They were as glassy as if she had taken strychnine. She was in shock, but somehow managing to go on, to function.

Time passed and the doctor failed to arrive as he was supposed to. The room was hot and the air was thick with the sweet smell of honeysuckle. Ciela was becoming more and more frantic and over-whelmed with worry and finally snapped, running down the stairs and crying uncontrollably. Li sat in the corner of the room, as always, but once I saw his hands tremble slightly. I walked out onto the balcony and, for some reason, screamed as loudly as I could at the setting sun. It was my kind that had done this. It was my kind that was poisoning the lives of the two people I loved the most. It was not just the Fleur-du-Mal who was an "aberration." We, the Meq, were all an aberra-tion, a mistake, a flaw that would eventually act as a virus and destroy the whole grain, the "natural" beauty, the way things should have been without us, alive and undisturbed.

We waited. Each of us sat and waited. Darkness fell above and below and Carolina lit candles inside. The doctor never came.

Solomon awoke around midnight, just enough to open his eyes and call for me. I sat on the floor next to him.

"Zianno, come close now," he said. I leaned over so that his voice was in my ear. "On my way through the Milky Way, I will leave a trail. Will you be able to find it, Zianno?"

"I couldn't miss it. You are an excellent pathfinder, old friend."

"Then I shall do it," he said and took a quick, shallow breath. "Yes . . . that is it, Z . . . zis is good . . . zis is good business."

We shut his eyes for him. He simply left. I looked at Carolina and she was tearless. Sad, broken, and tearless. Li got up slowly, walked out of the door and down the stairs. A few minutes later, I thought I heard the door to his small apartment open and close. After several more minutes, I made Carolina stand up and I took her to her room. I gently helped her lie down and said, "Tomorrow we find Star."

"Yes," she said. "I know we will," but she was numb, inside and out.

I closed her door, put a blanket over Solomon, and walked out onto the balcony, overlooking the "Honeycircle." I breathed in the thick, oversweet scent. I wanted more of it. Without thinking, I leaped over the railing and dropped twelve feet, crashing into the edge of a honeysuckle bush and rolling in the grass.

Somewhere in the darkness, somewhere inside the "Honeycircle," a voice said, "Careful now, you could hurt yourself doing that."

I felt the net descending for certain. It was him. I got to my knees, then stood up.

"*Bonsoir,* Zezen."

I turned. He was standing in the opening. His silhouette was black against black. His teeth sparkled white.

"Why have you done this?" I asked. "You already killed her sister."

"Yes, yes," he said, moving slightly to his left. "I realized that when I saw her, quite by accident, a few months ago. I immediately thought of our last visit, brief though it was. I believe your words were, 'She's not the one you want,' or words to that effect. I could not resist the chance to right a wrong, so to speak. Do you see my point, *mon petit*?"

"I want the child back."

"Oh, such a simple wish and yet so difficult to grant."

"I want the girl!" I lunged at him and he seemed to disappear in the dark, then I felt a hot sting, first in my right shoulder, then my left. I tried to reach out and couldn't. He had slashed all the tendons at the top of my shoulders. Then, just as I tried to turn, I felt the same hot bite behind my knees, this time with pain. I went down without a step. I was bleeding heavily, but I crawled through the opening. He was waiting, standing over me. I could see his ruby earrings reflected in the candlelight from the carriage house. I kept crawling toward the stairs and the light. He walked alongside me, casually.

"Perhaps we shall meet again, Zezen, when your manners have improved. I should like to talk with you at length sometime, about the Meq. I think you would find it enlightening."

I kept crawling. "What do you care about the Meq? You had Baju killed and stole the gems from the Stones."

"I beg your pardon?"

"You know exactly what I'm talking about."

"Yes, but you have the wrong villain, *mon petit*. You will have to ask Opari about that one."

I looked up at him. He was smiling and backing away. His teeth were all I could see, but they were blurry and spreading apart. I was losing consciousness. I tried to get to the stairs, just the stairs. I made one more push with my elbows and hit something next to the bottom step. I rolled over in pain and everything began to go black. The last thing I saw was the wheel of Star's tricycle, spinning against the sky.

PART III

And now and then a son, a daughter, hears it.
Now and then a son, a daughter,
gets away.

—LEW WELCH

II

ZOR

(DEBT)

*When you have a great meal, do you owe your hosts for the experience?
Do your hosts owe the grocer for enabling them to obtain such wonderful fiber and grain? Does the grocer owe the farmer for supplying such a
high and constant quality of grain? Does the farmer owe the grain itself
for being such a strong and pure genetic strain? Does the grain owe the
light and rain for allowing it to ripen and multiply? Does the light and
rain owe the earth for tilting and spinning around the sun at just the
right speed and distance? Does the earth owe the sun and does the sun
owe a force of creation and destruction greater than itself for permitting
this to happen?*

Of course! But tell me, when is this debt ever paid?

As the Meq heal, part of us, the part of us that calls itself "I,"
must go into a waiting room, an annex of ourselves that is safe and
silent, completely inviolate and yet as empty as the space between
stars. I remember nothing of the five days it took me to heal. The five
days of mystical Meq restoration of tissue, fiber, sinew, and bone.
Willed or unwilled, our bodies are repaired and made new. Outside,
we awake unscarred and innocent. Inside, the ravages of time and
events are piling up in our annex, our waiting room, like stacks of un-
read letters and unopened bills.

Sometimes, the healing is ordinary, no more complicated than rest and bandages. It is nothing special, only faster, and we return physically as we were. Other times, it is far beyond ordinary, and we have "evolved," adding something to our senses and our unique arsenal for survival. It is awkward, clumsy, and always unpredictable. I discovered this as I awoke, not to sight, but to sound.

"I tell you, Carolina, he just vanished." It was a man's voice and it brought me to consciousness, though I kept my eyes closed. It sounded nearby, but somehow muffled. I listened harder and I realized the muffling was caused by a wall between wherever I was and the voice. A living wall. A deafening, roaring wall of cicadas. I moved my fingers, my toes. I could feel that I was lying on my side with my legs drawn up to my chest in the fetal position. "Not a word, not a note!" the voice said loud and clear. It was moving back and forth, as if the man was pacing. I opened my eyes slowly. I was in half-light, dawn or dusk, I couldn't tell which. I was staring at dots, dots in a long ragged line, and then, as I focused, one dot, one dot that became a star named Sirius, the Dog Star. I knew because it was written in bold red print outlined in gold. It was painted on the wall. I was in Star's bedroom, in the carriage house.

"Nothing! Nothing except that damn baseball glove."

"Nicholas!" a woman's voice shot back.

I sat up quickly with some discomfort, but no pain. My clothes were in the corner, stacked neatly on a chair. I was wearing someone's nightshirt and sitting on the edge of Star's bed. Everything came back to me at once—Solomon, Star, the Fleur-du-Mal—the sharp sting of the knife blade—everything, but it was all being drowned out in my head by a cacophony of sounds. The cicadas, dogs of all kinds, birds, street sounds, children playing, and the breeze barely blowing through the trees like a howling wind.

I stood, unsteadily at first, then walked to the chair holding my clothes and put them on. I checked my pockets for the Stone and found it. I walked out of the bedroom and around the corner to the small kitchen where I thought I would find them, the voices.

"I'm sorry, Carolina." It was the man's voice and he was moving again. "I just want her back. I don't understand any of this."

I heard him as clearly as if he were standing next to me, but he wasn't. He was at least forty yards away, behind thick brick walls, inside the kitchen of the big house. I walked out of the door and started down the stairs, but had to stop and kneel on the steps, covering my ears with my hands. The cicadas hit me in a grinding wave of noise, louder than anything I'd ever heard. My hearing was a hundred times greater than normal. Then I realized what was happening, and just as suddenly as I gained awareness, it went away.

Sailor calls them our "abilities." I would rather call them our "insanities." Some of us are born with them and some of us, like me, develop extreme ones after severe trauma. Ray was the "Weatherman," Geaxi had her amazing agility, and they both were faster than was natural. Now, I had discovered a kind of hyper-hearing, but I had no idea when it would arrive and depart, or how I would live with it if it stayed. It was madness to hear that much sound at once. I wasn't sure if it was a new weapon or an old warning, but either way, I would need to learn it and learn to use it. As the cicadas died down in the darkness, and I sat on the steps staring across the driveway at the big house, I realized that I had awoken from my healing with something else. Something burning bright and cold without rage or panic. Something pure, honed, and yet involuntary as an eyeblink. It was natural to me now. Ingrained and immediate. It was an efficient, working obsession to find the Fleur-du-Mal. I would find him and kill him. There was no other choice.

I drew in a breath and glanced up at the sky. I found Orion and let my eyes drift to the southeast, to the constellation Canis Major and the brightest star in the sky, Sirius, the Dog Star. I reached in my pocket and felt the Stone. There was no other choice. I stood up and started for the big house. I was alone with it now, alone with my cold, new companion—hate.

The tricycle that was usually at the bottom of the stairs had been removed and put away somewhere. I walked to the back door leading to the kitchen and opened it silently, standing in the entrance, listening. What I thought before were loud voices were just emphatic whispers. He was pacing the kitchen and she was standing at the end of the long table.

"Why not?" he asked.

"No," she said, "there will be no police, Nicholas. There is only one way. Believe me."

He saw me at once, but she had turned toward the stove and had
her back to me. His mouth dropped open beneath his mustache. His
eyes were red and weary. He wore a wrinkled dress shirt unbuttoned
at the collar. His sleeves were rolled up and his suspenders hung loose
at his sides. He didn't say a word, nor did I. She sensed something and
turned sharply, finding my eyes and holding them, searching for what
she needed to know. She looked haggard and drawn. They both were
beaten down, exhausted. She was holding a pot of coffee with both
hands. "Are you . . . all right?" she asked in a clear voice.

"Yes," I said, "I feel like your Stanley Steamer ran over me, but yes,
I'm fine."

There was almost a smile on her face, but it never surfaced. She
walked to the long table and set the coffeepot down, then sat down
herself. Nicholas had not moved a muscle. She looked at me. She
spoke again and her voice was suddenly sad and defeated. "It was him
again, wasn't it? He was the one who cut you."

I waited a moment. "Yes," I said. "But he will not harm Star, Carolina. He will not kill her and he will not torture her." I glanced at
Nicholas. His mouth had closed and he was listening from a different
place. I went on. "That is not . . . that is not how he wants you to suffer."

Suddenly Nicholas started walking the length of the table, never
taking his eyes off me and finally standing behind Carolina with his
hands on her shoulders, staring down and across the table. He was a
foot and a half taller than I was.

"All right," he started, "what I've got to say needs to be said and I
need to say it." His voice was hoarse from coffee and fatigue, and he
was nervous and maybe frightened, but he didn't waver and Carolina
let him speak. "I know who you are because Carolina has told me
about you, and I thought most of that was fairy tales, but I've watched
you heal from wounds that probably would have killed or maimed for
life any other . . . person. And Solomon told me once that I would
never have met her if it hadn't been for you. I owe you for that. But I
don't give a whisker about you or . . . your kind when it comes to my
daughter. If you or one like you is responsible, I want her back. And
I'll do anything to get her back. And Carolina will not suffer one day
because of it. I will not have it." He paused and wiped his mouth and

mustache. "I hope you don't take too much offense at my manners, especially before we've even met, but I wanted to say what needed to be said."

"I understand," I said without hesitation. "And I agree. One of us is responsible and I am leaving for New Orleans tomorrow morning to take care of that."

"Then I'm going with you."

"You can't."

"I can and will."

"You can't, you don't—"

"Sit down!" Carolina interrupted. "Both of you, please, sit down."

We did as we were told and after he sat, Nicholas started to say something, but she put her hand over his mouth and he stayed silent. I watched her compose herself. She was remarkable. Practically her whole world had fallen apart, she was as physically drained as I'd ever seen her, and yet she seemed as if she had seen it coming and knew what to do.

She took a deep breath and said, "Nicholas, this is Zianno. Zianno, this is Nicholas." We exchanged glances and a nod. I could tell he was a good man because he listened to her wholeheartedly and with faith. He had let her inside him to that place where deep and unquestioned trust is required. A place of no proof and no doubts. A place that is only held in place with love.

She gave us both a hard look. "Neither one of you is going any-where." She went on. "At least not in the morning."

"Carolina, I—"

"Hush!" She cut me off. "You are not ready to travel, no matter what you say, and two days will not make a difference if and when Star is found, and she will be. I have more to say to you about that, but not now. I wired Owen Bramley four days ago about Solomon, saying nothing about Star and only mentioning that you were here. He wired back that he'd be here in five days with 'extra cargo,' whatever that means. I want you to stay until then. I am going to hold a gathering for Solomon, not a service, more of a 'remembering.' I owe it to him. We all do."

"All right," I said, "I'll stay, but only until I've paid my respects to Solomon, then I'm gone."

"And I with him," Nicholas said.

Carolina turned and looked at him, almost breathing him in, she was so close. She reached up with her hand and traced his features with her fingers, then whispered to him, "You cannot help, not with this, my love."

He took her hand away and held it carefully in his. "Christ, Carolina, what am I supposed to do? She's my only daughter."

Carolina glanced at me for the briefest moment, turned back and said, "Stay with me, Nicholas. Please."

"But why?"

"Because I'm pregnant."

There was a full ten seconds of stunned silence. Nicholas was trying to make sense of so many mixed feelings, he couldn't begin to form a coherent thought or sentence. For some reason, I could only think of one thing to say, something I'd never said. I said, "Great Yahweh!"

"Yes," she said and rose up out of her seat. She picked up the coffeepot and felt the sides for warmth. She looked to the counter for cups and went to get them. Nicholas and I watched. "Yes," she said again. She came back with three cups, two hooked in one finger, and set them down. She reached into the pocket of her blouse, taking out a handkerchief and wiping her nose, which was as red as her eyes. She sat down again and gave her hand back to Nicholas. He still had not found a response. She looked over at me and said, "Another thing, Z. You cannot afford the luxury of what I see in your eyes if you intend to bring Star back whole and healthy."

I waited a moment, almost afraid to ask, knowing she would get it right, but also knowing there was no stopping it. Not now.

"What do you see?" I finally asked.

"You must let it go, Z, for Star's sake."

"What? Tell me."

"Hate. Hate and vengeance is what I see."

I watched her and watching her was like staring into moving water. You surrender, and in surrendering, are revealed. "I'll find Star," I said. "That much I promise."

She moved again, this time to the other end of the kitchen and a drawer in the sideboard. She withdrew something wrapped in a scarf and brought it back, laying it gently on the table. "You will need this, not just for your own peace of mind, but when you find Star, she will recognize this, no matter what she's been through. The scarf is hers too."

I unwrapped the scarf. It was silk and hand-painted with pictures of Chinamen caught in a storm at sea. Inside was Mama's baseball glove.

Suddenly Nicholas found his voice. He almost shouted, "Carolina, how long have you known you were pregnant?"

I looked up and she was still looking at me. "Is this what Nicholas found earlier?" I asked. "When he was talking about someone vanishing?"

"Yes," she said.

I turned slightly and looked at Nicholas. What I'd asked had made him curious. "How did you know that?" he asked.

"It's not important, not now anyway, but tell me, was it Li you were talking about? Was it Li who vanished?"

He sat down in the chair next to Carolina and dragged it closer to her, putting his arm around her shoulders. They leaned their heads together.

"Yes," he said. "It was Li, but I'm not surprised. He never said hello; why should he say good-bye?"

She started to pour the coffee and I stopped her. "No more coffee," I said. "It's your turn to heal."

Rain fell all the next morning and most of the day. It was a September rain and the air was chilled by it. Carolina and Nicholas slept in. I wandered the grounds and the neighborhood, staying close by in case Owen Bramley arrived, but he never did. It felt good to walk in the rain. I stepped into the kitchen of the big house to dry off and ran into Ciela, who was going shopping for Solomon's "remembering." I asked her where the other girls and staff were and she said Carolina had closed the "house" and let everyone go, but Ciela said she would not leave while the child was still missing; she owed Carolina that much.

Listening to her, I walked to the far end of the kitchen and noticed an alcove with a door just beyond it. I asked her where the door led and she told me it was the inside entrance to Li's room. I opened the door and walked into the tiny, empty space in which he had lived. I wondered about the odd man who had spent his life devoted to Solomon for a reason I never did understand. I wondered where he was and knew somehow that he was probably not on his way back to China. I looked out at the rain through the one narrow window and across to the "Honeycircle." I thought I would have a violent jolt of memory, but I didn't. I only thought of what I must do. I had to get to Unai and Usoa. Why had they told me the Fleur-du-Mal was in New Orleans when he was in St. Louis, most likely all along? I had to find some truths. I had to talk to Eder and find out if she might know what Baju had meant when he told me "this is not about theft." I knew what my heart felt about Opari, but I had to clear it in my head. And I had to find Star. If I was going to kill the Fleur-du-Mal, I had to find Star first. Sailor, Geaxi, even Opari, would have to wait. I leaned my head against the window and watched the raindrops run down the glass. One drop ran into the next, then the next, and the next.

I stayed in Solomon's room that night and, for the first time in years, slept with Mama's glove as a pillow.

There was a reason deeper than mere recognition of Solomon's passing in Carolina's gathering, her "remembering." She knew instinctively the emptiness that others felt could and should be filled, if only temporarily, by sharing memories of the old man's presence, his ability to fill up space and give it color, movement, life. "That's what people needed to remember," she said. "They owed some of their best memories to Solomon's presence."

And they came by the dozens, some with tears, some with smiles. Every one of them was greeted with charm and no outward signs of stress relating to Star. Carolina had had an informal meeting earlier with Ciela, Nicholas, and me and let it be known that the standard reply would be, "Star is in the park with Li."

They came on foot, in taxis, a few in automobiles, and one group composed entirely of musicians arrived in an elegant parade-dress, horse-drawn carriage, driven by none other than Mitchell Ithaca Coates, who was resplendent in an oversized tuxedo and top hat. He handled the horses well and brought the carriage to an even halt under the stone arch. I walked out with Carolina and Nicholas to greet them and felt a smile on my face for the first time since I'd healed. I glanced at Carolina and Nicholas and they were smiling too. It was as if Solomon were arriving for his own "remembering."

I helped Mitch with the door and he introduced each of the passengers as they stepped down from the carriage. There was the big man, Tom Turpin, who gave his condolences to Carolina from himself and everyone else downtown who was "in the shuffle." There was the stunning woman, Yancey, who I'd seen with Solomon at the roulette table. She was decked out from head to foot in black lace and chiffon, and even wore a black veil, which she held across her face. She simply nodded toward Carolina and Carolina did the same in return. There were two more pianists and two horn players, followed by a Creole man Mitch introduced as Bernie de Marigny, the grandson of "Johnny Craps," the man who had brought the game that took his name to America. The man bent over and took Carolina's hand, but stopped short of actually kissing it. Then, in a raspy whisper, he said, "Solomon liked to live life on the Yo," which Mitch said meant the number eleven. "It's a difficult roll," de Marigny went on, "but it pays well." He smiled and I could see the light catch the diamond embedded in his eyetooth. The last person to step down was a black man of about average height, wearing an inexpensive but neat and clean black suit and bowler hat, which he removed after stepping down. Mitch was beaming when he said, "This is my teacher and the king of ragtime, the eminent—"

"I am previously acquainted with Mr. Joplin, Mitchell, but thank you for the courtesy," Carolina cut him off. "We are old friends and I'm only sorry Miss Lily could not be here to greet him," she said, giving the man a warm embrace and taking his arm in hers. I could tell he was a shy man and he only smiled a little and said, "I'm so sorry, Miss Carolina, about Solomon. I just lost someone myself not two months ago." Then he extended his hand to Nicholas and they shook hands. "That goes for you too, Nick."

"Thank you, Scott. He believed in you, you know."

"I know," the man said, "I know."

Mitch nudged me in the ribs. We were just two kids in the background. "That's my teacher, man. That's Scott Joplin. He's teachin' me to read music . . . write it down too . . . He's the best, Z, the best there is."

Carolina led everyone into the large dining room and main salon where people were already mingling and enjoying the food, wine, and beer that Ciela had prepared and laid out. There wasn't any formal design or shape that Carolina had planned for her "remembering." She believed things would take care of themselves. "Solomon's presence is everywhere in this house," she said. "Let him decide."

The musicians all gathered around the Steinway grand piano in the main salon along with most of the others. It was the first time I'd noticed the absence of Georgia's old upright. As Ciela replenished refreshments, Carolina rearranged the furniture so that everyone could be closer to the piano and the music. She asked Nicholas and me to move some couches, sofas, and chairs, which we did almost without complaint and without speaking. Nicholas was having the obvious problem of not knowing how to relate to someone who looked twelve years old, but was older than him in reality. It wasn't easy and I wasn't helping. Then an odd thing occurred.

The two of us were trapped for several minutes behind the couches and sofas as a line of people resituated themselves with their food and drinks. We were both awkward in the moment and neither of us knew exactly how to make it better. We started to talk about long lines and waiting in general, but especially at the gate of any good baseball game, then about the frustration of the fans with prices and conditions, then the state of the game itself, the current standings, Cy Young, pitching, fundamentals . . . everything, anything that related to the new friend we had in common, the one that eliminated our differences and allowed us to become direct and easy friends—baseball. Baseball is the one great communicator. Baseball overrides it all.

Carolina encouraged the way things were going. She joined in as Tom Turpin sat at the piano and played several of "Solomon's favorites." Every room was filling up and a path had to be cleared for the horn players to get to the piano. In the crush, Scott Joplin turned and gave me his bowler hat, saying, "Would you mind finding somewhere safe for that, son?" I said I would be glad to and slipped through the crowd to an alcove under the stairs with an empty bench and a door I hadn't seen before. I left the hat there and found Mitch listening to the music, nodding his head. Scott Joplin was at the piano. "That's called 'The Chrysanthemum,' " Mitch said. "It's just published, brand-new!" Mitch knew all the particulars about him. He'd found his hero and teacher in the same person. The piece came to a close and Scott Joplin turned on the piano seat and Carolina took his hand. He dedicated the next composition to Carolina and "the missing lady," calling it "Leola." It was slow and haunting, and as he played, Carolina made her way back through the people, greeting everyone cordially, keeping her real terror somewhere deep inside herself, but it was taking its toll. I caught her eye for a moment and she knew I'd seen her weariness. I felt as guilty as if I had surprised her naked. I had done this to her. I had put her in this role where she had to assume all grief, inside and out, grief that should never have been hers in the first place.

I took a step toward her and felt a gentle tug on my sleeve. I turned, confused for a moment, then recognized the Ainu woman and her grandfather from the train ride to St. Louis. In so many words, she told me it was Solomon who had paid for their trip and allowed them to join their people at the Fair. They never got to thank him properly and felt the debt would go forever unpaid. I told her not to worry, Solomon would have considered their presence as payment. She asked if I had known him well, and as I was about to answer, the old man interrupted with his low, growling belches. He was looking at me, but speaking to the woman and she responded with a puzzled look. I asked her what exactly he had said. I told her not to try and make sense of it, but just to translate, literally, if she would be so kind. She said, "My grandfather asks for you to 'name what you keep alive.' " I looked at the old man and knew there was only one answer. "The Meq," I said, "the Meq is what I keep alive." He seemed pleased and lowered his head in acceptance. I did the same. The woman smiled, embarrassed that she had missed something. I asked her name and she introduced herself as Shutratek and her grandfather, Sangea Hiramura. I told her my name was Zianno, and looking at the old man, told him I would keep his name alive in my memory. He belched and she said he said he would do the same.

I turned to look for Carolina and instead saw Nicholas was waving me over to meet the Cardinals', player-manager, Charles "Kid" Nichols. Between us there were cardsharps and rabbis. I saw two bakers from the old Freund Bros. Bread Company and the tiny, five-foot tailor, Ira Stern, whom Solomon used to visit every day on his rounds. I saw the Deputy Police Commissioner, several old riverboatmen, and caught a glimpse of Annie Dunne, young Thomas Eliot's nurse from down the street. Every room was alive with color, movement, music, and stories. It was the river of Solomon and somewhere across it, above it, I heard my name being shouted. It was Carolina.

Like the suddenness of being stung and the time it takes to realize it, I was aware of my new "ability," my hyper-hearing. The clutter of noise and conversation became deafening, but I focused only on Carolina and found her the next time she shouted my name. As I started toward her, the "ability" went away, but just as it faded I thought I heard another voice, a voice as familiar as a younger sister's would be, if I'd had one. It was Meq, I was positive. It was saying something about the Ferris Wheel and how beautiful it was, but vanished as a mirage does, probably some side effect of the "ability," I thought.

I got to Carolina and her jaw was set tight in a false smile and there was a trace of panic in her eyes. She was standing with two men, one of whom I remembered from years before. Thankfully, he did not remember me. His name was Gideon Boehm and he'd worked in St. Louis for years as a sometime lawyer, sometime promoter of horse races and prizefights. His reputation was marginal at best, but it wasn't him who Carolina seemed worried about. It was the other one. He was a plain man, taller than average, about sixty years old, with a strange but not unpleasant expression on his face. He seemed out of his element, yet completely at ease with it, as if he'd felt that way half his life.

"There he is," she told the men, pulling me to her and putting her arm tight around my shoulders. "He was Solomon's favorite grand-nephew, this one," she said, patting me on the arm, then standing away, looking at me hard and keeping her smile in place. "Zianno," she said very slowly, "I couldn't let these gentlemen leave without having you meet one of them. I know how much you love history in school and, well, I just couldn't let this moment pass." She paused again, keeping her smile frozen. "Zianno, I'd like you to meet Frank James."

I stared back at her and she nodded, assuring me that I'd heard correctly, and in that moment we asked each other silently the same question . . . did Frank know Solomon had taken Jesse's stash?

I looked up at the man and he smiled, extending his hand. "Nice to meet you, son," he said.

We shook hands and I told him it was a real pleasure to meet him because the history books were doing him a disservice and not telling his side.

"It doesn't really matter," he said and he glanced at Carolina. "Both sides pay in the end. Besides, son, it's not history keeping me from talking, it's the governor of Missouri."

The other man laughed at that and I sneaked a glance at Carolina. I said, "Mr. James, did you know Solomon? Is that why you're here?"

He looked down at me and he answered, but as he spoke he continually looked at Carolina. "No, I can't say I knew the man. I heard his name once or twice, after the war, a card game, I believe, and maybe one other time . . . later on. No, son, I am here with Mr. Boehm and tomorrow I will fire my pistol to start a horse race. It is the only time the state will permit me to use a firearm."

Carolina seemed to let out a breath that she'd been holding and thanked both men for coming, especially Mr. James for talking with me. They turned, and as Gideon Boehm led the way out, Frank James paused and spoke back over his shoulder to Carolina privately. "I don't know how he did it," he said and he winked at Carolina. "Never have. But I'll tell you one thing. Jesse would have thought it damn clever."

We both watched him disappear in the crowd without a word between us.

"Come on," she said. "This 'remembering' is over. Solomon just said good-bye."

She scanned the crowd and took my hand, weaving through the people until she found Nicholas near the music. Tom Turpin was back on piano and the woman, Yancey, was leaning on his massive shoulder. Carolina whispered something to Nicholas and we moved again, toward the stairs and the alcove with the door. On the way, she found

Ciela and told her to clear the kitchen and the smaller rooms graciously. Nicholas was going to announce that it was time for things to wind down. She kept my hand in hers and led me through the door into the little room.

"I call it Georgia's room," she said.

It was a kind of office, study, and sanctuary all in one. There was a window in one wall with the curtains open and a beautiful cherry wood desk in front of it and a Tiffany lamp on the corner of the desk. Books in oak shelves lined two other walls from floor to ceiling, and against the wall closest to the door was Georgia's piano. Outside, I heard Nicholas's voice above the others, thanking everyone for coming, but now gently encouraging them to leave. Carolina sank into the chair behind the desk. She was completely spent. She looked up at me and in the smallest voice asked, "What will that evil one do with her, Z?" Star had never left her mind.

Just then, there was a light knock on the door, which was still open. It was Scott Joplin.

"Miss Carolina?"

"Yes, Scott. Please, come in."

He hesitated, then stepped inside. "I don't want to bother you," he said, then glanced at me. "I've got a favor to ask you, kind of private."

She saw where he was looking and said, "Don't worry about Zianno. He's family. Now, what do you need?"

"Well, I'd like you to keep this for me," and he handed her a manuscript. It was titled "A Guest of Honor—an Opera." "It was meant for Lily to sing," he said. "I just don't see any reason to pursue it until I know she's all right. She has that voice, that voice that drips just like honey, and I can't hear anyone else in the lead role."

"I know, Scott. I have heard her singing to Star on many occasions. She has a lovely voice."

"Well, I'd like you to just keep it here with you, then. Safe and secure. And if you hear from Miss Lily, I would be grateful if you'd find me or leave word with my publisher. I want Lily to know how I feel, Miss Carolina. I am serious about this piece and I am serious about her singing it."

"I will be glad to keep it for you, Scott, and it will stay with me until I hear from Lily or you tell me otherwise. I miss her too. She had a lot of promise. My daughter, Star, she always loved to . . . she always . . . she—" Carolina broke down and covered her face with her hands. Scott Joplin asked if she was all right and she nodded behind her hands. He asked if he'd said something wrong and she shook her head. He looked at me for some kind of assistance or explanation. I said, "She'll be fine, she's just exhausted. Would you like me to get your bowler?"

He took the cue and turned for the door, saying, "Yes, son, thank you. Young Mitchell Coates will be looking for me."

Carolina suddenly uncovered her face and looked up. "I like Mitchell," she said. "I could use someone just like him around here."

Scott Joplin stopped at the door. "Well, I believe he's available, Miss Carolina. He's a hardworking boy, bright, and he might be a good player someday. I will send him by."

"Thank you, Scott, I mean it. Solomon always believed in you. Always."

"I know," he said, "I know."

I slipped past him into the alcove and reached down for his bowler resting on the bench, and as I grabbed it, another bowler spun through the air and landed on my hand. A much older, nastier, and uniquely familiar bowler.

"Bull's-eye," the voice said.

I looked up and he was smiling, almost as brilliant and white a smile as the Fleur-du-Mal, only a thousand times more welcome. Ray Ytuarte. "What's the matter, Z? It looks like you seen a ghost."

Behind him stood Owen Bramley with Eder and Nova, who was almost as tall as Ray, only a hundred and ten years younger. Owen Bramley said, "It seems we've missed most of the festivities."

I looked back at him, then over to Ray. I turned and looked at Scott Joplin, then past him to Carolina sunk in the chair behind the desk. I looked behind her through the window past the "Honeycircle" and beyond that to the shadow of a beautiful doubt and the echo of a whispered word, "beloved."

"Yes," I said. "You have."

★ ★ ★

Twelve hours. It was just twelve hours from the time Ray had tossed his bowler that we were both boarding a train for New Orleans. Yet, in that short span I was witness to something so rare that Eder told me later it had never happened in all her time among the Giza. She had only heard mention of it through her parents in legends and stories from the Time of Ice.

It began with embraces and awkward introductions in the alcove, and Scott Joplin assuming we were family. Then Mitch rounded him up and Ciela cleared the house with shouts of "Out! Out" (in English). Nicholas helped show the last of the stragglers out with the utmost courtesy.

Carolina decided to leave the house as it was and clean up in the morning. She suggested we all gather in the kitchen around the long table, which we did, and Owen Bramley immediately began a long explanation for their late arrival, which was not unusual. Since I had known him, he had never been anywhere at the time he was expected to be there. "When I heard the news from Carolina about Solomon," he said, "I was damn near inconsolable. However, when she mentioned that you were already in St. Louis"—and he nodded at me—"then I remembered that Ray had asked me to wire him if I ever heard you were back in the States. I had trouble with a man in Boise, but after I told him . . ."

As he rambled on, I looked around the room. Ciela was busy at the stove, oblivious to the fact that anything at all was out of the ordinary. Nicholas stayed close to Carolina, first standing, then sitting beside her. He was still sorting through new realities and fears though he was handling it well. Without warning, his world had assumed a missing daughter, a pregnant wife, a dead friend and mentor, and now his kitchen was full of beings out of some fairy tale he might have read to his daughter. He listened to Owen Bramley, but rarely looked at him. In fact, neither of them looked very long or very often at the other, but they were always more than cordial to each other. Owen Bramley mostly paced as he talked, wiping his glasses when he paused. I'm not sure what Nicholas thought of Eder. He might not even have thought of her as Meq, even though he knew she was Nova's mother. He would have seen a woman, about Carolina's age, with slightly exotic features, who could easily have been from Spanish Town on South

Broadway. I know Carolina was fascinated with her. This was the first time she had ever met an "adult" Meq. And Nova broke her heart when she handed Carolina a carefully wrapped bundle of sprigs, saying, "It's Solomon's seal. It's a herb that will come back every year and bring back the memory of your missing friend." When I heard her voice, I knew I'd heard it before, recently. She was the younger sister. She was the one I had heard talking about the Ferris Wheel. She had been blocks away and probably talking to Ray and I had heard it. I knew then that I must harness my new "ability."

Ray was Ray and his presence felt good. He'd found a spot on the countertop instead of a chair and sat there with one leg pulled up against his chest and one leg dangling, swinging back and forth. He was smiling, winking at me, and making faces at Nova, who ignored him. Domesticity had only changed one thing that I could see; instead of wearing his bowler, he was twirling it on his finger. Watching him, I made a decision. I decided not to tell him about the "Pearl," about Zuriaa. I don't know why, maybe I thought I had to know more, more of the truth, before I told him. I have never known why we sometimes decide on behalf of the ones we love what they should and should not know. It is a mistake. In the end, we are all found out. I glanced at Nova and marveled. It was apparent she had a quick intelligence and an innate capacity to focus and concentrate, read between the lines of the moment. She was listening to Owen Bramley, but I could tell she was more aware of Carolina, and even me, as I watched and thought about her. Owen Bramley was just finishing his long tale. "So in the end," he said, "even with the additions, the solution lay in packaging, not logistics." I had no idea what he was referring to, but then he suddenly changed the subject and said, "By the way, Carolina, where is Li? And where is Star? For God's sake, I have only seen her in photographs."

Carolina looked at Nicholas, taking his hand, then she looked at me, wondering what to say. It was impossible to keep it hidden any longer.

"The Fleur-du-Mal kidnapped her," I said. Eder let out a small gasp and glanced at Ray, who returned her look and dropped his smile, confirming something between them. Even Carolina looked a little stunned. She had never heard me refer to him by name. I went on, "I don't know why he has taken her, but I have an idea. I am going to New Orleans tomorrow. That is his home, of sorts, and that is where I will find her . . . and him. Li has disappeared."

Owen Bramley stopped pacing. "Who in the hell is the Fleur-du-Mal?" he asked.

I looked at Eder first, then Nova, then Ray. He shrugged his shoulders. "You got the stage, Z, tell the man," and he waved his bowler in front of him as an introduction. I glanced again at Eder and she nodded her head slowly. This was reckless, maybe even dangerous to her. She had never before shared information like this with the Giza. To her, we were still Meq, even the worst of us, and our safety had always been our silence.

"He is . . . one of us," I said. "He is one of our kind, but he is also different. He is supposedly an assassin by trade and has been for a very long time. He might, he probably does, have a vendetta against me. All I know is, he has Star, he's responsible for Solomon's death, he killed Carolina's sister and Mrs. Bennings"—and I paused, looked at Eder and Nova, thinking of Baju—"and he may have been behind some other things. I don't know." Eder gave me a quizzical look.

Owen Bramley took his glasses off, wiping them furiously and looking back and forth between Carolina, Nicholas, and me. "Did Solomon know this Fleur-du-Mal?" he asked.

I looked at him. Until then, I hadn't thought about it. "No, why?" I asked.

"Because if he had, this would make more sense. But it does not, it does not make a damn bit of sense. Why haven't you brought in the police on this one?"

"You know better than that, Owen."

"But this is Carolina and Nicholas's daughter! For Christ's sake, Z, this is not Vancouver!" Then he stopped as if he'd been shot or had shot himself. His freckles all merged into one red blotch and he looked at Eder in panic. "Eder," he said, "I'm sorry, I never meant—"

"It is all right, Owen. I know what you meant," Eder said evenly.

"Vancouver?" Carolina asked. "What's Vancouver?"

"That's where my papa was killed," Nova said and all eyes in the room looked to her, even Ciela's. Nova looked back, one by one, into each and every face. The only sound I could hear was the hiss of a gas jet from the stove behind Ciela. In those few, strange, silent seconds, something happened to everyone in the room. Through the innocence and wisdom of Nova's eyes, we all drank from a common pool, a quiet place of loss and restoration, and realized one by one a common trust and hope. Without having to say a word between us, we became what Eder said had only been legend—a family—an extended family of Giza and Meq. Not a family formed through time, geography, and circumstances, as we had with Kepa, but a family of strangers, formed in a few moments with love and blind trust.

Nicholas stood and cleared his throat. He put his hand on Carolina's shoulder and spoke to Eder. "I don't know if you were planning on staying in St. Louis or not, but if you are, then Carolina and I wouldn't have you stay anywhere but here. You, Nova, Ray, and you too, Owen, if you have to," he said, but he wasn't looking at Owen or even Eder, he was looking down at Carolina. "We're going to have another baby in the spring. I won't have our baby being born in some big, empty house. No, ma'am, I won't have it."

Carolina looked up at him and smiled. "I agree," she said.

Ray jumped down from the counter and pulled a chair up next to mine. Owen Bramley sat down too, next to Nicholas. "How do we find Star?" he said. "What can I do?"

Ray said, "Get me and Z to New Orleans." Before I could say or do anything, he added, "You're gonna need me, Z. It's my town."

So we sat at the long table making a plan and setting up a network of communication. Owen Bramley assured me I would have no problems traveling to New Orleans now or at any time in the future. And I could stay anyplace I chose. Solomon had left me a quarter of his estate and it was so well invested and diversified, he said I would only get richer. The other three-quarters had been willed equally to Owen himself, Carolina, and Star. "A bank account will be set up for you in New Orleans in a matter of hours," he said, "and there is no need to worry about your youthful countenance. Not with this much money."

I asked him if he still had the name and address of the French photographer on board the ship in Vancouver. He said he probably did, he'd have to look, and asked what that had to do with finding Star. I told him I wasn't sure, maybe nothing, and I felt Ray watching me, wondering the same thing.

Then I asked if there had been any word from China and Owen Bramley said he'd received one telegram with one line from Sailor, which he couldn't figure out at the time, but it said, "Have lost Zianno—gone searching."

Finally, after a long day and night, Carolina called a halt to the gathering, saying she was exhausted, mentally, physically, and spiritually. Nicholas put his arm around her waist and asked Ciela to show everyone to their rooms. Carolina said, "Don't leave before I say good-bye, Z." I watched her walking away and I said, "We'll find her. I promise."

But there were no good-byes. I sneaked into Ray's room at dawn and woke him up with my hand over his mouth. I whispered, "Let's go," and within minutes we were out of the door and standing under the stone arch in the driveway, shivering. The temperature had dropped twenty degrees and it had begun to rain again. The seasons were changing. Ray pulled his bowler down low over his eyes. All he said was, "Damn, Z."

I noticed two huge wooden crates stacked under the arch, side by side. As we passed them, I asked, "Yours?"

"Don't ask," he said. So I didn't.

Our train snaked its way down through Missouri and the eastern edge of the ancient Ozark Mountains. The rain stayed with us the whole trip and once, during a stop in the lowlands of Arkansas, I asked Ray if he could tell how long it would last.

"No, Z. I got no idea."

"But you can tell when it's coming, you can 'listen' for it, right?"

"No, it don't work like that, either."

"Well, how do you know then, what makes it happen?"

"I don't know. I never have. I just sorta get a vision. I see the whole thing at once and I know when and where it's going to change. I sorta see the mind of the storm, I guess. But I can't tell where it's going after where I see it. I only know what I know close-up, like somebody's face right up against you. You see them real good, but you can't see anything else around them."

"And you can't do it on purpose? You can't will yourself to see something?"

"No, I don't have nothing to do with that."

I looked at him a long time while both of us stood there on the end of the platform like two kids, two brothers or cousins, watching the rain and waiting, waiting for something.

"Do you ever think it's a curse?" I asked him. "Not just being the 'Weatherman,' but the whole thing, being Meq, I mean."

"No, I try not to think about it like that."

I put my hands in my pockets and turned to look at the flat cotton fields surrounding the station. I felt the Stone that I still carried there, cold and silent. It never gave me a reason or an answer. "I wish I felt about us the way Sailor or Geaxi does," I said.

"You sure you want to?"

"I don't know. I don't know what I feel these days."

He bent down and picked up a penny from the platform in front of him. He turned it over in his hand, then tossed it side-arm through the rain somewhere deep into the cotton field. "You ain't lived as long as they have," he said. "Give yourself another hundred years and then ask yourself how you feel."

When we boarded the train and were back in our seats, he turned to me and said, "By the way, are you gonna tell me or not?"

"Tell you what?"

"Did you find her? Did you find Opari?"

"Yes and no."

"Yes and no?" He paused, looking at me with streetwise eyes that had seen every kind of bluff and con there was. He took his bowler off and adjusted what was left of the brim, then set it on the seat next to him. I watched him, then turned and looked out of the window at the flat land and flimsy shacks that reminded me of ones I'd seen up and down the Yangtze. I turned back and told him everything, the whole story, and I told him as rapidly as I could, so that when I left out the part about Zuriaa, I hoped he hadn't noticed. And I told him about the "Honeycircle" and everything that happened there. And then I told him that I was going to kill the Fleur-du-Mal as soon as we found Star.

Ray picked up his bowler again and examined it carefully, looking for any imperfections, of which there were many, and then slowly set it on his head at just the right angle. He looked straight at me with clear green eyes. "Well, Z," he said. "It seems like that son of a Carthaginian's got it comin'."

I almost laughed out loud. "Where did you hear that phrase?" I asked him.

He looked back with a blank expression, then we both sniggered and started to laugh together, loud and long enough to draw attention from the other passengers. "I heard Kepa say it," he finally answered. "I thought it kinda rolled off the tongue."

I laughed again and then asked him about Kepa, Miren, Pello, and the others. He said Kepa was still as strong as barbed wire, but he and Pello were worried about the future of the Basque way of life in the territory. More and more, the sheepmen were being forced off free-range land. They had formed mutual aid societies in Boise and other places, but Kepa was not optimistic. I asked him if that had anything to do with him bringing Eder and Nova to St. Louis and he said no, that had been Eder's idea. Nova would begin the Itxaron the following year and Eder wanted her to know more about the world than just the high desert and the womb of protection that Kepa and his Basque tribe provided. When Ray mentioned Nova, I noticed his concern for her was as great as Eder's, maybe greater, but he agreed that she should live among the Giza and learn their ways. He said he thought Nova could "see things," but he didn't explain it further and I didn't ask. I did ask if Eder had told him anything of Unai and Usoa, since he had never met them and it was they who we would seek first in New Orleans. He said Eder thought the Wait had taken its toll on them. They had been together so long, she said their only thoughts were for each other.

I looked out of the window of the train and tried not to think of what that meant. Thoughts only of each other, only of your beloved. I could not let myself think that way, not if I wanted to find Star. I looked at the live oaks and cypresses, some thick with moss, and the tangle of rotted logs and brush beyond. We were approaching New Orleans from the west, skirting the edge of Lake Pontchartrain. Suddenly the image of Captain Woodget came to mind and I remembered that Usoa had said he was living there, somewhere across the lake. I promised myself to try to find him, if and when I could.

We wound through the outskirts and finally stepped off the train well after midnight. Ray had not been to his "town" in over forty years and New Orleans, in the fall of 1904, was no longer anybody's "town." It was a wide-open and well-lit city with an international port and a legalized red-light district. However, it didn't take Ray long to adapt. Within twenty minutes of me telling him I knew only that Unai and Usoa lived somewhere near the Vieux Carré, in a house owned by a man named Antoine Boutrain, we were in the French Quarter and he was asking all the right questions in just the right way, streetwise and elusive, vague and straight to the point. He was a master at it and within another twenty minutes we had a description and an address.

The house was less than two miles away on a street just off St. Charles Avenue. The street was dark and claustrophobic with heavy, overhanging limbs on both sides. "Orange trees," Ray said. "The Creoles loved 'em." The house itself was stuccoed brick and set back from the street. It had a wide front door and four sets of long, rectangular windows, floor to ceiling. There was a single gas lamp burning faintly by the front door and in the pale light I could see the house had once been painted yellow, but the bricks were now chipped and weatherworn and the color was mostly a memory. Ray said, "Your move."

I took a step toward the house and stopped. I was certain I heard singing. I looked at Ray and could tell he had heard nothing. I listened harder and even though there was melody, the singing wasn't really singing, it was more like breathing. Then it stopped abruptly.

I nodded to Ray and he followed me along a brick path around the house and through a trellised arbor of bougainvillea to an open courtyard. In the middle there was a circular, tiled fountain and pond and lying near it, either unconscious or dead, was the woman Isabelle.

"What the . . ." Ray said and started toward her.

"She prefers to fall asleep and wake up in the same place, monsieur." It was Usoa and she appeared out of the blackness like a ghost. "Most often, that place is her own boudoir, but other times, as is now the case, she finds somewhere else to run from her dreams. We always make sure she is safe and wait for her to wake."

She turned to me and smiled. From behind me, a shadow moved and another voice said, "*Bonsoir,* Zianno. Again, you surprise us."

Unai walked over to Usoa silent and barefoot. Indeed, they were both barefoot and wearing long, beaded tunics made of muslin, which looked to be simple nightshirts, but I knew they were more than that and probably from somewhere I'd never been. Usoa reached into a pocket hidden in the folds of her tunic and then took Ray's hand, placing the traditional cube of salt in his palm. *"Egibizirik bilatu,"* she said.

Ray glanced at me, then mumbled, "Uh . . . well . . ."

"You are Ray Ytuarte," Usoa said softly. "We have heard of you through Eder and we welcome you. I am Usoa Ijitu—"

"And I am Unai Txori," Unai finished.

I noticed they introduced themselves informally. It was unusual for old ones and their whole demeanor seemed more relaxed. Their names together meant "Gypsy/Bird" and standing there barefoot in muslin tunics they seemed just that.

Ray glanced again at Isabelle, who was snoring peacefully on the ground. Usoa smiled at him. "Damn," he said.

She turned and took Unai's hand in hers, then lifted it to her lips and held it there, nodding once.

"We have something to tell you," Unai said. "You will be the first to know."

"What is that?" I asked.

He paused for only a moment, then said, "We have decided to cross in the Zeharkatu. For eleven hundred years, we have waited and soon the Wait shall end. Next year, in Spain, there will be a Bitxileiho. It is near our home, our ancestral home, and we will use the circumstances to cross. It is right. It is time."

My mind raced. I had question after question, but I only asked the first one. "Why now?"

Unai laughed and Usoa kept his hand tight against her lips. He said, *"Le cœur a ses raisons que la raison ne connait point."* Usoa looked up and translated. "The heart has its reasons that reason knows nothing of."

He turned her head slightly and kissed her on the lips. I saw the blue diamond in her ear flash in the low light as she turned. Another question I had was being answered. I was envious of their openness and tenderness but realized those very things had made them lose their vigilance. Eder was right—their only thoughts were for each other.

They had not lied to me or given me any false indications. They had simply been fooled.

"What about the Fleur-du-Mal?" I asked.

"What about him?" Unai answered. "We are weary of the Fleur-du-Mal, as were Yaldi and Xamurra. He has *'nostalgie de la boue,'* a homesickness for the gutter. We are tired of watching. Besides, you say you have found Opari. The Fleur-du-Mal is irrelevant and obsolete."

"What if he is stealing children?"

Usoa let go of Unai's hand and took a step toward me. "He has stolen children before," she said. "You know that, so why do you ask, Zianno?"

"What if he stole Carolina's daughter?"

She was standing directly in front of me. She reached up and touched my cheek with her hand. "This is why you come, is it not? This is what has happened?"

I hesitated. I saw so many things in her eyes at once. She looked back at Unai and I followed her. I saw the same things in him. They had survived so long, living with the seed of a powerful, rare, and almost supernatural love, keeping it hidden and suppressed, waiting for the time to let it germinate and live, and then at that moment that same love somehow betrayed them and made them weak, vulnerable. Love, guilt, risk, consequence.

"Yes," I said.

On the ground, Isabelle groaned and rolled over onto her back, leaving her mouth open and slack. There was saliva running out of the corner of her mouth and the angle of her head made her look as if she was snarling. Everyone looked down at her and for some reason Ray said, "She ain't no Queen of Hearts, is she?"

Usoa knelt down and gently rolled Isabelle back on her side and replaced a small silk pillow under her head.

"What will he do with her?" I asked.

"If he lets her live, he could do many things. He has in the past," Usoa said, rising. "But I think this may be personal and, therefore, he may take his time. He is unpredictable, but this is his favorite game of all."

"What? What is?"

"The corruption of innocence. And pulling your heart out by the roots."

Unai stepped up beside Usoa and put his arm around her waist. "Our watch is over, Zianno," he said. "This information only proves it. We have made mistakes before, but none this egregious and untimely. We regret it and pledge on your mama and papa's memory to help you any way we can. If I could change the way events have transpired, I would. *Tout de même,* we owe you, Zianno. We owe you."

"You owe me nothing," I said. "The Fleur-du-Mal owes me the return of a little girl who has nothing to do with this. And in return for her, I will take his life."

"What can we do?" Usoa asked.

"We begin tomorrow. Ray and I will need your insight and knowledge, your memories and maps of his haunts and habits. We are no longer watching. We are after him like dogs."

Unai clutched the Stone beneath his tunic. I looked down at Isabelle sleeping, dreaming there on the ground. She smacked her lips once and made me think of a doll, a dreaming doll being kept by two children older than any place her dreams could ever go.

Ray said, "Dogs?"

We checked in to a hotel that same night. It was an old hotel well past its prime, but centrally located and still run with discretion and an emphasis on privacy. There was cast-iron grillwork all around with thick vines weaving in and out. Ray and I liked the old place and the fact it was called the St. Louis made it a good fit.

I gave them my real name at the desk but registered under Owen Bramley's and told the management he was the executor of my grandfather's estate. There was no problem and the date of our departure was left open.

The next day, at about noon, Ray and I began a ritual that was to last much longer than either of us had anticipated. I awoke before him to the overpowering smell of fresh-baked bread and pastries coming from a bakery below our windows and not half a block away. Our rooms in the suite were separated by a sitting room, but each opened

through louvered shutters onto a balcony that ran the length of the
suite. I dressed and made my way downstairs and to the bakery, where
I picked up a dozen assorted croissants and rolls with fresh butter and
jam. When I returned, Ray was awake and waiting for me on the balcony, drinking chicory coffee that he'd ordered from room service.
That in itself, a twelve-year-old kid ordering coffee, would have been
out of the ordinary anywhere but in New Orleans, where the unusual
becomes the ordinary. We sat on the balcony sharing the rolls and coffee, speaking little and watching the street life of New Orleans pass
around and below us. Eventually, we planned our strategy for the day.
We were searching for the Fleur-du-Mal, who was referred to by several names in countless countries, but whatever name was used, he was
actually known to only a few. Ray, in his manner, decided to start in
the French Quarter, then make his way to the far side of the Quarter
and Storyville, the red-light district. My plans were slightly less practical and a lot more vague. Ray said, "Where you goin', Z?"

I said, "Everywhere. Nowhere."

Ray found out more that first day, on his own, than he ever did following any name or place that Unai and Usoa gave him later. It was
not their fault, really. Ray had known the underworld, especially the
kind of vice, deceit, and shifty deals that was New Orleans, most of
his life. Unai and Usoa's life, until they had been watching the Fleur-
du-Mal, had been quite different. That evening, I found out some
of it.

We met at Isabelle's, as we would many, many nights thereafter. I
only saw Isabelle herself infrequently. As usual, she was in her boudoir
preparing for a grand ball that didn't exist, and when I did see her, she
was in a panic and yelling to Usoa that they would be too late, she
would have to cancel. She was quite mad and Usoa always told her
they had more than enough time and not to worry, she looked lovely.
I asked Unai how long she had been this way and he said it had been
a gradual but increasing decline, probably due to her love of absinthe.
He said he had seen it before, the Giza destroying themselves from the
inside out, as had most Meq. At the mention of the Meq, I thought of
Sailor and Geaxi and asked if he had heard from them. He said no, but
that was normal, he had once gone a century without hearing from
Sailor. Impulsively, I asked him when and how he had met Usoa. He

laughed out loud and sat down in a beautiful wicker chair with broad armrests and a wide, fanned back. He looked so tiny in the chair. A child in high leather boots and yet, when he spoke, when I looked in his eyes, I knew he spoke from twenty lifetimes before the chair was even made.

"I owe it to Charlemagne, *de bonne grâce,*" he said. "And his ignorance of the Basque. But I also owe Adelric, the great Basque chieftain, and his ignorance of love."

"Was it sudden?"

"Was what sudden?"

"Your realization of it, your . . . connection."

"Ah, I see," he said. "No, no, Zianno. Our realization and our connection were *à tort et à travers,* or rather wrong and crosswise."

I sat down in a wicker chair opposite him and leaned forward. I caught a glimpse of Ray moving in the shadows, finding a place on the ledge of the fountain, and I thought of Opari, appearing out of the shadows and into my life, changing everything in an instant. "Tell me the story, Unai. Please."

He looked at me strangely and asked, "Where should I begin?"

"At the moment you knew she was your Ameq."

He turned his head and stared into the darkness of the courtyard and then looked up, focusing his black eyes on the night sky above us. "You want to know of the Isilikutu, the silent touch, the Whisper, only our hearts can hear."

"Yes," I said.

"All right," he said. "I shall begin there, but first, I must tell you where 'there' was.

"I was staring at the sky as I am now. I was in the Pyrenees, hiding among the boulders above a narrow pass called Roncesvalles. The year was AD 778. It was the first time I had been back to the Pyrenees in over two hundred years. I was summoned, or more properly, Sailor was summoned in North Africa by his Aita and I was traveling with Sailor at the time, so we decided to return together, more out of curiosity than anything else. Charlemagne was in retreat across the Pyrenees, making his way to the safety of his Frankish kingdom. He had discovered that the Basque, even most of the Christian Basque, did not want his presence in their homeland, and he was about to suffer the worst defeat and humiliating military campaign of his entire career. He would be ambushed in the narrow pass and cut off from his rearguard and supplies, all of whom would be killed and the supplies scattered in ravines by the time his massive army and entourage were able to turn and bring relief. He had underestimated the Basque and their ability to join separate, fiercely independent tribes into a cohesive fighting force. And in the Pyrenees, with their heavy weapons and armor, Charlemagne and his men would be no match for the Basque. In the mountains, the Basque could become ghosts.

"Sailor's Aita, Bidun, had summoned him to witness the occasion and very possibly, in case something went wrong, use the Stones, though he must have also known Sailor would never do such a thing.

"The point is, we did witness it, and in the midst of the carnage, while the air was filled with Basque arrows and the screams of men and horses being pierced and blinded, I stared up at the sky and suddenly felt the presence of something else, something unknown and yet as familiar as my own heartbeat. I heard her breathing. I heard her breathing rapidly. I was six hundred and forty-four years old and had been in the Itxaron for six hundred and thirty-two of them and I knew instantly I was in the presence of my Ameq. I looked down fifty feet below and at the head of the baggage train was a caged caravan breaking away from the others and making a run for freedom along the narrow ledge. Behind the bars of the caravan were several men, women, and children, all Christian Basque who had resisted Charlemagne. And there was one other among them who resembled a child, but of course was not. The caravan struggled, passing and pushing oxcarts and packhorses into a three-thousand-foot drop. Then, just as the caravan broke free and moved away, she grasped the bars and looked up among the boulders, searching for me. Amid the screams and chaos, she had heard my heartbeat and felt my presence. I stood up from my hiding place and looked for the first time into the eyes of Usoa. She whispered one word which I heard with all my being. She said, 'Beloved.' In another instant, she was gone and the caravan disappeared around the rock cliff. I stood staring, *sans souci* and oblivious to the battle raging below.

"Later, Sailor had to tell me what had happened, that I had experienced the silent touch, the Whisper, what the Meq call the Isilikutu."

Unai stopped talking and rose from the wicker chair in silence. He took Usoa's hand and held it to his mouth, kissing her palm. I had not heard her approach. She sat down in the chair and, except for the blue diamond in her ear, could have been his twin.

"Do you know the story of Pyramus, Zianno?"

"No," I said. "I don't think so."

"It is the story of a legendary youth in Babylon who dies for love of Thisbe, his beloved. The details are unimportant, but for the next twelve years, Unai nearly became my Pyramus. Using passion instead of reason, he endangered himself constantly, finally cajoling and manipulating Bidun into convincing Adelric to take him along in his entourage to Worms, where Adelric had been summoned. Charlemagne wanted an explanation for the abduction of Count Chorzo of Toulouse and Unai wanted to find me at any cost, though he told Adelric he was acting as a spy at court, where, everyone knew, children were ignored. But once there, he was no child. He stalked the grounds of the assembly and foolishly used the Stones almost at random on guards and emissaries until he found me.

"Ironically, it was Unai's entrance that secured our safety and eventually gained us favor. Originally, I had been captured along with some Basque families from Navarra as punishment, but after Roncesvalles I was put into service as a handmaiden to one of Charlemagne's own daughters, Berta. She thought of me as a charmed being and a good luck omen for her. When she heard the commotion of the falling soldiers, who had been 'charmed' themselves by Unai, she burst out of her chambers and saw the two of us embracing. I told her it was Unai who had saved me from an assassin and thereby saved her. With that act and Berta's natural belief in fortune of all kinds, we were both made a part of her permanent entourage. Adelric returned to the Pyrenees thinking he had planted the perfect spy and Charlemagne welcomed us as magical angels of good luck and fortune. In fact, we were merely two Meq in love. But the ruse worked and we stayed in the courts of Charlemagne for many years, traveling through Aquitaine and the rest of his empire at will. We even became elephant handlers, taking care of Abul Abbas, Charlemagne's pet elephant, until it died in Saxony in the year 811. I could tell you story after story about Unai and that elephant. Later, of course, we had to leave that world and

move on, as the Meq always do, but that is when and how we met and
soon our long journey and Wait will end. The Zeharkatu awaits us
like a gate to a place we have only named in whispers."

From deep in the shadows by the fountain, I heard Ray say,
"Damn."

I never said what I felt that night. Not that night or the next or the
next. I let it burn up inside me and drift away on its own like smoke.
I was honored to have heard Unai and Usoa's story, but inside I felt
only melancholy and confusion. What had happened in China was
real, I knew that now. It was common to us, it even had a name. Isilikutu. But what had happened in St. Louis and what it meant was
more confounding than ever. If I was going to find Star, I had to let
it go.

In the days and weeks that followed, Ray and I stuck to our routine:
"breakfast" at noon on the balcony and then off to follow our separate trails and sources of rumors, clues, and bits of information about
the Fleur-du-Mal, then a brief meeting with Unai and Usoa at Isabelle's, dinner somewhere, and then back to the French Quarter or
Storyville for our nightly tour of hotels, clubs, whorehouses, saloons,
pool halls, poker rooms, docks, markets, and the streets themselves.

Physically, it seemed to rain more and the temperature dropped a
bit, often dramatically, at night. But I noticed no change in the seasons
to speak of. New Orleans is a season unto itself, especially at night.
Storyville never closed, and it was there that we concentrated most of
our attention. The Fleur-du-Mal was an assassin, but as Unai and Usoa
told us, for centuries he had also trafficked in young girls and women
in a complex network between the Muslim East and the Christian
West. White slavery had become his stock-in-trade. New Orleans,
with the only legal red-light district in America, was a natural hub of
that wheel.

Ray and I made acquaintances with most of the "players" in the
district; the gamblers, bartenders, pimps, and some of the madams.
Even though we were "just kids" in their eyes, we were streetwise and
it was New Orleans, a place where life didn't always need distinction
between such things. We moved freely and easily and Ray knew the

game well. With just the right amount of laughter and bluff, he could
steer a conversation into a gentle interrogation. "Countess" Willie Piazza, the colorful madam who spoke seven languages and wore a
monocle, made the first actual reference to the Fleur-du-Mal, and
even that was an alias we'd not heard before. Ray had simply asked her
if she knew any characters that looked like us. She laughed out loud
and took a drag from a cigarette lodged in a holder as long as her arm.
"Oh, yes, honey, I certainly do," she said. "The Genie, that's what I
call him, always poppin' up out of nowhere with teeth as white as
milk and eyes as green as pine trees. But I don't like what he's sellin'."

"What's that?" Ray asked.

"Girls, honey. Girls younger than he is, younger than you. Girls
that should still have a real mama."

"Well, when was the last time the Genie popped up?"

"It was at the opera," she said and took another elaborate drag on
her cigarette. "Somethin' by Mozart, I believe. Anyhow, between acts
one and two, he came up to me with that cagey smile and asked me
about Jelly Roll Morton, of all things, and if he was still playin' at my
place. He was in a custom-tailored little black tuxedo with that black
hair slicked back and tied in that green ribbon. But like I said, I don't
like what he's sellin' and I politely took my leave. That was just after
Mardi Gras, honey, last March or April."

Through the end of the year, that was as close as we got to the
Fleur-du-Mal. It was a frustrating, empty time. A chase without a
starting place. A game that he was playing and probably enjoying, but
a game that Star never asked to play. He was using her life without per-
mission.

I wrote to Carolina and Nicholas every other day, trying to sound
positive and sometimes making up leads when I had none. I knew
Carolina would read between the lines, but I did it anyway. Ray even
wrote to Eder, and Nova especially, something I never thought I'd see.
I heard from Owen Bramley occasionally, as did the hotel management. He helped legitimize our stay and keep curiosity to a minimum.
He also said he was moving to St. Louis from San Francisco. Nova had
insisted and would not allow any other decision, some doom and
gloom prospect in the city's future, she had said. And he mentioned he
had contacted the French photographer and was in the process of ob-

taining the prints and negatives I had requested. They were old, but they were there, they existed. No one heard a word from Sailor or Geaxi, not Owen Bramley, Eder, or Unai and Usoa, who were already preparing to leave for Spain and an end and a beginning that was unlike any other. We entered the year 1906 frustrated, separated, and in some ways helpless. Unai's toast on New Year's Eve was apropos: *"Aide-toi, le ciel t'aidera,"* he said. It meant, "Help yourself and heaven will help you."

Ray was a good friend, companion, and the closest thing to a brother I'd ever had. We laughed a lot, enjoyed the same food, and shared a love for music, particularly what was going on in New Orleans. On our rounds, we always caught "Stalebread" Lacoume's Razzie Dazzie Spasm Band wherever they were playing. Jelly Roll Morton was a regular at Willie's and he was doing things very similar to what Scott Joplin and Tom Turpin were doing in St. Louis, only his music was looser, more danceable. And at the Economy, a tiny club that seemed never to close, we stood outside and listened to a form of music that affected us deeply. Players from all over the South came through the club and they were all playing the "blues." I was hypnotized. Each player took a common theme and structure and made it their own, made it unique. And when they played together, the music became timeless in a way Ray and I understood instinctively. Complex in its very simplicity, it was an enigma. Through the music, the players themselves shared a joy and camaraderie, almost a secret, acknowledged with a grin or a common nickname. You could feel this music, almost touch it and taste it, or as Ray said, "This is gonna last, Z."

It was a guilty pleasure for us, but it did yield information about the Fleur-du-Mal, even if it was always in the past tense. Several people said they'd seen "the kid with the smile," or "the quiet kid with the green ribbon," but few could remember when and none had a clue where he lived.

We both loved the music, but Ray also loved the crowds, the noise, the late nights, and the constant ebb and flow of strangers in New Orleans. When the crush of Mardi Gras came, I stayed at Isabelle's for two weeks. I needed a break and I needed to know anything they might have forgotten to tell me about the Fleur-du-Mal, anything I might have missed. Ray stayed put in the St. Louis Hotel and immersed himself in the smothering chaos of Mardi Gras.

The peace was welcome and so was the time spent with Unai and Usoa. These were the last few days and weeks they would be as they were, as they had been for so long it was difficult to imagine. They had spanned an immense length of time with a conscious, living bridge of denial and survival and were on the brink of burning that bridge with another conscious decision that would both confirm their love and trigger their own mortality. The Zeharkatu. It was perhaps the greatest mystery of the Meq and the one I knew least about. I wasn't even sure what to ask. When I did bring it up, I was surprised at their reluctance and shyness, as if they were as ignorant as I, but didn't want it revealed.

"Where will you go?" I blurted out. "What happens next?"

We were sitting in the courtyard in the wicker chairs. It was a beautiful morning near the end of my stay. The sun was shining through the live oaks in warm pools of light and Usoa was pouring each of us a cup of rich chicory coffee. After a moment, Unai leaned forward in his chair, but before he could speak Usoa gently pushed him back and spoke for both of them.

"We follow in the footsteps of your mama and papa," she said. "In the old way."

"And how is that?" I asked.

"We were with them when they decided to cross. We will do as they did."

She paused and looked at Unai, who took her hand in his.

"Go on, please," I said. "Where were you?"

"We were staying on the island-city of Kilwa, across from Tanganyika on the East African coast. It was 1859. Your mama and papa arrived with the favorable winds from India, trailing a man who had supposedly done business with Opari. Ironically, it was the same man we were watching because we knew he did business with the Fleur-du-Mal. It was ironic because none of us ever found the man, but it was with us that Yaldi and Xamurra made their decision. The man's name was Hadim al-Sadi and he was the current 'sultan' of an old Muslim family of trader-merchants that dealt in anything from gold and porcelain to silk and slaves, as long as it was profitable. Hadim's family was said to have discovered an ancient trade route, older than the Sahara, that connected East Africa with West Africa through the kingdom of Mali. For centuries, the Fleur-du-Mal has been obsessed with Mali. Why, we have never known. The point is, we thought we had a link between the Fleur-du-Mal and Opari and we were excited. We thought we might find a way into her invisible world.

"But as the months passed and we watched and waited, Yaldi and Xamurra became more abstracted and distant. Their interest waned, and, looking back, it is clear they were at the end of a much greater Wait, the Itxaron, only none of us knew it.

"Then, late in the year, Baju and Eder came through Kilwa from the west on a Portuguese ship. Baju said he was making a survey of the stars in the southern hemisphere and seeking the lost African tribe that worshipped Sirius, the Dog Star. His interests were eclectic and ever-expanding and their visit was a surprise, but not unusual.

"One morning, not unlike this one, we were all sitting on the abandoned walls of the old Gereza fortress, watching the everyday traffic of the harbor, when Baju casually mentioned there would be a Bitxileiho, a total solar eclipse, in Spain the following year. The news was not extraordinary, but for your mama and papa it crystallized every emotion and focused every vague yearning they had experienced for months. They looked at each other for a moment, smiled, then Yaldi announced to everyone that he and Xamurra would sail to Spain and cross in the Zeharkatu the old way, in the Pyrenees. His statement was shocking and grand. No Egizahar had crossed in hundreds of years and no one in our lifetime had crossed in our homeland, in the old way. I remember being a little jealous and greatly puzzled. You see, no one, including your mama and papa, knew what 'the old way' meant. When to go? Where to go?

"Finally, Sailor had to be tracked down and asked what to do. It took another two months, but a day before their last opportunity to sail in fair weather, we got word from Sailor. His note said simply, 'Sail to Biarritz . . . Trumoi-Meq will find you.' "

Usoa paused and took a sip of her coffee. The sunlight streaked her cheek and flashed off the blue diamond in her ear. "And we shall do the same," she finished.

"Trumoi-Meq?" I asked. "I heard Eder mention his name once, but I assumed she was speaking of someone dead."

"Quite the contrary, Zianno. He is an old one, perhaps as old as Opari, and the only one who knows the mountains and 'the old way' of the Zeharkatu." She leaned over and placed her other hand on top of Unai's. "Finally," she said. "He awaits us."

"But how . . . how did you know it was time?"

Unai spoke from deep in the wicker chair. "It is like taking a breath," he said. "How do the lungs know when they are full? I do not know, but they do, *n'est-ce pas*? We have breathed in long enough. We are too full of time and experience. It is right to let it go. It is right to breathe out."

"What about the Gogorati? The Remembering?"

He shrugged and said, "You have found Opari, no?"

"Yes and no."

"Well, we now know she exists. And as Baju and Eder, your own mama and papa, and now Usoa and I have discovered, we look forward to our son or daughter being there, fresh and strong and less than a hundred years old. That is our wish, our dream. It is clearer to us now than it ever was imagining ourselves being there. It is best. It is right."

I stood up and walked to the fountain. Thoughts and images of Mama and Papa, questions and doubts about Opari, history, and mystery were all mixed up and racing in my mind one into the other like brushfires. I could not allow it. I turned and changed the subject.

"What about this place?" I asked. "What happens to Isabelle?"

Usoa looked over at me and laughed slightly. "You will be amazed to learn that he has asked and she has accepted."

"Who?"

"Captain Woodget," she said. "He has asked her to marry him and she has accepted, even though in her lucid moments she still considers him socially inferior."

I laughed along with Usoa and once again promised myself to go and see the old man. "How is he?" I asked. "And where is he, where will they live?"

"He is fine. Crusty and ornery, but fine. And they will live on his family's plantation, old property deeded to them after Andrew Jackson left. It lies on a tributary to Lake Pontchartrain, past Mandeville, and on the way to Covington."

"Covington?"

"Yes. Covington, Louisiana. Why? Is there something odd about that?"

"Maybe, maybe not," I said. "It's just ironic, that's all. The kind of irony that the Fleur-du-Mal might love. Has he ever been seen there? In that area?"

Usoa looked over at Unai, then back to me. "No. Not that we know of," she said and paused slightly. "But, as you know, we have made mistakes."

"No, you have not," I said and walked over to where she sat in her wicker chair. I knelt down and took her hand in mine. "The Fleur-du-Mal is the mistake."

"*Ecrasez l'infâme!*" Unai grunted.

I looked up at Usoa and she said, "Crush the loathsome one."

Three days later, I watched them set sail for London and Biarritz, their final destination. Farewells had already been exchanged, and as they boarded, I thought it was remarkable they still only carried two pieces of luggage: two finely crafted pieces of Italian leather, at least four centuries old. I watched them and thought of that moment as being the last time I would see them as they were, as I was. Then I thought about the chance of seeing them after whatever awaited them and realized they would be the only Meq I had known before and after the Zeharkatu. I smiled and looked forward to seeing them again, although I had no idea when or where that might be.

I walked back to the St. Louis Hotel, making my way through the aftermath of Mardi Gras, where the exotic and the profane still lingered in every sight, sound, and smell. An ascent and descent bound so closely together, one was hardly distinguishable from the other. An almost alchemical blend of real beauty and real beasts.

Ray was waiting for me. I saw him from a block away, pacing the balcony outside our rooms and looking more agitated than I'd ever

seen him. When I got within earshot, I called to him. He turned, located me on the street, and shouted, "I think I might of found somethin', Z, you'll have to tell me."

I kept walking toward him. He was gripping the iron railing so hard
his knuckles were changing color. A spike of fear hit me in the chest.

"What do you mean?" I asked. I was directly under him and he was
staring down. I could tell he hadn't slept much since I'd seen him last.

"Come on up," he said. "It won't happen until later, anyway. I'll tell
you all about it."

"About what?"

"Come on up," he repeated. "You ain't gonna like it."

For the next few hours, Ray told me about what he'd discovered
and he was right, I did not like it. I was shocked and more frightened
with every detail, but never prepared for what I actually saw later.

We waited until after midnight, then walked to Storyville. Ray said
the "show" was only held once a night at around one A.M. We stood
in the shadows of an alley behind Emma Johnson's place on Iberville.
She was probably the most notorious madam in Storyville, known
for anything sexually out of the ordinary. The "Parisian Queen of
America" they called her. She was a trafficker in practically everything, but specialized in young virgins and supplying young boys for
aging homosexuals. There was no perversion too repugnant or difficult for her, no crime too low. She also produced what she called "sex
circuses," where deviations of all kinds were performed on a raised
stage, surrounded by an audience. It was one of these we waited for,
only this "show" involved a much younger girl—a child—a child Ray
thought I might know. "It could be her," he said. "It could be Star."

Security was tight. There were three doors on the back of the
building and all three were guarded by various bouncers and thugs.
Two of the doors were legal fire exits and well lit, but the third was off
to the side and kept dark. It was the "stage door" and the one we
wanted. Ray had already "greased the wheel," he said, by incurring a
debt from the two biggest members of the security force, who he said
were "suckers for three-card Monty." They both thought letting Ray
and me slip in to see the "show" was easy payment. At precisely five
past one, their backs were turned as planned and Ray and I walked out
of the shadows and through the unattended door.

Once inside, we instinctively found a corner of the room where we could watch without being seen. It was dark, as dark as you could get and still find your way. The only continuous light was a single, bare, blue light, hanging from a twenty-foot-high ceiling over a round stage in the center of the room. Matches flared occasionally in the darkness around the stage, lighting a cigar or cigarette and outlining the leering faces of the audience. In the brief flashes, they looked like ghouls to me. There was no way of telling how many there were. It was too dark. I asked Ray how many times he'd done this and he said, "Once." Then the music started.

It began with rattles and shakers, then the slow and steady beat of a conga drum, then another conga with a deeper tone, playing fewer beats, and finally a hum of voices, all male and chanting an obscure African dream song.

The far end of the room was really a curtain. Two black men walked through, naked to the waist and carrying a ten-foot log between them, hoisted on their left shoulders. In their right hand, each carried a burning candle. Wrapped around the log, and clinging to it like snakes with their heads entwined, were a man and a woman, completely naked and glistening with oil from head to toe. They were motionless on the log, as if they were sleeping. The woman seemed to be a quadroon or octoroon and the man was coal black. They made their way slowly to the stage, through the audience, which was beginning to stir. I heard at least two low whistles from somewhere in the room.

Once on the stage, the first man holding the log turned to face the other and they stood that way in silence for several moments, then the rhythm of the drums changed pace slightly and two more men appeared, carrying stone posts, which they set on the stage at precise positions and the log was laid between, then secured, so it was resting a few feet above the stage. All four men turned and walked back through the audience and disappeared behind the curtain. The human snakes on the log remained motionless and silent under the single blue light.

A female voice; a lilting, beautiful soprano began what sounded like an aria over the tribal chant. Finger cymbals were added, then a lone violin came out of nowhere, weaving its way melodically through the rhythm of the congas. It was East and West, good and evil, pain and

pleasure, discordance and harmony. I glanced at Ray. He was extremely uneasy and shifting from one foot to another, as if he could
run away without moving.

I looked back at the stage and the blue light flickered out, followed
by the sound of a gong that reverberated through the room. The
drumbeats picked up tempo and five red lights descended from the
ceiling slowly, until they stopped in a circle above the stage. At the same
time, something was rising out of the stage, directly opposite the sleeping snakes. It was in the shape of an oyster, maybe four feet wide and
three feet high. When it came to a rest, the top half of the oyster unlocked and began to open. The sleeping snakes awoke, then fondled
each other and began writhing and undulating on the log in very
much a human fashion. Three-quarters of the way open, I could tell
there was something in the oyster, something or someone where the
pearl should have been. I took a step toward the stage and Ray grabbed
my arm.

"You make sure you're sure, Z," he said. "This ain't no place for
mistakes."

I took another step and stumbled, tripping over an outstretched leg.
I fell to the floor in the dark. Whoever I tripped over kicked me with
his boot and said, "Scram, kid!"

On my hands and knees, I looked up at the stage; the oyster was
completely open, exposed in the circle of red light from above. When
I saw what I saw, my body jumped, as if I'd been electrocuted. I felt
rage, shock, terror, and pity all at once, and violation in the deepest
sense. There was Star, dressed as a miniature Aphrodite in a white
gown, sitting on a raised bench inside the oyster, staring across at the
human snakes achieving every possible sexual position on and around
the log beam. Her eyes were glazed, but not from drugs. It was something else, something worse. It was as if she were sitting at the bottom
of a dry well, staring up at a light, an escape that was too distant to believe in or hope for, a light without salvation.

I screamed inside at the Fleur-du-Mal and his evil, his "aberration,"
as it had been so delicately described. I stood up and started for the
stage again, grabbing the Stone in my pocket as hard as I ever had.
This could not go on.

Suddenly the drums became thunder in my head and the finger

cymbals sounded like great glass panes crashing to the ground. The beautiful soprano voice was shrill and loud as a siren. The low sighs and moans of the audience became a snorting, slobbering herd of beasts. I could hear the skin of the human snakes slapping as they increased their tempo and passion. I could hear the log itself groan against the stone posts. I could hear Star breathing. I turned and glanced at Ray. He was a frozen silhouette in the darkness, watching me.

I took another step toward the stage. Then, from somewhere in the middle of the cacophony of music and noise, I heard my name. "Zezen," a voice said in a low whisper. I stopped where I was and waited, focusing. "Zezen," it said again and this time I knew the source. I looked up at the stage behind Star to a narrow opening, a slit in the oyster shell, and peering back at me through the shafts of red light were two familiar green eyes.

"*Bonsoir, mon petit,*" the voice said, slow and steady. "I thought you might acquire this ability sooner or later."

I looked left and right.

"No, no, *mon petit*. Do not try and deny it. You can hear me easily, can you not?"

I stared back. "Yes," I whispered. "And I suppose you can hear me just as easily. Correct?"

"Of course, of course. An ability that is a necessity if one is to survive against all odds." He paused. "You look upset. Not because you are already missing your sycophantic little Meq watchdogs, I pray."

I waited and tried to gather myself. "Why do you do this?" I asked. "This is sick and unnecessary."

His eyes darted briefly to Star in front of him. "It is never too soon to start an education. You should know this, *mon petit*."

I pulled the Stone out of my pocket. I was gripping it so hard, I could feel it almost piercing the skin on my palm.

"I would reconsider using your precious Stone, Zezen," he said. "Look to the left of the child, by her throat."

I looked and there, not two inches from Star's jugular vein, was the point of a stiletto sticking through another slit in the oyster shell. I knew he would use it without a moment's hesitation. "Please, I beg of you," I said. "End this. End this now."

"Oh, but now would be too soon. Just listen to that voice, Zezen."

The soprano was in full throat, building to a crescendo. "She could be Pamina in *The Magic Flute,* no?"

I looked at Star's face. She had the same blue-gray eyes as Carolina, even down to the same flecks of gold in them. The same mouth and hair and freckles, but her expression was lifeless, traumatized, and lost.

"When will you let her go back to her mama?" I asked. "And deal with me. You know I won't relent. I will not quit. I will find you."

"You shall only find me when I wish you to, Zezen, and you shall never find me when I do not. In revenge, I am afraid you are a novice and compared to some Arabs I have known, you are truly a child."

"You must release the girl," I said. "How could she possibly interest you? She needs her mama and her mama needs her."

He laughed his low, bitter laugh. "I do not think so. I think her mama will be busy soon with another little Giza abomination."

My heart froze. He knew Carolina was pregnant. He knew all about it.

"Surely, you won't, I mean, you don't plan to—"

"No, no, *mon petit,* I could not care less."

I couldn't figure it out. What was the point? "Then, why?" I asked. "Why do you want Star?"

He laughed again. It cut through the drums, the soprano, and the sudden cry of release as the black man reached orgasm.

"The grandchild, you idiot," the Fleur-du-Mal whispered. "I want the grandchild."

At that moment, the red lights dimmed and a curtain began to descend from the ceiling. In a few more moments, the entire stage would be covered.

"Wait," I pleaded.

"No, *mon petit.* I do not wait. That is where we differ greatly. I suggest you go off and chase something else. Perhaps Sailor will send you after the sixth Stone, or has he neglected to mention that to you?"

"What?"

"Oh, yes, it is true."

I thought he was trying to distract me and somehow use my confusion to escape.

"There is a sixth Stone?"

"*Oui.* Ask Sailor where he got the star sapphire in his ring. Ask the annoying monkey, Usoa, where she got her blue diamond. Chase the truth there, Zezen, but do not chase me. That is pointless and will prove fruitless. *Au revoir, mon petit.*"

The curtain dropped the last few feet and covered the stage all around, followed almost immediately by seven or eight huge men who surrounded it. Lights in the back came on, and before I realized it, Ray had me by the arm and was leading me to the exit.

"It's best we get on out of here, Z," he said and glanced in my eyes.

We squeezed through the crowd and darted out of the door, not stopping until we were three blocks away and Ray pulled me in under the limbs of a magnolia tree.

"It was her, wasn't it?" he asked, already knowing the answer.

"Yes," I said. I could hear my own voice sounding like a stranger's. "It was her."

By May, Carolina had indeed given birth to a boy, Solomon Jack Flowers, born the evening of April 26 and named after our Solomon and an outfielder for the Chicago Cubs, Jack Murphy, who threw out three Pirate runners at the plate that day and is the only major leaguer to have done so.

Ray and I had not mentioned seeing Star to anyone, especially Carolina and Nicholas. At that point, it would have done no good and neither of us could have found the words.

We heard nothing from Sailor or Geaxi and I needed to ask him a few simple questions, to say the least. Ray and I had discussed what the Fleur-du-Mal had told me and both of us were in the dark. I knew the Fleur-du-Mal was mad, but I wanted to know if there was madness in what he'd said. Nothing made sense.

Adding to it, coincidentally or not, on my birthday I received a gift from the Fleur-du-Mal. There was no card attached, but there was no doubt as to who had sent it. A phonograph player and a single playing disc were delivered to our rooms with the explanation that it had been left for me at the desk by a beautiful woman no one knew. I didn't make the connection with the Fleur-du-Mal until we played the disc. It was a woman, accompanied by a piano, singing an aria, "The Abduction from the Seraglio," from a Mozart opera. She was a soprano, the same one I'd heard singing over the drums at Emma Johnson's. Every month after that, on the same day, we received another phonograph and another disc with the same voice singing a different aria. It was his way of letting me know he could find me anytime he wished, while I could only sit, wait, and guess. Eventually, I had to move my bed to make room for them. I told the management our family were big collectors.

We expanded our search west as far as St. Charles and east along the Gulf coast to Mobile. On July 21, 1905, the Board of Health announced that yellow fever had broken out in the city and there was a general panic and exodus from New Orleans. The disease didn't affect us, of course, but we thought the Fleur-du-Mal would try to protect Star, now that we knew his long-range motivations. By September, we had combed every port and bayou we could find and come up empty. In New Orleans, there had been 3,402 cases of yellow fever and 452 deaths, but it was over. They had oiled and screened thousands of cisterns and salted miles of gutters to get rid of *Aedes aegypti,* the mosquito that carried the disease. It was a transition point in the medical history of the United States and the last time a killer disease would sweep through a city.

In October, I kept the promise I'd made to myself to visit Captain Woodget. I crossed Lake Pontchartrain by steamboat and followed the meager directions given to me by Usoa. Outside Mandeville, after several inquiries, I was told it would be easier to find his property on water than land, taking Cottonmouth Slew to where it met the Bogue Chirito just below Covington. "You cain't miss it, boy. It's the damnedest thing you ever seen," they said. I hired an old shrimper to take me there, and by noon as we rounded a bend in the channel, I knew what they meant.

There, anchored and resting between scaffolding erected on a long private dock, was an exact, scaled-down replica of the *Clover,* complete with sails, brass fittings, teak wood decks, and a new name, *Little Clover,* painted on her bow. Climbing down the mizzenmast was a white-haired, bearded man in faded trousers and undershirt, with a long-stemmed pipe hanging from his mouth. The tam-o'-shanter had been replaced by an old straw garden hat. Captain Caleb Woodget, master seaman and smuggler. It was almost a decade since I'd seen him last.

I paid the old shrimper and jumped onto the dock before he'd even come to a stop. Captain Woodget watched me walk the fifty feet or so between us. He removed his garden hat as I got close and leaned on the railing of his ship. I stopped and admired the *Little Clover;* the craftsmanship, detail, and obvious man-hours he'd put into her.

"I heard you'd retired," I said with a grin I couldn't conceal. "But I thought gardeners planted seeds, not clipper ships."

"Holy Trident!" he shouted. "If it did not walk and talk, I would think it a ghost."

He scrambled down a makeshift ladder and we embraced warmly. He was older, thinner, but his eyes were bright and he held my shoulders with hands as strong as any that still worked the sea.

"The last time I saw you, lad, you were spinning a good yarn to a customs agent."

"I still do, on occasion."

He laughed and stepped back, running his eyes up and down me. Aye," he said. "You wee people amaze me," and he looked around him, then up at the sky. "God in his infinite wisdom and all that, I suppose."

I smiled and said, "I suppose." Then I asked for a tour of his ship and he showed me everything, top to bottom, all fifty-three feet of her. He was proud, but hesitant and slightly embarrassed, as if I might think the project crazy. It was crazy; crazy and beautiful.

I asked him if he missed his old life, and just as on the first night I met him, he paused and filled his pipe before he answered.

"I miss nothing about that damn business, Z, but I miss the smells, all of them, good and bad, on the ship, in a thousand different ports and especially the smell of the open sea itself." He lit his pipe and took two long pulls. "Do you think I'm over the top, lad? Should I be scuttled before it becomes too obvious?"

"I don't think so, Captain, not yet." We both laughed. "And I agree with you about the smells, except for a few places in China."

"China?" he asked. "So, you've been to China, have you?"

I nodded and he put his arm around my shoulder and led me on a walk through his property and gardens, which covered several acres to the north and east toward Covington. As we walked, he told me the names of hundreds of flowers and gave me a season by season history of plantings and cutbacks. We walked by trellises of roses in every color and under long arbors of bougainvillea. At first, it seemed a wild and random maze, but soon I saw the overview, the grand plan of wildness within order. He told me of his love for Isabelle and how it grew along with his chaotic gardens, unplanned and unavoidable. He said when he walked with her through the disordered beauty, it was the only time she felt peace. Somehow, that made more sense than anything else.

He showed me through the mansion, which had seen better days, and around sunset he cooked a savory meal of catfish and fried potatoes. Isabelle never made an appearance, but I did hear her singing on and off from somewhere in the upper rooms.

He asked me to stay the night but I refused, telling him I still had business in the city that evening. As usual, he inquired no further and drove me to the ferry in Mandeville without my asking. I caught the last crossing of the night and promised to return. Inside, as was usual for me, I had no idea when that would be.

Ray and I were invited to St. Louis for the holidays, but we refused, giving various and vague excuses. Ray even passed on a chance to see Nova on her twelfth birthday, an event I was sure he had promised to share. We were both burning out from our complete lack of success in finding even a trace of the Fleur-du-Mal.

Owen Bramley finally moved to St. Louis from San Francisco in March 1906, just ahead of the earthquake. Ray reminded me of Nova's prediction and Owen Bramley said his building had indeed been in the center of the collapse and fire. We both agreed Nova may have been born with an "ability" rare for Meq and Giza alike.

We continued to make our rounds in Storyville and the French Quarter. Ray established new contacts in places like Mahogany Hall and the San Jacinto club. Meanwhile, the New Orleans summer seemed to turn everything, even time itself, into a thick, slow-moving syrup.

I was tired of questions and secrets and I felt the weight of not telling things, not telling Ray the truth about Zuriaa, and not telling Carolina the truth about Star. Self-loathing was gaining on my hatred for the Fleur-du-Mal. Even Ray was showing the strain. We rarely laughed or enjoyed much of anything.

Then, in September, Owen Bramley came for a visit and quite by accident, almost as an afterthought, everything changed.

He arrived by train on the afternoon of the fifth and, after a brief meeting with the hotel management, joined us on the balcony outside our suite. The heat was stifling. He wore a three-piece suit, but within minutes had removed his jacket, tie, and vest and resembled the Owen Bramley I remembered, wiping his glasses on his white shirt and complicating the obvious.

"Much warmer here than it should be," he said. "I've talked with several meteorologists and they all agree there is some sort of bulge in the Gulf—overlapping lows or something to that effect."

"Drink some iced tea," Ray said and he poured out a tall glass and handed it to Owen Bramley. "It seems to help."

He drank the entire glass, asked for another, and got right down to business.

"I brought the photographs and negatives of the man who shot Baju. I would have delivered them sooner, but I wanted a friend of mine, a detective of sorts in San Francisco, to see what he could find out first. He found out two things—the man is nearly a ghost and he is not freelance; he works for a single person, a woman, although her identity is unknown."

My pulse jumped and quickened. Maybe the Fleur-du-Mal had told the truth, maybe the man was working for Opari.

"The problem is," he went on, "the photographs are ten years old. The damn man has disappeared."

"Does he have a name?" I asked.

"No, not a proper one, anyway. Evidently, several years ago in Macao, he did some particularly nasty work that the locals referred to as 'the work of the Weeping Widow.' He is half Portuguese and half Chinese and supposedly an ex-eunuch, if that is even possible."

I took the photographs and stared at the fuzzy image of the man with the razor-thin eyes, caught in the act of murder. I was hoping to find some reason or truth hidden somewhere in the picture, but I saw none of that. I only saw a killer.

Ray asked about Eder and Nova and Owen Bramley assured him

they were doing fine. He said Eder, and especially Nova, did wonders
for Carolina, keeping her spirits high and rejoicing in the new baby.
Owen himself, though he masked it well in his speech, showed new
lines of concern in his face around the eyes and mouth, and there were
streaks of gray in his red hair. I couldn't help but think that if I had
been Giza, I would have shown the same lines and streaks.

At one point, he happened to notice the five phonograph players
crowded together in my room and he asked about them. I glanced at
Ray, who shrugged, and I had to tell him they were "gifts" from the
Fleur-du-Mal, part of a game of psychological torture he was playing
where the "gifts" served as a reminder that he could find us, but we
could not find him.

Owen Bramley asked if they had come with any notes or messages
of any kind and I told him about the discs and the same woman
singing from different operas. Then, after we had exhausted every
angle and nuance as to what they might mean, he asked if he could
take one of the discs with him, "just for the hell of it," he said. I carefully packed three of them and the next day they left with Owen
Bramley and his luggage on his return to St. Louis.

Exactly two weeks later, on September 19, I was awakened by two
loud raps on my door and told there was an urgent telephone call for
me at the desk. It was ten o'clock in the morning. The temperature
had dropped at least twenty-five degrees overnight and gusts of wind
were blowing in through the open doors to the balcony. Ray was nowhere in sight. I closed the doors and dressed as quickly as possible,
then ran down to the lobby and the telephone. There was static on the
line, but I could hear Owen Bramley shouting at the other end.

"Z! Is that you? Can you hear me?"

"Yes, yes," I said. "You're breaking up, but I can hear you."

"Good. Listen to me. I have amazing news." He was excited. His
voice was a full octave higher. "The girl's name is Lily Marchand. Do
you hear me? Lily Marchand," he repeated.

"What? Who? What girl?"

"The girl on the disc, the girl singing the operas. Carolina even
knows her, for God's sake."

"What? You'd better start at the beginning, Owen. I don't understand."

The static on the telephone line was getting worse. I glanced out of the front of the hotel where anything loose in the street was blowing away.

"I was playing the discs," he said. "I was alone in Carolina's office, Georgia's room she calls it, and Scott Joplin burst in shouting, 'I know that voice! I know that girl!' He was visiting Carolina, you see, and just happened to be there, he just happened to hear it, Z. Well, of course, I said, 'Who is it?' and he said, 'That's Lily, Lily Marchand. She used to work for Carolina and disappeared right before the World's Fair. I been lookin' for her for two years!' I asked him if he knew where she lived and he said he had only heard it was somewhere around New Orleans, but, and this is why I called, Z, this could be a break, he said a woman named Willie Piazza had known the family for years and might know how to find her. Do you know of this woman, Z, do you know Willie Piazza?"

"Yes," I shouted. The line was almost all static.

"Find her," he yelled back. "Find her and you might find—" The line went dead and Ray burst through the front door of the hotel, out of breath, which I'd never seen him, and soaking wet. Outside, sheets of rain were blowing sideways.

"Damn, Z, I missed this one," he said and shook the water off his bowler. "I didn't see it, feel it, nothin'!"

"Missed what?"

"The hurricane," he said. "And she's comin' right now."

The manager of the St. Louis Hotel was standing nearby and over-heard. He turned to Ray.

"Did you say hurricane, son?"

"That's right, sir," Ray answered. And she's a big one—still ain't hit landfall, but she will soon and if I was you, I'd get all them shutters shut around this place."

The manager glanced out of the window, then back at Ray. Ray held his gaze, stone-faced, and even though he wasn't sure why, the man did as the "Weatherman" requested, clapping his hands and scrambling the staff to close the shutters and prepare for a hurricane.

I grabbed Ray by the arm and told him, hurricane or not, we had to find Willie Piazza now. Without asking me why, he slapped on his bowler and said, "Come on."

We made our way to Storyville as best we could, corner to corner, street to street. The wind was fierce, blowing in gusts of seventy to eighty miles an hour, but it was the rain that caused the most havoc and danger. I had never seen so much rain fall so hard. Whole streets turned into rivers within minutes. Abandoned carts and automobiles were picked up and washed into buildings, causing balconies to tumble, lampposts to splinter, and windows to crash and break into shards, which were swept away in the water like flashing knives.

Somehow, we found Willie. She was hanging on to what was left of her double front doors, standing in two feet of swirling water and debris, and yelling at three men in two different languages. The men were bound together by a long rope that was anchored to the main building. All three were trying to save Willie's big sign, which had toppled from the roof to the street and was being sucked into the rushing waters. They were fighting a losing battle.

When we got close enough, I tried to get her attention. "Willie!" I shouted. "Willie, I've got to talk to you."

"Not now, honey," she shouted back. "We got a world of trouble here."

I kept on. I was only a few feet from her, but I still had to yell. "Do you know Lily Marchand?" I asked. "Please, tell me if you do, I've got to find her."

"Not now, honey," she said again. "I've got to save that sign, *coûte que coûte.*"

"Just tell me if you know her, that's all."

At that moment, the sign broke loose from the men and disappeared under the water, finally bobbing up in broken pieces half a block "downstream." Willie watched it go.

"Tant pis," she said. "God must have wanted poor Willie to buy another one."

"Do you know her?" I repeated. "Do you know Lily Marchand?"

"Yes," she said finally. "Yes, I know Lily, or I should say knew her. Haven't seen her or her pitiful brother, Narciso, for three, maybe four years. Old Creole family, honey. Lost all their money a long time ago."

"Do you know where she lives?"

"I know where she used to."

"Where?"

"Across Pontchartrain, somewhere near Covington on the Bogue Chirito. A run-down plantation called 'The Vines,' if I remember right. I told the Chinese man I couldn't be sure, but 'The Vines' sounded right."

"Chinese man? What Chinese man?"

"The one that came lookin' for Lily last week, same as you. I told him 'The Vines' was most likely it. It just sounded right."

"Were his eyes like two slits, two razors?"

She laughed. "Honey, they all look alike to me."

It was my turn to say "Come on," and I waved to Ray, who was standing in the doorway with several of Willie's "nieces." I thanked Willie, then Ray and I ran through the rising water on Iberville and across town.

Luckily, we caught the last ferry crossing Lake Pontchartrain. The storm slowed as it made landfall and the north side of the city had not yet felt its full force. Still, we were pelted with driving rain and Pontchartrain was rough with whitecaps all the way across.

Just before we docked, Ray said, "Who is Lily Marchand?"

"She's the one singing the operas," I told him. "And the same voice I heard at Emma Johnson's."

He arched an eyebrow and tugged on his bowler.

"I got a feeling, Ray. I got a feeling this is it. This is where he is. This is where Star is."

The rain filled the brim of his bowler and spilled over the sides. He ignored it. "Then, let's go get her," he said. "Let's take her home."

Our luck ran out once we were in Mandeville. We were out of transportation. The few people we saw were all seeking shelter. Except for about twenty or thirty lost chickens, we were the only ones still on the street. I had no idea exactly where to go or how to get there, but I knew who would.

We set out for Captain Woodget's on foot and arrived at nightfall. Both of us were shivering and as wet as I'd ever been at sea. The captain and Isabelle, who was in one of her lucid periods, met us at the door and rushed us to the fireplace, where Isabelle reminded me more of a worried grandmother than a madwoman, drying our hair with towels and telling the captain to make us tea while she found us clothes. I was sure she had no idea who we were.

I introduced Ray to Captain Woodget and then explained as much as I could about who and what we had to find. I told him it could be dangerous. The captain said he knew of the old place, but there would be no way to reach it at night and in "this breeze."

"This *breeze*?" I asked.

"Well, you know what I mean, lad. You and I have seen much worse than this."

"That we have, Captain, and that's why you don't have to do this. You owe me nothing."

He paused for only a moment. "Oh, but I do, Z. I owe you for changing the way I thought about this world, the way I was overlooking the mystery of it, what was beyond what I took for granted, and what was inside as well. I owe you for that, but I am most indebted to you for the life I have now. If I had not met you, I would not have met the biggest damn mystery of all—Isabelle."

I tried to assure him I had nothing to do with his love for Isabelle, but he wouldn't hear it. We were fed, clothed, and given hot tea to drink, which the captain spiked with añejo rum, and thereby ruined both the tea and the rum.

He offered us each a bedroom for the night and Ray accepted. I asked if I could stay where I was and bed down by the fire. I didn't know whether it was the hurricane or the anxiety of finding Star, or both, but I was dog-tired with fatigue. I knew we were close. I knew we'd found a flaw in the Fleur-du-Mal's plan. What I didn't know or understand was the possible presence of "Razor Eyes." He was a cold-blooded murderer and his arrival, for whatever reason, put Star in twice as much jeopardy.

Isabelle brought me a pillow and a pink goose-down blanket. I welcomed both. We all said our good nights and I stretched out by the fire.

Outside, the hurricane never slept. The wind rose and fell in swells and the rain pounded through the night, constant and hard. I stared at the fire. I waited for sleep . . . I waited.

I heard a voice. I was being called . . . summoned.

I was with some others. We were walking toward the opening in a cliff, the mouth of a cave. We were invited. We were the painters, they expected us. They were taller than we were. They led us deep into the cave with tiny lamps held in their palms. They stopped and said we would know where to go from there. We went on, we knew where to go. We set up our scaffolding and brought out our rubbing cloths and ochre. We painted the beasts as they ran through our minds. I went ahead. I saw a light and heard a thundering roar. They told me to stop, but I went ahead and the light became another opening and the roar was a waterfall in front of it, blocking what lay beyond from view. I put my hands in it. I spread the curtain of water and instead of a river below, there was another opening to another cave. I walked through the space in the water and there was a fire inside the cave. It was a small fire that had been burning for days. The ashes were spilling out of the pit. I saw something in among the ashes. I reached in and flicked it out, watching it tumble and roll on the floor of the cave. It was a skull, a child's skull. It was not Meq.

"Z!" the voice shouted. "Wake up, lad."

It was Captain Woodget standing over me with Ray leaning in at his side.

Ray said, "You look pretty good in pink, Z."

They were both fully dressed. It was still raining and there was little light, but I could tell it was morning. Where I'd been I didn't know and there was no time to think about it. It was September 20, 1906, and the hurricane raged on. Even the captain said he'd never seen anything like it. "Most of them move on in a few hours," he said. "But this one's in love with Louisiana."

We discussed our options for getting to "The Vines" and there were none. The roads were completely washed out. Our only chance was by water—up a low backwater river that was already out of its banks, in a hurricane, on a half-sized sailing ship that had never been used. The captain said he could do it.

At the dock, Ray and I fashioned rain slickers out of scraps of canvas and the captain wrestled with the scaffolding. Eventually, we had to tear it down entirely in order to get the *Little Clover* righted in the channel and ready to sail. If the scale of the ship had been any larger, we couldn't have done it. The captain shouted his orders through the rain and Ray learned to sail on the job.

Amazingly, there was traffic. Mostly fishermen in small craft, making a dash for home or helping the stranded. We saw one barge that had no choice but to go on and try to make it to port and one steam-driven trawler with no lights burning, traveling in the opposite direction at a reckless speed. As it passed, I had a strange sensation, a buzzing in my head, like static on a telephone line. I looked over at the trawler, but the distance and the rain between made it impossible to see any faces.

We pushed on, tacking often at severe angles. We couldn't hold a good line for longer than a few minutes, but the captain remained steadfast and the rain never bothered him.

After three tight, difficult bends in the river, he waved to me, pointing at a dock on the opposite shore and shouting, "The Vines."

It took all our efforts and another half hour to turn the ship against the current and secure it to the dock. We walked up to the main house on a wooden walkway with missing boards and broken railings. The cypress trees on both sides had taken a beating and still were. The wind tore at them from every direction and the rain never let up.

The house was dark as we approached, except for a light in one of the back rooms. It was a big house, an old plantation mansion with columns in front and a veranda all around. It looked as if it wouldn't make it through the storm.

We watched and listened.

Suddenly, faintly, somewhere between the rain and wind, I heard music. I turned to Ray and the captain.

"Do you hear that?"

They both looked at me and then at each other.

"Hear what?" Ray asked.

"Lily Marchand. It's her, it's her voice. She's singing."

Neither Ray nor Captain Woodget could hear what I heard. My "ability" had awakened. I concentrated and pinpointed her voice to one of the front rooms, one of the rooms in the dark.

We walked up a short rise and stepped onto the veranda. I could hear something else behind the singing, a hum or a churning, maybe a small engine. The door was wide open and the rain was blowing in, soaking the floorboards of the entryway.

We passed into a hallway that was dark except for a light at the end, the one we'd seen from outside. There was no furniture. Ray found some candles against the wall and gave us each one. Captain Woodget had matches and lit the candles. Two rooms appeared off the hall. The one on the left was completely empty, but the one on the right was filled with sofas, chairs, rugs, lamps, and, most of all, phonograph players. There must have been fifty of them, stacked and squeezed into every niche and corner of the room. And one of them was playing Georges Bizet's *The Pearl Fishers,* with the role of Leila, the priestess, being sung by Lily Marchand.

They were gone. We'd missed them, I knew it. I looked around and found the phonograph player, the one I wanted, easily. I followed the hum, which was a generator supplying the phonograph player with power until it ran out of gas. I took the needle off the disc and there was silence in the room.

Captain Woodget said he was going to check out the room in the back, the one with the light. Ray and I stayed and looked around.

We saw plates and dishes with food still on them, saucers and coffee cups, all recently used. Phonograph discs and pornographic studio portraits were strewn everywhere. Sadomasochistic contraptions and devices, things I'd only seen in places like Emma Johnson's, were lying about. In the corner of the room, there was a giant cage or playpen. Inside the playpen, on top of two Persian rugs, was a mattress and a small blanket. This was where he kept her. This was where she slept.

Suddenly there was a loud crash and Captain Woodget was shouting, "Holy Trident and dammit to hell!"

Ray and I ran down the hall, toward the light. We pushed through the door and Captain Woodget was standing over a wine decanter he'd knocked off a long wooden table, a table similar to Carolina's.

He'd stumbled into it when he saw the man and woman sitting at the table, across from each other, their faces flat against the wood, their arms and hands splayed out on either side. Their throats had been slit. The table was covered in blood and pools of it swirled at their feet. The man's shirt had been ripped open, as had the woman's blouse, and both their backs were covered with a bloody rose, carved into the skin with the point of a stiletto.

I knew it was Lily Marchand and most likely her brother, Narciso. I looked up and Ray's face was frozen with disgust and disbelief. I remembered that neither of us had seen the Fleur-du-Mal's handiwork and unmistakable signature since Georgia and Mrs. Bennings.

"We missed him," I said. "He must have known. He must have known we were coming."

"You better come down here, lad," the captain said. He had regained his balance and was standing at the other end of the table. "There's another one—a Chinaman."

"A Chinaman?" I bolted for the end of the table and looked down to see what the captain had found. I expected to see "Razor Eyes." I saw Li instead.

He wasn't stripped and carved up like the others. He'd been stabbed just below the heart and his throat was partially slit. There was a green ribbon stuffed in his mouth. I had no idea where he'd been or how he had got to where he was. We'd never seen a trace of him the whole time we were in New Orleans.

Ray reached down and pulled the green ribbon out of his mouth, and as he did Li opened his eyes and saw me. He was alive. I knelt down and he tried to grab my leg and missed. He made a raspy, coughing sound and then he spoke directly to me.

"She . . . go . . . ma . . . lee"

It was the first time he'd ever spoken to me and the last. His mouth went slack and his eyes dulled.

I leaned over to close his eyelids and Ray said, "Who's Molly?" That triggered something in my memory, something I'd learned about the Fleur-du-Mal from Unai and Usoa.

"It's not a who," I said. "It's a where. The Fleur-du-Mal is taking Star to Mali—the country." I looked out of the window at the never-ending rain. The wind rattled the window in its casing. "How?" I said, almost to myself. "How did he know?" Ray was wrapping the green ribbon, first around one finger, then around another. His expression was black and lost, like mine. "We'll never catch him now," I whispered.

Captain Woodget knelt down beside me and ran a fingertip through Li's blood, which was spreading on the floor. He looked at me. "This blood is fresh, Z," he said, then he winked at me.

At first, I didn't get his meaning. Of course it was fresh, I thought, Li had just died. Then it hit me.

"Captain," I said. "Do you recall the trawler we passed in the channel?"

"Aye, lad, and going at a fair rate of speed, not minding the weather."

"That's the one," I said. "Can you catch her?"

"If we can make it to Pontchartrain and she's not yet all the way across, I know I can. I can play this breeze in open water. The trawler won't be able to." He gave me another wink.

I insisted we take Li with us. "I don't want to remember him here . . . like this." Ray and the captain nodded in agreement.

The three of us carried Li's body to the *Little Clover*. The only place we could secure him was on a bench in the stern, in an upright position, tied to the railing. Whatever obsessions had driven him to this end were at rest now. He resembled Buddha at the center of the storm, sleeping and dreaming.

We set out for Lake Pontchartrain. It was late in the day and we were losing what little light we had. Without paying heed to channels, currents, or traffic, the captain steered us on a course that brought us critically close to one bank, then another. The rain was dense and constant. The trawler was nowhere in sight.

Then, as we spilled into Lake Pontchartrain, the captain caught the wind and made a good line almost directly for New Orleans. He guessed we were doing twenty to twenty-five knots. The *Little Clover* was well made, but I could feel and hear the strain on her hull.

The rain and fading light obscured the horizon by the minute. I couldn't tell if we were gaining on the trawler. I had Ray tie a rope to me and I climbed up the mizzenmast, hoping to use my "ability" to listen for the trawler. Ray helped the captain hold the wheel and fight to keep the line. The rain felt like tiny knives and the wind whipped my canvas slicker like a handkerchief. I heard a foghorn and turned, but it was too far in the distance, too far west.

Then slowly, like a pulse or heartbeat, I heard the steady chug-chug of a steam engine, plowing through the wind and water. We were close, closer than I thought. I yelled to the captain, "Port, ten degrees!"

He managed the slight change in direction and we gained even more speed. Suddenly I could see the trawler. It was a faint black dot, bobbing on the horizon. Smoke poured out of the smokestack. It was no more than a mile ahead of us.

We closed the gap. A thousand yards . . . five hundred . . . one hundred. Then, just as I thought I saw a figure on board the trawler, I heard a ripping sound. Our foresail was shredding and the ship jolted from side to side. I heard a crack, followed by another crack, louder and longer. The *Little Clover* was coming apart.

Ray pulled the captain out of the way just before the mainsail fell on them. I tried to slide down to the deck and was thrown overboard as the ship actually snapped in the middle. The waves tore at the opening, and piece by piece, the *Little Clover* disintegrated.

The rope tied around me was still attached to a section of the mizzenmast and I used it as a raft while I looked for Ray and Captain Woodget. I could see the trawler steaming away and a single figure on deck, staring back. I could even hear him. He had a white smile and a familiar, bitter laugh.

I found Ray holding on to Captain Woodget, who was unconscious. He was struggling to reach something with his free hand and barely staying afloat. I helped him with the captain and he finally snatched what he was after—his bowler.

The last thing I saw of the *Little Clover* was a section of the stern, a bench with Li still strapped to it. Within minutes, he disappeared into Lake Pontchartrain and it seemed like an appropriate grave. He had paid his mysterious debt to Solomon in full. The rest, the running tab he kept inside himself, was anybody's guess.

Three days later, we were on the balcony of the St. Louis Hotel, waiting for the weather to finally break. Captain Woodget was in hospital recovering from a collapsed lung and exposure. We swam four miles to shore that night, through rain and debris, and the experience took its toll on the captain.

I talked to Owen Bramley several times and told him what I could, but no matter how I worded it, the story had the same conclusion. I asked him to come to New Orleans and check on Captain Woodget and make sure he had the money to rebuild the *Little Clover* again.

I informed him that Ray and I had booked passage to Africa. Everything else was unknown.

The hurricane of 1906 lasted five days and killed three hundred and fifty people in Louisiana and Mississippi. The assistant to the mayor of New Orleans said in a public statement that his city owed a great debt to the unfortunate of the city of Galveston, which had lost so many lives to the hurricane of 1900. "If all those folks hadn't died," he said, "we wouldn't have learned what we learned and then we would have had more people die last week."

I have always wondered if he knew what he was saying.

12

GEZUR

(LIE)

Have you played the game? The game where all sit in a circle and you whisper something to the one sitting next to you, who whispers it to the next, and so on, until it has made the round of the circle and comes back to you—a new whisper, a new "truth," a tale that, somehow in the transfer, evolves and mutates into something that bears no resemblance to the original. How can this be? Is it willful, accidental, inevitable? Can truth be so easily turned, folded, pierced, twisted, and tossed like a toy from one to another?

If played honestly, the game is always good for a laugh. Truth has many masks. A lie, only one.

Ray and I left New Orleans with no fanfare or ritual. We were both in it now, both deep in the obsession. Ray no longer thought of New Orleans as "his town," or anyplace else. For us, it was just another stop, another place on the map. We were disappointed, but not discouraged. We were still in it, still on the Fleur-du-Mal like dogs. We had only momentarily lost his scent. The problem was with the word "momentarily." A moment for us could equal weeks, months, even years in the lives of Carolina, Nicholas, and Star. Ray knew this as well as I and even though, if I was honest, I had to admit we were following a hunch at best, we both felt the urgency of finding Star, if she was ever going to know her parents or have a chance at a normal life.

My hunch was really a deduction with a leap of faith at the end. Li told me Star had gone to Mali and the Fleur-du-Mal himself had told me he wanted "the grandchild." In his way, he had hinted at her future education and training, as sick as it was. Usoa had also mentioned Mali and the Fleur-du-Mal's centuries-old fascination with it, for reasons never known to the Meq. I knew Star could not have a child for several years. I knew the Fleur-du-Mal was unpredictable, but something told me he would not have the patience to wait for that event. He would instead keep her somewhere remote with someone he trusted, while he followed his other pursuits and interests. This was my hunch. The leap of faith was that we would find the somewhere and someone in Mali, somehow.

Our ship sailed just before sunset on the evening of October 7. It wasn't much of a sunset. The light was low and flat under a cloud cover and it spread and faded into darkness without inspiration. Ray and I stood by the railing and watched in silence. There was nothing to say. We were both in it, I knew that, but still I couldn't help feeling guilty for bringing him into it. Earlier in the day, I had read a story in the sports pages about Ty Cobb and his teammate, Ed Siever. The day before, during a game, Ed Siever had cursed Ty Cobb for not hustling in the field and they got into a fight. Cobb knocked him down and kicked him in the head. Ray was more than a teammate to me and he would never curse me for not hustling, but standing there by him in the fading light, feeling his blind trust and determination, I felt just like the honorable Ty Cobb.

Neither of us knew much about where we were going. In all my time at sea, we had rarely dropped anchor, and then never for very long, anywhere off West Africa. The ancient kingdom of Mali was a complete mystery. I wasn't even sure of the languages we would encounter, let alone the dangers.

Ray had scoured the streets in the days before our departure trying to find connections, names, and places of anyone we could use. He came up with nothing. The only time he had heard Mali or any other country in West Africa mentioned was in a tale told by a grandchild or great-grandchild of a slave. Every connection and transaction between New Orleans and West Africa had at some point, in some way, involved slavery. Ours was no different. She was only one child, and white, but she was a slave. Even our route would be close to the routes of the old slave ships; New Orleans—Havana—Puerto Rico—Dakar. The irony was complete when we changed ships in Puerto Rico and boarded a small passenger steamship named the *Atalanta*. The name was that of a maiden in Greek mythology who challenged and defeated all of her suitors in footraces until she was tricked by Hippomenes and stopped to pick up the three golden apples he had dropped along the course. It was also the name of a Spanish slave ship that had sailed into Havana in 1821 with 570 slaves still alive. The deaths at sea had been uncountable.

We were sailing east, toward Africa. It was late 1906 and the evil of slavery had long been abolished and we were going back, back to where it had begun. Times had changed, but Ray and I knew evil had not.

I stood by the railing and looked at him out of the corner of my eye. Ray was strong. What he didn't know, he learned fast, and what he couldn't change, he accepted—to a point. In our preparations for leaving, the only thing he sought for protection was a talisman, a good luck charm. A woman he knew, a voodoo priestess, gave him a collection of small bones, "directions for your dreams," she called them. For my part, I had exchanged bank drafts for brand-new double eagle gold pieces and assorted small gems. Enough, I hoped, to buy protection, false identities, bribes, tolls, whatever it took to survive and locate Star. Ray had found two money belts to carry the gold and gems. They had been difficult to find because they had to be small enough for us to wear, yet sturdy and secure. When I noticed Ray stuffing one of the pockets on his belt with the bones, I asked him if he didn't think that space should be used for gold rather than bones.

"Damn, Z," he said. "It's as clear as a tear, ain't it? We can get more money, but I don't want anybody stealin' our luck."

On the Atlantic crossing, I watched Ray enjoy the open ocean almost as much as he had the mountains. He gained his sea legs early and we ignored the Meq custom of staying out of sight and wandered the decks at will, watching the sea spray by day and the star spray by night. Whenever asked, Ray was always willing to talk and tell our story, which got longer and further from the truth with each telling. His white lies changed color depending on the interest of the listener. I don't remember exactly how far he went with it, but his original story was that we were cousins from New Orleans; Spanish Catholics being sent by our parents to visit our dying grandfather in the old country. He was good at it and I could see that it gave Ray a wicked, but harmless, thrill to spin his tales for the Giza, giving them what they thought they wanted, just enough to quell their curiosity and spark their interest at the same time. In two days, half the passengers had become our adoptive "travel" parents. We were covered in the kindness of strangers.

Ray was unpredictable and reliable at once. A rare quality, but perfectly suitable, even necessary, for survival. He confronted the Giza and the world at large spontaneously, knowing and trusting in his ability to respond. No doubts, few fears. Confront, that's what he did. It made me think about something I hardly ever thought about, something that never seemed to matter—the difference between Egipurdiko and Egizahar.

I really only knew two Meq who were Egipurdiko. Ray and the Fleur-du-Mal. Their natures and character, morality and beliefs, were as far apart as they could get, but there was one trait they shared. They both confronted the world of the Giza, used it, manipulated it, were at home in it. The other Meq I knew, all Egizahar, avoided the Giza's world whenever possible and certainly never felt at home in it. I was Egizahar, I carried the Stone, I had a power the Egipurdiko did not and yet it was Ray who wrote to St. Louis, telling the right lies, shading the truth, protecting Carolina and Nicholas from losing hope. I didn't do it. I avoided it. I thought it would break my heart to lie again to Carolina. Ray knew instinctively that without a word, truth or fiction, Carolina's heart would break long before mine.

I watched Ray as we sailed east. I watched him carefully and tried to learn what he had to teach. He was an open book and an easy read.

Still four hundred miles from Dakar, Ray told me we'd probably turn north soon. I asked him why and he said there was a "big blow" coming up from the south. I wondered if the "Weatherman" still had

his "ability." He'd missed the one in New Orleans, after all. Forty-five
minutes later, the *Atalanta* made a sharp turn to the north and increased her speed by seven knots. I looked at Ray and he was grinning
under his bowler.

"Damn," was all I said.

Usually, captains of passenger ships are conservative without ex-
ception. I was expecting our captain to be no different and tack hundreds of miles to the north and northeast in a long arc until he made
berth in Dakar, maybe three or four days behind schedule, but safe. He
surprised me by turning due east after sailing north for only one day
and half the night. He was in a hurry, as if any deviation in his
timetable was more important and more dangerous than the weather.
We did hit rough seas, but it was due to the strong currents from the
north that run down the coast of West Africa. I remembered them
from my time with Captain Woodget. The captain of the *Atalanta* was
lucky. We missed the storm and made port on the morning of December 25, 1906. However, we were not in Dakar. We were at least a
hundred miles north in the port city of Saint-Louis at the mouth of
the Senegal River. Whether it was fate or circumstance, I have never
known, but because of the way we arrived to what happened afterward, from that day on my concept of Christmas changed forever.

We anchored at the end of a long gangplank connected to others
that were all secured to the main docks. The sun was a fat gold ball
hanging over the river to the east. The sky was blue and cloudless except for a single white hump far to the south. It was eighty-five degrees and felt like paradise. The air was filled with the smells of the
savannah surrounding the river. Trees, grass, flowers in the distance.
Land. Ray took a deep breath and filled his lungs with it.

The captain gathered all passengers on the gangplank and explained
our situation. Ray and I hung back and stayed to the rear as everyone
crowded in to listen. We had sustained two minor cracks in the boiler
in our race against the storm to the south, he said. There was no way
they could make Dakar. The repairs would have to be done here; there
was no choice except to chance blowing the boiler. It would take
some time—two weeks at the most—but all who wished to continue
would be accommodated by the company—on board ship or ashore.
All who wished to disembark in Saint-Louis would be provided with

their luggage and a modest rebate. I glanced at Ray. There was really no choice for us. Two weeks was not an alternative. Besides, what difference did it make where we started? Our destination was Mali and Saint-Louis as a starting place seemed like a good omen. We talked about it and Ray reminded me I'd said the same thing once before and it hadn't turned out so well, but he agreed that lost time was more important.

We kept our true intentions to ourselves and told the captain we preferred accommodation on shore during the delay. We were kids. We needed to play. "Why not?" he said. "It's Christmas."

The first mate was ordered to retrieve our luggage and personally escort us through customs, making sure we were registered and established in a secure hotel. We walked the long gangplank to the customs house with several other passengers and both of us had a smile on our faces. Ray gave me a wink. "Good start," he said.

It was slow-going through customs. There were only two French officials available and they were in no hurry. Their tunics were unbuttoned and neither wore their caps. The first mate said that most of the Christian population was in the city watching the annual Christmas parade. Waiting our turn, Ray and I walked back to the gangplank to watch the gulls, herons, and flamingos in the distance.

Suddenly I felt pinpricks in my skin. I actually looked down at my arms and hands. It came on so fast, I didn't recognize it. The old feeling of fear and presence—the net descending. I instinctively turned in a circle, searching, watching for the eyes watching me. Nothing. I asked Ray if he could feel it and he said, "Feel what?" I looked at each of the passengers, but none was paying us any attention. I looked out over the river but there was little traffic. Two Arabs in a single-masted fishing boat were standing and staring our way, but not at us. I turned and looked past Ray to the end of the maze of gangplanks. The only activity was on the deck of a well-appointed private yacht flying two flags. The top flag was a crest of some sort and the lower was the national flag of Germany. Deckhands seemed to be preparing to leave. None of them was looking our way, but I felt something, something very dangerous. Just then, the first mate from the *Atalanta* called for us. I looked at Ray.

"Why have you got that out?" Ray asked.

"What?" I said and then felt it in my hand. Unknowingly, I had taken the Stone out of my pocket and was holding it as tight as I could. "I don't know," I said.

Ray put one arm around my shoulder and made a sweeping gesture with his bowler toward the customs house. "Then, let's go and see Africa, my friend."

We made our way up a long, slow rise to the center of the old city and our hotel, the Cour Royale du Senegal. The streets were unpaved and we tried to use boardwalks where they were available. The first mate carried our small amount of luggage and Ray and I followed close behind. I kept myself from turning around. The fear I'd felt was unreasonable, I told myself. There was no way for anyone to know Ray and I were landing in Saint-Louis. It was unscheduled.

The streets became more and more crowded. As we approached the hotel, we had to detour around the Christmas parade that was in progress right in front of our entrance. French soldiers and police were scattered among the people, but most were slouching in groups and leaning against walls, relaxed and out of the way. The sun was bright overhead and it was a beautiful day for celebrating and rejoicing. Every Christian family, French and African, was either in the parade or watching. Ray was fascinated by all the different headgear. I noticed that even the Islamic community had closed their shops and markets to witness the pageantry. Children of every shade were tugging at the robes and blouses of their mothers to get even closer. Suddenly Ray and I were just two more kids among a thousand others.

The first mate barked at a group of French Catholic nuns to let us through. They did, but not without a few words for the first mate and stern looks all around. He told us to wait on the stone steps of the hotel while he took our luggage inside and made sure of our accommodation with the management. There were three gradated steps leading up to the hotel. Ray and I found a space at the far end of the highest step to wait and watch the parade.

The parade itself was a feast of color. Everyone in the procession, European and African, adult and child, wore their finest formal dress and each carried a symbol of faith. For most, it was a small cross made of gold or ivory, but several people carried long hand-carved wooden crosses festooned with anything they felt was holy. Feathers, garlands of flowers, bells, even symbols from another faith. I saw the crescent of Islam attached to the top of at least twenty crosses. It didn't seem to matter. It was a holy day, a joyous day, and they were celebrating the anniversary of a miraculous birth.

Ray grabbed me by the sleeve. "Look at that," he said.

I followed his eyes to our left, away from the parade and the main body of onlookers. Several Senegalese women dressed in cotton robes of bright greens and golds with elaborate turbans on their heads were in a panic and carrying a younger woman into an alley leading to the service entrance of the hotel. She had lost her turban and was obviously in labor. They were all talking at once in high-pitched, cackling voices. The younger woman did not cry out, but she was shaking her head back and forth frantically and holding her stomach, as if she could keep the baby inside her with sheer will.

I couldn't look away. I wasn't sure if I should even be watching, but I couldn't look away. They tried to find a place for the younger woman to lie down. One of the cackling women found some large sacks of peanuts and lined them up against the wall. They were helping the younger woman down on the sacks when one of the sacks split and peanuts spilled out underneath her. She cried out finally. It was too late. She was having the baby. I looked around and the parade was still moving. No one had noticed. There was a troop of Catholic girls approaching, dressed as angels and singing French Christmas songs. I looked at Ray. He was speechless.

I turned around and walked down two steps. I had to get closer to the struggle. I could not look away. Two of the older women held the younger woman by the arms. She kept trying to get up. They were all yelling and one of them finally broke away and ran to find help. Another woman, the one with the finest jewelry and beaded necklaces, unwrapped her turban and placed it under the younger woman's legs, just in time to catch the tiny dark life that dropped onto it.

I could tell the baby was probably premature. It was too small and not able to breathe. The younger woman, the mother, looked down once and fainted. One of the other women began to wipe the baby off and pinched it gently on the legs and arms, trying to make it cry and take a breath. Nothing. They all started cackling again and waving toward the woman who had gone to get help.

She had disappeared in the crowd. Seconds ticked away and I knew if someone didn't do something soon, the baby would surely die.

I started to turn and ask Ray if he knew anything about this when someone rushed past me, spinning me halfway around on the step.

It was a young black woman of about twenty or twenty-one years old. She wore no turban or skull cap and her hair was cropped close to her head. Her robe was plain, rough cloth and only covered one shoulder. Without a word, she separated the cackling women and knelt down over the baby. One of the women shrieked at her and she glanced back, silencing the woman instantly with a fierce gaze. She bent down again and executed a series of rapid movements with her mouth and hands. In fifteen seconds, she rose up and spat something against the wall and the baby cried out. It was a thin, ragged little cry, but it was life. Divine or not, I was certain I had witnessed a miracle.

I watched the young black woman more closely. I could only see her in profile and I knew it made no sense, but there was something familiar about her. She was carefully cleaning the baby's face with her own saliva. She wore no rings on her fingers and her touch was tender and efficient. She wrapped the baby in the rest of the turban and helped rouse the mother by gently laying the baby in the mother's arms.

Then she looked directly at me. It was a sudden, instinctive movement and seemed to surprise her more than me. I stared back. Her eyes were chocolate brown and lighter than her skin, which was smooth and unmarked, except for three raised horizontal lines on each temple. There was a single silver pearl piercing her left nostril. She opened her mouth slightly and whispered a word to herself, as if she couldn't believe what she was seeing. I heard it easily. "Meq," she said.

That was the last thing I expected. I took a step toward her and her expression changed from surprise to terror. She raised one arm and pointed somewhere behind me, then bolted for the hotel. I turned in time to catch sight of Ray in the middle of a duck-and-run. Two sailors, surrounded by several others, and all of them in foreign uniforms and wide-brim flat hats, were trying to strike and grab him from behind, but he was much too fast and disappeared into the crowd before they could touch him. All the sailors held what looked to be shortened oars and were gripping them like baseball bats. Just then I felt a sharp pain in my lower back that knocked all the breath out of me. I knew I'd been hit with one of the oars. My knees were buckling, the colors of the crowd swirled, then another blow sent me forward and down. As I was falling, I saw Ray's bowler hat tumbling down the steps and I reached for it, somehow catching it in a last grasp. I could hear him yelling in the distance, "Come on, Z! Move!"

Sprawled on the steps and barely conscious, I tried to rise and run toward his voice. I couldn't. My legs would not respond. I had no pain anywhere, except where I'd been struck, and yet I couldn't move anything below my waist. Seconds passed, then minutes, and I tried not to panic. Dazed and facedown on the steps, I could only breathe and listen. The sailors gathered around me, shouting at the crowd and each other. They were speaking and yelling in German. Through the legs of one of them I saw the split sack of peanuts spilled in the alley. The women and the baby were gone. I tried again to turn and rise, but the effort was useless. Another voice, a high-pitched male voice with a strange accent, broke through all the others.

"*Du hast ihn gelahmt, idiot! Ich kann kein ein benutzen hat gelahmt!*"

I fought to concentrate and remember the little German I'd learned with Solomon. The voice had said, "You've crippled him, you idiot! I can't use a cripple!"

I panicked. That meant they, whoever "they" were, wanted me and weren't going to be careful about it. I reached for my pocket and the Stone, then felt the sole of a boot clamp down on my elbow and wrist, pinning my arm to the step.

I lay still and waited. With my face buried against the step, I couldn't see who was above me. The boot moved, then raised and kicked me in the legs. I never felt it. The kicker bent down and whispered in my ear. It was the same man who had screamed at the sailors, but to me he spoke slurred English with a Chinese accent. "Not this time, not this time," he repeated, then pulled the Stone out of my pocket, thrusting it down in front of my face to let me know he had it. Before I could ask who he was, he stood up and began speaking German again to someone behind him. I understood enough of the conversation to know they spoke of "contracts" and "damaged goods" and the necessity to decide whether to take me "as is" or do something here and now, something quick and final before the police or anyone else arrived.

I had no legs, no Stone, and I was out of options.

"I think I'd leave him be," a voice said suddenly from in front of me. I glanced up and it was Ray. He gave me a wink, then walked past me toward the others and spoke calmly, as if he'd been there all along. "I think I would, if I were you, leave him alone right here where he is . . . and take me. He ain't no good to you now—not this way." He paused and I heard him walk up behind me, then move me around, shoving and kicking me, just enough to get his point across. "Once one of us is broken . . . especially like this," Ray said, "well, he just don't come back. You might as well take me and let him lie here. If you take him, he'll be nothin' but trouble for you." Ray paused again, then added, "I'm tellin' you the truth and you know I am, don't you? You do and you know you do." He kept rambling on as if he was stalling for time. Then it hit me. That's exactly what he was doing. He could have stayed somewhere in the crowd, invisible and uncatchable. Instead, he had walked out into the open, putting himself in grave danger and staging some kind of crazy game, trying to buy time. I figured there must be help on the way, but where was it?

"Seize him!" someone shouted in German. Ray almost let them take him, then wriggled free and pretended to fall, landing next to me on the steps, where he could see my eyes.

"Who are these guys, Z?" Ray whispered.

"I don't know. What are you doing back here?"

"Ah, don't worry about that," he said, as if he had all the time in the world. "I think I might know one of them—the Chinaman—I just can't remember where or when." Two sailors reached for his arms and he slipped out easily. "Listen up and listen fast," he said, "I talked to that black girl, the one who delivered the kid. If we don't make it out of here together, then just do what she says. You're messed up, Z. She can help you heal."

"What? Who is she?"

"I don't know." Two more sailors joined in trying to hold and secure Ray. He went on talking while he was letting himself be taken. "Just don't worry about me and don't worry about her. Find Star, Z.

Do that first." He paused, then winked one of his green eyes and said, "Some Christmas, huh? Damn."

Just then we heard several whistles and shouts coming from the top of the steps. The high-pitched voice barked out a command and the sailors all turned at once, fleeing back into the crowd, toward the docks, and dragging Ray with them. He was smiling, then he yelled back at me, "And try and learn a little somethin' about the weather, would you? You're gonna need it."

Once again, maybe because I was Meq, or maybe because I had a friend like Ray Ytuarte, I knew instinctively that somehow I would see him again, and he knew the same. He had sacrificed himself for me. He knew that if one of us hadn't been captured, then they most probably would have hunted one or both of us down—and that would not bring Star back. If he went with them, then it would be over and the search for Star could begin. I didn't have a clue why Ray was being kidnapped, or who his kidnappers were, but I had no doubt whatsoever they would have their hands full.

The whistles and shouts and commotion from the top of the steps became several men running past me, all waving their arms and brandishing kitchen knives and rolling pins and meat cleavers. They ran into what was left of the Christmas parade, shouting and threatening everyone and everything, yet going no farther than the street in front of the hotel. They were certainly not the police, as I'd assumed. They looked more like an entire kitchen staff gone mad, which was close to the truth. The young black girl Ray had spoken of appeared just then from above. She knelt down next to me on the step. In English, she asked, "Are you all right?"

I nodded and grunted, "I can't walk."

"We will fix that," she said, then added, " 'I sing the body electric.' " I looked up at her. She smiled and said, "Walt Whitman—the great American poet," then stood up and shouted over to the men still waving their kitchenware at the unknown assailants. The German sailors were long gone. She spoke in a local language and French, mixing the two as she went along. When she finished, the men all stopped what they were doing immediately and trudged back up the steps toward the hotel. Most of them seemed slightly disappointed they had not engaged the enemy.

"Friends of mine," she said. "All of them work for the hotel, the kitchen staff. They were there and they came to help. Good friends each one." Suddenly she dropped her smile. "Your friend—the other one—was he taken?"

"Yes," I answered, and left it at that. I had too many questions for this woman, but this was not the place to ask. I was paralyzed from a severe blow to the spinal cord and I had no idea how long it would take to heal, if at all. I had to find shelter and find it quickly. There were still a few hours of daylight left and I wanted to be as far away as possible by nightfall. Ray had told me to trust her and I trusted Ray completely. The decision came instantly. "Can you get me out of here?" I asked. "Can you take me somewhere safe?"

"I will take you to PoPo, to our home, and . . ." She paused and straightened up, tapping her finger on her lips and turning in a slow circle. "And I will take you in a wheelchair." She almost laughed, then started up the steps. "Give me a moment," she said, "I must borrow something from the hotel with the help of one of my friends. Do not move. I will not be long." She stopped and covered her mouth with both hands, then dropped them slowly. "I am sorry. That was in bad taste, was it not?"

"Just hurry," I said. Then with a smile, "Please."

Less than fifteen minutes later she returned with one of her friends from the kitchen staff. She was pushing a crude wheelchair and he was carrying my luggage along with Ray's.

"What about the sailor from the *Atalanta*?" I asked. "Did he have any questions?"

"I never saw him," she said. "My friend, Bakel, retrieved all of your belongings. Should I inquire?"

"No. Let's go on . . . let's leave now." She helped me into the chair, arranging my legs and strapping me in. She was quick and efficient. "What is your name?" I asked quietly.

Without looking me in the eye or slowing down, she said, "Emme . . . Emme Ya Ambala." I told her my name was Zianno, but she could call me Z. When she was satisfied I was secure, she glanced up and, in a curious mix of question and statement, said, "And you are American."

"Yes," I said, "and you speak English—better than most Americans."

"Truly?"

"Yes. Truly."

She laughed out loud. " 'Who might you find you have come from
yourself, if you could trace back through the centuries?' " Then she
looked over at Bakel and said something in the local dialect. We set out
around the corner and down a narrow street at a rapid pace. Emme
was pushing the wheelchair and Bakel was trailing, carrying our luggage. After a few blocks and several changes in direction, we finally
slowed down. I turned as far as I could in the chair and caught her eye.

"Walt Whitman," she said, never hesitating. "The great—"

"American poet," I finished.

"That is correct," she said, then laughed again.

The two of us spoke little the rest of the day and Bakel never spoke
at all. By sunset, Saint-Louis was far behind and we had trekked almost
five miles upstream on the Senegal River. We stopped for the night in
the first settlement where it was possible to get riverboat passage to
Kayes. Emme said we could transfer there to the one and only railroad
connecting Kayes to Koulikoro on the Niger River. Where we were
going from there remained a mystery. The day had been the longest I
could remember. I'd lost my best friend, I'd lost the Stone, I'd lost the
use of my legs, and at the end of this longest day, I was lost in Africa,
completely at the mercy of a young black woman who wore a silver
pearl in her nose and quoted Walt Whitman. I still had no idea why
she was doing what she was doing, or how she knew I was Meq. Then
I thought of Star and how lost and helpless she must feel. After that,
the damp mat I was sleeping on seemed like a featherbed. I closed my
eyes and waited for a dream, any dream, and let the long day go.

The next morning came too soon. Emme shook me awake and told
me we had to leave right away. She handed me a flat biscuit and a bowl
of something that resembled oatmeal, and I gobbled it up as if it were
a gourmet meal. As I ate, I stared at the wheelchair and wondered how
this would ever work. Bakel had already arranged for our things to be

transferred to the riverboat, and once there, handed his duties over to another man named Masaka. While we were waiting to board, I asked Emme if she needed money for our trip, for Bakel, for Masaka, for anything. She said, "No, no, no," brushing off the idea with a wave of her hand.

"You have many friends," I said. "Is it like this for you everywhere in Africa?"

She laughed and pointed to the three raised horizontal lines on each of her temples. "It is because of these," she said. "These signify to others that I am a granddaughter of a wise man, a holy man. For that reason Bakel and the others wish to help. By doing so, they believe it will enhance their own lives."

"Is it true? Are they better off for it?"

"I think so," she said, "but only because of Obongelli. He has true powers."

"Who is Obongelli?"

"My grandfather. He is also called PoPo. He is the one I take you to see. He may be able to heal you. I know he will be overjoyed to see you."

"That explains why everyone is helping you," I said, "but why are you helping me?"

"Because of this," she answered, changing her expression and pointing to the silver pearl in her nose. "It is Meq. It is from one of your Starstones."

"What? How in the world do you know about that?" I involuntarily reached down for the Stone in my pocket, then remembered it was gone.

Emme smiled and said, "I will let PoPo tell you about this truth. It is only right, and he should be the one." She pushed me and the wheelchair on board the riverboat, which was badly in need of repair, then leaned over my shoulder saying, "Now we go home and you must tell me all about America on the way."

"Where is home?" I asked.

"Dogon land," she said, "deep in the Federation of West Africa."

"Is that anywhere near Mali?"

"Yes, more or less. We live south of the Niger River and north of the Volta River, on the edge of the Dolo Valley."

Without explaining or mentioning Star or the Fleur-du-Mal, I
managed a faint smile built on faint hope, and said, "Good."

For the next two and a half weeks, we traveled in a generally eastward
direction, leaving the green world and humid climate of western
Senegal for a landscape that occasionally reminded me of Kepa's camp
in America—dry, reddish brown, and remote. Masaka stayed with us
until we reached Koulikoro, where he told Emme he must return to
his family. As far as I know, he never once inquired about who I was
or why she was caring for me. From there, we took another boat ride
north and east, downstream on the Niger River, until we disembarked
and began our journey overland. Emme procured two donkeys for the
trip, securing me, our luggage, and the wheelchair to one of them,
while she led the way on the other. The donkeys were thin and old,
but they served us well, and three weeks later we were nearing Dogon
land.

Emme and I talked often along the way about Africa and her life
there. She was opposed to the French presence in her homeland, but
she was also obsessed with a Frenchman, a doctor she referred to as
A. B. or Antoine. It was obvious she was in love with him, although
she never expressed it openly. He was the reason she had been in
Saint-Louis. She had wanted to apologize to him. "For what?" I
asked. "For not believing in something," she said. "Not believing in
what?" I asked her. "In him," she answered quietly.

My own obsessions I kept to myself. I thought about Ray almost
every day and worried about Star every night. I wondered why I
wasn't healing and constantly had to tell myself that I would, that my
Meq blood would eventually find the source of the injury and renew
all damaged nerves and tissue. That's what I told myself, but as each
day passed and my legs remained paralyzed, I wondered more and
more if it was still true.

The mystery of who had attacked Ray and me, and why, had
plagued me since we'd left Saint-Louis. Since I had never seen who it
was, I could only make wild guesses, and none of them made any
sense. I only knew that the man in charge, the man who had stolen the
Stone, knew me and knew what I was carrying. Emme and I rarely

spoke of the attack. Then, only a day before we entered her village, she said something that triggered a connection, or at least the possibility of one. We were halfway down a sandstone cliff overlooking a dry and desolate valley. The ridge of sandstone ran five miles on either side of us. The sun was setting and everything had the look of either the first or last place on earth. She was talking about her grandfather and how my presence, my existence, would vindicate him and his long-standing story about the Magic Children, a tale she had heard since early childhood, a tale she never quite believed until the day she saw me, Ray, and the man behind us.

"Who is he?" I asked.

"I call him Snake Eyes, but PoPo knows his real name and has always warned me of him. PoPo says the man also knows of the Meq, and would like to steal the Ancient Pearl. He is an evil man, a trader in flesh and murder, and he smells."

That's when something dawned on me. Ray had said he thought he knew the man, the "Chinaman" he called him. "Snake Eyes"—"Razor Eyes." It had to be. "Is the man a Chinese-looking man?" I asked.

"Yes," she said. "Do you know him?"

"I might," I said, thinking back to that long-ago day when Baju had been murdered, and the man who had done it—"Razor Eyes."

That night and most of the following day we stayed in a cave that Emme said PoPo had shown her when she was a girl. It would be a good place, she explained, for us to rest and clean ourselves before the end of our journey. She left the wheelchair on the donkey and carried me in her arms. The entrance to the cave was almost invisible, even from a short distance away, and had not been altered in any manner, except for a few symbols carved in the stone. Farther in, I saw the outline or imprint of hands on the walls. Tiny hands, the hands of children, hands like mine. Emme said there were other caves in the area with similar carvings and drawings, but this was the only one with a hot mineral spring. Twenty yards from the entrance was a natural cavity in the rock floor where the spring formed a pool. Emme lowered me into the steaming, mineral-rich water, then lit several candles that were hidden in niches and crevices around the pool. The effect was immediate and I felt better in five minutes than I'd felt in five weeks.

"The best surprises are the simplest pleasures," Emme said, climbing in next to me.

I glanced over at her. "Whitman?"

"No," she said, laughing and splashing water in my face. "Me."

We both laughed and that was the moment I chose to ask her where and when she had learned to speak English. Her expression changed instantly and she looked away from me, staying silent for a full minute. Then she turned back and said, "It is a little complicated."

"Believe me," I said, "I am used to that."

For the next hour I heard the most improbable and unlikely story I could imagine—a story of shipwreck, slavery, love, betrayal, and heartbreak, involving her mother, Libe (now dead), a desert warlord named El Heiba, and her father, a black American engineer who called himself Ithaca. Someday I will retell it in its entirety, but the essence is that Emme and her grandfather learned to speak and read English from her father and three books he left behind—two books of elementary grammar and a copy of *Leaves of Grass* by Walt Whitman. When she finished, it was evident that her father's appearance and disappearance was an unseen driving force in her life. I asked her if he was still alive and she hesitated, staring into the water, then said simply, "I do not know."

The following day we rested, bathed, ate, and did very little else. Emme said we would stir up less commotion by arriving after dark. We waited for sunset, then left the cave for the last few miles of our journey. The air was almost cool as we descended the cliff. It turned pitch-black quickly and even though I couldn't hear any sounds of wildlife, I knew we were in a vast and wild place. Overhead, a river of stars burned in silence.

We arrived at the edge of her village and were met by several children who seemed to be waiting for us. They ranged in age from about six to twelve, but it was hard to tell in the darkness. They were smiling and giggling. Emme said they had seen her care for many strange orphans in nature, but never a white child. When they saw her help me off the donkey and into the wheelchair, their speech became more animated. Emme had to quiet them and eventually scold them, waving her arms and making them scatter back into a maze of dwellings.

She wheeled me in through what I took to be the back door of a structure that was very simple and unusual at the same time. It was two-storied, perfectly square, and made out of mud bricks. It was small, maybe twenty by twenty feet around. The roof was banded straw or reeds in a pyramid shape and seemed to top the dwelling like a hat. Close by, there were other structures, some in the shape of cylinders, but it was too dark to tell who or what they housed.

She showed me the place I would be sleeping, a simple pallet that she raised with mud bricks to a level where she could easily get me in and out of the wheelchair. Once our belongings were inside, I stacked my two small suitcases against the wall and rested Ray's bowler on top. I knew that inside one of the suitcases I had Mama's glove wrapped in Star's scarf. Under my shirt and around my waist, I still wore my money belt full of shiny American double eagles. I suddenly felt lucky. I was alive and conscious, and even though I was barely mobile some-where in the most remote part of the world, I knew I had all I needed, the reason and the means to heal and keep going. It was stacked right there in a small pile against the wall.

Emme helped me onto the pallet and straightened my legs.

"Emme," I said, "I am more than grateful."

"It is nothing," she said. "It is I who am grateful because tomorrow PoPo will come to see you. I doubt he ever thought he would see one of the Magic Children again."

"Again? What exactly does that mean?"

"I think PoPo should answer that," she said. "Tomorrow."

There are horseflies in West Africa—big ones. Wherever man and his animals go, wherever their food, their shelters, their droppings are, the horsefly is their companion.

I awoke to one crawling on the curve of my ear. I jerked my head involuntarily and it buzzed away. I was lying on my side staring at a drab brick wall. Behind me, over my shoulder, I heard someone stifle a laugh. I turned my head and saw him sitting on his haunches not three feet away, staring back at me. I assumed it was PoPo. He was an ancient black man with a narrow face and enormous ears. His eyes were large and watery, but very much alive and intense. He wore a strange four-cornered hat with flaps hanging over his huge ears. He almost laughed again, then held a monocle in front of his face. It had a hairline crack in the glass and was attached to the end of a stick, which he held regally. He leaned forward, and behind the monocle, his left eye looked twice as big as his right. Then he set the monocle down and spoke.

"Sometimes I am awake all night," he said directly to me, not waiting for introductions, "and cannot sleep because I am consumed by the number of lies I have told in my life—lies that got me into trouble, lies that got me out. Lies that came and went as easily as slurred speech and lies that stayed and decayed like rotten teeth. It was lies that followed me and lies that led me on."

He slapped his palms together, so quick and sharp I jumped, then opened his hands and from between them the dead horsefly dropped on the dirt floor. He winked at me and spat at the horsefly, missing it and making a small wet circle in the dirt next to it.

"There we are," he said.

Then, for reasons I have never understood nor have they ever been explained to me, I stood up on my own two legs. They were wobbly, tingling, and not yet capable of running, but definitely awake and healing. I looked over at the old man.

"What did you do?" I asked.

"Nothing. I did nothing," he said. "Your body awoke with your mind, that is all. It is common."

I thought of Sailor and his explanation for ghosts. I never quite believed him and I was certain the old man was being more than modest. Whatever the explanation, it felt like a miracle to have my legs back and I took a few tentative steps. The old man watched me as if he were watching a dream come alive. Standing by a stone hearth, Emme was watching too, only she was watching her grandfather as much as me. I was what he had told her about all her life. I was the lie made true. I turned to PoPo.

"My name is Zianno Zezen," I said, then hesitated, but only for a moment. "My name is Zianno Zezen, Egizahar Meq, through the tribe of Vardules, protectors of the Stone of Dreams . . . please, call me Z."

This time he could not contain his laughter. He rolled on his side and called to Emme. His hat tumbled to the floor and she came to his aid, but merely to rub his bald head affectionately. She looked over at me and smiled. "Do not be offended," she said, "he is only overjoyed."

She helped him onto the pallet that was my bed. He wiped his watery eyes and asked Emme for his monocle, then he composed himself and crossed his legs under him as if he were about to begin meditation. His posture was extraordinary for such an old man.

"Are you a young one or an old one?" he asked.

"A young one," I said, not at all sure where this was going. "What do I call you? Your granddaughter has given you two names."

"Call me PoPo. I would be insulted if you did not."

"But your formal name is Obongelli? Is that right?"

"Yes. Obongelli Ambala. I am also Hogon, which is 'the oldest.' I have many names and I answer to them all, but I prefer PoPo. Po means 'smallest seed' in our language, so I am the smallest of the smallest seeds. I prefer it that way."

He seemed to be searching my eyes as he spoke. I reached down and retrieved his hat and handed it to him. "How do you know of us?" I asked.

He put his hat back in place, then decided against it and set it down. "I have always known of you. Unfortunately, I have only seen one of you once before, when I was a child myself, and it was only for an instant." He leaned forward and searched my eyes again. "I am sorry," he said, "my eyesight is weak and I wanted to see if your eyes were green."

"Why is that?"

"Because his were."

I felt a chill as sharp and sudden as a knife blade on my neck. "Did he also wear his hair tied back with a green ribbon?"

The old man's watery eyes cleared and focused on a single event, probably seven or eight decades earlier. "Yes," he said, and his eyes widened slightly. "He did indeed wear a green ribbon."

That proved it. At that moment I knew Usoa's information and my hunch were correct—the Fleur-du-Mal had been to Mali. There was a connection, or at least there was one in the past. Whether he had come again, I had to find out. I thought starting at the beginning, PoPo's beginning, would be a good place. "Please tell me about the one with the green ribbon," I said, "and everything you know about the Meq, PoPo. I need to know what you know."

Emme walked over with two large silk pillows and a small rug rolled up under her arm. She spread the rug on the dirt floor and gently placed the pillows on top. The rug matched the primitive surroundings, but the silk pillows were hand-embroidered in intricate Arab geometric designs and were obviously not Dogon. She anticipated my question. "My mother obtained them," she said. "They came from the harem of Hadim al-Sadi. Would you like to sit while PoPo speaks?"

Emme and PoPo waited for me to take my place on the pillow, but I told her no, I would rather use my legs, and I paced the small room while PoPo spoke.

"Many years ago," he began, "my grandfather took me on a pilgrimage. I say pilgrimage, however, my grandfather never used that word. He merely said there was a meeting he must attend. He sounded more professional than spiritual and referred to the meeting as 'good business.' It was a pilgrimage to me because I knew I might get the chance to meet one of the Magic Children. He had just revealed your existence to me a few weeks before. It is one of the oldest secrets of our 'deep knowledge'—the existence of the Meq. I must tell you now that only two of our people know of this truth at the same time in each generation—an old one and a young one. Usually, they are in the same family, but not always. Families sometimes dwindle to one, then the truth must not only be kept and passed from old to young, but leap across to another family, as one would use faith and trust helping another across a stream. It is never too difficult. The choice is always clear. Emme and I hold this truth now. It is all the lies surrounding this truth that make it worthy of great laughter. Do you agree?"

I laughed and though I had no clue what he meant, I answered, "Yes, of course." Not since Solomon had I felt so immediately comfortable in a stranger's presence. "Please . . . go on."

He made an odd grunting sound and then continued. "We traveled north across the Niger to the tents of Hadim al-Sadi. He was camped outside Walata. As a child, it was the most exotic place I could imagine and I could not wait to arrive. In reality, it was harsh and cruel.

The sand swirled constantly and stung the eyes, and the camels smelled worse than goats. My grandfather told me to be silent and not complain. 'Stay out of harm's way,' he said, 'because someday, PoPo, you will also make this journey.' He made a vague reference to a pact that had been sealed centuries before between three parties—our ancestors, the ancestors of Hadim al-Sadi, and a single Magic Child. My grandfather called him the 'little wolf,' but also told me he had been called other names in other times.

"I wore the Ancient Pearl in my nose, as Emme does now, and my grandfather said the 'little wolf' must not see it. I was to stay far away from the meeting and remain there. Of course, as a curious child, I did not obey and followed him secretly to the meeting. Hadim traded in slaves and dealt with many black tribes, so it was not unusual for a black child to be seen around his tent. I wandered among the camels and horses at first, then found a place near the entrance where I became no more than a shadow. I could not see inside, but I could listen. I understood little of their conversation. They spoke in low voices and often in Tuareg, a language I did not yet understand. However, I knew my grandfather's voice well and after only a few minutes, he said something that was answered by a bitter laugh. It was a child's laugh and yet it was not. I have never forgotten the sound of it. That was followed by something being kicked over and then the entrance to the tent, a curtain of embroidered silk, was flung back. A child, a white male child, rushed out and then paused a moment. He seemed to sense my presence and turned his head slowly. We were not ten feet apart. He was my height and stared at me eye to eye. He had green eyes. Then he noticed the Ancient Pearl in my nose and he smiled— a white and frightening smile. The moment passed and he was gone. I knew who he was. He was the 'little wolf' and he was Meq. As he walked away, I now remember seeing the green ribbon. I can see him disappearing through the sparks of the campfires."

PoPo stopped speaking and inhaled slowly. He was an old man and reliving the old memory had surprised him with emotion. I let time pass and glanced at Emme. She nodded gently to assure me that he was fine.

"Why was he at the meeting, PoPo? Can you tell me?"

"The Prophecy," he said. "The Prophecy and the Lie." A single tear formed in the corner of one eye and then he smiled. "I have all my life longed for and feared that he would return to hear it from me, just to laugh at its truth, as he has always done in generations past."

"What is the Prophecy?" I asked. "And what is the Lie?"

"They are one and the same according to my grandfather, each a result of the same event long ago. The one with green eyes came to Mali in the 1300s when Mansa Musa, the king of Mali, returned from his pilgrimage and brought Arab architects and merchants with him. The one with green eyes was among them. Being the only white child anyone in Mali had ever seen, he was treated with a blend of curiosity and respect that enabled him to be granted nearly anything he wished. When he heard of the Dogon and our cosmology, he asked to be taken into Dogon land and introduced to the head priest. This was an odd request for anyone, especially a child, but Mansa Musa approved it and the child, along with Hadim al-Sadi's ancestors, made his way to Dogon land in the upper Sanga. Two of my ancestors were there to greet them. They went to the mineral cave and others like it where Meq handprints were shown to the 'little wolf.' He told the priests that he was Meq, and to prove it, he cut himself and asked for poison to drink. The priests were horrified, but his wounds began to heal in front of them and the poison only made him belch. Then my ancestors made a mistake. They told him about the Starstone."

PoPo paused and followed me with his gaze. I was still pacing the room. "Go on," I said.

"It was told that long ago, when there was only Water and the Word and the Meq came to visit, they left a Starstone in one of the mineral caves. When they held the Starstone in their hands, it was said they had power over Nature and were able to make the animals sleep. Only the Meq could do this, so the Starstone was buried in the water, but the gems that adorned it were passed among the elders of the Dogon. The Ancient Pearl is the last remaining gem. The others have been lost in time.

"The one with green eyes wanted to know where the Starstone was buried, but the priests had no real knowledge because the Meq were already ancient lore—an auxiliary myth. The 'little wolf' suddenly became furious and bade Hadim al-Sadi take two daughters of the priests into slavery unless the priests led him to the Starstone. The priests pleaded their ignorance and begged for their daughters, but the one with green eyes lost his patience and slit the throats of the daughters in front of the priests. In return, the priests issued a curse on the evil one in the form of a Prophecy. They foretold that he would die like the bastard Nummo in our cosmology—at the hands of twins. They said, 'You will kill a twin whose other will have a child that will have a child that will kill you.'

"The one with green eyes laughed at them and vowed to return in every future generation of their families to laugh at them and what he called the Lie. If the priests did not appear when he summoned them, Hadim and his descendants would kill their daughters and their daughters' daughters.

"So, there it is—the Prophecy and the Lie."

PoPo stopped talking and I nearly stopped breathing. I sat on one of the silk pillows and the pieces to an enigmatic puzzle started falling in place. Incredibly, I realized the Fleur-du-Mal's madness in abducting Star had its source right where I was. Whether the sixth Stone existed or not, he believed it did, and even more, he believed the Prophecy. All the needless death and suffering came down to simple superstition and pride. When he found out he had murdered the wrong woman and Carolina was Georgia's twin, he waited for Star to be born and now he was waiting for Star's child—*his own killer.* The challenge and irony of confronting and manipulating "fate" had become his obsession. That was why he had not yet summoned PoPo. The joke was missing its punch line. To the Fleur-du-Mal, the Lie was coming true and he would be waiting for it. But where was he? And more urgently, where was Star? And what, if anything, did "Razor Eyes" have to do with it? The questions tumbled one into the other. I looked up and PoPo and Emme were staring at me. I had one more question for PoPo. "Why did your ancestors refer to twins in their Prophecy?"

"Because twins have great significance for the Dogon. The starting point of creation is believed to be in the twin star that revolves around Sirius, the Dog Star. The Dogon have known this as long as they have known of the Meq. My ancestors called on the power in the smallest and heaviest of all the stars for potency in their Prophecy and curse." He paused and leaned forward on the pallet. He reached out for my hand and I gave it to him. His dark skin was leathery and he held my hand in his as he would a butterfly. "Is this important information to you?" he asked softly.

"Yes, PoPo, it is. You see, that is why I came to Africa—to find the one with green eyes."

"Ayiiii," he yelped and started laughing hysterically. He clapped his hands together and turned to Emme. "And what do you think now, my granddaughter?"

"It is a small world, PoPo," Emme said. "It is a small world."

"I need more information, PoPo," I told him, "about both the past and present if I am to do what I need to do. I will need your help." I paused and looked at Emme, remembering I had no Stone in my pocket and no real understanding of where I was or where to go. "I will need your help too, Emme."

PoPo glanced at his granddaughter and I could tell he was not sure what her response would be. His big ears seemed to lean toward her and his eyes widened. Her expression gave nothing away, then she smiled and picked up the old man's strange hat, placing it carefully on his bald head.

"I would be honored," she said. "We had hoped there was another kind of Meq than the one with green eyes. PoPo has always believed in this. We have been waiting for you."

For the next several days I walked. I walked with Emme outside the village along ancient trails that were red in color from the decay of rock older than the trails. I wanted to see all the caves where they had found children's handprints on the walls. The trails were rough and wound through desert scrub and stunted trees. Every day my legs grew stronger and Emme took me to another cave more remote than the last. Some of the caves had handprints spread throughout and some had only two or three in a small circle. Most were made from colored ochre, reds and yellows, and some were outlined in black. A few of the handprints were missing fingers. Emme said the Bambara, a tribe similar to the Dogon in fundamental principles and metaphysics, also had knowledge of such caves and handprints.

"Do they refer to them as Meq?" I asked.

"No," she said. "Only PoPo and I know of the Meq by name."

I walked with PoPo too. He was the most amazing walker I have ever seen. He always seemed to be walking backward because he never looked ahead and yet never ran into anything. The Dogon had a complex system of division and direction in their village. Everything was laid out in a north–south arrangement that symbolized the human body. Every space was accounted for and had to be traversed with care. Popo made his way laughing and talking, without care and without even looking.

I told PoPo everything I knew about the Fleur-du-Mal and the kidnapping of Star. I saw no reason to hold anything back. I had to find answers and connections. I showed him the old photographs that I still carried in my luggage of "Razor Eyes" from the awful day in Vancouver. PoPo recognized the man, as I'd hoped, though he said he looked much older now and was partially paralyzed in the face. PoPo called him by the single name Cheng, and said the man was well known in the slave trade from Lagos to Timbuktu and beyond. He always bought, never sold, and it was always girls. He sometimes traded with the sons of Hadim al-Sadi—Mulai (the elder), and Jisil (the younger). It was Jisil who had revealed to one of PoPo's acquaintances that Cheng sought the Ancient Pearl. Jisil had also let it slip that Cheng was merely a buyer for someone else, someone never seen and only referred to as "the girl from Peking."

We walked and talked at length and the time I had lost and my sense of it passing became acute. The more I learned, the more frustrated I became. It was Star I was after, and that was all. At times, I found myself wishing I could be Giza. I wanted to be large and strong, barging headlong into the desert, making people tell me the truth, by force if necessary. My hate was gaining ground again, but it wasn't focused or sharp. I was thinking like a victim and the Fleur-du-Mal would only find that amusing, never threatening.

After ten days, I was healed completely. My legs were strong and I took even longer walks with Emme. It was easier to concentrate when we were on the old trails and it kept the fuss over my presence in the village to a minimum. While we were on one of our walks, another of PoPo's acquaintances, Jean-Luc Leheron, formally Captain Leheron, arrived in the village unannounced. I was later told that he

was the man, according to Mulai and Jisil al-Sadi, who had killed their
father, Hadim, somewhere in the northern Sahara in 1902—an unfor-
givable act. For that reason, Jean-Luc Leheron had kept one eye on the
comings and goings of the two sons ever since. It was his retirement
and exploration of the upper Niger that originally brought him and
PoPo together. Their mutual respect for the legendary revenge of
Hadim's family kept them in touch. Anything unusual or unexpected
they reported to each other. PoPo said it was a good thing that Jean-
Luc had already departed before Emme and I returned. He would
have asked unanswerable questions about my presence, and I would
have been unable to contain my reaction at the news.

"News of what?" I asked.

"News of a girl, a blond girl called the 'bluebird,' seen in the camp
of Mulai two months ago."

My mouth dropped and PoPo stifled his urge to laugh.

"And Cheng was there," PoPo continued. "Jean-Luc said several
Tuareg chiefs were angry because they were expelled from Mulai's
camp when the girl arrived. The chiefs were given no reason and
Mulai then headed north into the desert at a time of year that is tradi-
tionally spent near towns and trading centers. Cheng disappeared just
as quickly."

It had to be Star. I was excited at the news, then suddenly a thought
occurred to me that I had ignored until then—diseases. There were a
thousand different ways for her to get sick in Africa. "Was the girl . . .
all right?" I asked. "Did he say anything about her health or condition?"

"No," PoPo said. "He only reported that she was seen."

I walked past PoPo and glanced at Emme. She had been washing
her face and hands while PoPo told us the news. She stared at me with
the towel folded in her hands. Unconsciously, I picked up Ray's bowler
and began to twirl it on my finger while I paced. What did the Fleur-
du-Mal plan to do? I turned to PoPo. "Did anyone mention seeing the
one with green eyes?"

"No," he said flatly.

That was no surprise, but what was "Razor Eyes" doing there? And
why had he stolen the Stone and kidnapped Ray? Even with the news
that Star was alive, I was more confused than relieved. Staring at the

old frayed bowler as it twirled, I felt helpless and sat down on a bench next to PoPo. Emme must have been thinking along with me because she was the one who put it together.

"If the one with green eyes is as you say he is," she began, "and he is indeed the same one who laughed at our ancestors, then he is trading with Hadim's sons to fulfill and control the Prophecy." She set the towel down even though her face was still wet. "Without a doubt, slavery is the key and the lock he will use to ensure it," she said, looking straight at PoPo. It was evident this was an issue they tried to avoid.

"What do you mean?" I asked.

"Mulai and Jisil keep slaves . . . and a harem. They are a closed society, as closed as any in the world, and they are in constant motion throughout an area as remote as any in the world. The one with green eyes stole the child knowing who she was, knowing that she could be the mother of his executioner. He raises the child himself until she is strong enough to travel and has forgotten her past. Then he hands her over to Hadim's sons to be raised as a slave and impossible to trace. The girl grows to be a woman and has her child, the father of whom is also chosen by him. He controls the girl, the baby, and in the end, the Prophecy. He then kills the baby at his leisure and sells the girl, now a woman, into further slavery—"

"To Cheng and whoever he works for," I interrupted.

"Yes," Emme said. "The deal has been struck. That was the purpose of their meeting and the reason for Mulai's sudden departure."

"But why did Cheng attack me and abduct my friend?"

"That I do not know," Emme said. "However, being aware of his habits and his history, I would say he sold your friend to someone and pocketed the profits."

I let Emme's words sink in, then turned and looked at the old man. He was watching me carefully.

"If you choose to go after her," he said slowly, "it will be extremely difficult."

"I have no choice, PoPo. I promised her mama I would find her."

PoPo glanced at Emme, exchanging something common in their history with his eyes, then spoke in a low whisper, to himself as much as me. "Then find her soon," he said. "She will not remember her mother long."

* * *

I wanted to leave the next day, but that was impossible. It took Emme another three weeks to gather and pack the provisions we would need. Finally, we left Dogon land some time before my birthday, in 1907. I had no idea of the exact day or week. I would soon find out that days, weeks, even months, had little significance where we were going. The hard fact that Star would turn seven years old that same calendar year made my own birthday meaningless. Sailor might not have agreed, but that's the way it was.

PoPo insisted on going along as far as Gao, on the Niger River, which made Emme insist on bringing two cousins with us to assist PoPo on the return journey home. The donkeys were loaded down and our progress was slow and tedious. I brought a single suitcase stuffed with my things and Ray's. I had to flatten his bowler slightly, but it was not possible to leave anything of his behind. I wore the money belt under my clothes and around my waist at all times. The gold and gems would be necessary for everything from information to camels. Emme thought we should travel poor and keep to ourselves, but I remembered something Solomon had taught me long ago— "Poverty often ensures no response, while gold is an international language."

Outside Gao, Emme unpacked one of the bundles on her donkey and laid out several robes and scarves. They all had a deep blue sheen and were the traditional color and cloth of the Tuareg, the "blue men" of the desert. In another bundle she brought out an assortment of bracelets and earrings made of silver, all inlaid with colored stones in geometric patterns. She put two big silver loops in her ears and handed me a short dagger made of serpentine.

"What do I do with this?" I asked.

"All Tuareg men wear it above the elbow of the left arm. It is called an *ahabeg*."

"But I am supposed to be a boy."

"Wear it anyway," she said.

She carefully arranged a blue scarf on her head, leaving her face uncovered. The scars on her temples were not visible, but the Ancient Pearl in her nostril stood out against her dark skin and the dark scarf.

Then she began wrapping the turban-veil, which she called the *tagel-must,* around my head and face. Only my eyes were left exposed. She told me that it was more than just protection from the desert sand and sun. Tuareg men never removed it in front of others as a show of respect and also believed it repelled "jinn," or evil spirits. It would be a perfect disguise and keep my identity hidden without arousing suspicion. She explained how the Tuareg were feared throughout the Sahara because of their legendary capacity for revenge. Being a young woman and young boy traveling alone, acting as Tuareg might lessen the chance of attack. It was good logic and the clothes were loose and comfortable.

I briefly thought back to China and how uncomfortable Geaxi and I had been in the heavy monks' robes that Sailor had made us wear. For another moment, the first in a long time, I smiled to myself and wondered where they were and what they would be doing. Then I thought of where I was and what I was doing and I could barely answer that. I decided I should at least send a letter to Owen Bramley.

Emme and I walked into Gao while PoPo stayed on the edge of the desert with the donkeys and the two young cousins. He told us he had no desire to see any more towns. "They are only sinkholes of gossip and money," he said, "and I have no need of either."

The outpost town was tiny and we easily found the one government building that served all civil purposes from jail to mail. I sent Emme in to post the letter. It contained few words, almost no information, and little truth. It was the best I could do. The letter was this: "Dear Owen—I'm still alive and so is Star—I will find her—it won't be long—Z."

I asked Emme how much time it might take for the letter to reach St. Louis. She said there was no way to know for sure, but it could take five or six months. Five or six months, I thought; maybe I could beat the letter with a telegram that said I'd found her.

Emme seemed to read in my eyes what I was thinking. "Do not think ahead," she warned, "the Sahara will not allow it."

Later, outside Gao and near sunset, we said good-bye to PoPo. The old man made a formal farewell, sitting straight, as always, on the back of his donkey. He removed his strange hat and then looked down at me through his monocle-on-a-stick. He said, "I wish you well, Zianno

Zezen. I know you prefer 'Z,' but one does not call the first drink of water from a deep well by a nickname. Please, if you can, watch over my granddaughter and ignore her complaints. She is a proud girl, much like her mother. She has a keen mind, but her heart wanders."

PoPo stayed where he was with the two young cousins while Emme and I headed north into a haze and horizon that had no definition. I turned and waved farewell, thinking I would surely see the old man again someday. It is a simple thing you tell yourself, not even a thought, really—more of a notion, a feeling that time and events will bring you back together in a future that is taken for granted. It doesn't always work out. After that last glance and farewell, I never saw PoPo again.

It is difficult for the Meq to talk about Time. To the Meq as individuals, time is not a question of gain or loss, and saving time is absurd. Without physical change, time is an internal concept and only distance, whether from a person or from a goal still unaccomplished, feels like a loss of time. Perhaps there is a crossroads, a paradox, a place where strangers, both Giza and Meq, wait in the twilight and the loss of time has no bearing at all on the only thing that can be found in Time and truly missed—love.

In the first few months of going deeper and deeper into the central Sahara, and traveling now on camels instead of donkeys, my thoughts continually revolved around Time. We were chasing Mulai and Jisil al-Sadi, and any information concerning their whereabouts became harder to get and less specific. It was more frustrating than it had been in China searching for Zeru-Meq. Their entourage included hundreds of people, camels, horses, and everything that went with them, all moving at will across political, geographical, and tribal boundaries like ghosts. The word Sahara is Arabic for "sand sea" and the al-Sadis seemed to sail through the desert on an outlaw ship with its own charts and ports. Emme asked questions and often got nods of recognition and stories about Mulai, Jisil, and sometimes Hadim, but not a single direction.

For many months we traveled, generally heading west through

Araouane and Tichit, never finding their camps or coming close. Emme refused to get discouraged and we drove each other on. She was concerned, however, that as time went on, Star would not welcome us as friends or liberators. In her mind and body, even spiritually, she would be nothing more than a slave to Mulai and Jisil. Emme was certain of this. Star's captivity by the al-Sadis became something we rarely talked about, never doubted, and followed obsessively. The drone of distance, time, and silence became a cocoon and a companion. We lived day to day, season to season, and eventually traveled in every direction without calendars or clocks. From the Ahaggar in the east to the Adrar in the west, we journeyed and searched, year after year, never relenting, never stopping.

In the beginning, we both seized any opportunity to send a note or letter, Emme writing to PoPo and me to Owen Bramley mostly. I wrote one letter to Carolina, but after reading it I tore it up because there was nothing in it. I never mentioned Ray in my letters. I rarely mentioned myself. The letters were more like postcards from no one describing nowhere. As the letters from both of us became shorter and less frequent, our obsession grew. Obsession is a clever and insidious drug. It drove us on and isolated us simultaneously. Human contact only served as a source of information and fuel for the pursuit. The extremes of heat, cold, wind, distance, and especially time affected us less and less. We were insulated in our cocoon, our obsession, and obsession is an amazing eraser of time.

I remember the night we were camped to the west as far as we had ever been, in a bleak and desolate stretch of desert beyond any traditional or commercial trade routes. Emme said we were only miles from Nouadhibou, or Port Etienne, as the French had renamed it. The sun was still an hour from setting and I turned toward the west and stared at the endless dunes and hills. Emme was tying the camels outside our tent and the only sounds to break the silence were our own voices and the groans from the camels.

"Look there," she said, and pointed low on the horizon.

I looked and saw a string of black dots weaving in the air over the dunes, flying north to south.

"Ringdoves," Emme said, "migrating down the coast." She paused and we watched the birds until they were gone, then kept staring into emptiness. In minutes the temperature had fallen fifteen degrees. I found blankets for both of us and we sat in silence while the sky darkened like a bruise, then filled with light. Emme's eyes seemed to glaze slightly, but she wasn't crying. She looked up at the great Milky Way and pointed at the bright dancing star that was Sirius. "The earliest Egyptians called it Sothis," she said. "They believed it was the home of departed souls. The Dogon believe the same thing." She wrapped her blanket tighter around her shoulders and looked at me. "What do the Meq believe, Z?"

I only hesitated a moment. It was an easy answer or, as Ray liked to say, clear as a tear. I said it once, then realized how very true it was. I heard myself say it again. "I don't know," I said. "I don't know."

Several weeks later we were gathering fresh supplies somewhere outside Tindouf, a traditional stop on the old caravan routes and a place where many tribes crossed paths for trade and gossip. I asked Emme if the man we were trading with could tell us the month and year. When he answered, I was shocked but Emme showed no reaction. Maybe it was because she was used to the natural, internal changes of her own body. Or maybe she had seen in her reflection the aging around her eyes and in the hollow of her cheeks, all things that never occurred to me—the boy, the Meq, the one who should not have been surprised. The man told her it was January in the year 1916.

Almost nine years had passed and we were still searching for the al-Sadis and Star. Nine years of crisscrossing the desert and its wells, trading centers, oases, and caravan routes, asking questions that were dangerous, hiding the gold that I carried, watching Emme get us in and out of places no western traveler would ever see. Nine years of learning to navigate by wind and stars, and learning a nomad life of survival that had not changed for millennia. Suddenly, for that one brief moment, it seemed time, distance, and the Sahara itself had swallowed all of us up.

My despair lasted the rest of that day and the next. I wandered through the open markets alone and sat for hours by a crumbling stone wall, staring at a lone acacia tree on the horizon. It was bent with the wind, permanently twisted and stretched, bare and isolated in the landscape, yet surviving. I thought continually of Star and her life. I thought of the Fleur-du-Mal and myself, then just before sunset of the second day I stood up and turned away from the tree and ran to find Emme. I had a hunch and, ironically, that was all we needed.

Emme had mentioned years earlier that Mulai and Jisil al-Sadi bred, trained, and traded *mehari,* the racing camels dating back to the earliest caravans. While I was loitering in the streets and markets, I overheard several excited conversations, some in Berber, some in Tuareg, between various groups of nomads, concerning a wedding and a camel race that would follow the celebration, occurring outside Tindouf in one week. The best and fastest camels from many tribes and distant points of the Sahara would be there. My hunch was that the al-Sadis would be among them. After I told Emme, she was amused at first, thinking it more than a long shot, then changed her mind and admitted it was at least a possibility.

The week passed quickly and on the morning of the wedding Emme and I were up early and scouting the race grounds and surrounding camps, still wearing our Tuareg clothing, but steering clear of all Tuareg encampments. By midafternoon, the wedding party arrived in clouds of dust, loud cheering, and clanging cymbals. The races began shortly after, with fifty or sixty camels and their drivers, snorting and yelping and coming off all at once from the starting line, which was a quarter of a mile across. Emme and I found a place to watch, standing next to a ragged group of camel drivers and slaves. The drivers were Tuareg and two of them nearest to us wore gold rings in their ears and bracelets made of ivory, silver, and turquoise up and down their arms. None of the others wore jewelry as rich and plentiful. It was unusual and Emme and I stayed near them just to listen. With our Tuareg turbans and veils masking our faces, they spoke freely without fear of an outsider's presence. Their dialect was one I had never heard. Emme said it was archaic and used by only a few tribes, including the al-Sadis. She translated as they spoke, but two minutes into the race I didn't need it. I distinctly heard one of them yell "Mulai!" and saw him point to the man who was leading the pack. I only managed to turn and look at the man for a few seconds before the whole group passed and he became invisible in the dust and sand. He wore dark blue from head to foot and gold strands were woven into the cloth, making it sparkle in the bright sunlight. Then Emme leaned over and translated what I couldn't understand. They were also yelling, "My chief! My chief!"

Finally, we were in the right place at the right time. I glanced at Emme and she gave me a quick look, then stepped over to one of the camel drivers and grabbed his sleeve. I had no idea what she was doing or that she was going to do it. She lowered her veil and told the man that our chief wished to buy camels from Mulai al-Sadi—good camels—*mehari;* we would pay in gold. The man stared down at Emme and looked her over slowly. The other man came closer and looked at me, then focused on the pearl in Emme's nostril. This was dangerous business. I knew they would either believe her now, or not at all. If they believed her now, we would have many doors open for us. If not, we had been exposed once and for all, and would most likely be killed by decapitation as soon as we left Tindouf.

Emme's gaze was too powerful for the first man to doubt her and the other man stared at her pearl and thought of gold. The ruse worked, but only to a point. Neither of them had the authority to fi-nalize any deal without the complete knowledge and approval of their chief. A meeting here, at the races, was completely out of the ques-tion. Emme kept after them. She was lying, of course, dropping names and telling them our chief had been under El Heiba and now wished to quit the resistance and return to his homeland and race camels. The drivers paused and stared at each other for just a moment, then the conversation changed in tone completely. She had finally come up with a name common to them all. This enabled the camel drivers to verify their trust and at least tell her the exact location in which Mulai would be pasturing his camels along with his prize Arab horses the following year, without ever having to say or use his name. It was an elaborate and baroque deal, but a deal nonetheless.

Emme never mentioned the "bluebird" by name but at the same time steered the dialogue toward a blue-eyed white girl our chief had sold to Jisil al-Sadi years before. Emme asked if Jisil had sold her yet; being so white and skinny, Emme thought she would never adapt. One of the men said that Jisil only wished he could buy and sell the girl. She was not his, the man said, and she never would be. He added that the problem would solve itself in little more than a year, when the girl would be sold—then their chief could get back to the business of camel racing full time. Emme asked if the girl ever traveled with them to events such as this. One of the men said no, never, that it could never happen. Then the other man interrupted him with a stern look and brought the conversation back to camels.

The races went on until early evening. Emme and I left long before that, but we now had what we needed—a time and a place. We would meet them there. We would be waiting.

As we were leaving, in the midst of shouts and swirling clouds of sand, I started laughing and couldn't stop.

"Why are you laughing?" Emme asked.

"I don't know," I said. "It's not that funny. I was remembering something."

"What?"

"Another day similar to this one. The first time I rode a camel."

Emme watched me for a moment, then reattached her veil. "Where was that?" she asked.

"In St. Louis."

"Senegal?"

"No. Missouri."

"When?"

"A lifetime ago . . . the day Star was stolen. The day an old friend died."

"Look at me," Emme said, unfastening her veil again, so I could watch her say the words. "We will find this girl, Z. She may not be Star anymore, but we will find her and free her."

"I know . . . I just never thought it would be with camels."

Early the next day Emme posted a letter to PoPo, telling him our good news and giving him our route and probable stops along the way, then we left Tindouf and began traveling in a zigzag, easterly direction. We were in no hurry and our final destination was still far away in the central Sahara and massif of Tassili-n-Ajjer. Our spirits were high and we talked at length about what the camel drivers had said and what it meant. It seemed clear that Star would be sold in just over a year, and that would be the same date the Fleur-du-Mal would do whatever it was he had in mind to do. What was not clear was Star's relationship with Mulai and Jisil. Somehow, in some way, she had come between them.

For six long and uneventful months we had good luck with both the weather and the animals. We ran into no sudden storms and the camels stayed healthy. We even purchased two goats along the way. Why not, we thought; we were rich with hope. Emme talked often of the future, not only scenarios for Star's rescue and escape, but for herself afterward. She said she might rethink a decision she had made concerning the mysterious A. B., the Frenchman from Saint-Louis in Senegal. She didn't say what the decision was and I didn't ask. I never asked about him because I never mentioned Opari. It had always been an area of mutual silence between us and seemed a fair trade.

Finally, on a clear but windy morning, we came within sight of In Salah, an ancient town in the heart of Algeria. It had been a crossroads for caravans, wars, and warriors for centuries. That day, although there were a few stragglers like us, it seemed desolate and nearly abandoned. Emme stopped an old herdsman who was leaving just as we were arriving and asked if there had been sickness or a threat of some kind to the people. In Berber, he replied, "No, no, only an Englishman, a soldier who has fled the war in the east. The people think other English soldiers will come after him. They want nothing to do with him, so they stay inside and wait for him to leave, but he doesn't leave. He only sits in the shade and smokes Turkish tobacco. Very unpleasant, very bad."

The old man waddled off and Emme shrugged her shoulders. We knew there was a war going on in Europe, and we knew there was fighting in Africa, but that was thousands of miles away, mainly in East Africa and South Africa and nowhere near the central Sahara. Emme thought that it was of no concern and told me to tend the animals while she went to post a letter to PoPo. I agreed without telling her what I really intended, which was to find the English soldier. I wanted news, English-speaking news.

I combed the markets and alleys of In Salah until finally, under the awning of an empty stall at the very edge of town, I found him, sound asleep in the shadows. He was snoring loudly and looked to be about twenty or twenty-one years old. His face was unshaven, but his beard was blond and barely more than peach fuzz. Either he or someone else had torn all the insignias off his ragged uniform. They were lying in a pile beside him, along with several papers, including a British newspaper. I figured he must be a deserter; there was no other reason for him being alone and so far from anywhere. I tried to find out what I could without waking him. I knew there was nothing I could do for him—not here and not now. Among his papers I discovered he had been in the Second Battalion of the Nigerian Regiment under Lieutenant Colonel Austin Hubert Wightwick Haywood. The name sparked a memory. I had heard the colonel's name before in other remote parts of the desert. He was known as the only Englishman in recent years to have crossed the Sahara. I looked down at the sleeping young soldier and wondered if he had heard the same thing, maybe even tried to do the same thing. I would never know. I took the British newspaper and ran back to my goats and camels and began to read.

Minutes later, I discovered the United States had entered the war in Europe. That was no surprise. Sailor had always said the Giza would eventually find a way to fight a world war. The rest was not news, not really, just reports of what was in fashion—economically, culturally, spiritually. Two things did catch my eye. One made mention of a new American poet on the scene—Thomas S. Eliot—and I wondered if he could be the same boy on the bicycle who had been so infatuated with Carolina, then dismissed the thought as impossible. The other was an article, with pictures, of a new biplane that was going to be tested in Scotland as a seaplane. I could not believe how far men had come, once they learned to fly. The machine looked remarkable. There was something familiar about the name of the pilot, and I was squinting in the sun, trying to place it, when Emme's shadow interrupted. I looked up and knew immediately something was wrong.

"What is it?" I asked.

She was trembling slightly. She handed me a letter, but it never made the exchange. It dropped in the dust and I picked it up.

"It was waiting for me," she said slowly. "It has been here more than a month."

I opened the letter and looked at it. It was in French and I only understood a few words. However, I could read the signature at the bottom clearly—Jean-Luc Leheron.

"What does it say?" I asked, then changed my mind. "No, what does it mean?"

"It means I have to leave, go back to Dogon land—now—today."

I knew there would be only one answer to my next question, one small seed of an answer. "PoPo?"

"Yes. He is . . . not well. He is . . ." She stopped, then swallowed hard. "He is dying."

"Then I'll go with you."

"No, you will not. You will go on and stop this abomination. You must—we have never been this close to her. If you left now, you might not get back in time . . . many things might happen, many things. You will free that girl. She will fear you, she will have another name, but you will free her. You must! You will free her as you would a bird. You will do this because you were meant to do this. You have no choice, as I have no choice. PoPo is my blood and I know you understand this, Z, . . . more than I."

I looked at her and knew without a doubt she meant what she was saying, and that what she was saying was true. There was no other way for it to be. Any delay was just that. "Then I think we'll only say a temporary farewell, Emme Ya Ambala. I have not yet seen enough of you in this world."

"I feel the same, Zianno Zezen. There will be a day somewhere, somehow, and you will introduce me to Star. That will be a good day."

We embraced in the sand with grit swirling around us. The wind was coming from the west and picking up. I heard dogs barking in the distance. The sun was low, but the sky was still bright with several hours left in the day. Emme loaded her camel with supplies, then climbed on, ready to head south.

"You will have to learn some new dialects," she shouted down at me.

"I will talk backward," I said, "it always works." Then something else came to me. " 'I, now forty-seven years old in perfect health, begin, hoping to cease not till death—' "

"I am impressed," she said, " 'Song of Myself,' but the correct age is thirty-seven." She was laughing. "You are crazy."

"Someone else told me that once. Do you know what I told her?"

"No, what?" Emme shouted back. She was already moving, swatting at the camel and straightening the reins. The camel groaned and balked as always. I walked alongside.

"Egibizirik bilatu."

"What does it mean?"

"Something about truth," I yelled. She was pulling away.

"I will remember that," she yelled back. "Is it old?"

"Yes," I shouted, but I knew she couldn't hear me any longer. She was only a blue dot melting into a shimmering, shapeless horizon. "It is very old," I whispered.

I left In Salah two days later, moving north and east, slowly at first—one day, one night at a time. As I crossed the oldest north–south caravan route from Ghadames to the Niger, I traveled even more slowly. I bought two more goats and a donkey. It was twice as slow and twice as convincing. By the time I got to the sandstone cliffs and hidden canyons of the Tassili-n-Ajjer, I was a full-time goatherd.

Mulai and Jisil's "property" was neither legal nor defined by boundaries in any way. It was what they could hold on to and defend. However far that defense was extended was their current "property" line. Sentries on horseback and in pairs usually patrolled the entire remote area surrounding the al-Sadi camps. Occasionally, one sentry would be posted for a few months at a time near strategic passes and lookout points. My goats and I found one of these passes at the northern end of the Tassili range. There were two small streams and ragged pastures nearby and in the cliffs all around were caves and grottoes where I could camp and make myself familiar with the sentry, who would be lonely, hungry, and angry at being posted so far from his main camp. At least, this was what I hoped for, since disenchanted soldiers sometimes say more than they should. I had to find out anything I could, in any way I could, about the "bluebird." It was still early in what passed for spring in the Tassili-n-Ajjer, but the deadline the camel driver had mentioned was only months away.

I started out making my rounds with the goats at a good distance from the pass itself. Gradually, daily, I let the goats stray closer and closer. I was in luck. The sentry who was posted to the northern pass was not hungry or angry, far from it, but he was lonely and one day called out to me. I played mute, waving my arms and making hand signals. He took pity on me and we struck up a friendship, of sorts. He did all the talking and I nodded my head. To keep him talking, I often brought tobacco and dates, things I kept with me for trade, but never imagined would be used as bribes for information. In such a fierce and friendless place, they were better than my gold.

He was named Idris, after Idris Alooma, the sixteenth-century ruler who brought firearms to the Maghreb. This Idris was heavyset, which was unusual in the desert, and I never saw him look at his rifle, much less use it. He was jolly and gregarious and he still had a small spark of innocence left in his eyes, though he was anything but innocent. He had killed many men. Death, especially as a warrior for Mulai and Jisil, was common to him. He could slit a man's throat and still take time to sample the dates the man had been about to swallow. He would fondly remember the dates, never the man.

He spoke a common Berber dialect, which I understood, not the difficult archaic speech of the camel drivers. Since I always brought gifts and never spoke back, he encouraged my visits and even used his hands more for expression, as I did. When I pointed at my eyes with two fingers and made a fluttering motion with my interlocked hands, imitating a bird, a "bluebird," he shut his eyes and waved his hand across his face, telling me this must not be seen, not be discussed. It was a forbidden subject. I knew that no female, more specifically a female slave, would have become a forbidden subject unless the chief or chiefs had made it so. Star may not have known she was the daughter of Carolina Covington, but her blood did.

I began staying longer, returning sooner, and generally becoming a friendly nuisance until I was virtually living at the pass with Idris. He showed me hundreds of caves in the area and most of them were decorated with paintings and engravings from ancient times. Idris had no idea who had put them there or what they meant, but he pointed out that some of the older engravings were of animals that now only existed in the south—rhinoceroses, giraffes, elephants, crocodiles, hippopotamuses. In Berber, he said, "Many rivers, long ago." Most amazing was a cedar tree near one of the caves, its limbs spread and twisted, reaching fifty feet up and out between two rock walls, rooted in what was the riverbed, maybe three or four thousand years ago. It was still alive.

I began sleeping in the tree. There was a crevice in a gnarled limb where I could stretch full-length and even watch Idris as he kept his watch in the pass. He did little. There was little to do. No one came through the pass in either direction for weeks. Idris said sometimes the sentry of the northern pass could live through the entire length of his watch and never see another human.

I waited, watched, and listened. My Meq "ability" to hear at great distance increased dramatically the first night I slept in the old cedar tree. I was learning to focus, turn it on and off, and even listen in my sleep. It was more than an increased intensity of a sense. It was more like another one.

It was during this strange sleep-listening on the night of a new moon that I first heard the horse of Jisil. Idris confirmed it for me the next day, nervously, because Jisil had been alone and this was never done. Somehow, I had known it was Jisil when I heard the hooves. He stopped for only a moment in the pass, so Idris could recognize him, then headed north at a full gallop. Three nights later he returned. He was alone again and charging hard back to his camp. I was worried. Something urgent was driving Jisil, but it was still weeks before the season Mulai's camel driver had spoken of, the season the "bluebird" would be sold.

The next day I stayed close to Idris and the pass. Around sunset, I gave him the last of the dates and herded the goats back to my camp. I fed the donkey and the camels and climbed up into my perch in the coiled limb of the old cedar. As the Milky Way spread itself overhead, I watched Idris sit by his small fire. His silhouette was the only thing that moved in all directions. Then something began to happen. Something that proved forever what Sailor had told me years before. "Chase a whisper," he'd said, "and you will find the wind."

I heard a sigh. I turned my shoulders toward the source of the sound and I was staring into empty space. At first, it seemed to come from space itself, from somewhere near Sirius, the Dog Star. I waited and listened for it to come again, but it did not. My eyes drifted to the rock face opposite the cedar and just beyond the farthest outstretched

limb. The moon cast light and shadow against the stone at precisely
the right angles for me to see something I had never seen in the rock
face before—an opening.

The sigh returned and doubled in strength, then tripled. It was as if
one sigh had found a gap in the silence and the others were following,
curious and crowded behind each other, anxious to come through and
spill out from wherever they were. And they were all coming from the
opening, which was forty feet up the rock face and fairly small, so that
only a child could enter without difficulty.

I put some candles in my pocket, climbed down from the cedar,
and made my way across the ancient riverbed. In the dark, scaling the
sandstone cliffs would usually have been impossible, but once again,
because of the angles of light and shadow, I was able to see footholds
and handholds clearly. I climbed slowly and surely toward the opening. The sighs had become so numerous they seemed to flow like
water from a spring or fountain.

I found a ledge that ran in front of the opening. It was very narrow
and could have been invisible from the ground. I lit a candle. I peered
into the black space of the opening. The air was dry, as dry and light
as ashes. The opening itself was no more than three or four feet high
and wide. I followed the sound and flow of the sighs.

The passage wound into the mountain and gradually increased in
height, but remained narrow. The walls were smooth and as I ran my
hand over the stone, I could feel engravings at different points along
the way. I shone the light on several and they were all in languages and
symbols I had never known or seen before. The sighs sounded more
and more like water.

Abruptly the passage ended. There were no other ways in or out,
only the one narrow passage that ended in a domed stone room in the
natural shape of an oval. I set one candle down in the sand and lit another. The walls were covered with more engravings of symbols and
animals, some of which I knew were extinct. At the narrow end of
the oval there was a dark opening in the stone that was the source of
the sighs. Water was flowing from it, clear and sparkling, disappearing
into the sand where it fell.

I was suddenly thirsty. I had to drink from that water. There was no
other thought as strong. I walked toward the dark space and the water

and knelt down and bent forward, placing my palms against the stone on both sides of the fountain. I opened my mouth for the water, closed my eyes, and leaned into it.

But there was no water.

I opened my eyes and the dark opening that had been the source of the water and the sighs was actually a circle in the stone, indented and stained black, and my palms were not in some random resting place against the stone. I had unknowingly put them in handprints exactly my size that had been there for millennia, carved or worn into the stone in exactly those positions. I leaned back and looked at the wall. Around the black circle and engraved in a language I had never seen written, but understood intuitively, were two intersecting lines. They were written in Meq. The script Eder told me we had lost, the script that had been scrawled into the bone barrettes she wore in her hair. Translated, they read like this:

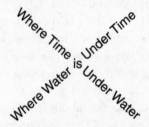

I looked around for more. There was absolutely nothing else in the room. No pottery, no tools, no remnants of any kind. I scanned the walls again and something caught my eye to the left of the black circle in a small and tight script. I held the candle close to the wall. It read:

> *Dream of light*
> *We are*
> *Silence of water*
> *We are*
> *Blood of time*
> *We are*
> *Will of stone*
> *We are*

Memory of truth
We are

And it was signed. The name was Trumoi-Meq.

I don't know why, but I suddenly thought of Mama and the train ride to Central City. When I had asked her how we were different, she had said, "We are more than just Basque, we are older." I hadn't understood and I remembered how she had looked out of the window and let out a long sigh. Was that what I heard coming first from the skies, then the cave, and now from a nonexistent fountain? Was it the sighs of a whole species trying to explain itself?

I sat in the sand of the ancient room and listened. I tried to feel a connection with what I'd discovered, but I'd never felt so distant, so lost and alone in my life.

I rose and walked back through the passage, leaving the lit candles in the room. I followed the faint shafts of moonlight to the opening and stepped outside on the ledge. The sky over the Sahara seemed to be blazing with stars. I wondered if all the others before me, the old ones, had stepped out of the cave and onto this ledge and felt the same sense of relief and loneliness. I took a deep breath of air and let it out slowly. It was a paradox of awe and despair.

I turned and looked toward the pass and beyond. Idris was in his place by the fire, still eating dates. What teeth he had left were stained and the rest were missing because of his love of dates. The trail to the north sloped down and away from his lookout, but was visible for at least a mile in the moonlight.

Then I heard the hooves. They were coming from the south, at a trot, not a gallop, but I knew the sound. It was Jisil. And he was not alone. There was a voice saying his name, speaking in another language, but a voice I knew well, a voice that sounded as if it could be Carolina's twin, only Georgia was dead. It was Star and she was very frightened.

I tried to find them in the darkness and couldn't. From the sound of the hooves, I knew they were near and both riding the same horse. I had to make a decision whether to start climbing down the rock face or wait and watch them ride through the pass. I decided to wait.

Idris eventually heard the sound of the horse and recognized it also. He stood up slowly and walked to the edge of his lookout.

Jisil and Star appeared almost at the same moment. His horse was a solid gray Arab stallion and they were only slowing down, not stopping. My pulse quickened and my heart pounded. Finally, she was flesh and blood, alive and right in front of me. So many times I had doubted this would ever happen. I could not see her face and she never spoke, but I knew it was her. She rode on the saddle in front of Jisil and wore simple white robes and a turban with a veil. Under the veil, she was breathing rapidly. I could hear her easily with my "ability."

Jisil wore a dark turban and veil that seemed to sparkle in the faint light. Gold strands had been sewn in with the cloth. He glanced up at Idris as they passed and waved his arm once in an arc. I couldn't tell whether it was a greeting or a farewell. They disappeared down the north slope as quickly as they had arrived and Idris went back to his fire and his dates.

For a moment I was frozen on the ledge. I don't know why. In the same moment I heard the hooves of another horse, far to the south, but approaching fast and in full gallop. This time I didn't wait. I started for the end of the ledge and began my climb down the rock face. I had only gone a few feet before the rider from the south was already in the pass. Clinging to the rocks, I glanced at Idris as he rose from his seat by the fire to greet the rider, then dropped his bowl of dates where he stood, and pointed north. The man wore a dark turban and veil like Jisil and his horse was the same color gray, only mottled slightly with whites and darker grays. He carried something on his back, which he slung around in one motion and held to his shoulder. I couldn't quite make it out, but the motion was familiar. It was a rifle and he was aiming down the north slope, down the trail that led to Ghadames, down toward Jisil and Star.

In the moonlight and because of the distance, it was a difficult shot, but he only fired twice. The two cracks were close together and were quickly swallowed by silence. His horse never moved. The man rested the rifle on his thigh and watched the darkness to the north. Nothing moved, not the horse, the horseman, Idris or me. A full minute passed, then he slowly turned his horse and addressed Idris in that archaic dialect I did not understand. The only words I did understand were names—"Mulai" and "Allah."

Then he raised his rifle and shot Idris between the eyes. Idris fell and toppled along with the dates over the rocks and into the pass. The horseman looked back to the north once more, then turned south and rode back the way he had come, this time in a slow and arrogant trot, the trot of a chief and the arrogance of an assassin.

I scrambled down the rock face, slipping, losing balance, going much too fast. I ran across the riverbed and found my packs. I untied all the animals and wished them well, then ran and stumbled my way up to where Idris had pastured his horse. I secured the packs and saddle, fumbling with every buckle and strap. I tried to calm myself and slow down. As I rode north, away from the pass and down the slope, I held the horse to a trot. At a gallop, I would never see them, dead or alive.

I found Jisil's horse first. He wasn't far off the trail and he was pacing nervously. As I slowed to a walk, he bent his head and nudged something, then backed away, shaking his reins and snorting. When I got close enough, I looked down. It was Jisil. He was sprawled facedown in the sand. He had been shot through the spine and heart. I never saw his face. His dark turban had wrapped around him and whipped in the wind above his head. I was watching it when something broke loose from his hand and flew up like a handkerchief. I reached out and caught it. I couldn't tell what it was, but there were drawn lines and words in Arabic and it seemed to be a map. I tucked it away and listened, as hard and focused as I ever had, I listened.

I let my "ability" spread and deepen. The two horses shuffling and snorting sounded like a stampede. I concentrated and narrowed myself, centered myself like the small black circle in the oval room of the cave. The wind was raging. I could hear it scraping the rocks clean. I had to go under it, underwater, under time, under the wind, to find her.

I heard a sigh.

I turned and ran toward the source. It came from the opposite side of the trail in a mass of brush and sand. I looked down and saw the white muslin veil. The sigh came from behind it. I pulled the veil back slowly and stared down at the face, the mouth, that had made the sigh.

In the moonlight, I could see enough of her features to tell that her eyes were closed, but her lips were parted and she was alive and breathing. There was a ring in her nose, a gold ring in the center attached by a chain to another smaller ring in her left nostril. That was attached by another chain to another, larger ring in her left ear. But it was not the rings or chains that caught my attention, it was the freckles. Carolina's freckles, all across her nose and cheeks. I was certain that under her closed lids, the eyes were blue.

I lifted her head gently and she sighed again. She had been shot through the shoulder, probably knocked from the horse by the impact and then rolled into the brush. I wasn't sure if she was conscious and less sure what to say to her. I had never thought about it in all the years I had been looking for her.

"Star?" I whispered.

Her eyes fluttered and opened about halfway, then found mine and opened wide. She tried to speak, saying something in Jisil's archaic dialect, then fell back into unconsciousness, either from the sight of me or the pain of her wound, or both.

I dragged her out of the brush roughly. There was no other way. I pulled back her robe and looked at her shoulder. It was still bleeding, but I knew it would stop. The bullet had not lodged and the wound was clean. I bound it tightly with her veil and mine, then stood up and looked for Jisil's horse. There was no chance of getting out to the south because of Mulai's camp. The east and west only promised more desert. The only way of getting out was to the north and that would take a good horse.

I found him near Jisil's body, still skittish and watching me as I approached. The wind tore at Jisil's turban and stung my face and eyes with sand and grit. The animal was a chief's horse and ignored the wind. To him, the wind had never been an enemy, only an ally, and that gave me an idea. I tore off the part of Jisil's turban that was loose and blowing. I started walking toward the horse, deliberately, and wrapping the cloth around my own head at the same time, slowly. I stopped within five feet and waited. After a cautious snort and whiff of me, he lowered his head and shook his reins. I turned and walked back toward Star, not looking once over my shoulder. When I had almost reached her, I heard his hooves crossing the trail of crushed stones

behind me. It was a gamble and I had been lucky, but Jisil's horse, one
of the finest Arabs I had ever seen, never questioned it.

I loaded and strapped my things on first, then with great difficulty,
I managed to get Star on the horse and in the saddle behind me. I literally tied her to my back, even though she was taller and heavier. It
was not her weight that gave me problems or concern. It was what I
discovered when I first picked her up. It changed the way I touched
her, moved her, and it had probably changed everything for Jisil.

Star was pregnant, very pregnant.

We traveled at a steady pace along the trail to Ghadames and the
oldest of the caravan routes. Jisil's horse knew the way when I didn't.
Star remained in a semiconscious state and only took water with the
aid of my fingers.

Somewhere outside Ghadames, we rested near a grove of palms. It
was midday. There were mounted and motorized patrols in the distance. What army for which country, I couldn't tell. I found water and
traded for biscuits, helped Star to a place in the shade, then sat by her
and took out what I'd caught in the wind from Jisil, what I hoped was
a map.

It was a map and a little more. Jisil had outlined the north coast of
Africa from Tripoli to Tunis. He had marked two places on the coast
by name and symbol. The one to the east was named Sabratha and
marked with an X. I had never heard of this place. He also had a trail
of arrows that headed west, avoiding Sabratha and ending in the other
place, which he had marked with a circle. The name was Carthage. In
the margins he had scribbled notes and several names, all in Arabic,
except one—"Cheng."

I looked over at Star and it came to me. I remembered Jisil's two
midnight rides a few days before. He had been making a deal. The
new pieces fitted into the old puzzle. Jisil had fallen in love with a
slave—Star—and was trying to save her and the baby from a deal that
had been sealed long ago, a deal that Mulai would not break, a deal
with the Fleur-du-Mal. I figured Cheng would be working for the
Fleur-du-Mal or against him. Either way, he could lead me to him.

I had heard of Carthage and I definitely knew of Cheng. There
was no choice but to take Star there. She needed to be free and safe
to have her baby. Her shoulder I knew would heal. I could end the

madness there, in Carthage, because Cheng would be expecting Jisil, not me.

I followed the map generally and asked directions occasionally. Sometimes I spoke in my rough Berber, sometimes in French, and once in English. I no longer cared about any pretense or disguise. Star continued to drift in and out of consciousness. I tried to stay behind her when she woke, so my presence wouldn't startle her. She drank more water, but she was weak from the loss of blood. Without being aware of it, she often held her belly when she slept.

South of Gàbes, a day and a half later, we came out of the desert and the mountains. Birds circled overhead, and even though we couldn't see it yet, we could smell the salt and the sea air of the Mediterranean.

We camped that night near a rocky outcrop on the high plain between Gàbes and Sousse. Star was pale and drawn and I couldn't seem to make her comfortable. Her sleep was more delusional. I tried to think of what Emme would do. Sirius was as bright as a streetlight in the sky. Star opened her eyes once and stared at it, then mumbled something in the old Berber dialect and fell back into her restless sleep.

Then, as if someone had whispered it to me, I remembered something, something that had once been a pillow of dreams for this daughter of Carolina, something I still carried with me—my mama's glove. I reached in my pack and pulled it out. Carolina had said she would never forget it. I unwrapped the old scarf with the drowning Chinamen and held it in my hand. I put my other hand inside the glove and pounded the pocket with my fist. Everything worked, everything felt good. I slipped my hand out of the glove and placed it under Star's head. I put the scarf in her hands and covered her with a blanket. The rest would have to be magic. It was the only medicine I had. I had already decided that if she didn't improve by morning, I was going to find a town and a doctor.

As soon as I awoke, I knew something had changed. Star was awake and staring at me. It was not hostile or even lively. It was as if she was searching for something underwater and couldn't quite get the physics right, couldn't quite reach it. But she was alert and conscious. I rose up and faced her, sitting cross-legged the way Carolina, Georgia, and I used to. Neither of us spoke. She saw Jisil's horse not far away and, without taking her eyes from mine, nodded toward the horse. I slowly

shook my head and she looked down once, but that was her only reaction. She reached one hand up from her belly and held it over her
wounded shoulder, asking me with her eyes if I was the one who had
attended to it. I nodded once. I showed her Jisil's map and pointed to
Carthage, asking her with my eyes if that's where we should go. She
nodded once. I smiled and she didn't. She hadn't decided yet if she
trusted me, but she held on tight to Mama's glove and the old scarf. I
stayed silent and we traveled that way. The fact that I was still a child,
still "physically" the same, was a blessing and a curse. It would help her
remember her past, possibly, but never explain her present. I stayed
silent and tried to let the present win her trust. The past would come
later.

We rode overland and off the trail the last fifty miles approaching
the ruins of Carthage. Only Jisil's horse had drawn any real attention.
Our skin color and appearance seemed to have little effect on the few
people we saw. It was another world to the one in the deep desert. Star
had to dismount twice along the way because of the pain, not in her
shoulder but in her belly and back. We were walking with the horse
between us when we stopped on a natural rise that opened up two
views around us. It was twilight and the sun was setting in the west
over what I assumed were the Atlas Mountains. To the north and east,
in the long shadows, were the fields and pastures, roads and ghosts of
roads leading to what had once been Carthage and the harbor beyond.

It was a good place to camp and let Star rest. I had no idea of the
final arrangements in the deal Jisil had made. I knew I'd never seen
Cheng work alone and I didn't expect him to now.

The site was not inhabited nor was it deserted. There was evidence
of excavations begun and abandoned. Some fields had been plowed
and sowed around the broken stones of temples and markets. Robber
trenches from centuries past crisscrossed the various sections of the old
city. It was haphazard and ragged. The Romans hadn't left much
standing and time since had given it no dignity. The wind blew in
from the north. The Mediterranean was a dark blue band in the distance. I smelled the faint scent of goat in the air and looked down the
rise toward the remnants of a stone gate or tower. Foraging in and
around the ancient foundations were a few goats and sitting on one of
the stones with his back to me was a boy about my size, the goatherd.

He seemed harmless, but I didn't want any surprises. I was going to leave Star where we were and try to find Cheng somewhere among the ruins, before he found us. I decided to find out who the boy was. He might have heard or seen the movements of someone like Cheng. Another boy, another goatherd, would not intimidate him and any information he gave me would be more than I had at the moment.

I helped Star lie down on her side and covered her up, making sure she was out of the wind and had Mama's glove under her head. She held her belly constantly and grimaced at times, but never made a sound. I knew she would need attention soon, the kind of attention I knew nothing about. I waited for the last rays of light, then walked slowly around and down the hill, toward the goatherd.

I had barely rounded the hill when I felt it, more acutely and more powerfully than I ever had before. The impact literally hit me like a blow to the chest and I changed my gait, slowing to a single measured step at a time. It was the presence of Meq, and more than one, I was sure of it.

I looked down at the goatherd. He hadn't moved. He sat on the stones facing west, but his goats were nowhere in sight. I walked silently, listening with my "ability" and drawing closer. He wore the heavier cloth of the northern tribesmen, with no turban. There was a hood instead, attached to his robe and gathered at the back of his neck. He kept his head averted. I could not see his face. When I got to within ten feet, I stopped and waited.

"Where have you been?" the voice asked.

Suddenly an arm and a hand reached out from the robe. The hand waved me over. There was a small ring on the first finger, a star sapphire mounted in silver. It was the same hand that had come out of the darkness of a carriage long ago in St. Louis and helped me in. It was Sailor.

I sat down on the stone next to him without a word. As he turned to face me, I noticed his high-laced boots under his Arab robe. His star sapphire sparked with color in the starlight. I looked at his face and in his eyes. The same. His "ghost eye" winked at me.

"I think it was Mencius, the Chinese philosopher, who said that a great man is he who does not lose his child's heart," Sailor said. He smiled faintly. I was staring at him, speechless.

"I think he meant to say 'a great-looking man,' " he finished with a broad smile. "Do you not agree, Zianno?" He posed in profile, then laughed out loud.

I was still in a stunned silence.

"I felt your presence as soon as you came around the hill," he said. "I was hoping you would come soon. I have been expecting you for some time and I could have used your help."

That woke me up. "*You* could have used *my* help," I said. "Do you know where I've been?"

"No, that was why I asked."

He acted as if I'd seen him only yesterday. At first I was angry, then just as quickly I realized that time and its passage were different for Sailor and all the old ones. The desert had taught me something, but I still had much to learn from my own kind. Sailor was not alone, however, and I could feel the presence of another. It was strong and familiar. I finally smiled and Sailor and I embraced warmly. As we did, I whispered in his ear, "We're not alone, are we?"

"No," he whispered back. "There is another and she is the reason I knew you would return."

I pulled back and stared at him again. What did he mean? Who did he mean?

"Why are you here, Sailor? I mean here, in this spot, now?"

He paused for only a moment and unconsciously turned the sapphire around his finger. "Because I have found Opari," he said. "And she is here."

"Opari?"

"Yes."

"Why would she be here?"

"To buy a slave. She has done it for years. I have followed her since that night in the Forbidden City. Zeru-Meq discovered her escape and I began following her in Macao. She has always bought slaves, traded in them, but never personally made the transaction. This is a first. I have already seen her here with that baboon of a eunuch who usually buys them for her. They are waiting for the slave now. A girl, I believe, coming from the south with an Arab chief."

I looked back toward the hill where Star was resting. I listened hard for anything out of the ordinary.

"They are waiting for me," I told Sailor. "The Arab chief is dead and I have the girl."

"Then we shall use the girl as a Trojan horse, so to speak, and confront Opari."

"No," I said. "This girl will be no slave for anyone any longer."

Sailor gave me a studied look and his "ghost eye" clouded slightly. "Why?" he asked.

I told him who Star was and the condition she was in. I told him of her connection with Jisil, the Fleur-du-Mal, and the Prophecy. And I told him of the promise I had made to Carolina, a promise I would keep. I told him whoever was trying to buy Star and her unborn baby was either doing it behind the Fleur-du-Mal's back or he was behind it all. He was obsessed with breeding his own assassin.

"The Fleur-du-Mal believes this?" Sailor asked.

"Yes."

"I always thought his aberrance did not affect his intelligence. I was wrong."

I didn't respond. I was struggling to try to make sense of everything. One thing did not make sense at all and went against everything I felt in my heart. Opari. How could she be doing this? Even in that one moment we shared, I learned enough to know that she would never have had anything to do with someone like Cheng. Or would she? The heart is not a predictor of anything to come or a lie detector for what has been. Love can make mistakes. If Opari was doing this, then I would do what I had to do to keep Star free. Star was the truth. All I had to do was follow the lies.

"Where did you see them, Sailor . . . this eunuch and Opari?"

"Come with me. We must be cautious, but there is something odd."

"What?"

"She seems not to be aware of my presence, and yet I can feel hers even now."

I didn't say so, but I felt it as well, strong and catlike, somewhere around the walls of everything else, on the move, watching.

I followed Sailor down the slope only a few hundred yards to one of the old wall lines of ancient Carthage. Sailor had a pack hidden there with several things inside. He pulled something out and handed it to me.

"You left this in China," he said. Then he glanced up at the moon and down to a distant point on the hill. "Take it out and I will tell you where to look."

It was Papa's telescope in the old cylindrical case that Kepa had given to me. The brass was polished and the two pieces locked solidly in place. Sailor told me to look downhill near an abandoned excavation where wooden shacks had been constructed during the dig, then left to the elements. All were missing windows and some had no roof. One had a gas lamp inside that was lit and casting light on a young girl in Arab dress and a sickly, yellow old man. He was not wearing a bowler. He was bald except for a few straggly gray hairs. His face was sunken and his body was hunched over and leaning to the side where he sat. His eyes, the eyes I had seen for so long in my mind, were no longer razor slits. They were swollen, dark, and sagging. It was Cheng. I swung the telescope over to the girl's face and focused in on her eyes. Her green eyes. I had seen the face and the eyes once before.

"Do you see her?" Sailor asked.

"Yes, but that is not Opari."

"What?" He grabbed the telescope and pointed it down the hill, focused in, then backed off. "Explain this to me, Zianno. I do not understand," Sailor said very seriously.

"That is a girl named Zuriaa. Did you not look at her eyes? They are green."

Sailor looked startled, unnerved, like something given had been inexplicably proven wrong. "No," he said. "It was the presence. The presence was always too strong for me to doubt. She has the presence of a very old one. I can feel it now. Do you not, Zianno?"

"Yes," I said. "More than ever."

"Why is that?"

"I don't know." I looked at Sailor and he was deeply troubled. If anything, he knew what the Meq could and could not do. I wondered what he would say about the possibility of a sixth Stone. "I know the old man too," I said. "His name is Cheng and . . . and . . ."

"And what? Why do you hesitate?"

I realized that Sailor had not put the two men together—the one
he had been watching and the one who had murdered his good friend
and brother-in-law.

"He is the same man, Sailor. The same evil whose presence we felt
at the train station in Denver. And he's done a few other things since."

He never changed expression, but Sailor's "ghost eye" began to
swirl with clouds. He was Umla-Meq, the Stone of Memory, and he
felt he had been betrayed by his own memory and instincts. It had
been almost three millennia since he'd actually seen Opari, but how
could he have mistaken her presence? I'm sure he felt he should have
recognized Cheng also, though he'd never actually seen him before in
his life.

Sailor closed the telescope and handed it to me. I was setting it back
in its case when we both heard an agonized, guttural scream from up
the slope and behind the hill. I knew it was Star.

Neither Sailor nor I hesitated. We turned and sprinted through the
darkness, first up a winding trail, then to a shortcut between the brush
and scree.

"You care greatly for this girl, this Star?" Sailor shouted as we
climbed.

"Yes," I shouted back.

"She is like family to you? Like blood?"

"Yes."

I was getting winded and worried. I kept tripping over rocks and I
hadn't heard another sound from over the hill.

"Then you have found family?" Sailor yelled.

"Yes."

"Do you think Eder and Nova have found this family? Do you
think—"

"Yes," I said and grabbed his sleeve to stop. We were near the crest
of the hill and I wanted to go on quietly from there.

We caught our breath, then started a slow crawl to the very top of
the rise, directly above the place I'd left Star. Sailor kept rambling on
about the last time he had been in Carthage, the last time he had
crawled to peer over a ledge in this city of the Phoenicians. It was unlike him to keep talking, especially under the circumstances. He asked
if I knew the story, if I knew what had happened. I was only vaguely

paying attention, but I said yes, Eder had told me. Then he asked if I knew who had been with him, but before I could answer we reached the lip of the rise and leaned over to witness something that neither of us ever expected. It changed my life forever, and Sailor's too, no matter what he would like you to believe.

Below us, my one and only oil lamp was lit and secured in the sand, and protected from the wind by Jisil's saddle, which had been propped on its side. Jisil's horse was nowhere in sight. The saddle was being used as a backboard for Star to lean against and hold on to for support. Star was lying on her back with her head and shoulders leaning forward. She was dripping in sweat. Her eyes were open and glazed. She was staring between her legs at a young girl who was bent over a naked, motionless baby, born premature and not breathing, just like the one I'd seen born in the alley in Saint-Louis. The young girl was performing the same cleansing of the baby's mouth and throat that Emme had. She moved rapidly and with great expertise until she had cleared a passage, then she leaned down and carefully, purposely, breathed life into the child. Within sixty seconds, the baby let out three fierce and tiny cries. The young girl wet her little finger and gently wiped the baby's eyes, nose, and mouth. Then she wrapped the baby in Star's old scarf with the drowning Chinamen and helped her lean back against the saddle, placing the baby in Star's arms. She bunched several blankets around them to keep out all wind and drifting sand, then sat cross-legged in front of them, waiting for the new life to take comfort and take hold.

She never looked up at us, even though she was aware of our presence. I watched with a fascination that only began there and has never since ceased. It was Opari.

I couldn't see her face, but her hair was shining black and still cut straight at the shoulders. She wore loose, white cotton trousers that were tied at the ankles with the straps of her sandals and at the waist with a wide leather belt. Her arms were bare and hung from something resembling a shawl, but heavier and covered in designs I had never seen anywhere.

After several minutes, Star and the baby were breathing evenly, sleeping and possibly even dreaming. Opari turned slowly in the sand and looked directly into my eyes. It felt as though I had been struck in the center of my chest and every atom in my being had been charged with light and grace.

"Hello, my beloved," she said, as simply as life itself. She had an accent, but it only seemed to soften the language, not confuse it. "You must forgive me," she said. "It is berri, no, I mean new to me, the English. I will learn well, in time."

"Yes," I said, but my voice was a whisper, choked and barely audible. I cleared my throat and said, "We have time."

She looked to my left and I followed her eyes as they met Sailor's. They had not spoken in almost thirty centuries.

"You look well, Sailor," she said.

"And you, Opari," Sailor said quietly. Then the answer to the puzzle that had unnerved him spread across his face. "So it was you following me all these years," he said. "And you let me think the other was the presence."

"Yes," Opari said, then waved for us to be quiet and pointed to a curved shelf of rock, exposed to the wind on one side and sheltered on the other. She wanted us away from Star and the baby.

We met her at the low shelf of rock and all huddled close together, out of the wind. Opari glanced at me once and looked over at Sailor to speak. I watched her lips as she formed the words and they moved out of her mouth. I could not believe I was where I was.

"There is no time to hear reasons," she said. "Zuriaa and the eunuch have heard the baby being born. They will, how you say, *ikertu?*"

"Investigate," Sailor answered.

"Yes, they will investigate."

"I will not lose Star and the baby," I told her.

Opari looked at me and reached up with the tips of her fingers and touched my lips. "This is the girl and the child they wait for, is it not?" she asked.

"Yes," I said, and took her fingers in my hand and felt her skin for the first time.

"What is this?" Sailor asked, dumbfounded. "No one told me of this," he said, nodding his head toward my hand holding Opari's fingers. "When did this happen? Is this why you left China, Zianno?"

"No, not quite."

"Then why?"

"It is complicated."

"And who is Zuriaa?" he asked.

"She is Ray's sister."

"Who is Ray?" Opari asked.

"He is my friend. I think Cheng might have—"

"Never mind," Sailor broke in. "Opari is right that we have no time to hear reasons. We must save the girl and her baby. The Fleur-du-Mal and his obsessions have inadvertently created a good thing. I may be able to get us out of Africa tomorrow—all of us. Why all of us are here, now, is no longer important. The fact is, we are Meq. These things occur. Our reasons will be shared later."

"How can you get us out?" I asked.

"You would not believe it."

"From where?" Opari asked.

"From the old harbor," Sailor said, and he looked at Opari, "near where the Topheth stood."

Opari's dark eyes narrowed and her eyebrows bunched together. Though Carolina was blue-eyed and blond, I had seen her do the same thing occasionally at the mention of Georgia's name. Then I remembered the Topheth from Eder's story. It was the place where they had sacrificed slaves and children, where Sailor had held his hands over Opari's eyes to keep her from seeing her sister, his Ameq, slaughtered in front of them. Opari reached up with her other hand and circled Sailor's "ghost eye" with her finger. At first, he flinched and backed off, then closed both eyes and went inside himself, letting her finger-tip follow the outline of his eye and cheek.

"I still see her, Umla-Meq," she said. "But only in my heart."

Sailor opened his eyes and he and Opari looked at each other for several moments, resolving something that had taken almost three thousand years to burn out and blow away.

Then she turned to me and said, "It is because of you—" She paused and smiled. "It is, how you say, *barre egin*?"

"A laughing matter," Sailor answered.

"Yes." She smiled again and said, "I have never said the name out loud. It is because of you—" and she leaned over and kissed my cheek, then my lips. "Zianno," she whispered.

Sailor smiled also. A rarity. "These things occur," he said.

The moment passed as quickly as it came. There were voices coming around the hill and only seconds to get Star and the baby out of harm's way. We all three ran to Star's side and Opari said something to her in the ancient Berber dialect she understood. Star handed her baby weakly over to Opari. Sailor blew out the lamp and I kicked it over on its side along with Jisil's saddle. I wanted it to look as if something violent had taken place, anything to confuse and delay Zuriaa and Cheng.

I threw Mama's glove in my pack and Sailor and I helped Star to her feet. She was able to stand and even walk, though it was slow and the voices were getting nearer. Sailor and I picked her up between us and we all ran for the low shelf and just made it around and down the hill before Zuriaa and Cheng came into view.

Once we had descended a few hundred yards and were sure no one was following, Star wanted to be let down and we walked at her pace the rest of the way. She was pale from loss of blood and trauma of all kinds, but she never spoke out or complained. We followed Sailor through the darkness, winding back and forth down the slope and stopped at the place where he'd left his pack with the telescope and other things. A little farther on we stopped again and he picked up a second pack. From there, not fifty yards away in a grove of pine trees, we detoured and stopped to pick up Opari's things.

"You were that close?" Sailor asked.

"Yes," she said.

Opari rearranged her pack so that the baby could ride inside and strapped the pack on her shoulders. The baby was safe, tight, and warm between her shoulder blades. We started toward the old harbor and she took Star's hand in hers. The way was long and tedious and mostly in the dark. We used no lamps or torches and stayed close to the sound of Sailor's footsteps. Along the way the young mother and the ancient young girl never dropped hands. Our final stop was an old fisherman's shack next to what had once been a deep water port and was now marsh and lagoon leading out to the sea and the breakers of the Mediterranean. There was a long wooden walkway extending from the shack far out past the lagoon into open water. I saw a light in the east, but it was only a glow, a false dawn. The real one was still an hour away. I had plenty of time to think about the next day and that thought gave me a strange realization. I knew the year was 1918, but

I had no idea what month or day. For some reason, I thought about the enigmatic message I'd read on the wall in the cave—*where time is under water, where water is under time.* I realized that I had no idea how I'd got to where I was. Then I realized it didn't matter. When I looked around, I saw Sailor, Opari, Star, and her baby. Then I remembered that I didn't even know if Star's baby was a boy or a girl and realized that didn't matter either. It was the living who mattered.

Sailor stayed busy checking the walkway for missing planks and broken boards. Opari was looking after Star and the baby. She spoke to her softly in that old dialect and at one point Star's eyes opened wide in a kind of shock, then accepted something. She turned her head to the side and calmly let Opari remove the rings and chains in her nose and ears. In a few minutes, I saw only the blond hair, the blue eyes, and the freckles. She looked down at the baby in her arms and smiled for the first time, then turned back to Opari. I could have sworn it was Carolina.

Just then, I heard the hooves of horses. Only seconds later, Opari heard them too, and outside the shack I saw Sailor looking up the rutted road that led back to the ruins.

I glanced at Opari. "Is it them?" I asked.

"Yes," she said. "I would know Zuriaa's presence from years away, and easily when she is filled with this much, how you say, *gorroto*?"

"Hate," Sailor answered as he raced in from the walkway.

"Yes," Opari said. "She is hating."

What happened next, happened quickly. Opari made sure Star and the baby were safe and out of sight, then stood in the open doorway of the shack and told Sailor and me to stand behind her and wait. In moments, two horses approached down a short rise between the remnants of a gate and came to a halt ten feet from the shack. I saw the faces of the riders in the first few rays of real dawn. One was pathetic, paralyzed, sagging, dying, and empty. It was Cheng. The other wore no veil, looked exactly like Ray, and burned with fury behind her green eyes—Zuriaa.

She yelled something at Opari in Chinese. I had no idea what she was saying, but I could tell she was offended at Opari's presence, as if Opari had no business being there. Opari remained calm and told her to speak in English.

"English?" Zuriaa shouted.

"Yes."

"Why English?" she asked again and dropped her voice slightly, leaning forward in her saddle and finding me standing behind Opari.

"You," she said, staring at me blankly.

Opari took a step forward. "You lied to me, Zuriaa."

"No, I did not."

"Yes, you said you would leave alone this business . . . this selling of the children."

Zuriaa paused a moment, then she spat out the words, "I was made to do it."

"By whom?"

"You know the one, the only one who would."

"The Fleur-du-Mal?"

"Oui."

Opari stood a moment in silence, then turned and glanced at me. "Why does he want this child, Zuriaa?" she asked over her shoulder.

"I do not know."

I stepped forward next to Opari in the doorway. "But I do," I said, "and you can tell him this will not happen."

"I . . . I cannot do that," she stammered. She had trouble speaking to me, then I realized she thought I must be the only one who knew who she really was.

"You will tell him that," I said. And you will tell him who told you to tell him that."

"Where is he, Zuriaa?" Opari asked. "Where is the Fleur-du-Mal now?"

Zuriaa glanced at Cheng, who was having trouble staying in the saddle, then together they spurred their horses to make a charge at the doorway. In the same instant their heels struck the horses, Opari and Sailor reached for the Stone that each wore around their necks, and held them out, tight in their fists, at arm's length toward the horses. The horses snorted and stumbled, refusing to go forward, as if they sensed a cliff and a chasm and had the good sense to go no farther.

Opari and Sailor had reacted instinctively. I'm not sure at the time if they knew what they were doing or if it was going to succeed. But it did and it made me think of the loss of the last true gift my papa had given me—the Stone—and I remembered the one who had taken it.

"Zuriaa," I shouted. "Does Opari know about the gems that Cheng stole from the Stones of Geaxi and me?"

"What?" Opari turned and asked.

"And that Baju was shot and killed by Cheng?"

"What?" Opari and Sailor said in unison.

"And do you know, Zuriaa, that Cheng stole the Stone from me in Senegal? . . . The same place he probably sold Ray to a German, like a slave."

"What?" Zuriaa shouted from her horse.

She whirled in one motion and threw the gems that she kept in her pocket into the air in the direction of Opari and the doorway. She spurred her horse and raced by Cheng, stabbing him in the heart as she passed. I never saw her reach for the stiletto, but it hung and dangled from Cheng's chest before he and the knife fell together and the knife was dislodged, along with something else that rolled out from under him like an ugly black egg—the Stone.

Opari bent down to pick up the gems. I watched Zuriaa disappear up the rise and back through the ruins, then I walked out to where Cheng lay dead and picked up the Stone. I tossed it to Sailor, who had to hold one hand up against the rising sun to catch it. Opari watched the black thing fly through the air and couldn't believe it.

"These things occur," Sailor shouted to me.

"Are you going to be saying that now, I mean, from now on?" I asked.

"Many times," he said. "Many times."

Then we all heard a strange sound that was growing louder by the second, coming in from the open sea toward the lagoon. A sound that made no sense to me, the sound of engines whining at full throttle over water.

Sailor said, "Look."

I looked and what I saw came out of a dream, but was real. My dreams could never have been that rich. I saw two biplanes outfitted as seaplanes with wooden skids hanging underneath, the kind I had seen a photograph of in the desert. They were at a height of no more than two hundred feet over the water, approaching and descending.

Sailor said, "Come on."

I grabbed all the packs and Opari helped Star and the baby. We followed Sailor out to the end of the walkway where the two seaplanes were landing in the lagoon. The big engines roared and the two planes fishtailed in the water as they slowed down and got their bearings. Then they pulled up one behind the other alongside the walkway.

When I tried to see the pilot of the leading plane, at first there seemed to be no one in the cockpit, then someone small leaped out and onto the walkway. She had short dark hair under a leather cap, which she yanked off with one hand. With the other hand, she removed her scarf and goggles. It was Geaxi.

"Hello, young Zezen," she said. "I did not expect to see you here."

"Well, these things occur, Geaxi," I said. "Where did you learn to fly?"

"Canada, actually," she said without hesitation. "But tell me, why are you here? Sailor said it would only be himself and possibly Opari."

"He was right," I said. "Only he had the wrong Opari in mind."

"What?" Geaxi asked.

"Never mind," Sailor interrupted.

Geaxi pulled her beret out of a vest and set it on her head, looking around for someone until she found her.

"You must be Opari," she said and they exchanged a long look loaded with information.

"Yes, I am Opari."

"You have been missing."

"Yes, but no longer."

Opari took my hand in hers and held it against her chest, near to where her heart beat underneath.

Geaxi looked at us both and smiled. "I see," she said, "but that still does not explain—"

"Never mind," Sailor said. "We will have time for this later. Time is not our problem. I need to know if we have too much weight for the planes to take off."

"That should not be a problem," Geaxi said, "but I will ask Willie."

She waved over the second pilot. He was a tall man, about thirty years old with a boyish face. He wore a British uniform, but everything was slightly unbuttoned or fitted him oddly. He had sandy hair and, except for a broken nose, a handsome face. He seemed completely at ease with Geaxi and was not startled to see other Meq around. There was something vaguely familiar about him.

As he came close, Geaxi started laughing.

"What's so funny?" I asked.

"I have just remembered something," Geaxi said, and with a deep bow and a wave of her arm, she introduced him. "Willie Croft, I would like you to meet my good friend, the Buddha, also known as Zianno Zezen."

Then the name and the face came together and rang a bell. He was the kid outside the train in China, the one Geaxi told I was the Buddha and he had believed it. The recognition was simultaneous and the tall man dropped his face, almost embarrassed.

"Hello, Zianno," he said.

"Hello, Willie, but you can call me Z."

"Well, then, hello, Z."

"We've got a weak and wounded mother and a newborn baby, Willie. Will it be too rough for them?"

"No, I shouldn't think so, just a bit long is all."

"Good. How did you hook up with Geaxi?"

"Well, it's a long story," he said. "Would you want to hear it now?"

"No," I said. "I don't think so."

"Do we have too much weight?" Sailor asked.

"No," Willie said. "We'll make it."

"Where are we going?" I asked Sailor.

"Tripoli, then Alexandria and on to England by ship, if it's safe."

Geaxi took off her beret and slipped her leather cap back on. She fastened her goggles and wrapped her scarf around her neck. "Who flies with me?" she asked.

Opari sat in the other plane behind Willie Croft, keeping Star and her baby warm and calm. I looked at her once as we took off and every other minute after we were in the air. The two planes stayed close and climbed to almost a thousand feet. Geaxi seemed born to fly and handled the experimental plane with ease. For a moment, I thought about Ray and how much he would have loved to be with us. In my heart,

I resolved to find him and free him. We headed south, hugging the coastline, then east into and under the sun as it rose in the sky.

Eventually, we flew over a strip of white sand that was scattered with the ruins of an old city. Broken stones and columns littered the area. The only structure I could identify was the remains of a Roman amphitheater. In the center, standing alone, was a small figure who looked up as we flew over. Even from a thousand feet, I could see the green ribbon and the white teeth.

"What is that place?" I yelled at Sailor. We were sitting close, but the noise of the engine and the wind made it difficult to hear.

"Sabratha," Sailor yelled back. "The Fleur-du-Mal was born there."

I leaned forward and tapped Geaxi on the shoulder, pointing down at the ruins and the figure standing among them. Geaxi recognized him and couldn't resist circling and waggling her wings. After one full circle, the figure knew who it was above him and what it meant. It was the first time I had seen his brilliant teeth bared in a grimace and not a smile.

We flew on toward Tripoli and I forgot about the Fleur-du-Mal within minutes. Flying does that. The Mediterranean seemed as blue as Sailor's star sapphire and the sky was bright and light. I looked over at Opari in the other plane and she was staring back, silently mouthing the first word she had ever spoken to me . . . "beloved."

I turned to Sailor and yelled, "By the way, do you know what day it is?"

"Yes," he yelled back. "It is your birthday."

He was trying to put on his goggles and having trouble with it. He finally tossed them over the side and let the wind hit him full face.

"That can't be true," I said. Then I looked over at him and whether he was laughing or crying from the wind, I couldn't tell, but his eyes were full of tears.

"It is not true," he said. "It just sounded good."

Then we both started laughing and he added, "I have no idea what day it is."

13

PAR

(LAUGH)

Think of it like the two miners who were trapped and realized, once the dust had settled, there was no hope of escape. After countless confessions and a thousand tales of pointless regret, they decided instead to tell each other jokes until the very end . . . just to see who got the last laugh. The two miners were never found, but the others, the saved ones, remembered the echoes of that laughter for the rest of their lives. They all agreed it was the most genuine and contagious laughter they had ever heard.

We stopped five times on our flight to Alexandria—three times for fuel and twice for Opari to look after Star and the baby. Opari said the bullet wound was healing and the loss of blood was a concern, but both mother and son were doing well under the circumstances.

"Son?" I asked.

"Yes," she said, then looked at me strangely. "Did you not know?"

"No!"

She laughed out loud and shook her head, then kissed me while she was still laughing. It was a rich, full laugh—not a giggle—and I laughed with her. I couldn't help it even though I was the source of the joke. She was beautiful. Her dark eyes sparkled and danced. Her mouth opened and I almost wanted to count her teeth, they were so white and perfectly shaped. The sound of her laugh was free and spontaneous and I was jealous of all the others before me who had heard it.

Much later, Opari would tell me it was the first time she had laughed in over a thousand years.

Sailor took charge as I expected and I was grateful for it. He had a plan, which he and Geaxi had already set in motion, and he merely fitted Star, the baby, and me into it. It was unclear what he had in mind, but Sailor was the one who made sure Star got immediate medical attention after we arrived, not Opari or Geaxi. He told Willie Croft where to take her in Alexandria and even held the baby while she was helped onto a stretcher. Star could have made the trip under her own steam, but Sailor insisted on taking every precaution. I had never known him to put the welfare of the Giza before that of the Meq. It seemed very unusual, and even more strange, it seemed genuine.

As he was handing the baby back to Star, the baby's hands found Sailor's single braid behind his ear, pulling Sailor's head down and finally grasping in his little palm the piece of lapis lazuli that hung from the bottom of the braid. Without hesitating, Sailor untied the lapis lazuli and Star was carried away with the baby still holding the gem tight in his tiny hands. Star looked back at Sailor and smiled. Sailor waved. I had never seen him wave before to anyone, anywhere. I had no idea how long he had worn the lapis lazuli. I knew it meant something unique to him, and yet he had given it away in a moment to the child of a Giza, a complete stranger. While he was waving, I noticed that even Geaxi seemed to look twice. Perhaps it was because he had finally found Opari and their differences had been settled. Or it could have had something to do with his questions about Eder, Nova, and their relationship with Carolina. Whatever his reasons, the change was a dramatic surprise to everyone. As for me, I was so happy I was useless.

We had made our final landing a few miles west of Alexandria in a makeshift safe harbor, completely isolated and obviously not part of a British base. A man in uniform, which he wore as casually as Willie, helped tie the two planes to a dock covered with a tin roof and palm fronds on top of that. The man seemed as unconcerned about being around the Meq as did Willie. It was sunset. The air was cool and the light was golden.

Everything seemed slightly surreal. The landscape was barren and the point at which it met the sea was unremarkable, but I felt as if we had landed in paradise. As long as Opari was there, I was sure of it. I

watched her as if she was in slow motion. I watched her help Star and
the baby out of the plane, the way no movement was wasted and no
touch in a place of pain or discomfort to Star. After Sailor took charge
and Star and the baby had left with Willie and the other man, I watched
her gather our things and help Geaxi with the planes. I watched her
hands. I watched the way she knelt and stood up, the way she turned
and smiled. I watched everything. Opari—my Ameq. I thought of
Unai and Usoa and wondered how they could have waited so many
centuries to cross in the Zeharkatu. As I watched Opari, I could not
conceive of it. Now that she was with me, that we were free and together, the Itxaron—the Wait—seemed absurd and unnecessary. Opari
was a rich and complex woman living in a girl's body. I thought I
knew everything about living in a boy's body, but I was learning something by the moment that neither Papa nor Sailor nor anyone else had
ever had a chance to tell me about being Meq, being male, and being
in love. It was a feeling as old as time, but brand-new to me.

"She has become more than a ghost, no?"

I turned as if I'd been caught stealing. It was Sailor. He had been
watching me watch Opari. His "ghost eye" actually winked at me.

Embarrassed at first, I relaxed, remembering his own connection
with Opari. "Yes," I said, then stammered, "she is . . . she has . . ."

"Her sister was equally as lovely," he said. He turned and watched
Opari himself, and for a brief moment, I knew he was seeing Deza,
then he turned back to me. His "ghost eye" narrowed and focused.
He twirled the star sapphire on his finger and spoke in a low monotone. "You will, you must, become accustomed to this feeling, Zianno. There is so much still to be done. I will tell you more later, but
remember, you are Meq, you are the Stone of Dreams. We will need
you. You must dredge your dreams, conscious and unconscious, good
and bad. In the muck of an ancient nightmare, you may find a diamond. In the bright blue of an imagined summer day, there may be a
hornet you ignored. It would be your mistake to miss either through
lack of curiosity."

"What about Opari?" I asked. "Have you spoken to her?"

"No, but she must do the same. She must stay the same. She is the
Stone of Blood. I am certain she thought of this before . . . before she
found us."

"Aha!" I said. "So you finally admit someone found you and not the other way around."

Sailor laughed once, but that was his only response.

Darkness came quickly and a breeze picked up. It was warm compared to the night air in the deep desert, but still cool and it blew the salt air in from the Mediterranean. Geaxi led us to a low stone building with a newly rebuilt roof and most of one wall missing. She said the British had used a nearby site for target practice two years earlier. A stray shell had caught the side of the building. I was amazed at the size of the hole and couldn't imagine the weapon that had produced it. Geaxi circled the one large room inside, lighting kerosene lamps along the way. There were only two windows at the top of one wall and none of the lamps was beneath them. There seemed to be no electricity and no running water. Several straw mats covered the floor and a few personal items lay around two of them. Another was off by itself, clean and sparse, with two blankets neatly folded on top and two black ballet slippers at one end. By looking at it, there was no way to tell if the occupant had been there a day, a year, or ten years. I smiled to myself at the almost invisible address of Geaxi. I turned to speak to her, but she and Opari were busy preparing a kind of nursery for Star and her baby. I found Sailor instead.

"What is this place?" I asked.

He looked around all four sides of the large room and up at the windows. His eyes moved to the roof, which was temporary at best, then to the blown-out hole in the wall facing away from the sea. He flared his nostrils and took a deep breath of the breeze that filled the room with the fresh and ancient scent of the Mediterranean. He closed his eyes a moment and stood still, holding the air in his lungs. Then gently, slowly, he let it slip through his mouth and lips and over his tongue, tasting it as it left his body. He knelt and felt the stones in the floor, tracing their outlines with the tips of his fingers.

"The Greeks built the floor," he said without looking up. "But not the Greeks who lived down the coast, the ones who built the Lighthouse and the Great Library. These Greeks sailed in darkness and kept no books. These Greeks traded with the last of the Phoenicians." He glanced up at me and his "ghost eye" was filled with clouds. "It was here," he said, then paused. "It was here where the trades were made."

Out of the corner of my eye, I noticed Geaxi and Opari had stopped what they were doing and were watching us.

"Trades in what?" I asked.

"Bones," he said. "The bones of the Meq who were slaughtered in their temples."

I turned to look at Opari and both she and Geaxi were now staring at me. Just as the question "why" was on my lips, Opari shook her head once and I understood. The "why" was irrelevant; it was the "where" that haunted this place for Sailor. I understood that we were probably standing on the floor in the room where Deza's bones had been bought and sold, traded among the Giza like so many pieces of silver. Looking across the room into Opari's living eyes, I wondered how many places were like this for him, how many times he ran into a past that haunted him, a past in which he was still a living presence.

"Young Willie Croft owns it now," Geaxi said, then she started toward us. "Nay, I should say the Daphne Croft Foundation owns it in the proper and legal sense." Her movements were liquid, graceful, almost weightless, and her voice brought Sailor out of the past.

"Yes," he said, rising to his feet and breathing in deeply once more, "yes, that is correct. This place is merely a stage, Zianno. One of many we are acquiring."

"We?" I asked.

Suddenly Geaxi burst into laughter. She was standing next to Sailor with her hands on her hips. She was wearing boots, not her ballet slippers, but she went into a pirouette, laughing hysterically and raising her arms, waving her beret like a drunken ballerina. Opari walked over and took my hand, smiling, but also asking me with her eyes what was going on. I had no idea. I looked at Sailor and he was staring at Geaxi, just as mystified.

"Is something funny?" he asked.

She stopped turning, but still laughing she said, "You must admit it is a bit absurd, Sailor."

"What is absurd?"

"The Meq acquiring property."

Opari and I looked at each other, both in the dark about everything. Sailor said, "It is time to tell our stories. There is much to clarify."

Geaxi nodded, but she was still smiling. "I will get the bread and

cheese and those wonderful olives and meet you there." She turned
and walked away, but laughed once more to herself. Over her shoulder
she added, "And boil some water for tea. This may be a long evening."

Opari and I looked at Sailor. He was watching Geaxi's back, shaking
his head. There was a trace of a smile on his face, then it disappeared.

"Follow me," he said. His "ghost eye" was clear and he spoke in an
even voice.

"Where are we going?" I asked. "I thought we were here."

"Under the sea," he said. "Or at least under where it was and where
it shall be. That was one of the pass phrases used by the Greeks. Clever
people, the Greeks, even their pirates, but riddled with riddles."

Opari squeezed my hand. "I know of this place from Zeru-Meq,"
she said.

"Zeru-Meq?" Sailor asked and both eyebrows arched high on his
head, then relaxed. "I should have guessed as much," he said, nodding
to himself.

"Yes," she went on, "I believe he called it 'The Shadow in the Shallows.' "

"He would know," Sailor said, then motioned for us to follow. "We
must make haste before the others return. Willie is not aware of where
I am taking you. No Giza is."

We left the way we had entered and then veered sharply to the
west, away from the path leading to the dock. We walked in a line and
followed Sailor through rock and brush and sand in a complicated
zigzag pattern that eventually ended in a tiny spit of sand that would
have been underwater had it been high tide. If it was a trail we had
taken, only Sailor knew it.

In moments, Geaxi appeared from behind us, dressed in black and
carrying a large candle in one hand and a netted sack stuffed with food
in the other. I never heard her approach. She was as silent as a shadow
come to life. Overhead there was only starlight. The moon was hidden behind a low bank of clouds. I glanced at Opari and then turned
to Sailor.

"What now?" I asked.

"Look out to sea," he said. "Not directly in front of you, but
obliquely. Watch the water. Watch the light on the water. Try to look
for—" He paused and smiled at Opari. "A Shadow in the Shallows."

I turned and faced north, trying to see everything and nothing. The Mediterranean stretched into darkness, but suddenly, not a hundred yards out, I caught the outline of a form, a shadow darker than the sea around it and rectangular. It was just under the surface.

"Now you have it," Geaxi said and splashed out in the water, stepping high and holding the candle and cache of food above her head. In seconds, she was standing on one end of the shadow, which caused the other end to rise up like a seesaw and Geaxi was underwater up to her chest.

The shadow was no shadow at all, but a single slab of stone, balanced and hinged, accessible only at low tide and weighted so that someone as light and small as Geaxi could easily make it move just by stepping on top of one end.

"Come!" she shouted. "Come quickly!"

Sailor walked into the water without a word. Opari and I glanced at each other and followed. When we got to the slab of stone, I could see that under the raised end there was actually an opening, a kind of trapdoor. The shallow water of low tide was disappearing down the opening in a descending spiral. Geaxi stepped off the stone and lit the candle with a match she had tucked behind her ear. In the flickering light, I could see steps, also descending in a spiral and a slightly diagonal direction.

"The water only follows the spiral for two fathoms," Geaxi said. "Watch your step and stay close," she added, then walked into the darkness under the stone and beneath the sea.

The light from the candle was weak and Opari held my hand as we tried to keep pace with Geaxi. Sailor pointed out niches in the walls that had once held oil lamps. I asked him who had carved the steps and niches and he waved us on, remaining silent. I felt as though we were winding our way down and through the empty shell of a giant nautilus, the mollusk I had first seen in the Indian Ocean.

After twenty steps or so, the passage began to level out and the water that had been descending with us gathered and swirled in a pool. The carved steps wound around the pool and beyond, ascending slightly. The pool served as a drain and collection point for another passage whose opening was triggered by the weight and volume of the water above it. That passage, Sailor said, connected with another, then another, and so on until all water was returned to the Mediterranean. Gravity determined its course, but I still had no idea where ours was leading.

"We are nearly there," Sailor said, reading my eyes.

Geaxi had stopped and was waiting for us only a few more steps up the incline. She was standing where the steps ended and the passage became completely level. The carved stone gave way to sand underfoot—old sand, dry and crystalline, reflecting the candlelight and leading to something ahead in the dark. The entrance to the corridor had been enlarged and bordered with huge, perfectly beveled, square-cut stones.

"The Greeks did this," Sailor said and he ran his fingers along the edge of one of the stones. "They discovered this place and thought it too small, so they carved away, thinking as always it was somehow meant for them. I am afraid they were mistaken. It was here long before they brought their chisels. Still, one must admire their attention to detail."

Geaxi led us on. Arcane signs and symbols appeared on the walls. Animals and birds and fish, real and imaginary, overlapped and joined, all drawn at different times and ages. A single Greek word was engraved over one of the drawings, an outline of a hand exactly my size. The word was "KTEMAESAEI." I pointed it out to Sailor.

"What does it mean?" I asked.

Without slowing down or glancing back, he laughed bitterly and said, "A possession forever."

Suddenly Geaxi's candle flared and I realized we had reached the end of the corridor and entered a higher, broader chamber. There was no other entrance or exit. It was a room, an oval room, and it was instantly familiar.

In the candlelight, I saw two wooden planks, roughly sawn and set on stones in the center of the room as a kind of table. Around the planks, resting on the sand, there were several mats like the ones in the bombed-out building above. Geaxi placed the candle on one of the planks and emptied the bread, cheese, olives, and what appeared to be two wineskins on the other plank. She smiled and removed her beret with one hand, waving it over the table, as if welcoming us to a feast. But it was Sailor who spoke first.

"Sit down," he said. "And let us speak of the Meq."

We sat down facing each other, all of us cross-legged on the mats. Geaxi began to split the bread and reached into her vest for a knife to slice the cheese. Opari and I held each other's hands. Behind Sailor, in the background at the deep end of the oval room, I caught a glimpse of a black-stained, indented circle in the stone wall. There were shadows of two small handprints on either side. There was something written in the stone in a circle around the circle.

"This—this place," Sailor began and he raised his forefinger and traced the circumference of the room in the air. His star sapphire shot back brilliant blues and greens as it passed through the candlelight. "This place is Meq. It is very old, from before the time of 'Those-Who-Fled,' possibly and probably from before the 'Time of Ice.' " He paused and glanced at Geaxi, then stared hard at Opari and me. "We are not sure of its purpose. We . . . we speculated that this place and others like it will lead us to the next Remembering. The Gogorati." He stopped again and made sure he had Opari's attention. "This was why we searched for you, Opari. This place is reason enough for proof that the Gogorati is not a myth. It will occur . . . no matter what Zeru-Meq believes. And since this place does exist, we must unite. Those who carry the Stone must be of one mind if we are to solve the riddle that is here, now, in this place. All five Stones are required at the Remembering. All five Stones will be required even to find it."

"I am here because of Zianno," Opari said softly. "But my heart has . . . *esnatu?*"

"Awakened," Geaxi translated and leaned over, offering us both an olive.

"Yes, awakened," Opari said, then she looked each of us in the eyes, ending with Sailor. "I have been sleeping, Umla-Meq. You must forgive me. Now, tell me of your riddle."

"I wish I could," Sailor said. "But, alas, we cannot read it, let alone determine its meaning."

"Who is 'we'?" I asked. "You mean Geaxi?"

"No. Another. The one who found this place long ago and two others like it in all the years since. He knows more about these oval rooms than any other."

"Who is he?" Opari asked.

Sailor smiled and almost laughed under his breath. "He has used the name 'Mowsel' for centuries, but his *deitura* is Trumoi-Meq."

"He lives?"

"Yes," Sailor said. "He lives."

"Ayii," Opari said, then she made a high-pitched trilling sound with her tongue against her teeth, a sound I had only heard made by women in the deep desert. I pressed her hand and she glanced at me, then turned to Sailor and spoke in her softest voice. "He was a ghost, a myth to us as children. We were never thinking he was real. Can this be true?"

"Yes, but I see him rarely," Sailor said. "And speak to him only when necessary. He found me almost two thousand years ago."

"To help you find Opari?" I asked.

"No. That was incidental to him. He has always sought something else, something a bit more difficult to find."

"What?"

"Who we are. The answer to the question all of us carry and never ask—why are we here? Why do the Meq exist at all? But even he cannot read the old script. He can read an altered version and even write in a later, transitional script, but not the old one—the original. No one can."

"Like the one behind you?" I asked. "In the circle around the dark circle in the wall?"

Opari looked at me while Sailor and Geaxi stared blankly at each other, then turned to me. It was Sailor who said, "Yes, exactly like that."

I walked to the far end of the room and knelt in the sand in front of the dark, indented circle. I put my two hands on the wall and let my palms and outspread fingers press into the spaces that fitted them perfectly, that were made by someone long, long ago. Someone with hands exactly my size, exactly *our* size. Then I ran one of my fingers around the circle and over the script. Without turning away, I said, "I can read it."

A good joke is always difficult to predict, but somehow easy to follow. It is the same with the truth. As I was kneeling in the sand, I thought back to the cold day in St. Louis when Ray had held Papa's baseball and drawn a circle within a circle on the frozen glass of my bedroom window at Mrs. Bennings's House. I remembered how I felt when he told me what it was to be Meq. I don't know how my eyes

looked to Ray, but as I turned and looked at Sailor, Geaxi, and even
Opari, I saw in their eyes a mirror image of how I had felt watching
Ray draw his circles on the glass and listening to his simple, powerful
truth.

I motioned for Sailor to come and kneel next to me. I took his
hand and the finger with the star sapphire and translated for him as I
traced the characters and lines in the script with his finger. It read as
follows:

Geaxi picked up the candle and the light in the oval room danced
and shifted. She and Opari walked over in silence and dropped to their
knees alongside Sailor and me. I let go of Sailor's hand and he continued to trace and retrace his finger over the old writing. I watched
him closely. Over and over, he said the words to himself, moving his
lips without speaking. I suddenly realized that in the heart and mind
of an old one like Sailor, I had given him a gift as great and simple as
the Meq could receive—connection with the past and hope for the
future.

I told him of the other room I had found in the barren waste of the
Tassili range and the script I had discovered there, along with the lines
written by Trumoi-Meq.

"Yes," he said, almost with a smile. "But you can read both. He
cannot."

"These things occur," I said, but no one laughed. I looked at Sailor
and he was staring back with an expression in his eyes I had never seen
before. A look a prisoner might have after a sudden and unexpected release. Slowly, another realization dawned. What I had done was more
than a gift—I had unlocked the door to his lifelong obsession, an
"ability" far more significant than hyper-hearing, quickness, or silence.
I could *read* the writing. I could do what no other Meq had ever done.

Opari took both my hands in hers. She was frowning and leaning forward to look at Sailor. "What does this mean?" she asked. "That Zianno is the one? That Zianno has the Gift?"

Sailor stared back. "It is time," he whispered. "No one knew it would be Zianno. We might have hoped or wondered, but no one knew." He paused and glanced at Geaxi. "We have less than a hundred years to find the Egongela, the Living Room, and prepare for the Gogorati. I long suspected someone would come in time, someone from among us I would least expect. Alas, someone comes and even he is unaware of the Gift he possesses. He reads the writing without study or preparation. It comes to him. He comes to us, the youngest child among the Children, and behold, it is Zianno."

Geaxi took off her beret and tossed it to me. I caught it with one hand. "You have done well, Zianno," she said. "Now that we know what it says, the real work begins. We must try and find out what this gibberish means."

We all turned to the wall and gazed at the stained circle and the two handprints on either side. Geaxi had stuck the candle in the sand and it shifted suddenly, spilling melted wax over one side and snuffing out the flame.

"Everything has changed," Sailor said and we sat very still in the silence and the dark. Over our heads, beyond the stone walls of the oval room, I knew there was a vast sea teeming with life, and beyond that, an even vaster sea of sky teeming with stars. Under all of that, inside all of that, I could hear all our hearts beating.

"Light the candle again," I said. "Let's tell our stories."

There is a unique synergism that takes place when the Meq share their stories. There is little reference to time in the usual sense, only in terms of its relevance to an action and whether that action is positive or negative in its completion, no matter how long it takes to complete it. We assume survival. The connection and exchange is as discrete as the blood in our veins. The stories are shared like bread and wine, sweetly tasted and swallowed. Sorrow and joy are tossed like grapes across the table. One tale becomes many and many intertwine. Time becomes a passenger, a paying customer, someone along for the ride through the long, tangled here and now. This is our wonderful and terrible essence. This is our strength.

Sailor said, "Then you begin, Zianno."

So I began and I covered it all, starting with Li Lien-ying handing me Carolina's letter in the Forbidden City. From St. Louis to New Orleans to Africa, from Star's abduction to Ray's abduction, through ports, places, facts, faces, reasons, hunches, yearnings, visions, dreams, and obsessions—I took them with me. When I got to Emme and PoPo and the Dogon myths and their secret, singular knowledge of the Meq, Geaxi and Opari leaned forward like little girls at camp, eager for the next word. Sailor sat in silence, unmoving, and twisted the star sapphire on his forefinger. I told them of the Prophecy and the reason behind the Fleur-du-Mal's obsession with Star, and Geaxi laughed out loud, while Opari seemed to withdraw and reflect on something deeply personal.

"He is beyond mad," Geaxi said.

"Yes," Sailor responded suddenly. "But not beyond dangerous."

It was then that I asked Sailor about the star sapphire in his ring and the blue diamond that Usoa wore in her ear. I told him the story of the Ancient Pearl that PoPo had told me, how it had originally come from a Stone of the Meq. I told him what the Fleur-du-Mal believed, that they all came from a sixth Stone, and I asked him if it was true. All eyes turned to Sailor and he paused before he spoke.

"No one knows," he said. Then he laughed bitterly to himself. "It is an odd irony. Geaxi does not believe it, nor Unai or Usoa. Trumoi-Meq does not and Eder does not." He paused again and looked directly at me, then continued. "Your mother and father never believed it, never thought it possible. The only one other than the Fleur-du-Mal who believes this is so . . . is myself." He laughed again. "Quite an irony, no? It is the only thing on earth, apart from being Meq, that I have in common with the Fleur-du-Mal."

I let his words sink in and glanced into the eyes of Geaxi and Opari. Nothing in their dark eyes and beautiful, innocent faces would tell a stranger anything about the mysteries within.

"What would it mean?" I asked. "If there was a sixth Stone?"

"There have been theories," he said, then shook his head slowly. "But no one knows."

I noticed when Sailor shook his head that the braid behind his ear was coming loose at the end and I remembered the lapis lazuli.

"Why did you give Star's baby the blue gem?" I asked him. "If you knew it was . . . if you believed it came from the sixth Stone?"

"Yes, Sailor," Opari said. She squeezed my hand and leaned in closer. "I was wondering this also."

"Because she is in this now. She and her child—" He paused and stared at me. "And Carolina and Nicholas and Jack, their son. And Owen Bramley. All of them. What is mine is theirs and theirs is . . . ours for sharing."

"What? You can't be serious," I said. "Have we not caused that family enough grief? I have thought about this and I think once we have safely returned Star and her baby to Carolina, we should get out of their lives forever—and take care of our own—take care of the Fleur-du-Mal!"

"You can blame it on Solomon, if you like," Geaxi said suddenly.

"Who?" I snapped. I stared at her and felt blood rushing to my face in anger. "What does that mean?"

"Calm down, Zianno," Sailor said. "Geaxi meant nothing derogatory in her remark. In fact, it is a compliment. We can *blame* Solomon for having the foresight to know what we would need to survive in the twentieth century. There is much above us, above this oval room, that has changed since you have been in Africa. Solomon saw it coming and thought of what we would need—what *you* would need—to live on and thrive. Owen Bramley has made Solomon's 'vision' a reality."

He stopped and watched me, his "ghost eye" swirling gently. "Perhaps I should explain," he said.

"Yes, perhaps," I said as sharply as I could, but I'd lost my bite. I turned and looked at Opari. She was holding back a smile and I suddenly felt silly.

"No—perhaps I should explain," Geaxi broke in. She picked up her beret and walked toward the center of the oval room. She turned to me. "I was mistaken to mention Solomon so casually, Zianno. It was careless. I know what he meant to you, nay, I should say *means* to you. I regret that I never knew him. Giza with real 'vision' are as rare as ourselves."

I was curious now. I wondered what Solomon could have seen

coming that Sailor had not. Even in death, my old partner loved surprising me. "Tell me what Solomon 'saw,' " I said.

"A network," Sailor interrupted. "A system of stations, places like this one, some remote and some anything but remote. 'Bases,' in Solomon's words."

"I thought you said no Giza knew of this place."

"They do not, at least not what is underground—only what is above." Sailor was excited. I could hear it in his voice. He looked at me and laughed out loud.

"What's so funny?" I asked.

"Nothing. I suppose it must be the irony. Solomon's words were so simple, yet so timely. Now that we know you are able to read the old writing—"

"What words? You keep saying Solomon's words."

Sailor glanced at Geaxi and Opari and dropped his smile. "He saw two things you and the rest of us will need—communications and safe passage. He saw a home base with satellite bases throughout the world, run by Giza, owned by Giza, and protected from the prying eyes and ears of Giza less enlightened than himself. He called it 'the Diamond.' A reference, I believe, to your game of baseball." Sailor paused a moment, then added, "It was in his will, Zianno. A codicil, all prepared and ready for Owen Bramley to set in motion. Owen Bramley himself will have to tell you how it all fits together. At this point, I am afraid he knows more about how it will work than I, but—" He paused again, breathing in slowly and gathering himself, then continued. "The old man cared about you very deeply, Zianno, enough to know you could not survive on your own and keep going. You, we, us—the Meq need a strategy to survive, to last in this world, this 'game' Solomon called it, a 'game' with no time limit. He even added a prophecy, a warning, of sorts. He said the Children of the Mountains will be sought more than ever before because of man's fear and confusion with himself and his own mortality. Soon, communication and safe passage will be the only protection from man's ravenous pursuit of the miraculous, which he already sees in himself, but cannot prove. His fear is great. His hunt will be relentless. The Children of the Mountains will be his prey and proof."

"Solomon said that?" I asked.

"Yes, well . . . something like that."

"Who is Solomon?" It was Opari. Her voice was soft and her eyes looked into mine. I stared back. The question was innocent enough, but the answer was not.

Inside, in an instant, I felt as if I had missed a step or a beat in some unseen rhythm. A simple question, an honest question that anyone might have asked on any given day and I would have answered—splat!—suddenly became unanswerable and lay like a stone in a still pond. "Who is Solomon?" I saw the ripples, not the stone. I heard Solomon's voice, something among his last words, "I will leave a trail. Will you be able to find it, Zianno?" *Will you be able to find it, Zianno?* I heard the words like a gong, a silent repetition I had been asking myself my whole life—*Will you be able to find it, Zianno?* The oval room became airless, suffocating. Even the shape itself became something else—octagonal or hexagonal—I couldn't tell. Everyone in the room seemed extremely large, much too large for the cramped space of the oval room.

Opari saw it in my eyes.

"We must tell our stories another time," she said, looking first at me, then at Sailor. It was the same look we had both seen in Carthage when she finally turned around after delivering Star's baby.

It was and is the softest sword I have ever felt.

Geaxi couldn't see Opari from where she was standing, but she could hear her and it was the same thing. She walked over to the rest of us and knelt in the sand. "In England," she said. "We shall leave this until England."

Without a word, without an outward or obvious sign from anyone, we all held our hands in the air, fingers spread and palms facing out toward each other, fingers and palms all the same size. In the candlelight, Sailor smiled. Our hands were casting shadows that exactly matched the ones stained into the wall.

"Zis is good business," he said.

Three days out to sea off the coast of the tiny island of Gozo, just north of the slightly larger island of Malta, it rained. I had almost forgotten the feeling of getting wet from the sky. I held my face up to it and let the liquid darts sting my eyelids, cheeks, and mouth. I opened my mouth and drank it straight from the sky, laughing and spitting. Rain. Africa and the Sahara had taught me never, ever to take it for granted. I thought back to Emme's words at the edge of the deep desert—"Do not think ahead. The Sahara will not allow it"—and standing there in it, feeling the rain again as only a scattered shower, as one among many to come, it was more than relief. It was return. But with return came an anxious, familiar habit—thinking ahead and looking ahead.

The ship was cruising west, ignoring the sudden squall and sailing through it. Star, Opari, and I were at the railing in the stern, facing east where the sun still shone. We were aboard HMS *Scorpion,* a frigate that was currently decommissioned and flying an Egyptian flag. It was a worthy ship that had been rigged and rerigged several times for transporting everything from troops and munitions to potatoes and raincoats. The first day at sea I had asked Willie Croft if he knew who owned the ship and he said, "Technically, an Egyptian from Cairo bought it for scrap from the British Navy. In reality me, my mother, and the Croft Foundation own it and we, in turn, lease it to the British Navy for . . . unofficial operations."

"Such as this one?" I asked.

"Quite. Rather neat and tidy, isn't it?"

"Quite," I told him.

I liked Willie from the beginning. I knew he had been formally raised and educated, but his whole demeanor suggested exactly the opposite. His speech was a curious blend of formal and informal, and physically, he was simultaneously awkward and graceful. I never saw him bump into anything or break anything, but I always expected it at any moment. He had a quick mind, an honest smile, and most of all I trusted him. I still didn't know the exact nature of the Daphne Croft Foundation and its relationship with the Meq, but I knew that I could trust Willie. I knew it because I had seen what was in his eyes when he returned from Alexandria with Star and her baby, only hours after the rest of us had returned from the oval room. I watched as he helped Star by holding her arm and elbow, though she hardly needed it. She looked radiant, even with a bandage on her shoulder, and beamed a smile across to Opari. Willie was grinning like a teenager and whether he knew it at the time or not, he was in love. It shone out from his heart straight through his eyes. Star wore a print dress he had found for her—a simple English dress. She had tied her old scarf around the waist and looped it through Mama's baseball glove so that it hung at her waist like a purse. She carried her baby in her one good arm and her blond hair hung loose over her bandaged shoulder. I knew then that I would trust anyone who loved someone who looked so much like Carolina. Star was the image of her mother as I remembered her. To Willie, she was much more than that. All that day and night Willie kept one eye on Star and one eye on his job, which was to secure and cover the experimental planes and get all of us out to sea for our rendezvous with the *Scorpion*. He did that and we set sail for England at midnight. Willie made sure Star and her baby were safe and warm before he ever thought about rest for himself. He did it unconsciously and without asking, as only love compels us to do. He knew nothing of her past or what she'd been through. No one did except me and one other—the Fleur-du-Mal. What the Fleur-du-Mal had done to Star could never be corrected or taken back. Her life had been changed forever. The time she spent in Africa and at Jisil's camp was now the core of who she was and would affect everything that came after. Jisil himself was in her memory and his child was in her arms. What that meant, no one but Star would ever know.

Two days later, standing in the rain and feeling resurrected, I wondered if Star would ever remember Carolina or Nicholas. She had not spoken to me, at least not in English, since I'd found her. She seemed to understand what Willie said to her, but only spoke to Opari in the old Berber dialect and even that was in whispers. She accepted the Meq intuitively and never addressed Opari as a child, but as an equal, a friend, the midwife of her own child. She had regained her spirit and strength completely. Willie had called it "simply remarkable" and it was, only I knew where it came from and I was not surprised. Opari had told me she would teach her English, that they would learn together. That was fine, I said, but what I really meant, what I did not say, was that I wanted her to remember not just her language or her name, but something much more elusive—her innocence.

For that to happen, the heart must allow the mind to remember and vice versa. It is tricky. It may never happen. When it does, if it does, who knows why? As Opari would say later, "All it takes is a crazy boy and a rainbow." Perhaps. I only know that as I stood by the railing that morning off the coast of those ancient islands, laughing and spitting in the rain, I suddenly remembered that it had rained the morning Ray and I left St. Louis in search of Star. And for some reason, just as my mind focused on two large wooden crates that Ray or someone had left under the archway of Carolina's big house, a rainbow appeared over our stern, stretching across the Mediterranean. Opari and Star had taken cover behind me and I heard Opari yell out, "You are crazy! You are crazy in the rain!" I turned toward her voice and I heard another one, softer, almost a whisper, coming from over Opari's shoulder. It was Star. She was repeating something again and again, as if she had just discovered the sound of a stranger inside herself. "Fierce Whale," she said. "Fierce Whale." I walked toward her. Rain was dripping in my eyes, but I could hear her voice clearly, and in English. It was the same voice I had heard the morning of her birthday in 1904, the voice of a little girl who wanted to ride the Ferris Wheel at the World's Fair—the voice of innocence.

She was watching the rainbow. I turned to look and the colors were actually dancing in an arc over the sea. I turned back and Opari was staring at me, asking me what this meant with her eyes. I couldn't answer. I knew this was the tricky moment, the one where the heart and mind awaken and discover themselves alone and together in one soul. What they decide is never certain and in Star's case I could only guess what she would see and what she would remember. I took another step toward her. She was out of the rain and standing partially in darkness. Slowly, her eyes looked down at me and I could see the same blue-gray with flecks of gold as in Carolina's eyes. A smile appeared, then a look of recognition and acceptance. Her freckles danced on her face with her smile. Softly, in slightly accented English, she said, "We ride the Fierce Whale, ZeeZee."

Just then, Willie came lurching down the stairs that led up to the captain's quarters. His shirt was drenched and his red hair was matted flat against his forehead. Before he could speak I said, "What day is this, Willie? What's the date?" I wanted to think of it as a new birthday for her, a new beginning.

"What? That's odd," Willie said. "The date is precisely what I ran down to tell you. Turns out it's become rather significant."

"What is it?" I asked.

"November 11, 1918. An armistice has been declared in Europe. The 'war to end all wars' has ended."

I looked at Opari and then Star. Their expressions were as blank as mine must have been. I had forgotten there even was a "war to end all wars." I continued to stand there, happy, empty, somehow unimpressed by the end of a world war. Then Sailor and Geaxi made a sudden appearance from their cabins inside. They squeezed by Star and stood next to Opari.

"You are standing in the rain, young Zezen," Geaxi said.

"Yes—yes, I am," I said.

Willie laughed to himself and scrambled back up the stairs, leaning down to catch a last glimpse of Star. From inside her cabin, Star's baby awoke and cried out for breakfast. Opari and Star both turned to leave and answer his call. Geaxi followed and Sailor and I were left staring at each other. I hadn't moved an inch. The rain had slackened, but I was still soaking wet.

"Are you all right, Zianno?" he asked without a trace of irony.

"Yes," I said, then added, "quite." I felt a smile just beginning at the corners of my mouth.

"I sent word to St. Louis," he said, pausing for a response, then going on. "I told them you had done it, you had found Star and we were on our way to England."

"Good," I said.

He turned to go back inside and waited for me. It took a moment, but I finally moved and came in out of the rain. As he opened the door to the cabins, Sailor nodded toward the sky behind us and winked.

In a whisper he said, "You conjured a beautiful rainbow, Zianno."

"Thank you," I said, walking in behind him and grinning like an idiot. Return. I had to laugh at the word and its meaning. It should feel like completion, game over, the end. But it always—always feels like beginning.

The news of the end of the Great War instantly changed the mood of every man in the crew and even changed the course of the *Scorpion*. We had been charting an unpredictable, evasive course and generally heading west, but with the news of the Armistice, we sailed straight for Gibraltar and England.

The days became mild and sunny and we made good time. In the evenings, Willie insisted we share our meals in the captain's quarters, though the captain himself was never present. We sat in a tight circle and Willie always, at the last possible second, managed to sit next to Star and her baby, whose name I learned that first evening after the Armistice was Caine. Caine Abel Croft. I found out Willie had a hand in that too. Geaxi held the baby as we ate that night and during the meal told me the story. She agreed that Willie must truly be in love because she had never known him to act so impulsively and get everything wrong while doing it.

In Alexandria, Geaxi said that while we had been in the oval room he had taken Star directly to Sailor's contact, who escorted them all to a British doctor the man said would look after Star and the baby and then look the other way. Star still spoke no English and Willie was nervous about leaving her alone, but he had another man to see about passports and identities for Opari and me. The plan was for all of us to be of the same family when we reached England. Star was now the fair peach among the basket of cherries. He had no idea what to do about her or the baby until he returned to the doctor's and was asked his son's name for the birth certificate. Willie looked at Star who seemed to understand and she whispered, "Kahin al-Jisil." Willie misunderstood her, but he did not want to hesitate, and he anglicized what he heard, writing down "Caine Abel," and then adding "Croft" without blinking, making him a father and husband on the spot. The doctor never mentioned the baby's dark eyes and tufts of dark curly hair, nor did Willie. The rest of Star's papers were filled in accordingly and she left for England, on paper at least, as Mrs. Willie Croft.

Geaxi said the ironic fact was that "Kahin" really did mean "Cain" in old Berber. It was one of the few biblical names that crossed into the Sahara. She doubted, however, that Willie or Star would ever care, but Daphne, Willie's mother, would definitely want an explanation for Star's third name—Croft—and the Mrs. in front of it.

I remember laughing along with Geaxi about Willie and thinking how wonderful it was and how close we were to returning Star to Carolina and Nicholas. They had waited long enough. Whatever had gone before and whatever lay ahead would be worth it. Their daughter was coming home and their grandson with her. Names, false or otherwise, would make no difference. Nothing would make a difference.

Three nights later, we rounded the big rock at Gibraltar and turned north by northwest into the Atlantic. Opari and I again stood by the railing in the stern. She wore her shawl with the unusual and exotic designs. It was well past midnight and cold. The temperature had dropped considerably since we'd left the Mediterranean. I tried to urge her back inside, but she wanted to stay out.

"I feel like a stranger," she said.

I held her close and told her, "That's impossible. We're together now."

"No," she said, "I mean a stranger to this ocean. I have not seen it or breathed its air in twenty-eight hundred years."

"Is that all?" I asked. "It seems like only yesterday."

She groaned at my sad attempt at humor, but continued to hold me close. She took my hand and put it to her lips, then held it against her cheek. The Atlantic rolled and swelled around us.

"Will it be a good life from now on, Zianno?"

"We'll make it so."

"Then breathe, my love . . . breathe."

I did and the air itself seemed to taste and smell of rebirth and new life. What neither of us knew was that at that very moment the air throughout the world was carrying something else—a killer—a deadly microscopic guest that traveled everywhere at once from who knows where, finding humans as hosts, hosts who rarely survived the visit. It still had no name, but it would have one soon, and it affected all of us, Giza and Meq, forever. It was later nicknamed "the Spanish Lady." I pray that she never visits again. Unfortunately, I am afraid she will. Beware if she does. Most warnings are fiction, jokes, or bluffs. This one is not—beware of "the Spanish Lady."

We arrived in the busy port of Southampton by midafternoon and had to wait until the next day to find a berth. Troop ships by the dozen were returning and all had the right of way. Most of the men I saw

disembarking were jubilant and singing or wailing to loved ones waiting ashore, but others had a distant, vacant gaze in their eyes, as if "return" was no longer a word with any meaning.

Willie handled our pass through customs and immigration with
great efficiency, considering the chaos around us. In the past, Sailor
and Geaxi might have entered on their own in secret, in disguise, or
both. The trust Sailor had in this new "network" of Giza and Meq
was a mystery to me, especially since there were four of us together
carrying the Stones. Then I thought of Solomon himself, and even
Owen Bramley. They had both proved their willingness to help the
Meq many times over. This new situation was only an extension of
that trust. If Sailor had harbored any mistrust of Willie, or thought he
couldn't manage the situation, we wouldn't have been there.

Our papers declared Sailor, Geaxi, Opari, and I were all of one
family. With our dark hair and eyes, and our slightly exotic dress, we
passed easily as a French family orphaned by the war and being taken
in by the Crofts. Willie said he was working on a better idea for the
future—diplomatic passports. I still wore my money belt and a con-
siderable sum hung around my waist under my shirt. Fortunately, they
weren't checking children for gold.

The weather had changed drastically overnight. The temperature
dropped twenty degrees and clear skies gave way to English fog. It was
wet, cold, thick as smoke, and Star was fascinated by it—as she was by
everything. She had gone through the entire process of customs carrying Caine at her breast, asking Opari questions, who in turn was
asking me questions. They were both speaking English at all times,
even to each other. Star was learning the language in great leaps and
bounds and Opari had a natural ear for all languages.

Willie made one last call on the captain of the *Scorpion,* then led the
way through the fog and squawking lines of cars and taxis, all spewing
exhaust that added to the foulness of the heavy fog. Willie offered Star
his arm and she took it, though she swung her head in all directions,
trying to take in everything at once. People shouted, waved, cried, and
laughed. The war was over and the homecomings had begun.

"Where is she?" Sailor yelled. "There! Over there!" Willie yelled
back, and pointed toward a long limousine, parked away from the other
cars and flashing its headlights on and off.

A tall figure emerged from the driver's side of the car and stood up. The figure was waving for us to come over. Through the fog, I saw long arms moving inside a very large black seaman's slicker. Was it warning or welcome? For a brief moment I thought of the first time I had seen Solomon, a scarecrow waving far ahead, a beacon in a black cape trying to tell us something.

"Mother!" Willie shouted.

We walked the short distance to the car and rain began to fall through the fog. We huddled in front of the headlights and Daphne Croft looked down on all of us with a strange, angular smile. She was a woman of about seventy or seventy-five with long, gray hair tied up at the back, not in a bun, but gathered at the neck and hanging down her back. She raised one of her arms inside the big slicker and shielded her eyes from the rain. Her eyes were bright blue, even in the fog and rain. She wore no makeup and the lines on her face were deep and well earned. She seemed surprised by the number of us, but not the *nature* of us. I knew she knew we were Meq. Then she saw Star.

"Who is this child?"

Star glanced around at everyone, then realized she was the one being addressed. She walked toward the old woman and stopped not a foot away.

"I am the one your son is choosing to love."

Daphne looked Star up and down. Star had changed her English print dress for a pair of trousers. She used her scarf as a belt and kept Mama's glove hanging to one side. Willie had found an extra leather jacket on the *Scorpion* and Star wore that to keep out the chill. She carried Caine inside the jacket and the back of his tiny head peeped out of the top. Star smiled at Daphne and the old woman was instantly disarmed. The long car was idling loudly and the rain was steady. Daphne stood speechless for several moments, then threw a quick glance at Willie, who laughed to himself and nodded.

"Then come," she said. "Come in out of this rain, child. My goodness! Come! Willie—help this child into the car, will you? My goodness, we shall all catch the flu."

"You shouldn't be driving, Mother," Willie said.

"Nonsense. I drive all the time."

"Precisely my point," he said, then turned to Opari and me. "I suppose intros and all that sort of thing will have to wait." Willie started toward the car to open the rear door. Just as his hand was about to reach the handle, the door opened.

"Oh, my Lord," Daphne said, "I almost forgot. Mowsel and another man, a Basque man, came along. I believe they are here to see you, Sailor."

Sailor, who had been paying little attention, turned at once to Daphne.

"What?" he asked.

He seemed more stricken than surprised. He glanced at Geaxi and I could tell this was not in any of his plans. At the same moment, a boy leaped out of the open door of the limousine. He wore leather boots laced to the knee with loose-cut trousers tucked in at the top. A navy jacket that was long past seaworthy covered his torso and arms, and a hood covered his head. He pulled back the hood and stood staring at Sailor eye to eye. He had dark hair that curled around his ears and glistened as the rain hit it.

"Greetings, you old Jack tar," the boy said. He smiled and I was drawn to his mouth. He was missing one of his two front teeth. Trumoi-Meq. The only one among us I have ever known to be missing a tooth. Also known for centuries as Mowsel, a name I later found out had everything to do with his missing tooth.

Without acknowledging anyone, he took Sailor by the arm and led him away from the car. As they huddled together in the rain, he spoke to Sailor rapidly and close to his ear, no longer smiling.

I turned and someone else stepped out of the car. He was wearing a red beret, and as he stood, he leaned slightly on a cane for balance. His eyes found mine and I knew them immediately.

"Hello, señor," he said softly.

"Hello, Pello."

Twenty-two years had passed since I had seen him last, waving to Geaxi and me from a wheelchair on the docks in Vancouver. The lines in his face told me they had not been easy ones. I could only think of those terrible moments when his brother Joseba and Baju were gunned down and he was shot in the leg—violence that was so quick, so permanent, so senseless. I glanced at his cane, then felt guilty about it. He saw what I was thinking.

"There is no pain, señor. Only a leg that refuses to listen."

"I'm sorry, Pello, I didn't mean—"

"*De nada.* It is common."

He smiled and it was the smile of a shepherd and a soldier. It was welcome, genuine, and I sensed not often shown. My thoughts turned to his papa and mine.

"Kepa," I blurted. "Does the old man still live, Pello?"

"He lives, señor. Miren has passed, however. It has made him very sad. He shrinks back in himself."

"I will come and see him. Soon."

"That would brighten his eyes, señor. Perhaps even the old bull on his chest would again swell with pride. He misses the old ways, the old life."

"As soon as possible, Pello, I will come and see him. Tell him so. Tell him I will come and we will watch the stars together."

"I will tell him, but please, if it is not an inconvenience, I must ask you to tell me something."

"What?"

"Why you are here, señor. I was not expecting your presence."

I was thinking the same thing about him, but I didn't mention it and turned to introduce him to Opari and Star. No one was there. Opari, Geaxi, Daphne, and Willie were helping Star into the other side of the car. Daphne seemed to be in charge, yelling something to Willie about notifying the motor car industry of the need for safety belts.

I turned back to Pello just as a taxi pulled up behind the limousine. The horn squawked twice and Pello took off his beret, bending over slightly. His hair was more gray than black.

"We must go, señor."

"Wait," I said, glancing at Sailor and Trumoi-Meq. They were walking fast toward the taxi. "Where do you go?"

"Kepa's camp, señor."

"In Idaho?"

"No, no, forgive me. We have all moved home."

"I thought home was in Idaho."

"No, señor. Our original home—the Pyrenees."

Pello wheeled in one motion, using his cane for balance, and walked toward the taxi. His cane was more than a crutch. Through practice

and determination his cane had become both arm and leg on his damaged side. He moved quickly and directly, meeting Trumoi-Meq and
Sailor at the door of the taxi and holding it open. Sailor stepped in
without a single backward glance. Trumoi-Meq was right behind him,
but he paused and turned his head, staring at me through the rain.
Without hesitating, I whispered, "Dream of Light—we are." They
were his own words carved in the wall of the oval room I'd found in
the desert; words I was sure he thought no one else had ever read. His
mouth dropped open enough to show the gap of his missing tooth,
then he was yanked inside and Pello followed, closing the door behind
him. The taxi backed up and sped away. The fog and rain swallowed
their lights, then their sound, and they were gone. Not a word of explanation had been given by anyone.

I spun around and found Geaxi staring up the narrow street where
the taxi had disappeared.

"What just happened?" I asked.

"I do not know," she said. Her voice was flat and stoic, but her eyes
met mine and I saw the concern.

I was worried and a little frightened. Something was wrong somewhere. I had never seen Sailor vanish quite like that.

"Why was Pello here?" I asked her.

"I do not know, Zianno. There may be a problem with Kepa."

But that didn't make sense, I thought. Pello had just told me Kepa
was alive, and though he was heartbroken, he was not sick or in trouble. I would have asked her more, but I still wasn't sure how much to
say in front of Daphne and Willie.

"Let's sort it all out inside the car," Willie interrupted. He was
holding the door open and Geaxi ducked inside. I stood a moment
staring up at him. His hair was matted down again and his clothes
were soaking wet. He smiled faintly and added, "It's raining, Z."

Opari grabbed my hand and pulled me in next to her. Willie made
certain the trunk was shut tight and then jumped in beside me. Daphne
was driving. Star was up front with Daphne, holding Caine in her
arms. The rest of us sat in the back, facing each other on two wide
leather seats. I leaned forward and looked out of the side window as
Daphne put the big car into gear. The window was steamed up and I
had to wipe a clear circle with the palm of my hand.

Outside, just as we pulled away, a soldier dropped to his knees, then fell into the path of a stranger walking in the opposite direction. He hadn't stumbled or given any warning whatsoever, and he was unconscious by the time he hit the street. As we disappeared in the fog, I caught a glimpse of his face. His eyes were hollow and his skin glistened, but not with rain. The rain only fell in his open mouth. He was drenched in his own sweat.

Opari shook my arm and pulled me back in the seat. "Z, Z," she was saying. It was the first time she had called me "Z" and it sounded good. I turned and wiped the rain out of my eyes, then looked into hers.

"Did you see him?" she asked.

I knew who she meant. It was not the soldier, or Pello, or Sailor. She was smiling and excited. The fact that Sailor had left without a word didn't seem to bother her. Then I remembered she hadn't seen Sailor until recently in over twenty-eight hundred years. Why should a sudden exit now cause any alarm? I smiled and said, "You must mean 'missing tooth.'"

"Yes," she said, laughing, taking my face in her hands, kissing me while she laughed. "I have known since you were born, my beloved, that you would find me, and since China, that I would be finding you. Once my . . . Bihazanu?"

"Heartfear," I said.

"Yes, heartfear. Once my heartfear was lifted, I knew I would find you through Sailor. But never, ever in my long living did I think I would see this one . . . the one with the missing tooth . . . Trumoi-Meq."

I took her hands from my face and kissed the tips of each finger, then I took her face in my hands and kissed her eyebrows and eyelids. I kissed her nose where her nostrils flared, her cheeks, her chin . . . her lips.

Suddenly, Daphne changed gear and the big motor car coughed and backfired, jarring us apart. Opari was laughing and, for some reason, I had tears running down my cheeks. I felt a weariness as heavy as the fog. I wanted to ask about Carolina and Nicholas, if anyone had heard from them, if anyone knew we had arrived. I wanted to ask about Sailor and Pello and Mowsel. The long car rolled through the market town of Romsey and then turned west toward Somerset. Willie was talking with Geaxi and I interrupted.

"Where are we going, Willie?"

I asked the question, but I had no real interest in the answer. I was almost falling asleep as I said it. I had my head in Opari's lap, resting on her ancient shawl.

"Home," he said. "Home to Caitlin's Ruby."

"And where is that?" I asked, closing my eyes.

"Cornwall," Willie answered.

I nodded in my mind and fell asleep. I'm not certain if my weariness came from the inside or the outside. Either way, I surrendered and slept, dreaming my way through most of Devon. I slept soundly and dreamed wildly, but still listened to everything around me the way I'd learned in the twisted limbs of the old cedar tree, waiting for the sound of Jisil's horse.

Opari slept with me for a few hours, stretching out beside me in the seat. Her breath was warm on the back of my neck and I listened to nothing else while we lay together.

It wasn't until we were far to the west and the big limousine stopped for gasoline that I awoke to something I heard, and even then I stayed perfectly still. Willie had just finished saying something to Geaxi about relieving Daphne behind the wheel and driving the rest of the way himself. He opened the door and a fierce wind blew in along with a man's voice, yelling to Willie from somewhere near the car, possibly a doorway or window. Willie yelled back. "What's that, Tom? Can't hear you in this wind." I heard the man clearly. "A middle-aged man," the voice said. "American, judgin' by the accent—askin' for you, Willie." "Was it Owen Bramley?" Willie asked. "No, 'twasn't him," the voice said. "I'd of recognized him. 'Twas a fellow with a gray mustache travelin' with a woman and child. Quite worked up, he was, sir." At first, Willie had no response, then he said, "Thank you, Tom," and stepped outside, shutting the door behind him. The man's words were still sinking in when the door opened again and Daphne Croft climbed in, speaking as she entered. My face was turned away from her, but I assumed she was addressing Geaxi. I was certain she was referring to Star.

"That wonderful child is in love with this weather. Can you imagine? My goodness, I've lived half my life on this forsaken boot of land and I've never met one like her. How delightful . . ." She paused and lowered her voice to a whisper. "Is he asleep? I should have noticed—"

"It is all right, Daphne," Geaxi said. "He sleeps through everything."

Willie put the car into gear and we continued west. Daphne ignored what the man Tom had yelled to Willie and spoke instead to Opari.

"Now," Daphne said, as if to calm herself, "you must forgive my manners earlier, my dear. I am always honored to meet another member of Mowsel's family. Each time is a miracle. Each one of you is a miracle, my goodness."

"I am the honored one," Opari said. "Willie has great praise for you."

"Yes, yes. Willie is a good boy, a good son. He is my youngest, you know. Born in China, a complete surprise, long after the others."

"I have lived in China," Opari said.

"Really? How long were you there, my dear?"

"A few years—longer than I expected," Opari said softly, then laughed and Geaxi joined her. It was the first joke I had ever heard her make, at least in English, and I almost laughed myself.

Geaxi interrupted. "Daphne Croft—I would like you to meet Opari. She travels with the one who is sleeping in her lap, Zianno Zezen."

The car jolted suddenly as it went over a rough patch in the road. Willie had picked up speed and Daphne turned to tap on the glass that separated him from us. I never moved.

Geaxi went on. "Tell Opari about where we are going, Daphne. Tell her the story of Caitlin's Ruby."

"Yes, do," Opari said, then added, "My . . . *irudimen*?"

"Imagination," Geaxi translated.

"Yes, my imagination has no compass in your land. Tell me of this place and, please, tell me more of Mowsel."

"Well then," Daphne began. "I shan't waste a moment. We'll be seeing Falmouth soon and Caitlin's Ruby is not far beyond."

I didn't move a muscle. I wanted answers to other questions, but

Opari was running her fingers through my hair, and besides, I'd always learned more from the story than the storyteller. Daphne's voice was high and clear, almost musical, and she spoke in rapid bursts.

"Where shall I begin?" she asked.

"With Caitlin herself," Geaxi said.

"Yes, well, of course. Where else? It all begins with Caitlin, doesn't it? Caitlin Fadle, the Irish beauty said to have had hair as black as a tinner's grave and eyes as blue and lovely as the first day of spring.

"No one knows where she was born. No one knows how she came to Cornwall, but she was first seen as a tiny lass in the streets of Truro, no more than six or seven years old, fending for herself, living on scraps, and sleeping where she could. By the time she turned twelve or so, she was known to have been in Penzance. It was the year 1595, the year Penzance was sacked by the Spaniards. Caitlin Fadle, it is said in one version, was merely one of many women and children stolen and taken by sailors, then sent to Spain. In another version, she is taken aboard, but only she, and only by the captain. In yet another, my goodness, she is slipped on board a Spanish gunboat and hidden below by a boy—a boy with a missing front tooth. In every version, she does not return for twenty years. She has been forgotten completely because she was never missed. She had no family in Penzance and yet, she returns—and here is the mystery—she returns saying she is searching for someone, but she never gives a name and never asks a question. She has many trunks in her luggage, all filled with clothes worn only at court and only by nobility. My goodness, she has suitors calling by the dozen and speaks to none of them. She has no money or letters of credit. For survival, she has only one thing—a ruby bigger than a man's fist.

"She leaves the ruby with a man who is a stranger to her, a Scottish blacksmith named Bramley, and walks the shore of the harbor around Mount's Bay and the inlets and creeks that empty into it. She walks the coast and cliffs to Land's End and back, nine miles going and coming, always alone, always searching, but for what, for whom—she never says.

"Then one day she asks the blacksmith, 'Who owns the property at the source of the creek that flows into Newlyn from the north?' It is property that is difficult to reach both by land and sea, it is so remote.

My goodness, the blacksmith tells her, that's no place for a woman, no place at all. She tells him to sell the ruby to the merchants on Wharf Road and buy the land in her name, Caitlin Fadle. 'Keep a tidy sum for you and your family,' she says, 'and I'll use the rest to build it.' 'Build what?' he says. 'The waiting place,' Caitlin tells him. 'Me home.' "

At the mention of the name Bramley in Daphne's story, I almost rose up and gave myself away. But I was able to remain still and she went on. Outside, I knew we were far from anywhere. The big car cut through the wind and weather and we neither met nor passed any other vehicle.

"And she builds it. Can you imagine? In the middle of nowhere, all alone, though some say a stranger comes and goes on occasion, rowing in from the open sea and up the narrow passage to Caitlin's home. No one ever sees him. The blacksmith never mentions it and even defends Caitlin against the self-righteous scoundrels in Penzance.

"Many years pass. Caitlin still walks the cliffs to Land's End and oftentimes is seen inland between St. Ives and St. Just, walking among the standing stones. She always wears a long, woolen coat and cape, dyed dark red like the ruby, and keeps it wrapped around her, tip to toe. She bears a child, unknown to the blacksmith, perhaps because he only sees her in the red cape. My goodness, who knows. He has a family of his own, but Caitlin asks him to raise the child, a boy, to give him a normal life among other children. The blacksmith and his family take the child in and raise him without question or shame.

"Caitlin grows old and one day she begins dying. The blacksmith comes first with a doctor, whom she sends away. Then the blacksmith brings a priest, who is whisked away before he says a word. Lastly, he brings a solicitor, who is asked to stay and write her will and testament. Her once raven black hair is now a tangled, wiry gray, but her eyes are fierce and still blue as mountain ice. She tells the blacksmith that all her land, the heather and broom, the stone and thatch, all is his with two provisions—he and his descendants must never sell the land, the place she calls Caitlin's Ruby, and her son and his descendants must always have a home there, to work and live in and do with as they please."

Daphne paused a moment. I couldn't see her face, but I could feel her turn and look out of the window. "Caitlin passes," she finally said. "And not a clue, not a whisper to anyone, including the blacksmith, of why she came, why she stayed, or for what she was waiting. Not a whisper."

Then Daphne laughed suddenly and Geaxi laughed with her. "Please, you cannot stop there, Mrs. Croft," Geaxi said. "You must tell Opari what occurred over the next two hundred and sixty years, or so."

Daphne continued. "The property is handed down from Bramley to Bramley. The maze of buildings, terraces, and pathways that Caitlin began is expanded. The real Caitlin Fadle is forgotten, but the legend and story of Caitlin's Ruby grows. The public of Penzance and all Mount's Bay believes to this day she stole the ruby and waited hope-lessly for its rightful owner, the Spanish captain, to come after it. But of course, he never did. The Bramleys always believed she waited for someone else, and it was his legend that grew among the Bramleys for generations. They always believed Caitlin waited for the boy with the missing tooth—the boy who saved her and many other children through the centuries."

"Mowsel," Opari whispered.

"Mowsel, indeed," Daphne said.

Willie had slowed the big car down and was making a series of tight turns. It was becoming more and more difficult for me to lie still and continue to feign sleep. Opari started to say something, then stopped. I knew what she was thinking. So did Geaxi.

"I believe Opari is wondering how you learned of us, Daphne," Geaxi said.

"Oh, my dear," Daphne said, her voice rising a full octave. "I never would have if it hadn't been for my nephew. You see, my maiden name is Bramley. My nephew is Owen Bramley. He brought Mowsel to me. He brought all of you to me, and you have all saved my life.

"My wonderful husband, William, who always believed in mira-cles, by the way, died suddenly after our long return from China. I was not prepared for the emptiness that came after. My children were all grown and gone, even Willie was away at school in Canada. Caitlin's Ruby became for me a beautiful prison, a beautiful prison with gen-erations of memories for bars. I was completely lost, heartbroken to a point I thought not possible. Even old Tillman Fadle, Caitlin's last direct descendant, couldn't cheer me out of it. Then one day, quite by surprise, my prodigal American nephew returned. My goodness, what a day that was. He told me the most outrageous and lovely story about his recent life and an old Jewish man named Solomon J. Birnbaum.

"There were two children with him who looked as if they were related. What lovely children I remember thinking, so quiet and well behaved. They were introduced to me by name—Geaxi first, then a boy with a missing front tooth that became apparent when he greeted me and smiled. Mowsel. Not only did the oldest Bramley myth and legend become flesh and blood, but my spirit lifted and soared, almost as if William was saying to me, 'See, you old fool, there are miracles!'

"Owen went on to tell me Solomon's plan of communication and safe passage and a little of what would be required of me and Caitlin's Ruby. In a way, I was reborn to this life and its mysteries. Old Tillman Fadle had always preached that someday we would know why Caitlin sold her ruby to live in a place so remote and lonely. 'Wait and see,' he always said. 'Wait and see.' He was right, as was my husband and, of course, that dear man I never knew, Solomon J. Birnbaum."

Just then, Willie came to a near halt and I felt the car turning and angling downward. My eyes were still closed, but I was wide awake.

"My goodness," Daphne said. "We are here at last." There was a tap on the glass from the front seat and Daphne added, "That lovely child is pointing for us to look at something." I knew she meant Star and I remained silent, but I could feel Opari tense slightly and lean forward.

"Where?" Geaxi asked.

"There," Daphne said quickly. "Just ahead, do you see? There ahead of us, by the gate, a man with his arms spread. He's waving, I believe. Dear me," she said and paused. "He looks like a scarecrow come to life."

I rose up as if I'd been struck by lightning. Only Daphne was startled.

"Hello," she said. "You are Zianno, I presume."

"Yes, I—"

Willie braked hard and stopped the car. "That must be the man old Tom was going on about," he shouted back through the glass.

I glanced at Daphne's blue eyes and she smiled. The smile was friendly, childlike, angular, and wide. All the lines on her face had to move and make room for it.

"Zezen! Look ahead!" It was Geaxi. "Do you know that man?"

I leaned forward and looked through the glass. Up front, both Willie and Star were staring ahead, straining to see the figure approaching. Willie was gripping the wheel and Star had Caine inside her jacket, holding him close. I followed their eyes to a man standing in the middle of the road, not twenty yards away, between two stone pillars and an open gate—the entrance to Caitlin's Ruby. He was wearing a long trenchcoat and trying to wave, but he kept losing his balance and stumbling forward. There was only a light mist falling, yet his gray hair and mustache were soaking wet. I thought he was alone when suddenly a woman and a girl appeared from behind the pillars. They ran toward the man, but the woman fell before she reached him. The girl helped the woman to her feet, then caught the man just before he buckled. The girl then stood between the two, holding them upright, and stared back at us.

"My goodness, who are they?" Daphne asked.

I was certain I knew the girl, but I had to look twice before I recognized the man and woman. They had both aged since I'd seen them last.

"It's Nicholas," I said.

"And Eder," Geaxi said, reaching for the door and opening it.

"Who is the young one?" Opari asked.

"Nova," Geaxi and I said, then climbed out of the big car together.

I've never been much of a philosopher on the "why" of things. To me, it's just a part of the game, never the game itself. I have always been fascinated, however, with the "when." Synchronism, coincidence, luck, fate—all are words for that place in time where the rules change and, whether we like it or not, so do our lives.

Geaxi and I ran and got to them first. The mist had settled and it seemed abnormally calm. Willie and Star were close behind and Willie rushed past me to pick up Nicholas, who had passed out completely just before we reached him. I knelt down to help and Eder saw my face.

"Zianno," she whispered, then slipped after Nicholas into unconsciousness.

Star leaned over to look at the stricken man and woman. She had no idea she was staring at her own father. As she bent down, she held the back of Caine's head with the palm of her hand. Nova made a quick move and stepped in front of her.

"Keep the baby away from them!" she said sharply. Her voice was clear and precise, not angry or demanding, but something was visibly wrong. She looked quickly at Geaxi and glanced at me. "Keep the others away," she said quietly, "and help me, please, they're very sick."

The light was fading by the moment and I thought I saw another man approaching with a lantern. No one else seemed to notice.

"Who are they?" Star asked. Her eyes were wide and frightened and she instinctively held Caine tighter, straightening up and backing away. "And who are you?"

Nova looked a little frightening herself. Her hair was short and black and parted in the middle with bangs across her forehead. She had some sort of oil in it, which created an odd sheen in the mist and fading light. She wore heavy eye makeup, unusual I thought for any twelve-year-old, but especially for the Meq, and it was dripping down her face like black tears.

"You're Star, aren't you," Nova said. It was more statement than question.

"Yes."

"And that is your child?"

"Yes."

Nova looked at Caine's dark, curly hair peeping through Star's fingers. "Take him inside. The two of you must stay clear of these two," she said, nodding at Nicholas and Eder.

"Why did you say the word 'him'?" Star asked. "How did you know my baby is a boy?"

"I . . . I just knew." Nova bent down and put Eder's limp arm around her own shoulder. As she did, she said softly, "Please, you must back away. My name is Nova. We'll talk later."

Suddenly Opari was in the middle of all of us. She looked at Nicholas and Eder, then pulled their eyelids back and ran her finger over their lips, which were turning purple and blue. "This is a virus," she said, then looked at me. "They are dying."

Daphne arrived just in time to hear Opari's last words. She was slightly out of breath and gasped, "It is . . . Spanish flu . . . took three souls yesterday in Falmouth . . . we thought it . . . came home with the soldiers, but my goodness . . . 'tis everywhere."

Geaxi turned to Opari. "I have seen this before, once before," she said. "It was in Constantinople during the thirteenth century. Have you seen it?"

"Yes, many times in one form or another. It is quicker than the wind—a black seed that kills fast and at random."

"A virus, no?"

"Yes, the worst kind. It can . . . *hegaz egin*?"

"Fly" Geaxi translated.

"Yes, and it mutates to survive."

The man I'd seen approaching with the lantern was an old man, tall and wearing a whaler's coat and hat. Willie yelled to him.

"This way, Tillman, quickly!"

The man neither hurried nor slowed down. As I was to learn, that was how he did everything. He was Tillman Fadle, Caitlin's last descendant. He stood a full head above Willie, probably six feet eight or nine, and as he held the lantern out, for just a moment, he looked more like a vulture than a man. I couldn't see his face. The lantern's light was too weak. It was antique, made of glass and brass with tiny holes in the top. The light came from a candle inside. The heavy mist was seeping through the holes and making the flame spit and dance.

"Thought it was you," the man said. His voice rose and tailed off at the end of every sentence. "Couldn't tell, couldn't see," he went on. "Knew it was, though, knew it was. Had to be."

"For God's sake, Tillman!" Willie interrupted. "Of course, it's us. Now help me with these people, will you?"

"No! Please!" Nova shouted. "It isn't wise."

Willie started to speak and Daphne cut him off.

"It is all right, my dear. Really, I assure you. If this family could be spooked by the flu, then we would have been gone from this place long ago."

Nova had been kneeling the whole time, still trying in vain to support her mother and Nicholas. Geaxi bent over and placed her beret on Nova's head, then wiped the mascara and black tears off her cheeks.

"Come, Nova," Geaxi said. "You must help us get them inside. It is safe here."

Opari reached over and took Nova's hand. She made sure Nova was looking at her before she spoke. "How long have they been sick?"

"Eder, only one day," Nova said in a monotone. "Nicholas, two."

"Were you searching for us?" Star asked suddenly, as if something had just struck her, but didn't quite make sense.

"No, Star," Nova said in the same flat, distant voice. "Not all of you. Just you." Then her eyes found mine and I saw more tears running down her cheeks, only these were real and clear. "For so long, Zianno," she turned and whispered, "I thought this day, this time, this moment, would be for rejoicing. Now it's here and . . . and . . . what is this? . . . why is it like this?"

I said nothing. I could hear Tillman's old lantern swinging on its brass hinges and the candlelight flickered and slashed across Nova's dark eyes. Everything else was silence, except for the big limousine, parked and idling behind us.

"Come," Geaxi said. "There is much to do."

All of us helped carry Eder and Nicholas inside, with Daphne leading the way. In the rush of the moment, even in the falling dark, what I remember most were the eyes and movements of cats, dozens of them, following us, darting in front of us, peering down from tiled and thatched roofs, from every window ledge, every doorway. Willie told me later that the farmers and fishermen in the surrounding country considered them good luck whenever sighted. The "Cats of Caitlin's Ruby," he called them. Legend said that on the day Caitlin died they began to appear, one by one, then stayed and multiplied. They never came inside and rarely gathered all at once. But they did that night. They were all there. I will never forget their eyes.

Daphne led us through an entrance hall and down another long hall flanked by stairs leading up on both sides. There were few lights along the way, but I could see the wide beams overhead, ancient and straight and still holding their weight in an even line. I could also see the sweat glistening on the faces of Eder and Nicholas as we carried them through.

Finally, we were able to lay them down on two separate beds in what Willie called his "quarters." There was a large stone fireplace in one corner with a fire already blazing.

Opari said, "Strip their clothes and burn them. Wrap their bodies in wet sheets. We must try to break the fever."

She moved quickly back and forth between the two beds, telling Geaxi, Nova, and me exactly what to do, then turned to Daphne and told her that she and Willie and Star and the baby had to leave—there was nothing they could do and it was indeed dangerous. Daphne agreed reluctantly and took Star and the baby upstairs. Willie said he would be in the kitchen and within shouting distance. As he was leaving, he asked, "Should I send Tillman for a doctor?"

Opari never looked up and said evenly, "No. I fear it is too late for that."

For several minutes, Opari and Geaxi did everything they could to break the fevers of Eder and Nicholas, who remained unconscious and struggling for every breath. Their lungs were filling with fluid and getting worse. Their blood could not oxygenate, and as a result, once their clothes were removed I noticed their feet had turned black up to their ankles. Nicholas seemed to be hallucinating. His eyes would open and shut at random and his body jerked and convulsed. His breathing became more labored than Eder's and I knew he was much closer to death. I tried saying his name over and over, hoping to wake him, but it was no use. Nova did the same with Eder, holding her hand and repeating in her ear, "Wake up, Mama, wake up now."

I caught myself staring at Eder's face and body. She was a woman in her forties, going gray in her hair and slack in her limbs. Her belly was rounder and her breasts sagged slightly to the side. The lines in her face were the same only deeper, more permanent. She was still a beautiful woman, but bore no resemblance to the girl she had been, to the Meq, to the child-woman who had lived for over two thousand years completely immune to the virus that was killing her now. It made no sense. There were three of us in the room, three Egizahar Meq who carried the Stone, and we could do nothing. This powerful, mystical Stone that could make animals and Giza change their minds, their reality itself, was impotent and unable to do the one thing that mattered—*heal.*

Opari stayed busy trying to make them comfortable. She mostly pointed and nodded at what to do, saying little and moving quietly. I did hear her whisper once to Geaxi, "Sailor should be here." Geaxi only replied, "Yes, but this was never expected. Never."

Just then, Nova turned and grabbed my sleeve with her free arm. "Where's Ray?" she asked. I knew there had always been something between them, more than I'd had a chance to see in St. Louis and more than Ray had ever let on in Africa. Still, her question caught me off guard.

"I don't know," I said. "I mean, he was kidnapped, stolen, I don't even know if he is alive. I'll find him though. The Fleur-du-Mal knows where he is, I'm sure of it. As soon as . . . as soon as—" I stopped and looked hard into her eyes. "Where is Carolina, Nova? Tell me. Tell me now."

Before Nova could say a word, the door to Willie's "quarters" burst open and Star was standing there wide-eyed and trembling. I am certain no one had told Star the dying man lying in the bed was her father, but when she appeared at the doorway, unasked and unannounced, I knew at a glance she had somehow figured it out. What happened next is still a mystery to me. The Meq have a word for it—*berrikutu*—the "talking touch."

Star had changed from her trousers and navy jacket to a long striped dressing gown, probably borrowed from Willie. Her hair was wild and tangled and slightly wet. She even held a towel in her right hand and it looked as if she'd run downstairs the moment the truth had struck her.

It had been fourteen years since she'd seen her father's face, and physically he had aged twice that, but she walked over to him and sat on the bed next to him and held his hand in both of hers. "Papa," she said in the softest voice. "Papa," she said again, then again and again as if the word itself had shape and weight and meaning beyond the sound. It was a word to her from another life, another self. It was a word she'd buried in order to survive, but used without speaking it aloud to protect her in Louisiana, in the camps of Mulai and Jisil, maybe even through our escape and the birth of her own son. It was her secret word, her magic word. "Papa" had power. "Papa" was the one word that kept her alive and the one word she never thought she would say again.

A single tear dropped from her eye and fell by chance on Nicholas's dark blue lips. One more time, one last time, Star whispered, "Papa." As if by magic, his mouth opened and his tongue went to taste the tear. His eyes fluttered and opened. He looked around wildly at first, then focused on Star's face. I have no idea how he got his breath because his lungs were filled with fluid, but he opened his mouth a little wider and almost smiled, then spoke to her, or at least to the woman he thought she was.

"Carolina, honey, I knew you'd be here. I told everybody. I remember . . . I remember—" He paused and looked away, squinting and blinking, but his eyes couldn't or wouldn't focus properly. "Where are we?" he asked, looking back at Star. "Where are we, honey? I'm a little cold."

Without saying a word, Opari handed Star a wool blanket. Star exchanged looks with her, then glanced at Nova sitting on the other bed and holding Eder's hand.

"Carolina is your mother," Nova said simply.

"And he is my father," Star whispered.

The two women held each other's gaze for several moments. One was not much older than a girl, yet had born a child herself, and the other was a woman nearing thirty, yet still in the body of a child. An "understanding" passed between them that was beyond age, gender, or species. A bond and trust were formed instantly through the timeless sense of love and the endless sense of loss.

Star turned and leaned over her papa and kissed him full and hard on his blue lips, not as herself, but as Carolina—the Carolina who was in his heart, his mind and memory, his last words. And she kept kissing him. No one stopped her. No one tried. She kept kissing him and crying and kissing him until it was over and Nicholas was gone.

Gently, Opari and Geaxi lifted Star away from Nicholas. I took the wool blanket and began to cover his body. Just as I pulled the blanket over his head, Eder moaned and coughed. She tried to speak and coughed again, only it did no good. Her lungs were too full and she was too weak. Her eyes were still closed.

"Mama," Nova said, then leaned over and whispered in Eder's ear, "do you know where you are?"

Eder coughed again, this time violently. Nova held her closer.

There was nothing she could do. Then, suddenly, Eder opened her eyes and she was staring at me. She moaned again and her eyes fought to stay open, then somehow she began to speak, and while she could, she told me what she saw.

"I see your mama and papa, Zianno."

"Where? Where are they?"

"Just ahead, oh, what is the name of that place, that old fort in East Africa?"

"I . . . I can't remember."

"Baju will know. He always knows where we are. Yes . . . Baju will know."

Eder never closed her eyes. She left as quickly and thoroughly as Solomon had and I closed her eyes as I had his. Nova laid her down on the pillow and sat still by her side for several minutes, staring at her mother's face and features. Behind me, Opari began a low chant that seemed at first to have no melody or words. I learned later that it was not Meq. It was older; a chant she had learned from her mother, who said the Meq had learned it from "others" during the Time of Ice. It was called the "Song of the Glacier." Her mother said the "ancient ones" sang it together at the passing of one of their kind. They sang it to give shape and sound to the departing spirit, which was like a new-born at death and needed the strength of the still-living spirits to begin its infinite journey. They buried the "old" body of the "new" spirit in the direct path of an advancing glacier and chanted the song, or prayer, for hundreds of miles to and from their camps.

It was slow and beautiful, a song of mourning, but there was no time for mourning or ceremony. Circumstances would not allow it.

I left Willie's "quarters" and found Daphne and told her what had happened. We both found Willie and his first concern was Star. Daphne assured him she would look after Star and the baby. Willie and Tillman Fadle then took the bodies of Eder and Nicholas into Falmouth for several reasons, but the most immediate was to confirm the cause of death. If there was danger to anyone at Caitlin's Ruby, most importantly the baby Caine, then all precautions must be taken. Opari stopped her chant as we lifted Eder from the bed and she warned, "The man 'old Tom,' the one who gave directions to these two, is in great trouble. The virus was still able to fly when they met."

"What about here? Now?" I asked.

"No danger," she said. "No danger now or when we found them."

Nevertheless, after Daphne had taken Star and Nova upstairs, we all agreed the wisest and surest thing was to have postmortems performed in Falmouth by a medical doctor. I knew that none of us—none of the Meq—could be affected, but everyone else was in harm's way.

The wrapping and removal of the bodies was tedious and difficult. Willie, being taller and stronger, took charge of the task. He was exhausted and confused. I felt numb and Opari said little except to tell Willie what to ask the doctor. Geaxi was completely silent. Afterward, Geaxi, Opari, and I sat quietly in Willie's "quarters" until we heard the doors on the big limousine open and shut, then the crunch of gravel under the wheels as Willie and Tillman Fadle made their way up the drive and through the gate. No one spoke. I saw the headlights flash by one of the old leaded windows and in the few seconds of illumination I saw the eyes of a dozen cats outside on the ledge, staring in at us. I turned to mention it and then saw the eyes of Geaxi.

Eder had been Geaxi's oldest and truest friend, a confidante, a sister, and more. Geaxi was the Stone of Will. She could run nearly as fast as Ray and escape almost every possible restraint. She was the Spider. She was graceful, silent, proud, and a master of acting in the moment. But when she was confronted with the death of a friend, something happened to her inside. She became frozen and her grief was so frightening, so deep, and utterly alone, she went to a place I have not been. Opari, fortunately or unfortunately, knew this place. She had been there.

"Do not waste your tears in that cold place," Opari said. "You must turn away and come to us. We must remain. We must. Blood of time, we are." Opari picked up Geaxi's hand. "Shed your tears now, Geaxi." She took my hand and joined it with her own and Geaxi's. "Share your tears here, now, with us, or they will be your poison." She paused and added, "You must do this."

Geaxi cried that night as I have never seen her, before or since. Her whole body shook and sobbed and Opari and I held her between us. Some nights pass quickly, some do not. Some are so long and sad and empty, they are no longer in time and they never pass or resolve. But they exist, and finally, eventually, end.

* * *

Do you know the sound of castanets? The sharp cracks of rhythm over a melancholy chord announcing the Spanish Lady is about to dance? I used to love that sound. It always filled me with excitement and anticipation. Whether it was outside or inside, concert hall or campfire, I always felt lightning was about to strike any second from anywhere and the castanets held it all in the balance. It was thrilling. That was before the deaths of Eder and Nicholas, before the rest of it, before the real dance of the Spanish Lady. Ever since, I have heard another sound announcing another, darker dance.

It began with a dream I was having while dozing on the sofa in Daphne's sprawling living room, waiting for the return of Willie and Tillman Fadle. In the dream, I was standing alone on a cliff near Kepa's camp and thought I heard the sound of castanets behind me. I turned, expecting to see the Spanish Lady, and saw instead a rattlesnake, coiled and ready to strike. I opened my mouth to scream and could make no sound. It was a hopeless, helpless feeling. I couldn't turn away and I couldn't stop the rattle. It was Daphne who shook me awake.

"Wake up, Z, my dear. You are dreaming." I looked up at her bright blue eyes and she winked. "Come," she whispered, "and come quietly." She pointed at Geaxi and Opari on the floor in front of the fireplace. They were sound asleep under the blankets and shawls that Daphne had thrown over them. I could see the gems embedded in Opari's Stone. Her necklace had fallen loose from inside her shirt and the firelight bounced brilliant blues off the tiny sapphire and diamond. I bent down and put the Stone back in her shirt. I knew Daphne had seen it, but she said nothing. As I was to find out, the secrets and mysteries of the Meq were unimportant to her. She was a Cornish woman first and last; a survivor. Magic was everywhere in Cornwall, in song and story, and she'd grown up with it, but she knew it could heal neither body nor soul. "Grief," Daphne told me, "is like a wound, and one treats a wound with tenderness and kindness, not magic. You let it heal in its own time from within. My goodness, it's quite simple, really. A living thing loves to live. It's the same with all of us, my dear."

She led me through the long and cluttered kitchen out of a rear entrance and along a path beside a low stone wall. I had to hurry to keep pace. The wind was blowing strong from the west and Daphne leaned into it. There was a faint scent of sea in the air, though I knew we were miles inland from harbor and coast. Low clouds kept the sky gray from horizon to horizon. Behind us, a few gray and yellow cats followed and watched.

She stopped in front of a combination stable and garage and unlatched two tall wooden doors, then swung them open. As she did, I blew on my hands and looked around quickly at the startling beauty of Caitlin's Ruby, even in November. On distant ridges I could see several cedar trees, rare for where we were, and everywhere there were paths leading off somewhere, lined with heather and wildflowers and marked at crosspoints with unique structures, lookouts, and shrines. Daphne put her hands on her hips and stared down at me. Her mouth opened in that odd smile, but her eyes were all business.

"I fear there shall be a quarantine placed on us."

"What?"

"A quarantine," she said, pausing. "Perhaps you are not familiar—"

"No, no, I know what a quarantine is, Daphne. It's just that I need to find someone now, soon, right away."

She let another long moment pass. "Is it Carolina?"

Her question stopped me cold. I stared up at her crooked smile. "I thought you didn't know who Star and Nicholas were?"

"I did not, but I know of Carolina through Owen. My goodness, he rarely mentions her by name, but I certainly know of Carolina. I also knew of her missing daughter and absent husband, but never by name until last night."

"Absent husband?" I was confused and wondered if we were talking about the same person.

"Yes, that's right, the poor soul of a man who slipped away last night. I assumed you knew him, Z."

"I do, I mean I did, but how did you—"

"Nova told me all about who was what to whom this morning and the . . . urgency you might feel to find Carolina."

"Where is Carolina?"

"I think you should ask Nova."

"Where is Nova?"

Daphne smiled again and turned toward the darkness inside the garage.

"With Star and the baby," she said. "That is my point. I think we should try and take Star and Caine into Penzance before the quarantine is imposed, for quick help if it's needed and, my goodness, to contact Carolina, finally. Do you agree?"

"I . . . I don't know."

"You and Geaxi and Opari could wait here for Willie and Tillman. There is an old milk truck in the garage. I've driven it before and it runs perfectly well. What do you think, my dear?"

"I . . . I want to talk to Nova first."

"Certainly" Daphne said. "She is right behind you."

I turned and saw Star hurrying toward us, carrying Caine inside her jacket and lugging a suitcase that seemed to keep coming undone, causing her to pause every few steps and pick up the falling contents. At least a dozen of Caitlin's cats brushed against her every time she knelt down. Not far behind, Nova followed at her own pace, looking out over Caitlin's Ruby as I had done, and even stroking a few of the cats as they appeared and disappeared along the way. Daphne said simply, "I've never seen them let any person do what they're letting Nova do."

I could tell at a glance that both Star and Nova had already put last night behind them and resolved something in their hearts and minds, especially Nova. She seemed to have transformed herself. There was a calmness in the way she walked and moved, the way she stroked the cats and scanned the landscape. It was as if she was "seeing" something else, something more. I suddenly remembered what Ray had said about her, that he thought she might be able to "see things." I knew at that moment he was right, though I had no idea what she was "seeing." She wore a hat pulled down low over her forehead that looked familiar, but I couldn't tell what it was until she stopped in front of the garage and turned my way. It was a bowler exactly like Ray's only without the wear and tear that his had seen. She wore red lipstick and dark blue eye shadow that made her look like an Egyptian. I almost laughed, and would have, except for the look in her eyes. It was all Meq. Compassion, mystery, trust, everything that usually came through the eyes of an old one, shone through Nova and out to me.

"Where is Carolina?" I asked. The worst thoughts imaginable were running through my head.

"She is . . . she was . . ."

"What? Is she dead?"

"No, no, Zianno, that is not what I meant."

"Is she sick with this virus?"

"No . . . at least not that I know of."

"What then, Nova? Tell me. Where is she?"

Nova took a deep breath and turned her head toward the garage where Daphne was cranking up the old milk truck. "Your friend," she said, "Captain Woodget?"

"Yes," I said slowly. "What about him?"

She turned her head back and looked in my eyes. "He passed away in New Orleans. It was only a week after the woman he lived with had died in her sleep."

"Isabelle?"

"Yes, and Mama was supposed to go with Owen to their funeral. Owen insisted on giving them a full New Orleans funeral with lots of pomp and circumstance. Carolina took her place at the last minute and Mama and I stayed in St. Louis with Jack and Ciela."

"Where was Nicholas?"

"Not at Carolina's. That's the ultimate irony, Z. We hadn't seen him in six years and he suddenly appeared, not ten minutes before Sailor's message arrived."

"Where had he been?"

"I don't know."

"Why did he leave?"

"It's complicated. I think Carolina should answer that. But there he was and he almost came apart when he found out about Star. He wanted to leave for England immediately, but Mama and I wouldn't let him go alone. He was a ghost of himself. We left that afternoon for New York and paid a shameless amount of money to get aboard the first ship out. We had no luggage and actually slept on the decks, but we made it, or thought we had. You know the rest. Somewhere en route, Nicholas and Eder must have contracted the virus."

I stood motionless and breathed in as much of the faint smell of sea as I could. There was no time to remember Captain Woodget now, but I promised myself I would find Caitlin's old path to Land's End and walk to where I could look out over the sea and remember everything about him.

"Z," Nova said softly. "I don't want to bury Mama here. Do you understand?"

"Yes. I'll have Willie take care of it. Don't worry."

Just then, Daphne drove the milk truck out of the garage and opened the door for Nova. She jumped up and in, holding her bowler by the brim. Star was in the middle and leaned out of the window as I shut the door.

"Come here," Star shouted over the noise of the old engine.

I had to step up on the running board to get near the window. Then she leaned out farther and kissed me on the cheek.

"I have no choice, Z. I must think of Caine. If he was to get sick here—"

"I know, I understand."

"Willie knows where we will be," Daphne yelled across the seat. "Tell him to come and get us if there is no quarantine. My goodness, let us hope that is the case."

I hopped off the running board and Daphne hit the throttle. The milk truck sputtered through the gate and slowly climbed up the narrow road that led to Penzance. Everything seemed absurd and backward. If Caitlin's Ruby was now under quarantine, that meant the only ones quarantined were Geaxi, Opari, and me—two girls and a boy who couldn't get sick if they tried.

I turned and started back toward the house. Halfway down the path I was overcome with images of things dissolving, falling apart, coming unraveled. I stopped to catch my breath and my eye caught something on the ground, wedged between the gravel path and the heather. I recognized it immediately, but it took a second to reason why it was there. Then I remembered Star almost running to the garage, spilling everything and trying to retrieve it all, while holding on to Caine. She must have dropped what I now found in the process. I walked over and picked it up slowly, sliding one hand inside and pounding the pocket with the other. It was Mama's glove, and as I walked the rest of the way into the house, I tried to remember the last time I'd had it on my hand. I couldn't do it.

I entered the living room through the kitchen and Opari and Geaxi were waiting for me. It was more evening than afternoon, but they were just waking up. I envied their yawns and puffy eyes.

"What was that noise?" Opari asked.

"A milk truck," I said, then told her what had happened and why. Opari disagreed vehemently with Daphne's conclusion, insisting that they were much safer where they were and should not have left. I told her we were stuck; it was too late. We would have to wait for Willie's return before anything could be changed.

I felt I was in a kind of trance. I looked at Geaxi and watched her folding her blanket and placing it neatly in a corner chair. She was unnaturally quiet. Opari walked over and touched my temples with her fingertips, making featherlight circles and then kissing the places she had touched.

"You are *nekagarri,* my love."

"Yes . . . I am."

"Come," Geaxi said suddenly. "We will lose all light if we do not leave now."

"I want you to sleep," Opari told me. "Geaxi is taking me somewhere, somewhere she wants to go, somewhere on this land. You must sleep while we are away, Z. You must sleep and dream deeply if you can."

I glanced at Geaxi and she was ignoring me, preparing to leave.

"Will you do this? Please?" Opari asked.

"I will do this. I promise."

Geaxi tossed a heavy coat and wool cap over to Opari. She put her own beret in place and started toward the door, then stopped and looked at me. We hadn't spoken a word to each other since Eder had died. I wasn't sure what to say, so I chose silence and hoped she was all right. Then she began to laugh—hard—as if she couldn't help it. It wasn't cynical, bitter, hollow, angry, or anything else. It was just a laugh and when Opari joined in I knew it was on me.

"Someday, Zezen," Geaxi said, "you must teach me to play."

It was then that I realized I still had Mama's glove on my hand. I pounded my fist in the pocket and joined in the laughter. "I will," I told her. "I will do this."

Geaxi reached in the pocket of her vest and removed a simple gold ring. It was slightly scratched and big enough to be a man's ring. Without her saying so, I knew whose it was. She had slipped it off his finger the night before while we were wrapping the body. She gave it to me without a word, then turned and opened the door for Opari.

"Now or never," she said.

They were through the door and disappearing up a path heading north within minutes. From a distance they looked a little like two schoolgirls out for a walk in the country, followed by a few stray cats. They were each and all anything but that.

For a few moments, I stood there with Mama's glove on one hand and Nicholas's wedding ring between the thumb and forefinger of the other. Silent, inanimate, haunting—they were only things, things made by hand and fashioned to fit another hand for a simple, specific purpose, and yet, what lives they had led; what secrets, dreams, fears, and hopes they held just because they were made and given to another. I slipped the ring over my thumb, the only digit that would hold it, and threw Mama's glove on the big couch in front of the fireplace. I put a few logs on the dying fire and fell back on the couch, stretching out and using Mama's glove as a pillow. The fire caught quickly and the flames looked like birds taking flight. I watched and wondered at what I knew and what I didn't. I turned the ring around and around and around and fell asleep.

I slept for what felt like only seconds, then woke to discover I'd been out for hours. The fire had burned down to embers and the whole house was dark and empty. I listened for anyone moving and heard nothing, then sat up and listened deeper, using my "ability." I could only hear the wind swirling outside and the old house straining against it.

Suddenly the hair stood up on my arms and I shivered from head to foot. It happened again, then again and again, like waves, until I had to shout out loud to make it stop. I was not frightened—the Meq can-

not afford superstition—and I was not cold. Still, something or someone had made the hair stand up on my arms.

I went to the fireplace and stirred the embers, adding new logs and
waiting for the flames to catch. I felt off balance, out of breath, and
something else I couldn't quite define. I knew I was awake, but everything seemed to be taking place in a slightly altered state and time—a
dream time.

Then, far away and barely audible, I heard the sound of tires on
gravel, the sound of someone turning down the drive into Caitlin's
Ruby and approaching the house.

I started to move toward the door and found I couldn't do it without tremendous effort. My legs and feet seemed long and thick, my
hands and fingers useless and unnecessary. I tried to think and couldn't
concentrate on any line of thought or single image. I wasn't spinning,
but I felt weightless and weighed down at the same time, as if I would
begin to spin, if I only knew how.

The fire popped and cracked and the new wood began to catch. It
sent shafts of light across the room and cast shadows of the furniture
on the walls and windows. The shadows became dangerous cliffs on a
dark coastline and I was being drawn toward them. I was adrift at sea
and I was going to crash for certain. The cliffs danced and beckoned.
I knew it wasn't real, but I was losing all perspective. One reality was
slipping easily into the other and I didn't know which was which
or even care. I was weightless, inside and out. A beam of light swept
back and forth across the cliffs or the walls, I couldn't decide, and the
lighthouse kept moving and coming closer. I could also hear it and
it sounded like a car, but that didn't make sense at sea, or did it? I
couldn't decide and it was so hard to think.

It was then I heard the cats. In slow motion, I turned toward the
sound and there were six of them on a window ledge, outlined clearly
by the beam of light and staring in at me. I heard a door slam on the
lighthouse, the car, the house—I couldn't decide and all sounds had an
echo and the echoes all had different origins.

I heard a voice repeating something. It was a woman's voice and she
seemed to be shouting, "Is me own home! Is me own home!"

I closed my eyes and tried to find what was real and what was not.

I knew I was fatigued, but that didn't explain what was happening. Where was the voice? Whose voice was it?

I heard another door open and a gust of wind followed the sound and brushed across my face. I opened my eyes and a woman in a red cape with a hood pulled over her head stood in the doorway between the shadows of the cliffs and coastline.

"Is anyone—" she started, then stopped when she saw me. She took another step inside the room. "Home," she said flatly, then added, "Z, is that you?"

I couldn't see her face clearly inside the red cape and hood, and I knew it made no sense whatsoever and probably proved me insane, but my first thought and explanation for what I saw was that she could only be one person—and that person had died long ago.

"Caitlin?" I asked in a whisper. "Caitlin Fadle?"

The woman slowly pulled the hood down from her head with one hand and unbuttoned her cape with the other.

"No," she said, taking another step toward me. The firelight framed her face and I knew in an instant why I'd felt that first shiver. "It's me, Z," she said. "It's Carolina."

There is no word in English, Meq, Basque, or any other language I know that can describe the feeling, the sensation, relief, warmth, surprise—the utter and infinite dumb joy I felt at that moment. Life has only a few moments that can stop the heart and empty the mind. Perhaps that's why there is no name for them. I only know I couldn't speak and could barely stand, so I sat down right where I was and stared up at her, and for the first time in years, I felt exactly like the child I appeared to be.

"Is it true?" she asked before I'd said a word. "Have you found her, Z? Have you really found Star?"

She spread her cape on the floor beside me and sat down cross-legged. She wore borrowed clothes—a man's sweater and trousers, and some kind of all-weather boots that were coming undone. In the center of the red cape was a red cross on a white background. It was the symbol for the International Red Cross Society and explained her cape, but not the rest of it.

I watched her adjust her sweater and run her hands through her hair. She was eighteen years older, in her late forties, and the years had not changed her beauty, they had only made it sharper and more permanent. Her hair was shoulder length and the color of winter wheat, with a few strands of silver among the gold, and the gold flecks in her blue eyes literally danced in the firelight. There were lines and creases around her mouth and eyes, and even they seemed sculpted and natural. She picked up one of my hands, keeping her eyes on mine, and held it gently between hers. I had not yet said a word. I glanced at her hands and after eighteen years and a thousand scenarios played out in my mind of what I would say to her, all I said was, "Freckles."

She looked down, puzzled at first, asking "What?" Then she looked up and began to laugh, saying, "Yes, yes, yes, they're everywhere. I've got families of them now, Z. You should see them, they're everywhere."

"Carolina, how did—"

She cut me off and put her fingers to my lips. "Shhh," she said. "You must tell me, Z, is it true? Have you found Star?"

"Yes, but—"

"I knew it," she said. "I knew it was true. I told Owen I knew it was true the minute we heard. I told him, I'm going to meet them, I'm going over there."

"Carolina—"

"Just a minute, Z. I want to tell you first that I am still angry about you and Ray leaving the way you did. You promised me—"

"I promised you I would find her."

"But you never wrote or wired or anything, not a clue . . . not to me, anyway."

"It's complicated."

She put her hand to her face and rubbed her eyes. She was exhausted and pushing herself to the brink. "Where is she, Z?"

I reached behind me and pulled Mama's glove off the couch and handed it to her. She smiled and held it close to her face and was about to say something, then opened her eyes in surprise and started to cry. I knew she was sensing Star's presence, touch, scent . . . something. Anyway, I'm not sure there is a name for that feeling either.

With more hope than truth, I said, "She'll be back soon."

"Oh, God, Z, can it be true, finally? So much has been lost. So much time and . . . so many other things." Carolina exhaled and drew in a breath slowly, trying to gather herself, then suddenly sneezed violently several times, almost uncontrollably.

I panicked. "You're not sick, are you?"

"No, no," she said, wiping her nose and eyes with her sweater. "It's those damn cats outside. How many are there?"

I laughed and reached for Mama's glove and she stopped me, grabbing my hand and turning it over until my thumb stood upright. I'd forgotten about the ring.

Her face went blank and her eyes glazed over. She slipped the ring off my thumb and held it in her palm, staring down on it as if it were the most curious and precious thing on earth. Then she closed her eyes and made a fist around the ring, holding it so tight her knuckles showed white through her skin.

"What happened?" she whispered.

"He was in St. Louis, at the house, at the moment Sailor's message arrived. He . . . he had to come . . . he wouldn't wait. He must have caught this strange virus on the way. He got here before us. He was sick, no, they were sick—"

"They?"

"Nova and Eder were with him."

"They were all sick?"

"No. It is impossible for Nova to get sick . . . remember? It was Eder."

We stared at each other in silence, then the tears started down over her freckles and I couldn't stop them. I watched them drop and fall off her chin as they ran their course, gravity pulling them on, forcing them downward through space until they hit the ancient hearthstones in front of us, in front of the fire. All the new wood I'd tossed in earlier had caught and the fire was blazing. The tears didn't last a second on the hearthstones, and each one disappeared faster than it had taken to fall.

"My God, Z," Carolina said. "My God."

Death is a mad seamstress, a drunken messenger with no plan or sense of order—no pattern. Life is nothing but patterns and patterns are everywhere in life, or seem to be. Geaxi finds them everywhere; rock gardens are her favorite because the patterns are oblique and subjective, but ultimately she pays them little mind. Sailor thinks they are absolutely essential and depends on them as he would wind and waves. Opari finds them darkly mysterious and yet useful—the trick, she says, is in discovering their interconnectedness, their weave.

Death is different. It has no pattern, no weave, no design. Death can go where it wants.

I propped pillows up against the couch and pulled all the blankets around us. Carolina lay with her head in my lap and held my hand next to her cheek. If there had been people outside instead of Caitlin's cats staring in at us, they might have thought they were seeing something very odd—the grandmother in the lap of the grandson perhaps—but it was never that way for us. It never had been that way and never would.

I asked if she wanted to sleep and she said, "Not now, not yet." We watched the fire and talked. She wanted to know everything about Star and I told her everything I knew, leaving out some of what I'd seen in New Orleans. When I told her she really was a grandmother, I thought her response would be wild and exuberant, but she only held my hand tighter and quietly said, "Good."

She asked about Eder, if she'd been in pain at the end and I said, "No, not at the end." She never asked any details about Nicholas—how he looked, what he said, none of that—and I never asked what had happened between them, but I found out anyway in so many words, or the lack of them. I could hear in her voice that whatever had happened was still a mystery to her. I could also tell she was deeply in love with him; she had never lost that.

Nicholas suffered from what she called "madness of loss" and it consumed him. She said Eder was familiar with the condition, knew it herself and, though she said it was rare, admitted to Carolina that many Meq had been destroyed by it or destroyed themselves because of it. From what she told me, "madness of loss" sounded just as deadly as the virus that actually killed him, only slower.

After the Fleur-du-Mal kidnapped Star and after Ray and I had gone chasing them, Carolina said Nicholas became more affectionate and caring than he'd ever been. At first, she enjoyed being waited on and pampered, but it was not his true nature, nor hers. He was trying too hard, and after Jack was born, he tried even harder. He bought things for both of them impulsively, things they would never need or use. He began remodeling Solomon's old room himself, though he knew nothing about carpentry. It was supposed to be Jack's nursery and eventually his bedroom, but Carolina said the room took on the size and smell of a gymnasium. He worked obsessively for months until one day he simply stopped. Nothing was finished and he left the room as it was, tools and all, and walked away. Carolina said he gave no reason and never discussed it. When she asked about the room, he told her there were many more things to do. "Too many," he'd said, "too many." He began to forget other things—birthdays, appointments, deadlines. His health deteriorated and he developed odd eating habits when he ate at all. His mood swings were wide and dramatic and he began drinking heavily to find a balance or forget there was one. Carolina said he withdrew from company, even hers, and as the months passed his only mood was not even a mood—he simply quit feeling. "His heart was not broken," she said. "It was frozen solid."

And it only got worse. In his lucid moments, he was aware of his downward spiraling life and spirit and hated it. He cried often and promised to change, staying sober for weeks at a time and teaching Jack to play baseball, even taking him to watch games at Sportsman's Park. But Star's absence haunted him like nothing ever had, Carolina said. It was a nightmare he locked inside himself with ever-changing keys, but none of them worked. The keys always dissolved or disappeared and the nightmare would spill out again, worse than before and obvious to everyone he loved. Nicholas was not stupid or insensitive and in his lucid periods he realized the toll his behavior was taking on those he loved, especially Carolina, and on Jack's seventh birthday Nicholas himself disappeared. Carolina said she sent Mitchell to look for him and he tracked his movements as far as New York before he lost all traces of him.

"Mitchell?" I asked. "Do you mean Mitch Coates?"

"The very same," she said. "He's been a life saver in many ways for us, Z, particularly for Jack."

I smiled and thought back to my favorite memory of Mitch. He was winking at me and catching the double eagle that Solomon had tossed him. I could still see the gold piece turning over and over in the air and the easy way he caught it, almost without looking.

"Where is Mitch now?"

"He's in St. Louis and doing well," she said, then she saw the smile on my face. "He's a good man, Z. You would like him."

"What does he do for a living?"

"A little of everything, I'm afraid, but his real passion is music. He owns three clubs downtown and the music is wonderful."

Talking about Mitch seemed to bring Carolina back to the present, except for one more statement.

"I wish I could have kissed him, Z," she said. "Just one last time."

I knew who she meant and I knew how much it broke her heart to think it, let alone say it.

"You did," I said without explanation. "You did."

Just then, the biggest log in the fire broke into pieces and shot several live coals and sparks in all directions, one of which landed on my forearm. I jumped, then brushed it off, howling in pain. Carolina rubbed the red mark it left, then blew on it gently and kissed it once for good measure.

"Do you remember, Z, when you cut yourself on purpose right there in that same place and made me watch until the wound began to close? We were in Forest Park and you had to prove to me who you really were . . . who you are. Do you remember?"

"Yes," I said, "and it hurt then too."

"But do you remember what I said?"

"Yes, I think so. You said it was like something out of the Bible."

"Well, I've changed my mind."

"What do you mean? How?"

"I mean after all this time and all these years, I've changed my mind. I was wrong." The mark on my forearm had completely vanished, but she kissed it again and said, "There is nothing like you in the Bible."

In England, during the last days of 1918, the number of deaths from influenza was staggering and yet no one seemed to be paying attention. The end of the Great War and labor disputes in London and elsewhere took precedence over the death dance of the Spanish Lady.

A cartoonist was the first to give the virus the nickname "Spanish Lady," probably because the first reports of death in great numbers had come from San Sebastian, Spain. It was an inaccurate assumption and cruelly ironic. The source of the virus was not in Spain and the chaotic nature of its appearance in all parts of the world among all parts of every population was anything but ladylike. The Spanish Lady killed roughly twenty million people worldwide in just seventeen weeks, then disappeared.

As Carolina and I finally fell asleep on the floor of Daphne's living room, we heard no castanets or sad guitars, but everywhere else in the world the Spanish Lady was still dancing; fast and silent, without rhythm or mercy, she was still dancing.

The fatigue I'd felt earlier overwhelmed me. I went deep into sleep and found myself in an old dream. I was standing on the mound in Sportsman's Park and everyone was waiting for me to pitch the ball. I looked down at Mama's glove and the ball was no longer there. I could feel it in my hand, but it wasn't there. I glanced up in the grandstands and saw Nova sitting between Nicholas and Eder. All three stared back at me in silence, then Nova lowered her head and closed her eyes. I heard footsteps and turned toward home plate. There was no batter or catcher and the umpire was walking toward me, taking off his mask, just as he'd done in the old dream. I knew him, I knew him well.

"Z," the voice whispered. "Z, wake up."

I opened my eyes and Willie Croft was standing over me, motioning silently with his finger and pointing toward a sleeping Carolina. I rose at once and followed him back to his "quarters."

Willie walked quickly and pushed the heavy curtains back from the windows just inside and all around the odd-shaped room. He bent down near the fireplace in the corner and for a moment I thought he was going to fall in, but of course he didn't. He stacked kindling inside and then backed away, lighting the fire with a long match and old newspapers. His red hair was wet and so were his clothes. I turned to look through the leaded windows and it was raining. I could barely hear it falling, but it was steady and gray, and I could only guess at the time of day. There was no sign of the limousine and I assumed it was in the garage. With or without my "ability," I never heard the big car return.

"Where's Tillman?" I asked.

"He dropped me off and drove back to Falmouth," Willie said and paused slightly. "To wait for the coffins."

"There's no quarantine?"

"Quarantine?"

"Yes," I said. "On Caitlin's Ruby. Opari was right, wasn't she? It was a virus."

"Yes. The Spanish flu . . . quite nasty, that."

"Daphne thought there might be a quarantine imposed."

"No, no, there is no quarantine on anything or anyone. There is too much indecision among the powers that be for that. But tell me, Z, where is Daphne? And where are the others? Where is Star, for God's sake, and Caine? And who is the woman sleeping in the living room?"

"You didn't recognize her?"

"No, should I have?"

"Well, let me just say that Star will look something like her in a few years."

Willie blinked once, then started to speak and stopped. He took in a quick breath and held it. He looked at me the same way he had years ago, in China, when he was still my size and leaning out of the window of a train. He was a boy then and it had all been a practical joke to Geaxi, but the look of wonder is ageless.

I nodded to him and confirmed that it was true and said, "They haven't seen each other since Star was a child."

He cleared his throat. "How . . . how did she get here?"

"I don't know yet, at least not all of it. I do know in some way or another she used the Red Cross."

"Is she aware that Star is here, or was?"

"Yes."

"Does she . . . I mean, have you . . ."

"Yes, if you mean Nicholas and Eder. I told her." I sat down on the side of the bed nearest the fire and something occurred to me. It had bothered me all along. I now knew why no one had seen Nicholas before; he had disappeared from everyone, and I knew why Star was a surprise—she'd been in Africa—but why was Carolina a stranger? It made no sense. "Willie," I said, "I'm going to ask you something

straight out and please, if you can, give me an honest answer. Why, if
you know about us, about the Meq, and you know about Solomon,
tell me why you and Daphne don't know Carolina? In all this time,
how could you not?"

Willie paused only a moment and never blinked. "We do and we
don't, Z. It goes back to Owen, really."

"Owen Bramley?"

"Yes, well, what I mean is we knew *of* her. When Owen first came
to Caitlin's Ruby and told us of Solomon and Mowsel's family . . . the
Meq . . . he also spoke of a remarkable woman who owned the house
where Solomon lived. We knew there had been some sort of family
tragedy there, in St. Louis, but he never went into any depth about it,
and as the years wore on, it surfaced less and less until he never mentioned Carolina at all. Both he and Sailor, who I saw rarely, became
obsessed with the future—property acquisition, communication, Solomon's 'Diamond' plan. Owen always said, 'We can't look back.' And
Sailor would only say, 'It will work itself out in time.' I simply left it
alone. So did Mother. But now . . . now it's quite different."

"Quite," I said.

I was even more confused. Had Owen been protecting Carolina or
was it something else? Sailor, on the other hand, I could understand.
But what did he mean by "work itself out?" I was sure that Sailor,
more than anyone, would have kept Carolina involved, because of her
closeness to Eder and Nova, if nothing else. The past was unraveling
with the present. I looked at Willie and he was not only confused, he
was anxious and worried. Then I remembered Star.

"Daphne said you would know where she'd gone," I told him. "She
loaded Star and Caine and Nova in an old milk truck and took off before I could talk her out of it."

"The Falcon."

"The Falcon?"

"Yes, it's a pub in Penzance. We own the apartment on the top
floor. Mowsel lives there at times. I'm sure that's what she meant. I
only hope Star and the baby are"—Willie paused and his eyes moved
from mine to a point directly over my head, toward the door—"all
right," he finished.

"So do I," a familiar voice said from behind me. It was Carolina. I had no idea how long she'd been there. She was looking straight at Willie. "Are you the father by any chance?"

"No," Willie said. "I'm the husband."

Sometimes life takes longer to explain than it does to live and the adventure coming home delays the tale until eventually it becomes the tale itself. Zeru-Meq takes all his visitors through potholes on his way to the palaces and shrines. It is the way and it is mostly unmarked. He says we are all strangers, unasked and unannounced, and we must greet each other along the way with humor and patience because we are always, each and every one with each and every step, a little late.

As Willie stood staring at Carolina and before she could respond, there was a loud crash outside coming from the direction of the garage. My first mental image was a milk truck slamming into the stone foundation. I saw the same fear in Willie's eyes. He bolted past me and out of the door. I glanced at Carolina for a split second, then we were right behind him. We ran through the living room and Carolina shouted, "Wait!" Willie ran on ahead, but I stopped and watched her put on the big boots she'd worn earlier. She was having trouble tying them and I said, "Come on, hurry." She said, "I'm trying, I'm trying." I looked down at the boots and they resembled some sort of military wear. "Where did you get those?" I asked. "From a Canadian," she said. "I bought everything he had, including his car." We glanced at each other and thought the same thing at once. That was the sound. Someone had crashed into the car that Carolina had driven and parked in the driveway in the dark. We raced through the kitchen and down the path, toward the garage. The rain obscured our vision and muffled the sounds, but I could definitely hear voices ahead of us, female voices, and they were laughing.

Suddenly Carolina stopped and let out a sound, a yelp, and I thought she might have slipped on the wet path, but when I turned to look she was standing perfectly still with her hand over her mouth. "My God, Z," she said, then lowered her hand and she was smiling. "That's her." "That's who?" I said. "That's Star, that's her laugh," Carolina said, then started laughing herself. I looked at her and told her she was crazy, there was no way to know that. "Come on," I said. "Someone might be hurt." "Wait here," she said. "Please, just wait for me. It won't take thirty seconds. Please, Z, don't go yet." She turned and ran back in the house and I looked toward the sound of the crash and the laughter, but stayed where I was. In thirty seconds, she was back and out of breath, beaming, grinning ear to ear, and soaking wet. "Come on!" she shouted and grabbed my arm.

We ran through the rain down the twisting path toward the laughter and finally out on the wide gravel drive in front of the garage. Then we heard Willie laugh somewhere to our left. We turned and the first thing I saw was Carolina's car. It was a black coupe with one headlight missing, but not from a crash, and parked at an odd angle where the drive split from the garage to the house. And just beyond the coupe, flat against the gravel without any wheels or frame underneath, was the cab of the old milk truck. All around it shards of broken glass from the windshield lay on the gravel and flashed in the rain. Inside the cab, unharmed but in a kind of shock, as if they'd just been dropped from outer space, were Daphne, Nova, and Star with Caine tight against her chest, laughing themselves silly.

It took a moment to figure it out. Daphne must have braked hard when she saw the parked car and the jolt, along with inertia, had broken the rusted cab loose from the body and sent them flying. They were more than lucky. Willie was laughing with them, probably to keep from crying. He was trying to help Daphne out and she finally stopped laughing long enough to let him. I ran to help Star, whose jacket and hair were covered with glass. Nova hopped out in front where the windshield had been and was the first to see Carolina. She said not a word.

"Well, there is no quarantine," Daphne said as she got to her feet. "But, my goodness, there is no more milk truck either." Then she saw Carolina and smiled. Once again, her blue eyes shone bright right through the rain. "Welcome," she said casually. "You must certainly be Carolina."

Wishes may or may not come true, I've never been sure about wishes, and I've never been certain about anything in doubt coming true simply because we "trust" it will. Reality does not work that way. There is a truth, however, a place, a feeling, a moment, who knows what to call it? It does not go by names. It travels though, and stops occasionally in the middle of our lives, if we're lucky. It happens when the longest-standing hope finds the most distant dream . . . and it lights the world.

At the mention of Carolina's name, Star raised her head and looked into her mother's eyes for the first time since she was a child. Carolina stared back and for an instant I felt something pass through me I had not felt since my papa found my mama's eyes in the moment before the moment that killed them. I felt the weight of their lives. But it didn't frighten or overwhelm me as it had before. The feeling that passed between Star and Carolina, and somehow through me, was only sur-render . . . surrender to something in time and yet out of time . . . something in the center of life realized at the moment it is being lived. It is the most peaceful and powerful feeling on earth.

"Mama?" Star asked.

"Yes," Carolina said and knelt down next to Star. She was crying, but her tears were drowned in the rain. She put her hands on her daughter's face and ran her fingers over her lips, then she saw Caine peeping out of Star's jacket and bent to kiss his dark curls. She turned and looked at me.

"It's a miracle, Z."

"No, Carolina. It's your family."

She was laughing, crying, trying to wipe her nose and hug Star all at once.

"Are you all right?" I asked.

She reached under her soaking sweater and pulled out what she'd run back into the house to get. "I guess I won't need this," she said.

I took it from her and put my hand inside and pounded the pocket.

"What on earth is that?" Daphne asked. She stood straight and tall and the rain seemed not to bother her.

"It's called a baseball glove, Daphne. I'll have to teach you how to play."

"My goodness, yes," she said. "I love American games, but let's do it on a slightly nicer day, shall we, Z?"

"For God's sake, Z, she's right," Willie broke in. "Let's get every-one inside. I'll take care of this mess later."

"Quite right, Willie," I said and with everyone helping everyone else through the broken glass, we all made our way back to the path that led to the house.

I hung back at one point and let the rest walk on ahead. I don't know why, I suppose I just wanted to watch them all walk together and listen to the small talk and, of course, the laughter. It was a wonderful feeling, a kind of nudge in the ribs, a wink from somewhere that suggested life was working. That's when I knew Nova really could "see things." She turned around at that very moment and gave me a real wink, a wink as clever and knowing as any Cleopatra ever gave.

I laughed and started to catch up, but I only took a step or two before I heard another laugh, a laugh I knew as well as my own. I turned and found Opari walking right behind me and Geaxi right behind her. I had never heard them approach.

"It is seeming you are always in the rain, my love, while others always take shelter. I hope the desert has not touched you permanently."

"Me?" I asked. "Where have you two been all night and day? And how long have you been back?"

"Long enough to see a miracle, no?" Geaxi said with a grin.

Opari took one of my hands and Geaxi took the other. They led me like a schoolboy up the path and toward the house. They were both wet, but neither was soaked nor looked the worse for being outside nearly twenty-four hours. "No, tell me," I said. "Where have you been?"

"In a shelter that is older than I," Opari said.

"A shelter?"

"Yes, Geaxi will take you there, or I will."

"But . . . what is it? I mean, why did you go?"

"You will see it soon enough, Zianno," Geaxi said. "When Sailor arrives. It has many long names in several languages; 'Lullyon Coit' is the Cornish name. It is made of granite, prehistoric granite, and we are not sure of its purpose. I like to call it 'the slabs.' "

"Is it far?"

"No," Opari answered. "It is quite near."

"At the highest point of Caitlin's Ruby," Geaxi added.

None of it made sense to me, but I felt too good to worry about it. I turned to Opari and said, "Come on, there's someone I want you to meet."

"I know," she said. "I saw her and now I am knowing the answer."

"The answer? To what?" I tried to stop walking, but they both kept pulling me on.

"I never knew," Opari said and glanced over at Geaxi, "I never knew why you left China . . . now I do." She leaned forward and looked into my eyes. I loved her more than I ever thought I could and I was only beginning.

"Good," I said. "Then you also know why it will not be possible ever to leave you again."

Suddenly Geaxi pulled me to a halt.

"What?" I asked. "What did I say?"

She dropped my hand and stood staring at me, her eyes bearing down like black bullets.

"I have heard some sorry attempts," Geaxi began, then drew in a deep breath and waited a moment. "I have seen some sorry attempts, Zezen, many, many times in my long, long life at grand professions of profound love, but . . ." She paused and let out a slow, lingering sigh that ended, "That was the worst."

I had to agree and we walked the rest of the way in laughing like children coming home from school.

Captain Woodget was the first to teach me about knots—knots of all kinds and complexities. Solomon taught me how to untie and slip out of many things, but not knots.

To Captain Woodget, knots had power and purpose. He had a sailor's knowledge of knots and a working relationship with the mysteries of strength and coiled tension. A length of rope, resting in the corner and wound around itself, had the potential for many things with the proper knots. It could sail a ship, save a life, raise and lower cargo, pull a woman on board, secure a chest left behind, hold a man at the stake, hang a sailor at sea—if the mind could dream it up, the rope could carry it out. If you knew your knots, it could be done.

The Meq are fascinated with knots and their secrets of tensions and strengths. Ours are just harder to see. They are learned in the blood more than the mind. They are learned on a rope of time and with trust that each will remain unbroken. But, of course, there is always a key to unraveling any knot. For the Meq, it always seems to be a simple twist of fate.

That first night together, we began telling our stories and connecting times, people, places, and events that only those in the room would understand. It was an impossible knot of hopes, dreams, and circumstance that ended in a bond only felt through blood and trust— the sense of family. Everyone there welcomed it, nourished it, let themselves come out of themselves and be a part of it. It was healing, it was spontaneous, and it lasted through to the next day and the next until the end of December and the end of the year, 1918. We did what the Meq do well. Along with Carolina, Star and Caine, Willie, Daphne, and even Tillman Fadle, we were letting time pass. We were not worried about the future, we were simply waiting for it.

There were unwanted tasks and necessary arrangements that still had to be made, such as the legal transfer of Nicholas's and Eder's bodies and coffins into Carolina's name, but even that was done without hesitation or remorse. Carolina used the trip to Falmouth as a chance to call St. Louis and go on a shopping spree for Star and Caine. She was remarkable, but so was everyone.

The Daphne Croft Foundation, as a "concept," was still a mystery to me. Neither Willie nor Daphne ever mentioned it. The Daphne Croft "household," however, I could easily understand. Every day the food was fresh and so was the linen. She found suitable clothing for Carolina and shared remedies and recipes with Opari. Geaxi and I helped Willie keep the firewood split and stacked and the constant smell of something baking filled the kitchen. Everyone helped take care of Caine. I've never seen more babysitters in one place than I saw at Caitlin's Ruby. Each day felt like a found day, a gift, and was filled with stories and small chores, long walks, loud dinners, and quiet good nights. Any talk of anything beyond the next day's needs was wasted. No one cared. It wasn't necessary.

I did find out a few things indirectly when I asked Carolina about Captain Woodget and Isabelle. She said that Isabelle was sick for some time, but after she passed, Caleb Woodget only lasted a week. He died quietly in his sleep with a pencil in one hand and a partly drawn diagram of a new galley for the *Little Clover* in his lap. Carolina said it was a beautiful, slow funeral with two bands and attended by hundreds, even though few of them knew the captain and none could remember Isabelle. Owen Bramley had staged and paid for the entire event, then accompanied Jack back to St. Louis after they got word of Sailor's message. The rest was a crazy voyage on a troop ship for Carolina, the first ship she could find sailing for England, and an anxious wait in St. Louis for Owen and her son. I had wondered where Owen was and why we hadn't seen or heard from him. Now I knew.

There were other questions I never asked, as there were for everyone. There was a question Nova almost asked and didn't, the same question I asked myself and couldn't answer—where was Ray? There was a question Carolina could have asked and never did, the simplest one—why? I was afraid she would because the answer meant it wasn't over, the Fleur-du-Mal was still alive and so was her grandson, so was Caine. And there was one other question even Geaxi dared not ask, the most obvious one—where was Sailor?

We didn't see much of Tillman Fadle. He seemed to come and go on a different schedule to everyone else and yet I was always vaguely conscious of his presence, similar to that of the vulture he resembled. I was told he was a good man, a gentle man, a fisherman by trade who was self-educated with wide and varied interests. He and Daphne had, of course, known each other since childhood. His residence was separate and somewhat secret. It was his way. Daphne said that when she was alone after William had died and before she met the Meq, Tillman taught her a great deal about faith. "Though I rarely ever saw him," she said, "I knew he was never far away."

On New Year's Eve, I finally got to talk with Tillman. The night was rare for many reasons as it turned out, but it started with Tillman Fadle and it was the last time I ever spoke to him. It was also the first time I heard the name Einstein.

We were watching the stars. It was the first clear night in weeks, and after a grand meal and two pieces of Daphne's apricot pie, I wanted to walk and look at the sky. I made an offer that anyone was welcome to go with me, but only Geaxi took me up on it. She said she knew a good spot, a place she thought was made for sky-watching. I found Kepa's telescope among my things and we set off along a path that Geaxi seemed to know well. The air was cold, but there was a new moon and even the wind was down. It was pitch-black and as my eyes adjusted to it the sky became a dancing diamond mine, a treasure ship spilling its jewels across a bottomless sea. I was startled by it. It reminded me of the sky in the desert and I was speechless.

"There's a good spot, a better'n farther on, there is," a voice said matter-of-factly from somewhere behind us. "But this is a good one too, it is."

Geaxi and I turned to find Tillman Fadle leaning on a walking stick. He was wearing a huge black slicker and he looked seven feet tall. We weren't listening for him, but neither Geaxi nor I was aware of him standing there. It was unusual.

"It is a big sky, it is," he said.

"Yes, it is," Geaxi said and waited.

He stared at the sky a full minute before he addressed us again. "The big sky, the big picture," he said enigmatically. "Same thing, though . . all of it . . . same thing."

"Do you often come here?" I asked him.

"Oh, most certainly, sir, as often as I can." He took a step or two toward us, and as he did, he turned his head and spat in the darkness. "You know, sir," he said, "I think there's a young fella took a snapshot of the big picture."

"What do you mean 'a snapshot'?" I asked.

"They'll be provin' it 'fore long." He spat again in the dark and reminded me of someone, but I couldn't recall who. "You wait and see," he went on. "The ancients knew it, knew it, they did. Couldn't prove it, though, couldn't prove it. Won't be long, sir, you wait and see," he said. "This Einstein fella is on the track."

"On the track of what?" Geaxi asked.

Tillman looked up in the direction of the constellation Orion, then tilted his head to the side and peered out of the corner of his eye. He held his thumb and forefinger in front of him and peered through the space between them. He spat one last time and I remembered who he reminded me of—PoPo.

"That," he said. "He's after that."

"What?" I asked.

"What gets through the cracks," he said.

"You mean the light?" Geaxi asked.

"I mean that what turns *on* the light," Tillman said and I think he smiled, but it was too dark to be sure.

Just then, we heard the sound of a car in the distance. It was coming toward Caitlin's Ruby and it was not one of Daphne's vehicles, I could tell from the constant backfiring of the engine. I turned and raised Kepa's telescope in the direction of the sound, but there was nothing to see, no headlights, nothing.

"That'd be Cap'n Uld," Tillman said. "Norwegian man . . . owns a few boats in the Scillys . . . owns the Falcon. He won't drive a motor car with headlights . . . same as at sea . . . won't have 'em, won't use 'em."

"Is he coming here?" Geaxi asked.

"Yes, I'd say he was, yes."

"Did you say the Falcon?" I asked him, remembering something Willie had said.

"Yes, the Falcon . . . in Penzance, it is."

"Would Mowsel be with him?"

"Yes, most likely. Comes and goes that way, he does, with Cap'n Uld."

Geaxi and I glanced at each other and knew in an instant there would almost certainly be another passenger, another boy who came and went that way—Sailor.

I closed the telescope and Geaxi said we'd better go, then I turned back to Tillman leaning on his walking stick in the dark.

"What was that fella's name again?" I asked. "The one looking for what turns on the light?"

"Einstein," he said. "Albert Einstein."

"Where is he looking?"

"Up there," he said and looked at the sky, but pointed his finger to his head. "Up there and in here," he added and smiled again, I think.

"It was a pleasure talking to you, sir," I told him.

"And you, sir," Tillman Fadle said. "And you."

Geaxi led the way back without a word and we were there in no time. She was as swift as I'd ever seen her and only paused when we reached the gravel drive. Coming from the direction of the house, we could both hear the strain of Daphne trying to sing, accompanied by an accordion. She was singing "Auld Lang Syne" and there wasn't a cat within fifty yards of the house.

Sailor was standing outside the house, on the drive next to the car with no headlights. He was standing in a swirling, rising cloud of exhaust from the car. I couldn't see Mowsel, but Cap'n Uld was behind the wheel with one arm out of the window. He was smoking a pipe and didn't seem to be getting in or out. Then a door slammed on the opposite side of the car and Cap'n Uld put the car in gear and lurched forward, driving away in the darkness.

We slowed to a walk and Sailor turned to greet us. Mowsel had his back to us and was walking toward the house and Daphne's voice.

We stopped not three feet from Sailor. The cloud of exhaust had blown away and he was standing with his legs spread and his hands on his hips. It was then that I felt something I had not felt for so long I'd forgotten it; an inner warning and presence of fear—the net descending. It was powerful and tangible. I'd noticed it and felt it increase the closer we got to Sailor.

"Come with me," he barked. "We must not wait. Geaxi, can you find Lullyon in the dark?"

"Of course," Geaxi said.

"Lullyon?" I asked. "You mean 'the slabs'? Now?"

"I mean we must not wait," Sailor said. His breath became steam in the cold air. He took a step closer and stared hard in my eyes. His "ghost eye" was milky and bloodshot. "We must not wait, Zianno. Believe me."

"Sailor," Geaxi said. "There is something I think—"

"Not now, Geaxi!" Sailor screamed. I had never heard him raise his voice to that level, even in China. Slowly, with dark emphasis on each word, he said, "This . . . involves . . . us . . . all." The night itself could have cracked, it was so brittle and silent, then Sailor whispered, "Please, Geaxi, do this. Take Zianno and I will bring Opari."

Perhaps it was the shock of hearing him speak to her like that or perhaps it was some other knowledge of him that only she possessed. I do know Eder had called her his "dark" companion and I do know what she was trying to tell him. She was trying to tell him that his only sister, Eder, had passed. Whatever it was that stopped her, it stopped her. Geaxi turned to me without a glance at Sailor and said, "This way, Zezen."

I'd been to "the slabs" once before, but not at night. Opari had taken me on a cold day with the wind coming straight off the North Atlantic. It was a long walk filled with switchbacks and false crossings—a path that I thought had to be seen to be followed. But that was me, not Geaxi.

From a distance, Lullyon Coit, or "the slab," looked like the "stone boys" I'd seen the shepherds leave on the farthest reaches of Kepa's land. They were a form of signpost or station for the Basque, both personal and professional. They were unique and each possessed a kind of power, a power of place and intelligence. Lullyon Coit possessed a similar power, only it was much older and much larger. The stones weren't picked from a field, they were quarried and lifted, cut, arranged, and designed. There were four of them—three great slabs of granite standing upright in a triangular configuration and the fourth lying on top of the other three. The whole structure seemed to be pointing in a westerly direction. Ancient shelter? Burial site? Who knows? Caitlin never said what she believed, but leading away from Lullyon Coit, out of brick and stone and beaten earth, she left six different paths to get there.

In the dark, without ever taking a false step or a wrong turn, Geaxi and I arrived by one of them. The entire way, she never said a word.

The wind gusted and seemed to change direction at will. We were on the highest point of Caitlin's Ruby and there were no trees or even brush around "the slabs." They stood tall, black, and silent as they had for thousands of years in this place, in these exact positions. There was only starlight overhead. Orion was low and close to the horizon and Venus was far to the west.

While we waited, Geaxi paced and I sat against the base of one of the stones. Geaxi wore boots, a jacket, and her beret. I wore boots and a jacket, but my head was bare. The wind was relentless and neither of us was prepared to be where we were.

"Why does he want us here, now?" I asked. "Especially here in this place?"

Geaxi never stopped pacing. "The 'now' disturbs me," she began. "The 'here' is because this place will have great meaning during the time of the Gogorati, the Remembering. We are certain of this, but we are not certain why. Sailor has always wanted this place to be the first place where all five Stones come together. He thinks . . . no, he is certain we will learn something."

"What?"

"We will find out."

"What about Eder? When will you tell him?"

"Later. Something is wrong, I am most certain of that." She stopped pacing for a moment and looked at me. "We should find this out first, no?"

"Yes," I said. I knew she was right. Sailor was more upset than I'd ever seen him and our news would only make it worse. The wind blew and I thought how long it might take them to climb the path, then I thought about where I'd last seen Opari, then I thought about where I'd last seen Nova. If Sailor walked in and saw Nova, then . . .

"There they are," Geaxi said. "I can feel them."

Sailor came out of the darkness first and Opari was immediately behind him, wearing a full cape and hood. Neither had made a sound. Opari walked over and knelt beside me. She smiled, but remained silent. I looked around for anyone else and there was no one. In the small space inside "the slabs" there was only Geaxi, Sailor, Opari, and me.

Sailor spoke almost at once, but he was hesitating, something I'd never heard him do.

"There has been a terrible . . . a multiple . . . an unexplainable tragedy, I am afraid . . . with possible consequences. I am not sure where to begin."

"Then begin with Pello," I said. We hadn't heard from him since he'd left with Pello.

"I could begin there, Zianno, but the . . . tragedy does not. No, not there . . ." Sailor trailed off a moment, then looked at Opari and back to me. "And the consequences . . . the consequences may affect you directly, Zianno. Believe me."

"But—"

"Let me go on, please. I do not know what to make of this. It . . .

it could mean . . . no, I am not sure what it could mean. That is why I wanted us all together—now, here, all five Stones together at last, in this place . . . to find out the meaning . . ." He didn't finish and began pacing.

"What has happened, Umla-Meq?" Opari asked in an even voice, a voice aware of Sailor's fear. "Tell us what you know."

"What do you mean 'all five Stones'?" Geaxi interrupted. "I do not see Unai. There are only four of us present. Is he—"

"No," Sailor said suddenly. "No, he is not dead. He is . . . in another state."

"Another state?" I asked. "What does that mean?"

"Please," Opari said to all of us at once. "Let Umla-Meq speak. He says there has been a tragedy. We are all . . . we are all Meq, first, last, and for all in between . . . we must remember this and listen, because in the end there will be no one else, no one. You Zianno, my love, you are too young to know this, and you Geaxi, you know a great deal, more than anyone, perhaps, but you too are young. You, both of you, do not yet know of . . . consequences. Now, please, let Sailor tell us what he knows."

"This is what I know," Sailor said. He continued to pace in a lop-sided figure of eight pattern and spoke as if he'd thought it over many, many times and distilled it into a few drops of information that still would not break down and yield anything that made any sense. "I know Unai and Usoa crossed in the Zeharkatu several years ago. They came to Trumoi-Meq to help them do it, in the old way, and they went into the Pyrenees, where it was done. It was done and their blood became like Giza. They conceived a child not more than a year ago and moved to the Balearic Islands, awaiting the birth. There is a fishing village on the coast of Menorca that Unai wanted their child to experience in the years before the Itxaron, and learn the life there. The war in Europe had not affected this village in any manner. It was a good place, a safe place . . . a good choice."

Opari took my hand in hers and held it tighter than usual. Sailor went on.

"Now Pello comes to Mowsel with disturbing news, at the very moment we are leaving Africa, he comes with news that Trumoi-Meq has never heard before, news that . . ." Sailor stopped pacing and

turned his back to all of us. "Pello told Trumoi-Meq . . . that the child
of Unai and Usoa . . . had died of influenza."

Opari began a low, rumbling growl that climbed octave after octave
until it became a high, whining trill. Geaxi joined her, like another dog
or wolf, and added a clicking sound with her tongue against her teeth.
It was frightening. I looked at Sailor and he stood where he was, staring away in silence. For a moment, I thought the slab of granite over
our heads had moved. I stretched my hand out and touched the stone
behind me. It was cold and solid. My heart was racing and my thoughts
tumbled and slipped. I had missed something. What was it? I couldn't
grab hold of it. I took a step out of the enclosure and looked up at the
sky. I focused on one star and then another, and then the space between
them, which became another star, and another. I turned back inside
and almost fell on Sailor. My voice felt disconnected.

"Will Usoa not be able to have another child?" I asked.

"No, beloved, no," Opari said. "Do you not see? Do you not see
the truth . . . the consequence?"

Then, like a crack between the light, Sailor's meaning came to me
and took my breath away. I said it out loud and Opari shed a tear with
each word. It was so simple and yet, for all these millennia, it was the
only true thing that separated us from all others. "Meq . . . babies . . .
do not die."

"That is correct, Zianno," Sailor said. "Meq babies do not die—
they do not."

"What does it mean?"

"It means we may be the last," Geaxi said. "The last ones."

"Not necessarily," Sailor said.

"But we only have our blood!" Geaxi shouted. "You know this,
Sailor. What is the Wait about but this? Nothing! Nothing but our
blood sustains us. Nothing!"

"Wait," Opari said firmly. She was the oldest and had been on her
own the longest. Even Geaxi calmed down and listened. "Sailor, why
do you carry Unai's Stone?"

Sailor reached inside his jacket and pulled out a cracked leather
pouch, gathered at the top with a thin leather strap. He opened it and
out rolled the Stone into his palm. The tiny gems still embedded in

Unai's Stone sparked and flashed like shooting stars as he turned it over and held it out. "He could not wear it any longer," Sailor said. "He has . . . drifted. He is very close to madness. Usoa does not even try. She is completely lost within herself and will not stay in any one house or dwelling longer than one night. They move about like child demons. Unai gave the Stone to Pello, telling him his heart was too weak to wear it."

"Sailor," Opari said gently. "What do you think we should do?"

"I . . . am not sure," he said and started pacing and retracing his figure of eight. "But . . . I feel somehow we should . . . we must find it here . . . there may have been something . . . possibly the Stones . . . together . . . I am not sure, but . . ."

"Sailor," Geaxi said, grabbing him by the shoulders, "you are rambling."

At that moment I saw a look in Sailor's eye that made me think of something Carolina had said when she spoke of Nicholas, what she called the "madness of loss." But it was only beginning. What happened next was a madness unique to Sailor, a madness I have not seen since, and a madness that is the reason Sailor is sought to this day. Prehistoric slabs of granite weighing several tons each do not move themselves. For the first time in my life, I was witness to the "ability" of Umla-Meq, Egizahar Meq, Stone of Memory.

"The old way will not work," a voice said out of the darkness. It was Nova. "The old Zeharkatu will not cross in the old way. The shift is soon. The light has been turned on." She walked inside the enclosure without explanation and was followed by a silent Trumoi-Meq. At the sight of her, Sailor seemed to do what I had done earlier. His mind tumbled and glanced, sorting through a thousand reasons why Nova would be there, how it was even possible, then landed in an instant on the right one, the real one.

"Where is Eder?" he asked.

No one said a word. All around us, the wind hammered at the ancient stones.

"Sailor—" Geaxi said.

"Where is Eder?" he asked, turning and walking within a foot of Opari. "Where is Eder, Opari?"

"She is dead," Opari said evenly. "In Nova's arms she died, Umla-
Meq . . . from influenza."

Opari watched Sailor and his movements, his breathing, his eyes.
"In Nova's arms, Umla-Meq," she repeated. She spoke evenly and
easily, as a shepherd to one of his flock about to bolt. "There is still
Nova, Umla-Meq . . . you must see this . . . there is still Nova."

"Yes, I see, Opari! And you are correct, as Zianno was correct. Yes,
yes, yes, there . . . is . . . still . . . Nova." He took three quick steps and
tossed Unai's Stone through the air in Nova's direction. She caught it
gracefully with one hand. "You wear that, Nova. You wear that and
remember its . . . travels," he said with a snort and a laugh. Sailor
turned back to Opari. "Is that all I should think, Opari? That there is
still Nova and not see what has happened, what is becoming? Am I to
ignore, after all our precious time among the Giza, learning to survive
their pettiness and viciousness, learning to survive and last despite being
maimed, ridiculed, tortured . . . beheaded! Now, in the very century before the Remembering, am I to ignore that their poison has
poisoned my own blood—our own blood! Yes, yes, yes, despite this,
there . . . is . . . still . . . Nova."

Sailor closed his eyes and his whole body shook and trembled. He
leaned his head back, then forward until his chin was buried in his
chest. And then I felt the rumbling. It was almost silent, and rolling,
like a hibernating bear beneath our feet turning in his sleep. I barely
felt the first one. Suddenly Sailor raised his head and looked at Opari.

"This place shall be the first correction," he said.

The rumbling became audible and a vibration began below us and
around us, causing the massive slabs of stone to move.

"I am ending this plan I foolishly conceived and believed in, the
plan I sold to Solomon and bought myself. Do you appreciate the
irony, Zianno? Solomon would. Well—there is less than a hundred
years until the Gogorati. I do not intend to let the Giza interfere with
this inevitability. What did Nova say? 'The shift is soon.' She is correct . . . and it begins here . . . now! I suggest all of you find safety at
once."

Sailor started walking west, the same direction in which the ancient
builders had pointed "the slabs." "Opari," he yelled. "You and Geaxi

follow Nova's progress and be patient. Zianno, you must serve the family . . . it is a good choice," he said and laughed. "I will not be back . . . the light has been turned on."

The sound of his laughter was drowned out by twenty tons of granite vibrating and beginning to fall as easily as a house of cards. And Sailor had done it with his mind.

Sailor disappeared, of course, even before the stones had ceased falling. There was no reason to discuss it or ponder it. It was clear what he wanted and it would have been impossible to find him, even if we'd tried. None of us was injured. Caitlin's six paths became our paths to safety. I checked Opari thoroughly, then listened for the last broken stone to settle and rest. I looked up and Sirius was rising in the east, and Opari's words came to me, "We are Meq . . . first, last, and all in between."

Sailor was gone, I knew that. Lost, found, shaken, driven, who knows? The best way to describe it might be the way Mowsel described it later. He said, "Sailor is sounding."

After that night, it took us just two weeks to sort out what to do. There was hardly any debate and no indecision. We even took a vote and had to stop, laughing, because we never got to the second choice. It was amazingly simple. Out of the chaos of that night, our path became clear—Lullyon Coit was forgotten and our "direction" was away from Caitlin's Ruby, west to America and St. Louis. Sailor used the word "family" and that's what we would be. Carolina's home would be the only place to do it.

There was no joy in our leaving. Daphne had become much more than a gracious host. Leaving her and knowing we might not see her again was painful, but not awkward. She was also attached to Caine like a fierce mother lion and promised "not to die" before he was old enough to remember her.

Willie decided to go with us. He had no choice, really. He was addicted to Star. Nova was a mix of emotions, as was Star, and both wanted to stay longer, or at least promise to come back often, and that's what we did. Solomon's "Diamond" could wait, but regular visits were promised and assured. If the Fleur-du-Mal was still in business, then he would find us, no matter where we were.

Tillman never turned up, as expected, and we left on a morning that was gusting with wind and rain, similar to the afternoon when we'd arrived. Daphne stayed inside until we pulled away, but I saw her sneak a last look through a window from the kitchen. I still have a dream that always begins with our departure from Caitlin's Ruby.

One unusual event occurred as we were leaving the country that has become more humorous with time. I don't think anyone has ever known the truth of what happened except me.

We had to stop briefly at the foreign desk of Lloyd's Bank in London, in order for Willie to make some transfers for Daphne and himself before we left. Willie went in alone, but Star and I were lingering in the lobby, watching the bank traffic and trying to keep Caine from grabbing my nose. I looked past Caine's little finger and through the glass and realized I knew the young man inside, the agent from Lloyd's Bank who was doing business with Willie. It was Thomas Eliot from St. Louis, the kid in love with Carolina. He was older and taller and wearing glasses, but there was no doubt.

I couldn't resist what came to mind. It was just too good and Ray would have loved it. I knocked on the glass until I got their attention. I told Star to play along, no matter what I did and no matter what Willie said, to stay silent and just nod if she had to acknowledge anything. She agreed. When we entered the office, Thomas Eliot was telling a joke and had his back to us. He had reached the punch line when he turned and saw something only he and I could see, an impossible time warp to him, but just family relations to me. He saw a young woman, Carolina to him, almost exactly the same age as the last time he'd seen her—impossible—and she was with the same dark-haired boy she'd been with that day. It was too much for him. Instead of finishing the joke, he laughed to himself. It was a laugh to keep from falling apart, a tiny laugh of last defense, and Willie said, "Dammit, Tom, if you were plannin' on tellin' me a joke, then end it with a bang, not a damn whimper."

I never told Carolina about it, but I smiled the rest of the way. Mowsel was waiting on the docks to see us off. His hair curled out from under his cap and around the collar of his old jacket. Willie left him with a thousand instructions and only stopped when Trumoi-Meq smiled and displayed the proud gap of his missing tooth. It seemed to be a signal Willie had long understood as the end of negotiations. I had only spoken to Trumoi-Meq twice between New Year's Eve and our departure—once to say we had much to say to each other and once to promise someday to do it.

On the crossing, I asked Geaxi what she might do. I knew she would eventually become restless at Carolina's. She said she had heard of something new in aviation called "barnstorming," and thought she might look into it. I said, "But you're still only a twelve-year-old girl." She said, "Exactly."

Carolina told Daphne before we left to keep the black coupe until Caine was old enough to come back and drive it. Carolina and Opari talked constantly about everything and Opari and Star never stopped asking Carolina about America, even baseball, and they all became mothers to Caine. Willie took care of Nicholas and Eder. They were secure belowdecks and beneath the waves.

The voyage west to America was cold and wet and we kept mostly to ourselves, as always. Just before we docked in New York, I took a walk on the deck, alone, and stared out at New York as it came into view. I was leaning on the railing and behind me a voice said, "Excuse me, son, would you mind looking after my things while I step inside a moment?" I turned and there was a thin old black man in a perfectly fitted and pressed black suit. "Not at all, sir," I said. "I'd be glad to." He turned and walked quietly through the door behind him, never looking back. His "things" consisted of two books and a train ticket to Ithaca, New York, stuck in one of the books as a marker. The books were *Leaves of Grass* and a well-worn Bible. I turned the Bible open to the page that was marked with the ticket. It was Matthew and read, "Except ye become as little children, ye shall not enter the kingdom of heaven." I thought about Sailor and wondered if that was true or could be true or was even relevant.

Just then, the old man came back through the door and smiled. "You religious, son?" he asked.

"Yes and no," I said.

He laughed, and looked familiar when he did it. "Where's home, kid?"

I hesitated for a heartbeat; I hadn't thought of it that way since . . . since I'd asked an old Jewish man the same question, a stranger who was taking me there anyway. I could still hear his voice in my head, so I answered the old man the way Solomon would have answered. I said, "St. Louis, kid . . . St. Louis."

I'll remember you, while you remember me;
I'll remember everything you wanted to be.
  So, please be a brave lad,
    My heart sails with thee.
And I'll remember you, while you remember me.

—FROM "CAITLIN'S SONG"

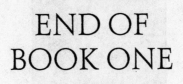

END OF
BOOK ONE

PHOTO: © JIM MAYFIELD

ABOUT THE AUTHOR

STEVE CASH lives in Springfield, Missouri, where he was born and raised and educated. After an attempt at gaining a college degree, he lived on the west coast, in Berkeley, California, and elsewhere. He returned to Springfield to become an original member of the band the Ozark Mountain Daredevils. He is the co-author of the seventies pop hits "Jackie Blue" and "If You Wanna Get to Heaven." For the last thirty-three years he has played harmonica, written songs, performed with the band, helped in the raising of his children, and read books. *The Meq* is his first novel.